OUT OF THE RED

David Bradwell

OUT OF THE RED

The gripping, twist-filled sequel to Cold Press.

Investigative journalist Danny Churchill is hot on the trail of Graham March - the disgraced former police DCI. The investigation takes him to Germany where he soon starts to uncover dark secrets and new depths of depravity.

Back in London, and aided by his flatmate - fashion photographer Anna Burgin - Danny's investigation intensifies, but as he gets closer to the truth, the body count starts to rise.

Help is offered from the most unlikely of sources, but if Danny accepts, is he doing a deal with the devil herself?

ABOUT THE AUTHOR

David Bradwell grew up in the north east of England but now lives in Letchworth Garden City in Hertfordshire. He has written for publications as diverse as Smash Hits and the Sunday Times and is a former winner of the PPA British Magazine Writer of the Year Award. Aside from writing, he runs a hosiery company with web sites at www.stockingshq.com and www.tightsandmore.com.

Get in touch at:
www.davidbradwell.com

OUT OF THE RED

A Gripping British Mystery Thriller - Anna Burgin Book 2

Out Of The Red was first published in 2018 by Pure Fiction
Copyright © David Bradwell, 2018
www.davidbradwell.com

ISBN: 978-1-9997099-6-9

For Philip Wolff.

PROLOGUE

Tuesday, April 5th, 1994

THE first line was exciting, full of daring, intrigue and the promise of the new. But nothing that came after could ever come close. He knew that. And that's why, despite the temptations, and the ease of access, he'd always resisted. Alcohol, yes. He'd get drunk with the rest of them, keeping up with the best of them. But he stayed away from anything stronger. He had a bright future. He wanted to enjoy it. He didn't realise that it would soon be no more than the basis of a tragic eulogy, and that within the hour he'd be dead.

Coralie Bruguière couldn't believe she could ever be happier. Three days earlier she'd come to London with her boyfriend, Olivier. It took a couple of days to acclimatise to the bright lights and noise of the English capital, compared to their quaint semi-rural life in the outskirts of Lille. But by Tuesday evening they were in love with the city, and even more in love with each other.

By day they'd explored the sights, walking hand in hand through Regent's Park, puzzling out the Underground, sheltering from the English rain and buying each other gifts on Oxford Street. They'd visited Buckingham Palace, countless museums and other places she never believed she'd see with her own innocent eyes.

It was a perfect break. She wanted it to last forever, but tonight, she knew, it was coming to an end.

Coralie had met Olivier at a Christmas party just over two years ago, and they'd been inseparable since. They were perfect for each other. Both had dreams of one day escaping to the bright lights of Paris. They'd met each other's parents and their relationship had gained approval from all concerned.

It had been an idyllic period in her life. Now, though, she had the sense that something was changing. Something for the better still.

Over dinner, in a restaurant just off the South Bank, the mood was light. It was late, and they were tired, but they'd been making the most of their last full day. Their money was running out, but they'd decided to spend the last of their funds on a special meal as a fitting final memory of their time in London. The restaurant manager had found them a table as other diners headed out into the night.

The waiter took their order. They skipped the starters to keep the price down, but Olivier insisted on ordering a special bottle of wine. Then, as they waited for their main courses to arrive, he took his girlfriend's hands and looked into her eyes. She smiled in delicious anticipation as he let go with one hand, and reached into his jacket pocket, pulling out a small velvet box that he'd been carrying for the last three days, waiting for this moment. He opened it to reveal a calibre-cut diamond on a white gold ring.

Three days earlier, Coralie had come to London with her boyfriend. The next day she'd be returning home with her fiancé.

It was after midnight when they left the restaurant, the good wishes and congratulations of the waiting staff still sounding in their ears. Rather than hail a cab, they decided to walk back to their hotel, holding hands along the riverbank, taking advantage of a break in the clouds and enjoying the calm of the cool night air. On the far side, they could see Big Ben and the Houses of Parliament. They turned right and headed towards the iconic Tower Bridge.

After a couple of minutes, Coralie stopped and pulled Olivier to her. They kissed, like characters from a Robert Doisneau poster. Olivier suggested she stand by the wall next to the river so he could take a photograph. She smiled at him. It was a beautiful pose, full of passion, hope and romance. He joined her by the wall and they held hands, looking out, across the river, watching the slow-moving water of the Thames, and listening to the sounds as the wake from a passing motorboat lapped against the wall.

They looked down to the mud bank as the water receded, and that's when they saw the body. And that's when the full horror hit.

Chapter 1

Four days earlier: Friday, April 1st, 1994

A RHINE riverboat edged slowly downstream, under the arched railway bridge that connected Cologne to much of the rest of Germany. Danny Churchill looked out of the window and then drew the curtains for the final time.

He turned back to his desk, pressed the power button on his IBM ThinkPad 500 notebook computer, and then went to retrieve his suitcase while he waited for it to boot. It would be good to get home. A shame, perhaps, that he couldn't stay longer, but this was a long-term project. He'd come looking for answers, but every answer led to further questions of its own.

Eventually the screen showed the now-familiar Windows 3.1 desktop. Danny returned to his desk and pulled out the chair. Almost immediately his fingers were gliding over the keyboard, nudging the trackpoint to move the cursor. He double-clicked on the CompuServe icon.

Electronic beeps and whistles gurgled from the internal fax modem while it established a connection. And then he was online. The sense of achievement never diminished, nor the feeling that he was crossing the threshold into a new network-centric world. Suddenly he wasn't alone.

He opened his mailbox and checked for new messages. When the download completed, there was only the one: a work circular with details of a leaving party for one of the picture editors. He started typing a new message.

Subject: Greetings from Köln!

Hi Anna and I hope all is well.

I'm just starting to pack up now and looking forward to seeing you tomorrow.

It's been a long day but I think I've made progress. I hope so anyway, although he's a sly bastard so definitive proof is still proving elusive. I can't say too much on here but I'll tell you what I can tomorrow. Dinner?

I should be back around lunchtime. Will you be home?

I saw a bit more of Cologne today. It's a lovely city. We should come here for a weekend. I'd love to just go off exploring and not have to worry about work. It's very photogenic too. You'd love it, I think.

I'd better dash. I'm heading down to the bar in a moment for a well-deserved nightcap, but then bed beckons. Missing you.

Take care and speak soon.

Danny x

He thought for a moment. Was there anything else to add? This whole electronic messaging thing - and indeed the ThinkPad itself - was relatively new, and he still couldn't quite fathom how it all worked. But as an investigative journalist for Britain's biggest-selling morning tabloid, the Daily Echo, he knew it was becoming ever more important to keep in touch with technology. A year ago, he'd got his first mobile phone to celebrate promotion from researcher to fully fledged writer. Now he had a notebook computer and an email address. The speed of progress was both relentless and accelerating.

He pressed send. The message made its way back to London, to the flat he shared with his best friend and confidante Anna Burgin. Would she still be awake? Probably, given the time difference. What would she be up to? He tried to picture her, on the sofa, watching TV, or with any luck, maybe working at the computer.

Despite the cost, he left the connection open while he continued packing. He'd worry about the hotel bill when he filed his expenses. The accounts department would be tolerant. He'd proved his worth, many times over.

A few minutes later a reply arrived.

Re: Greetings from Köln! - now Greetings from Camden!

Hi Danny,

Hark at you with the Köln thing. Can't wait to see you too. Yes, I'm here all day.

All's good back in the motherland. The women's air force has just merged with the RAF apparently, so I may have a career change and become a fighter pilot. I think I could fancy that if I'm tall enough, which I doubt. Life is so unfair.

In other news, I've had a lovely evening. I've just come back from a night out with Katie and Ben who are two of the writers at Harpers, although I fear the fourth glass of wine was an error, haha. I always assumed Ben was gay but apparently not, as he asked me out, and insisted on swapping numbers when I refused. Most unexpected!

You'd be proud of me though. I still managed to turn this thing on, although God alone knows how.

By "Dinner?" do you mean you're offering to take me to dinner or expecting me to cook for you? Very happy to accept if it's the former, but sod off if it's the other. :-)

Ooh, exciting news. I've got a surprise for you tomorrow if you're up to it. A big night out to relive your youth. I'm not saying any more now so hopefully you'll be keen to get home asap.

Safe travels and lots of love.

Take care. Anna x

Danny smiled. He cherished his friendship with Anna. They'd met at university and lived together since, although never quite crossed the line into romance. They trusted each other and looked out for each other. He had a sudden surge of homesickness as he pictured her struggling with the mouse, battling with technology. He sent a quick reply.

Hi again,

Lovely to hear from you. Thanks for the quick reply.

I could imagine you in uniform. :-)

Yes "Dinner?" meant invitation to dinner, my treat, but maybe lunch would be better if we're out at night? Sounds intriguing. I'll be there as soon as I can.

Sleep well and happy dreams.

Dx

He shut down the computer, and unplugged the modem and power supply. Ten more minutes of final packing in the morning and he'd be ready to take the train to Düsseldorf Flughafen, to catch the flight home.

With nothing else left to achieve, he picked up his key and left the room. When the lift arrived, he pressed E for Erdgeschoss. A moment later, the doors opened at reception. A guest was talking to the concierge, but otherwise all was quiet. The hotel exuded business-class calm and sophistication.

At the bar he ordered a Kölsch. The barman seemed glad of the custom. Highlights from a football match were on a TV screen at the end of the room, so Danny took his drink and made his way to a table with a better view of the game. The sound was turned off, not that he'd have understood the commentary anyway.

And with that, he allowed himself to relax for the first time in days, switching off from the constant stress and occasional danger of the investigation into the illicit sidelines of the corrupt former police Detective Chief Inspector, Graham March. One drink, then sleep. Then home for the weekend before battle resumed on Monday.

He closed his eyes, succumbing to fatigue. But then, suddenly, he was alert, on edge, sensing movement behind him. He tried to ignore it, but it seemed close, and the bar was otherwise nearly empty. He heard the rustle of clothing. Immediately he was wide awake. And then he heard a voice, softly spoken but unmistakeable. A voice he'd never expected to hear again.

"Hello, Danny," she said.

He turned, and looked straight into the eyes of a ghost.

Chapter 2

"OOH, that was good. You should take it up professionally."

Graham March lay back, sweat glistening on his 18-stone frame. Aurelia, his favourite Polish masseuse, opened a packet of baby wipes to clean up the worst of the mess and then picked up her tunic from the floor, moving to the side as it caught on a heel. She did up the buttons and then leaned over to check her appearance in the mirror that ran the full length of the table. She knew she was being watched from the adjacent room. It was all part of the job. All part of the humiliation.

"I'll leave you to get dressed," she said, trying not to catch his eye. "Can I get you a glass of water?"

"Yes, my darling, I think a certain amount of re-hydration is called for, if you catch my drift." His laugh was almost as sickening as the thought of what she'd just had to endure.

Aurelia left the room, and March sat up. He decided against a shower. He'd enjoy her scent for a little while longer. He was nearly dressed when she returned.

"Ah, there's a good girl," he said, taking the glass with one hand and patting her on the backside with the other. He let his hand roam down her thigh to where the hemline gave way to nylon. She tried to suppress a shudder.

"Mikołaj says he's ready for you," she said. "He's in his office when you're ready."

"Tell him I'll be there in five."

She nodded.

"See you again, Mr March," she said, turning to leave. The maintenance of courtesy took every ounce of her resolve. The maintenance of self-respect hadn't been so resilient.

Half an hour later, March climbed the stairs from the basement and emerged from the door of the Central Sauna massage parlour, onto the street that led back to Euston station. He frowned at the rain, his senses assaulted with the noise and pace of motion. It was suitably dark. He wouldn't be seen, not that it really mattered any longer. He'd survived far worse. Suspended, yes, but on full pay while investigations were ongoing, although he was confident he'd be able to annul those in the near future, once his version of the truth came out. And of course, some token good works and a word, or more, in the right direction. He raised his collar and allowed himself a small smile of satisfaction.

"I'm a changed man," he declared, raising his glass. "Cheers."

"You're full of bullshit, I know that." Despite the strong words, the woman on the other side of the desk was smiling.

"Seriously, Jacqui, I've discovered my charitable side."

"Right. Giving money to hookers doesn't count, especially if it's for services rendered."

March laughed and took another drink.

"If you weren't such a cynic you might actually have a bit

more success with romance, my dear. How's the casino business?"

"All the better now we don't have to subsidise your pension plan."

"And again, such misanthropy. That was merely a small recompense for turning a blind eye to what I like to call your more creative ventures."

"And again, full of shit. So, go on then, amuse me. What have you done? Giving cash to bookies doesn't count either."

"Jacqui. You do yourself a disservice. No, my darling, I have become involved with the homeless, protecting runaways and helping them to find a warm meal and a roof for the night."

Jacqueline Glover started to laugh, with a throatiness harvested from many years of nicotine addiction.

"Are you serious?"

"Never more so."

"Honestly, you're precious. Fornicating your way through London's waifs and strays does not count as charity. Christ."

"I'm shocked by your inference. Seriously, I have been dedicating my time to a homeless shelter. Telling you, it's enriching. Years and years I gave service to this community, until my current temporary reassignment."

"Suspension."

"Pure semantics, my dear. Anyway, it's good for the soul to make a difference in some other tangible way. You should try it."

"If I didn't know you better I'd almost miss the irony. And you're seriously trying to tell me you're not taking advantage?"

March smiled and finished his drink.

"I can't deny it's always a potential perk for the pretty ones."

They both laughed. Eventually, Jacqueline stood up, and walked over to the door. She closed it and returned to her desk. March watched her while she did so.

"You were probably quite a looker in your day," he said. "Obviously time has taken its toll."

"Have you finished?"

"Just teasing you."

"Yeah, well, it's time to talk business." In an instant her mood changed. March straightened up. He knew the perils of underestimating her. Of failing to acknowledge the ruthlessness at her core.

"So," she said, when she was back behind her desk. "Tell me everything I need to know about Mikołaj."

Chapter 3

DANNY looked at the woman in front of him, momentarily lost for words. It was so good to see her, yet it raised so many questions. There was a sense of relief, of a mystery being solved, yet immediately, equally, he was on his guard.

"Clare. It's a bit late in the day for April Fools," he said at last. "I thought you were dead."

She smiled.

"No, you didn't." She started to laugh, then indicated the vacant seat opposite. "Do you mind if I join you?"

Danny nodded, trying to take it all in. She looked well. Expensively dressed. Confident. Perfect make-up, despite the late hour. Deep down he was ecstatic to meet her again, but there was still unfinished business. And a deep distrust overlaying the sense of euphoria. What was she even doing here?

"Let me get you a drink," he said, standing, and pulling out her chair. "What can I get you? Assuming you have time?"

"Yes, of course. And thank you. Sauvignon? New Zealand if possible. Marlborough. If not any dry white would be perfect. Thank you."

"Coming up." He smiled, in spite of himself. "And don't disappear while I'm at the bar, because if you do, you're on your own this time."

"Touché," she said, with a glint in her eye.

He walked to the bar, hoping she couldn't see just how pleased she'd already made him - despite all of the trauma, the lies, the upset and betrayal. He'd imagined this moment, never truly believing it would happen. And now it had, all the scripts he'd rehearsed deserted him.

Clare Woodbrook had taken a chance on Danny when she was Fleet Street's most respected and feared investigative journalist. He'd joined the newspaper as her researcher but soon became an indispensable assistant. He idolised her. She mentored him. They made a formidable partnership. But then, last year, she'd disappeared on the eve of unveiling her biggest-ever story, and the quest to find her had nearly got Danny killed. By the time he and Anna tracked her down, everything he thought he knew to be true had collapsed around him. Before he'd had a chance to recalibrate she'd disappeared again - this time supposedly for good.

"I'm still here," she said when he returned with the drink. The wink was unmistakeable and playful.

"Clare, I just... Where to begin? How are you? What are you doing here? How did you find me? Is this a social visit? Just so many questions. The last I heard, you were killed in a helicopter crash, somewhere in Switzerland."

"Ah, Danny, the past is the past."

"I'm sorry, you're not getting off that easily."

"Shhh."

"What?"

"The past. Best forgotten. I'm thirty-two now, for heaven's sake. Older and wiser. Life moves on. What's happened has happened and we are where we are. Which, if I'm not sorely mistaken, is a rather splendid hotel in Cologne."

"Indeed. Nice hair, by the way. The brunette look suits you."

"I fancied a change."

"I'm sure. So, what are you doing here, exactly?"

"Looking for you."

"Are you being funny?"

"No, I just pass through occasionally and I heard you were in town so I thought I'd pop by and say hello before you fly home in the morning."

"I..." Danny stopped, laughed and shook his head. "Is there anything you don't know?" Clare was by far the most intelligent person he knew. Despite some obvious character flaws.

"I try to make sure there isn't."

"Okay."

"How's Anna?"

"You probably already know that too."

"Oh, you're good. But no, it's a genuine enquiry. She seemed a bit, well, frosty with me, last time we met."

"Do you wonder why? She got held up at gunpoint looking for you."

"I know. I'm sorry. Honestly. I feel terrible about all of that."

"Well she's fine, but I'm not sure you're on her Christmas card list. You're not on mine either, because I wouldn't know where to send it."

Danny paused, waiting to see if she'd acknowledge the implied question, but she didn't. She just kept looking at him. He tried again.

"How are you? Where are you living? What are you up to? Are you still dealing in artworks of dubious origin?"

Clare shrugged.

"I'm fine. Getting by. You don't really think I can answer the rest of that, do you?"

"I can dream. I've thought about you so much. I knew you weren't in the crash, though. I won't ask how you did it."

"Best not to."

"No, but... Hey, come here. It's great to see you." Danny softened. He reached across and gave Clare a hug. Previously he would only have dreamed of doing that, but now things were different. In many ways they were equal. And yet he thought the chasm between them would never be bridged. She was a dangerous woman. Ruthless, cunning, self-centred and not to be trusted, although he wanted to believe that deep down she still had a heart. That she still had values, however warped they might seem to others. That somewhere beneath everything, there was still a mutual respect and maybe, in some bizarre way, they were still on the same team. Her perfume was understated, but intoxicating.

"It's good to see you, Danny," she said. "I keep an eye on your career. You're doing well. And you did a good job on me."

"You gave me all the information."

"I know. But you turned it into something magical. I think my bridges are burned, career-wise, but that was always the case. Thankfully, I don't need to worry about taking a salary for a while."

"Crime pays?"

"You sound so cynical. But yes, if you want to put it like that. Although life has moved on now."

"I can imagine."

"How's Graham?"

"Now that you do know."

"Haha, of course."

"Well, you don't need me to tell you then." Danny shrugged. "He's slippery. He's suspended by the police but protesting his innocence. I thought we had him but we always need more."

"And that's why you're here." She indicated the hotel lobby.

"I can't tell you that. This secrecy thing works both ways."

"Ah Danny, I do admire you. I would never underestimate you."

"Although I feel a 'but' coming on."

"Maybe."

"Okay, enlighten me."

Clare smiled.

"I may be able to help you."

"Help me? Why would you do that?"

"Hold on."

She rummaged in her bag, and took out a packet of cigarettes. The health warning was in some unrecognisable language. Hungarian? Czech? Bosnian even? Surely she wasn't involved in that... She lit one and blew smoke at the ceiling.

"You're still not smoking then?" she asked.

"No."

"Good man. It's just one of my many flaws."

"Along with murder, theft, fraud..."

"Danny, please, let's not dwell on details. We do what we need to do."

"But some of us don't kill people."

"I've told you. The past is the past. I'm here in peace. I'm not going to shoot you."

"That's a relief."

"You're my protégé. I'm your guardian angel. It's a good arrangement, I think. This wine is nice."

She indicated to her glass. It was half empty already.

"Was that a hint?"

Clare looked up. The barman was already on his way, holding a bowl of mini pretzels.

"*Noch zwei Getränke bitte,*" she said. The barman nodded. Danny looked bemused.

"Two more drinks," she confirmed. "I said please."

"Pleased to hear it. You speak German now?"

"*Ein bisschen.* A little."

"A woman of many talents. So why do you think you might be able to help me? And why would I want you to?"

"Because, Danny, the former DCI March is a pet project of

mine. And I'm sure you're going to put us all out of his misery once and for all, but I'm equally sure I may be able to save you a lot of time. But obviously we'd need to be able to trust each other."

"Are you actually taking the piss?"

"Ah, so cynical."

"Can you blame me?"

"No, I suppose. But can we just start again?"

Danny paused to take a sip of his drink. To give himself time to think.

"Look," he said eventually, "I don't know what to make of this. Of you. I don't know why you're here. I don't know I can trust you. I don't know that you're not going to disappear again. I don't know anything about you any more."

"Okay, well, I'll be straight with you."

"But that's the point! Do you even know the meaning of the phrase?"

"Yes of course I do. You've got to get over this. Just humour me. But I will."

"Will what?"

"Disappear again. It's an occupational hazard. But we can stay in touch. You have email now."

"Yes, I do."

"It was a statement rather than a question."

"And you want my address?"

She laughed.

"Danny, I already have your address. Look at me. This is me. Clare. I'm on your side. Think of me as your secret weapon."

"I've seen what you do with weapons."

"It's a metaphor. The past is..."

"The past. Yes, I heard."

"Well then. So, can we agree we're going to help each other?"

"Whoa. Help each other? I thought you were helping me."

"Figure of speech. But let's just say we have some common

enemies and helping you may also work to my benefit, to a degree."

"Oh, it's all coming out now."

The second drinks arrived. Clare stubbed out her cigarette, gave the barman folded Deutschmarks and told him to keep the change.

"Listen, Danny." She reached forward and rested her manicured hand on his knee. She was still wearing a Ceylon sapphire ring, although it was bigger than the one he kept at home in her memory. "I can't blame you for doubting me. But think of all the good we did together. We were a good team before. The best. It's different now but we work well together. I promise you - look at me - *promise you* I will never lie to you. I'm not perfect. I get that. But you *can* trust me."

"Okay. And if I do?"

"Then I'll disappear again, but I'll stay in touch. And I'll help you, which in turn will help me, although in ways that are probably hard to explain. I won't ask for anything else in return, though. Nothing material. Nothing, well, illegal. I owe you that."

"You make it sound so easy."

"Ah, Danny. No. Nothing is easy. We move in murky worlds. But we can make it easier for each other."

"Okay." He wanted to believe her. Despite everything that had happened since they'd last shared an office.

"It's perfect symmetry, albeit inverted. You're now the boss and I'm your assistant. I'm not going to ask you what you have on March, or why you're here, and what you've been trying to find out about him."

"Assuming that's why I'm over here."

"Of course. Although we both know it is. But I assume it's to do with people trafficking, because if it isn't, it should be."

Danny smiled.

"You're too good," he said.

"I try."

Clare picked up her lighter and sparked a flame. Danny's eyes were drawn to it.

"What do you know about fire, Danny?"

"Fire?"

"Yes, fire."

"It's hot. It burns. I don't know what you mean."

"I'll tell you what I mean. Look at this. It's just a tiny flame. In itself it's almost meaningless. I can stop it now, look." She let go of the button, and the flame was extinguished. She lit it again. "But what if it spreads? Think how fast it grows, and how quickly it goes out of control. The biggest, most destructive forest fire, all from one tiny spark. Imagine if you could stop it now, and how simple and easy that would be. But imagine the devastation if you don't."

She let go and put the lighter on the table between them.

"That flame is March, Danny. Think about it. I don't know what timescale you're working to."

"And you said you weren't going to ask."

"I'm not. But I hear things."

"In your mysterious murky world?"

"Exactly." Her focused expression gave Danny a flashback to the days when she'd been at the peak of her newspaper career.

"And?"

"The general consensus is that time's running out. We're talking maybe a week, at best."

"Until?"

"He lights the touch paper, if you excuse the extended metaphor."

"It's very colourful."

"I'm being serious, Danny. But listen, you're the boss. It's your story. I'll leave you now but just know that I'm out there. Know that I'm a good person really. Whatever's happened in the past."

"I'd like to believe that. But really, after everything you put us through?"

"I'm going to make that up to you."

"Right. And if I need to speak to you?"

"I'll give you an address. A private mailbox."

"Like Rougemont?" Danny tensed, recalling the trouble caused during attempts to access Clare's private box at a security company the previous year.

"No. I mean email. You can message me. I may not always reply immediately. But talk to me. Come to me if you need me. And either way I'll do everything I can to help you."

She offered her hand. Danny thought for a moment and then shook it.

"Okay," he said. "Thank you. I think."

They both stood. Clare moved forward, to give him a hug. But as she did so, he caught her glancing at something, or someone, behind him.

"Just be careful, Danny," she whispered as they embraced. "Safe journey home."

She let go. He watched her, making her way through the lobby and out into the late Cologne evening. As he returned to his drink, he noticed the packet of cigarettes she'd left on the table. He thought of calling after her but it was too late. He couldn't quite shake the feeling that he might have just done a deal with the devil.

Chapter 4

Saturday, April 2nd, 1994

J UNIOR Home Office minister Samuel Elmhirst-Banks left his office in the Norman Shaw South building and made his way out onto Victoria Embankment. He crossed the road towards the riverbank and followed the path downstream, away from Big Ben and the Palace of Westminster.

The offices were quiet at weekends, but even so, discretion was paramount, especially with the omnipresent threat of a press leak. That was the very last thing he needed in the current climate. Once he was sure he wasn't being followed, he withdrew his mobile phone, extended the aerial, and tapped in a familiar number. It was answered on the third ring.

"I've followed as best as I can," she said, once the pleasantries were over.

"And?"

"Old habits die hard."

"That's no surprise. Where did he go?"

"Straight from the parlour to the casino. Victoria line from Euston to Green Park."

"It's good to see he's maintaining his interests. And then?"

"Probably about an hour there, presumably trying his luck with Jacqui if not on the tables. That was it then, though. Back out and straight home."

"Tube or taxi?"

"Taxi."

"Good. And no visitors afterwards?"

"Not before I left. I gave up about midnight."

"Okay. Good work."

"Should I keep following?"

"Please. I'll give it some thought. The press are circling."

"Understood."

He paused for a moment to let a jogger run past. He'd been in Government long enough to know how this worked, and he'd seen too many spy dramas to take anything at face value. The jogger glanced in his direction as she passed. It may have been innocent, but he'd risen through the ranks by knowing when not to take chances. There was a fine line between paranoia and due diligence.

When he was sure he couldn't be overheard again, he continued.

"Sorry about that. Have you heard anything on the grapevine about a shipment?"

"No, not so far."

"That's good. Let's hope it stays that way. That's got to be the priority. The minute that changes - if it changes - let me know."

"Shall do."

"Good girl. Keep the pressure on, then. If anything happens, or you get any sense that anyone's watching, anything at all, I want to know about it."

"Of course."

"Oh, and what's this nonsense about a homeless shelter?"

"Just that. It's a front. Pretty sure of it."

"Okay. Well, keep up the good work. It's hugely appreciated."

"Shall do. My pleasure. I'll do whatever it takes, you know that."

He terminated the call, turned left into Horse Guards Avenue and made a loop back to his office via Whitehall. There was some serious thinking to do. He was adept at dealing with pressure, but this time there was no room for even the smallest error. The rewards were there, but failure would be cataclysmic.

The time was getting closer, and the stakes were increasing with every tick of the clock.

I think I'm getting the hang of all this technology. Obviously, like most people, I mainly use the PC to play Minesweeper and Solitaire, but since Danny set us both up with CompuServe accounts I've been spending a bit of time online and - of course - discovering the joys of instant communication via email.

I was just re-reading his final message from yesterday when I heard the sound of his key in the door. Uniform indeed. I'll have to keep an eye on that. Or alternatively borrow a uniform from someone.

"Anna?" he called out.

I stood to greet him when he came into the room, wheeling a suitcase disproportionately large for the length of his latest absence. It was good to see him, and, as usual, it's any excuse for a hug.

"Good trip?" I asked, as he left my embrace in order to remove his jacket.

"I think so, but then the weirdest thing happened," he said.

"Sounds intriguing. Cup of tea?" I didn't really need to ask. I headed to the kitchen as I waited for him to reply.

"You'll never guess who I bumped into last night."

"Let me think. You were in Germany. The cast of Auf Wiedersehen, Pet, having a reunion?"

"I wish, but no. Weirder still."

I started to fill the kettle.

"A clue then?"

"A mutual friend."

"Really?" I tried to think. We didn't have many mutual friends. Mine are all decent upstanding people from the world of fashion while Danny seems to spend increasing amounts of time with shady journalists. It was futile.

"No idea," I said eventually. "Tell me."

Danny had a curious expression. Part smirk, part shifty.

"Clare," he said.

"What?"

"Clare," he repeated.

"*What?*" I repeated also. "Dead Clare? Clare your former boss, last seen in the obituary column?"

"The very same."

"And not, in fact, dead then, after all?"

"Very much not, it seems."

"And neither, by even the loosest of definitions, any friend of mine."

"No, but she was asking after you."

And so, Danny told me all about it. The summary of his latest enquiries into Graham March, who'd been suspended by the police under investigation for corruption, but seemed to be spending the days since then straying ever further. Then Clare's mysterious arrival. I wasn't very happy about it. I used to have a sneaking respect for Clare, back in the day, but that was before I discovered her darker side, and got held up at gunpoint in the process. So now my opinion could best be summed up as "good riddance". No, not happy at all.

"And then she just left?" That, I suppose, was something.

"Indeed. She gave me a hug and then disappeared into the night."

I was even less happy about the hug.

"Danny, this is not good news," I said.

"Well, it is. It means she's alive, at least. And she said she'd help me."

"And you trust her?"

"No, not really."

"*Not really*? Danny, she's evil."

"Evil's a bit strong."

"It isn't! She masterminded a fraud and then killed her colleagues, never mind the trouble she caused us. She even pointed a gun at you, Danny. A fucking great big gun. How much more evil do you want? If she's offering to help you I'd be very, very careful."

"I will. Anyway, I doubt I'll see her again."

"You doubt?"

"She'll disappear again. You know what she's like."

"But you'd entertain it if she doesn't? Jesus."

"Oh, come on. I thought you'd be pleased."

"*What?*"

I gave him a look somewhere between incredulity and contempt.

"Anyway, what was this secret night out you've arranged?"

"Oh, that. I'm not sure I'm in the mood now."

"Don't be like that."

I couldn't help it. Despite Clare's disappearance I'd still not managed to move the relationship between me and Danny up a gear. And knowing his infatuation with the woman, it seemed even less likely if she was suddenly back on the scene.

"I'll tell you over lunch," I said, "assuming the invitation's still open. And assuming I still want to accept it. I'm going for a lie down while you get unpacked." I had some thinking to do.

An hour and a half later we were being shown to a table in Cafe Delancey, just off Camden High Street. My mood had marginally improved. Despite everything, it was lovely to be back together.

"Do you remember Colette?" I asked him, once the waiter had left us to look at the menus.

"Colette? The name rings a bell."

"Colette Baca. She was a model back in the early days. Helped me put my portfolio together when I was setting up the studio."

"Ah yes, I remember. Amazing cheekbones."

I gave him a look.

"Yes. Anyway, I had a call yesterday. Her brother's in a band and they asked if I'd be happy to do some pictures for them. It's quiet at the moment so I said yes. Very happy to help."

"That's good."

"They're playing live tonight and we've been invited to go to see them, with a backstage pass, so we can go along after and meet them."

"Excellent, sounds like fun. What sort of music?"

"Ah, well, here's the thing. It's just Steve the singer, that's her brother, and two keyboard players. So, you'll be able to talk synthesisers and samplers and relive the glory days of Flag Day."

Danny looked embarrassed. He didn't like talking about his youthful aspirations to be a pop star, and the band he'd played in at home in Sunderland, before moving to London to be a student. That said, I could tell he was interested.

"Where are they playing?"

"God knows. Somewhere in Covent Garden. I've got it all written down back at the flat."

"Rock Garden?"

"That sounds like it. Anyway, are you up for it?"

"Definitely. Sounds good. What time?"

"Eight-ish I think. We can go for a drink first if you fancy it."

"Perfect." And then he gave me that look I find so adorable: crystal clear eyes beneath a floppy fringe. I had a moment of letting my imagination get the better of me but I still didn't feel quite my usual self.

Maybe it was a premonition of the horror that was about to unfold.

Chapter 5

I 'M not one to hold a grudge, normally. Actually, scratch that, maybe I am. I've never pretended to be perfect. And I certainly had a lingering resentment as far as Danny's old boss was concerned.

Now she'd annoyed me again, simply by not being as dead as she'd pretended, even though it was far from a surprise. Worse, though, I'd really been looking forward to a night out with Danny. I thought it would be fun and exciting, and a happy memory for the two of us. But the spectre of her reappearance hovered between us like a wasp at a summer picnic, and it was just so frustrating. I wanted the evening to be perfect. I really don't know why I bother sometimes. Maybe I shouldn't.

Still, it was brave face time. I didn't know much about the band apart from their name - Lumière Rouge - and obviously the identity of the singer. I knew there were two keyboard players, but had never heard any of their music. Colette described it as a kind of electro-goth crossover, which sounded vaguely terrifying. That said, I'd had a goth phase in my youth, albeit mainly with fishnets and eyeshadow. My big, backcombed '80s hair rather confused the issue. I'm a natural brunette and never really felt the urge to go black, or indeed purple, which seemed de rigueur at the time.

I think Danny was quite shocked by my appearance when we left the flat. Normally I try to make an effort, but it just wasn't happening, so I went for a simple uniform of jeans, Dr Martens boots and a black shirt, albeit with darker lipstick than normal. In fairness, he was in much the same (sans lipstick), although the black leather Belstaff jacket was a nice touch. He'd pissed me off, but I still couldn't stop myself from fancying him, as irritating as that was given his recent behaviour.

We took the tube to Covent Garden, despite my misgivings about that particular form of transport. It may be a nascent claustrophobia and the fear of being stuck in a tunnel with all manner of strangers, but most likely it's just the thought of relinquishing control to someone who grew up wanting to be a train driver, but now settles for burrowing through subterranean London like some sort of high-speed, uniformed mole.

Once back in the open air we sailed to the front of the Rock Garden queue by simple virtue of being on the guest list. That cheered me up a touch, especially as the rain was pelting down. Inside, I looked for Colette but couldn't see her among the crush. Danny did his best to lighten the mood by providing a succession of drinks, bless him. They started to have the desired effect. And by the time Lumière Rouge took to the stage I was in the mood for dancing.

It didn't last long.

The first shock was the band itself. Maybe it's latent prejudice, but I'd imagined them all to be young men, dressed in black, looking moody and magnificent. But the two keyboard players were girls, and they both looked amazing. One had flowing auburn hair, the other a shorter blonde cut. Both were in theatrical, monochromatic outfits that they'd clearly worked hard to prepare. That, in itself, should have perked me up because it would give me a lot to work with, photographically, but it was soon evident the men in the audience were fixated - Danny included. And stupidly I'd arranged for him to meet them afterwards. What is the point?

I remember being the centre of attention when I was a student, but now - as a supposed follower of fashion - I felt immediately and hopelessly underdressed.

The second shock was that they were actually bloody good, but the area in front of the stage became a heaving mass of bodies and I'm just too small for that kind of shenanigans. So, I moved back, towards the bar. Danny followed me.

"Are you okay?" he asked in the pause after the second song. I nodded.

"Are you sure?" he asked again. I just shrugged. But then the band started playing again, thumping out a chest-pounding drum track before the synthesisers cut in. I could feel Danny looking at me. He put his arm around me, but I didn't respond with my usual enthusiasm. I was beginning to think it was time to put my life in order. And that maybe I should have taken Ben from Harpers up on his offer while I had the chance.

Music, though, has a curious power to uplift, and as it continued I was genuinely impressed. I didn't know any of the songs but it really didn't matter. As they left the stage amid raucous calls for more, Danny tried again.

"What did you think?" he asked.

"Truthfully?" I asked. "They were amazing. What about you?"

"Fantastic," he said. But I didn't catch the rest of the sentence because a huge cheer announced the re-emergence of the band for the start of their encore.

When it was all over, and the crowd began to disperse, we moved to the front of the stage and I tried to attract the attention of one of the roadies, with minimal success. Thankfully I caught a glimpse of Colette at the side of the stage and waved. She waved back and a moment later she was heading our way.

"What did you think?" she asked, once the obligatory hugs were dealt with.

"Really genuinely impressed," I said, with Danny nodding beside me.

"Come on, I'll take you through and introduce you." She led the way, past a security man who looked like he could have crushed me by simply curling a finger.

Backstage was busy with various hangers-on drinking cans of beer and smoking. Steve was on a sofa looking particularly hot in more ways than one, his baggy white shirt drenched with sweat. Colette beckoned and he stood up to greet us. She did the introductions, telling him how impressed we'd been.

"So, you're the photographer?" he asked in a slightly croaky voice. "I've heard exceptional things."

"I try," I said, with a smile, "but good models help." I gave Colette a squeeze. Her own career had gone from strength to strength since we'd worked together all those years ago.

Colette looked at her watch.

"Sorry to leave the party early, but I've got to go," she said. "I've been offered a lift. I'll call you in the morning, okay?"

I nodded and we did the hug thing again. She left us with Steve. There was a momentary awkward pause, but then he filled it by offering to introduce us to the keyboard players. Obviously, I was hoping they'd be tongue-deep with their respective boyfriends, so that Danny got the off-limits message, but instead they were just together in an adjacent dressing room. Both had changed out of their stage attire and looked, frankly, a little bit spaced out.

"Holly, Leah, meet Anna, our new photographer," said Steve. "And, er..."

"Danny," said Danny. "I'm Anna's friend."

The girls shook hands but neither seemed particularly

friendly, much to my relief. And yet stupidly I still managed to cause myself unnecessary trauma.

"He's a keyboard player too," I said, and immediately regretted it. Danny looked a bit embarrassed.

"Ah, we'll leave them to talk synthesisers," Steve continued. "I've got a few ideas for the shoot to run past you. Can I get you a drink?"

"More the merrier," I said. And then hastily added "Ideas" in case he thought I was some sort of alcoholic. But then I accepted a drink too, and next thing I knew I was being passed a cold can of Red Stripe lager. It's not my usual but I'm not one to complain when on the receiving end of hospitality.

"Your voice sounds tired," I said, raising the can.

"It is a bit. It was hard work out there."

"I know. I saw. It seemed to go down well, though."

"It did, thankfully. There were A&R people out there somewhere, so hopefully they were impressed, but it's a lottery really."

"How's it all going?"

He paused for a moment. It looked as if he was unsure how to answer.

"It's going okay. It's just hard keeping the momentum, you know? Keeping everyone happy."

"The audience?"

He frowned. He seemed on edge, as though something was bothering him, but it could have just been the comedown from the adrenaline-rush of being on stage.

"Well, them, yes, but band members too." His eyes flicked to the girls. One - Holly I decided (my memory is appalling and I get easily confused after mixing my drinks) - was sitting back down, seemingly in a world of her own. I say sitting but it was more of a sprawl. She seemed completely out of it. Leah, I assume, by process of elimination, tried nudging her but just got a couple of fingers in return. Holly's eyes remained firmly closed.

Leah was talking to Danny, but even she seemed quite keen to get away. I heard words like "Jupiter 8", "Emulator" and "Prophet VS" but she kept looking past him and after a few minutes she came over to whisper something to Steve, and then disappeared. Up close she didn't seem anywhere near as glamorous. Her skin betrayed what I suspected was a far-from-healthy lifestyle. Danny came back to join us. There was definitely an undercurrent of something, but I wasn't quite sure what.

"So, the pictures?" I said once we'd watched this play out.

"Yes, sorry. Look, are you still on for tomorrow? Can we discuss it then? I'm going to have to shoot off and sort a few things."

"Yes, of course. Is everything all right?"

He nodded, but it wasn't convincing.

"Yeah, just the usual," he said. "I'd better dash. Great to meet you though. Looking forward to tomorrow."

We shook hands and then he left in the same direction as Leah. Holly remained on the sofa, largely motionless.

"Well, then," I said to Danny, in the absence of anything more constructive. I shrugged.

"Should we get going?" he asked.

I nodded. I called out goodbye to Holly but didn't get a response. Maybe she was just asleep. I don't know. Danny linked arms and we headed outside to hail a taxi. I wasn't sure what to make of it all.

"Mikołaj you old rascal, I don't mind if I do."

From behind his desk, the man gave a signal, and a moment later two glasses appeared in front of Graham March, followed closely by a bottle of Talisker single malt. A generous measure was poured in each.

"Thank you, Tomasz," said Mikołaj in heavily accented English. "You can leave us now."

As Tomasz turned, March couldn't fail to see the shoulder holster appear from under his jacket. Or the gun it contained.

"A toast, Mr March," Mikołaj said once they were alone. "To new arrivals."

March swallowed. It wasn't his usual brand but it was good, tarnished only by the overriding taste of menace in every drop.

Chapter 6

Sunday, April 3rd, 1994

DANNY was on the computer when I emerged from the shower. There was a packet of cigarettes on the desk beside him.

"Something you're not telling me?" I asked, nodding in its general direction.

"Ah," he said, looking even more shifty than he had yesterday.

I just raised my eyebrows.

"They're Clare's," he said eventually, as though trying not to upset me, but failing.

"Uh-huh," I responded, trying to affect nonchalance, but failing just as badly. I didn't know what else to say, so decided against saying anything, and instead left to make a cup of tea. A moment later Danny followed me to the kitchen.

"What's up?" he said. "You don't seem yourself."

"I'm fine," I lied. "Cup of tea?"

"Anna?"

"What?"

"Tell me."

"Tell you what?"

"What the matter is."

"Nothing's the matter."

"Is it Clare?"

"No."

"Right, so it's Clare then."

"God, you're annoying."

"Listen, I didn't ask her to reappear. I didn't ask her to help me. She just offered."

"But you accepted."

"Not in as many words."

"Ha. And what does that mean, exactly?"

Danny sat down, looking distinctly uncomfortable, while I poured hot water into two mugs and started stirring the PG Tips tea bags. I was *this* close to seeing if I could find him a leftover Typhoo instead.

"It means what I said. I was just as shocked to see her as you'd have been."

"Danny, if I'd seen her I'd have been calling the police or Interpol or at the very least hotel security."

"It just wasn't like that."

"I don't want to know."

"But it's bothering you. Why? I don't trust her either but what harm can it do?"

I just looked at him, trying to believe my ears were in some way disconnected from my brain.

"What *harm?*"

"Exactly."

"Are you being deliberately stupid or just trying to annoy me?"

"No, come on, tell me."

"For fuck's sake. The love of your life turns up when she should be doing a life stretch for multiple murders. *Murders,* Danny. She's an art thief, a self-confessed fraud, and seems to lack any sense of moral judgement. And she wants to be your friend, and she's giving you hugs, and now she's going to wheedle her way back into your life on the pretext of helping you, which is just about as likely as me becoming the next Archbishop of Canterbury, or a fucking professional basketball player or something. And you're asking me if I can see anything possibly even slightly suspect?"

"It's not like that!"

"Well, it looks like that from here."

"For starters, she's not the love of my life."

"Ha."

"Think what you want. And secondly, I'm investigating some seriously bloody dangerous people, so anything that helps is more than welcome."

"You're as bad as she is."

"I'm not! Jesus. Listen to yourself."

"Somebody needs to."

"Oh, Anna. Do you want me to get killed?"

"No, obviously."

"That's a start. Well then. Look, it's a serious business. And if she knows something then I'd be stupid not to at least take her seriously."

"Oh, so now she's your guardian angel?"

Danny laughed. Which annoyed me.

"What's funny?"

"It's just that's exactly what she said."

"What?"

"That she was my guardian angel."

"I fucking give up. Make your own tea." And I stormed off in a not inconsiderable strop.

Ten minutes later there was a knock at my bedroom door. I ignored it.

"Can I come in?" he said.

I ignored that too. He came in anyway, and sat down next to me on the bed. At least he'd had the decency to bring the tea, which was just as well.

"It's getting cold," he said, gesturing to the mug. I felt like ignoring it on a point of principle, but I like tea, and principles take second priority at times.

"Anna," he said, when I still didn't respond. "Please let's not fall out."

I looked at him. He looked genuinely upset at the prospect. I felt my anger start to soften, which is weird because that should have just annoyed me even more.

"I just don't see how her turning up is anything other than trouble," I said eventually.

"No, I understand that. But trust me. I'll take anything she says with a pinch of salt."

"And now you're talking in clichés."

"This is serious! No, I don't trust her. But she knows people. She may help. She may be completely useless. I don't know. But everything is worth considering. Do you think March is playing by the rules?"

"No."

"Exactly. So yes, I take on board the warning, and I love that you care, but I have to listen to her. I'd be stupid not to."

I rubbed my eyes with both hands, wishing I'd tidied my room before his arrival, and took a sip of the tea to give myself thinking time.

"And the cigarettes?" I asked eventually.

"She left them on the table in the hotel."

"And you kept them as what? Some sort of souvenir?"

"No. Because she'd written me a message in the lid."

"That's romantic. What sort of message?"

"Will you give it up with the romance? You were the one out swapping numbers with non-gay Ben."

"Yeah, well I may just ring him. What sort of message?"

"Her email address."

I sighed. Danny just looked at me. She was clever. I'd give her that. Too clever for her own good one day, perhaps.

"Okay," I said, feeling the fight go out of me. "Just promise me you'll be careful."

"I will." It came out as little more than a whisper. And then we hugged. And then his mobile phone rang.

Danny rushed to the living room to answer the call, leaving me to ponder my life decisions, but not coming up with thoughts of any particular clarity. A couple of minutes later he reappeared, looking shocked.

"Everything okay?" I asked.

"That was March," he said. "He wants to meet."

Danny left the flat about half an hour later. I told him to be careful, and he assured me he would be. They were meeting in a coffee shop near Mornington Crescent, in full view of the public. If there was any trouble there'd be plenty of witnesses. I wasn't happy but acknowledged he had no option but to go.

With the flat to myself, I had a call of my own to make. Not to Ben, although I was seriously tempted. Colette answered on the fourth ring.

"What's the deal with the girls?" I asked, after we'd said our hellos.

"In what way?"

"I don't know. There just seemed to be a bit of tension. And they looked a bit out of it. Are they okay?"

"How do you mean okay?"

"Just okay, okay. It was like they were spaced out. Excuse the lack of subtlety, but are they on drugs or something?"

I could hear Colette sigh.

"I don't know. Quite possibly. Why? What happened?"

I told her about Holly collapsing on the sofa and Leah acting weird.

"Leah's a funny one," Colette said after I'd finished. "Holly seems a bit posh. She's got a kind of public school background and definitely comes from money. I get the feeling she's only in the band as some sort of rebellious phase before settling down for a life in the country with a city boy."

"I know the type."

"Exactly. Leah, though... she's about as different as it gets. I think she was homeless. Maybe not sleeping rough as such, but living in a squat somewhere. How they all met each other I have no idea. I get the sense she's had it hard."

"Are they your friends?"

"No, not particularly. I've only met them through Steve."

"That's good. I'm not sure about them. Steve seems a lovely guy but they seem highly strung."

"When are you doing the pictures?"

"This afternoon."

"Best of luck then. See what you can find out. Let me know how it goes. Okay?"

"Shall do."

"I'm out of the country for a week on a job, but we'll catch up when I get back. Call me."

"I will. Have fun."

We hung up. I thought again about calling Ben, but I had too much to do, preparing for the photo shoot. What would I say to him anyway? "Hi Ben, I know I said I wasn't interested as recently as thirty-six hours ago, but how about a night of passion just to get my own back on my flatmate who's a pain in the arse?" And besides, I couldn't help worrying about Danny. Of all the unfathomable things in the world, what exactly was March up to?

Chapter 7

"DANNY, you're looking well. Can I order you a tea or something? Earl Grey perhaps? You look the sort."

Danny looked around the room, scanning for anyone who might be watching. Alert to danger. There were only three other customers. A couple seemingly in love, holding hands in the corner, and a mother with a pushchair near the counter. None looked particularly interested in the overweight man with the thinning grey hair, sitting on his own by the window.

"What's this about?" asked Danny.

"Just a little chat with my old friend. Take a chair, please. The lovely waitress will be over in a moment."

Danny sat down, against his better judgement. The last time he'd been opposite Graham March had been in an official police interview, during the hunt for Clare. It hadn't been cordial.

"So, how's life?"

"I'm doing well, Graham. Can I call you Graham? I gather titles are no longer appropriate."

"Ah Danny, you're a cheeky boy. It's just temporary, I assure you. Just a little misunderstanding, caused in no small part by your good self, but don't worry, I bear you no malice. I'm enjoying an extended paid holiday thanks to you. You've done me a favour."

Danny looked at the man opposite. They hadn't shaken hands.

"That wasn't the intention. But again, the meeting?"

"You're a bit eager. Patience, old boy. Your Uncle Graham has got a story for you."

Danny laughed.

"You're coming clean? Well that's a turn-up. Excuse me while I start the tape machine."

"Ah, not so fast. Make yourself comfortable. All in good time."

The waitress arrived. Danny ordered a cappuccino, without sprinkles.

"How old are you now, Danny?" March continued. "Twenty? Twenty-one?"

"Twenty-five."

"Really? And yet still possessed of such youthful innocence. I've read some of your work."

"You can read! Well done."

March ignored the jibe.

"Some interesting theories. A rather tasty hatchet job on your former boss, if you don't mind me saying."

"I'm not sure I'm interested in your opinion on anything."

"Have you heard from Clare recently?"

"No."

"You surprise me. Obviously we can agree the helicopter crash was a fake?"

Danny feigned a yawn.

"I'm not here to talk about Clare."

"No, of course, but it's interesting nonetheless. What I like to call a real-life mystery. The hunter becomes the hunted and then goes all Lord Lucan on us."

"Have *you* heard from her?"

"Me? Alas not, although she has my number if she's in town

and wants some excitement one evening. Even the enchanting Clare must have needs."

Danny looked for a trace of a smile but March looked serious. If he wasn't being ironic he was surely delusional.

"Listen, I'm sorry to curtail your daydream, Graham, but can you actually get to the point?"

"I'm building to that. And how is sweet little Anna. Are you two shagging yet or does she prefer them manlier?"

"That's none of your business."

"No, but the image makes me chuckle."

The coffee arrived. Danny reached for his wallet but March passed the waitress a five pound note.

"My treat. All things considered."

"Assuming it isn't poisoned."

"You could say thank you."

"I could."

Danny pulled the cup closer and scooped some of the froth with a teaspoon.

"One last question and then we'll begin," March continued. "Easter Bunny, Danny? Is that really the name you gave me?"

"One of many, but by far the least offensive."

"Ah, very good. And the rationale?"

"Because of your name, March. That's the Easter. And the Bunny because you were operating underground."

"Oh." March looked puzzled.

"What?"

"Ah, well, that is a disappointment."

"A disappointment?"

"Yes. I was rather assuming it was something to do with my prowess with the ladies. You know? At it like a rabbit, if you catch my drift. How thoroughly unexciting. And talking of which, have you spoken to the delectable DC Amy Cranston recently? Although I hear she's a DS now. Very impressive. I really do miss her."

"I'm sure it's not mutual."

March leaned forward and lowered his voice. Suddenly the mask of joviality slipped.

"Danny, I used to think you were an annoying little shit, but I appreciate I need to reassess that judgement, as you seem to have put a bit of weight on. You want to be careful with the pizzas. Get yourself to the gym perhaps, try to build some actual muscles. Either way, it's time to give you the benefit of the doubt. I'm here to do you a favour."

"A favour? From you?" Danny laughed, leaning back to put as much distance between them as possible.

"Well, I say a favour, but it's a chance, mainly, for you to atone for your earlier misjudgements."

"Right. And they are?"

"Don't be coy, Danny. You know you've said some horrible things about me."

"All of which were true."

"In your warped tabloid opinion. But now you can write a new story and set the record straight."

"The record's already straight. The only bit missing is the part where you get sent away."

"I'll ignore your naivety." March reached into his pocket for cigarettes, withdrew one and lit it, inhaling deeply.

"I didn't know you smoked," said Danny, making a show of wafting the smoke away.

"At last you make a salient point," said March, putting his lighter back in his jacket pocket.

"Which is?"

"The things you don't know about me. Specifically, viz, my charity work."

"Your *what?*"

"Ooh, very good. That's the spirit. The investigative journalist - and I use the term in its loosest sense - actually asking a question. We'll make a man of you yet, Danny."

"Fuck off, Graham. Are we done? I've got better things to be doing on a Sunday." Danny started to stand up. March reached out and grabbed his arm, pulling him back down. His grip was vicelike.

"You're forgetting the story, Danny. You'll want to hear this."

"I doubt it."

"Well, I'll summarise and try to speak very slowly. Make things easy for you. So, the next thing you don't know is that I'm volunteering at a homeless shelter. A leading light in the quest to provide safe accommodation for the disadvantaged, if you will."

"You're doing *what?*" Danny's question was part disbelief, part disdain.

"Exactly what I just said. And you get to write the story. Wrongly maligned senior police officer shows the caring side of humanity. It's good news for a change. Your readers will lap it up."

"Are you drunk?"

"I hesitate to acknowledge the insinuation."

"Well what the fuck are you on about? The only thing our readers are interested in, where you're concerned, is how long you're getting sent down for."

"So it's your job to change perceptions. I'm a decent man, Danny. Come with me and I'll give you an exclusive. And then, as a separate adjunct, I'll tell you about my work in the field of the arts. And not the kind of art your former boss used to nick, either."

Danny leaned forward, looking March straight in the eyes.

"I don't know what the fuck you're playing at, but play it with someone else, okay?" This time when he stood up March didn't try to stop him. Danny turned and left the building, heading out into the relentless rain without looking back.

The location for my photoshoot with Lumière Rouge was a derelict building close to Bromley-by-Bow tube station, which meant another trip on the loathsome Underground. I could have driven, and normally wouldn't have given it a second thought, but by the time I'd finished preparing my equipment I didn't have time to write a shot list or start sketching ideas, so I decided to take the train and do it on the way instead. It was a heavy-duty compromise for the sake of art.

Steve was there, with a bag over one shoulder, holding an umbrella, but there was no sign of the girls. We shook hands.

"So, what did you have in mind?" I asked.

"Quite straightforward, really. We just need a few publicity shots for gigs and labels. Apparently you're the best."

"According to Colette?"

Steve grinned.

"Of course."

"Well, she's got a point." I smiled back. "Do you have a stylist? Any requests from management or a record company?"

He shook his head.

"No, no stylist, sadly. And no manager either. It's just us. And we're still working on the record company thing but hopefully this will help."

"Fingers crossed. I'll do my best. Any sign of the others?"

"They're on their way, apparently." Steve sighed, as though this was a frequent occurrence. "Come on, we'll do a recce while we wait."

We edged through a broken gate, past a sign forbidding trespassers, and approached the main doors of the deserted building.

"Have we got permission for this?" I asked.

"Not exactly, but there's no security apparently. We'll be okay if we're careful."

I had my doubts. The doors had been kicked in, and unsuccessfully boarded up. I assumed it had once been an office block but now all the windows were smashed and nature had taken its course. Weeds had taken hold in cracks in the concrete floor. There was a steady wind, carrying in rain and catching an almost overbearing stench of decay and urine. One corner showed evidence of a fire. Empty beer cans littered the floor, together with the occasional syringe and used condom. Not my idea of a romantic setting, but I'm a traditional girl at heart.

"How did you find this place?" I asked, trying to keep cheerful rather than betraying my sense of distaste. And wishing my sense of smell was less sensitive.

"Leah heard about it. We're going for the distressed look."

"You've achieved that. Is it safe?"

"Should be. Just be careful where you're walking."

I crossed to the window. Shattered glass lay on the floor, crunching under the soles of my DMs. Outside, the traffic was relentless. I shivered. The place was creepy. Suddenly I felt very aware of my own vulnerability. What if Steve was a maniac and was here to murder me? What chance would I have? Nobody would hear my screams. I started to feel increasingly uncomfortable.

"What do you think?" he asked, moving towards me. My grip tightened on my camera bag. I wished I'd brought a tripod. I've used one of those as a weapon before.

But before I had a chance to answer, I saw movement from over his shoulder. The one I thought was Holly was making her way towards us. I visibly relaxed.

"Hi," I called, with perhaps disproportionate jollity. "Come and join us."

Holly didn't look happy, but at least she was upright and, best of all, she was here.

"What the fuck is this place?" she asked. A hello would have been nice.

Steve moved over towards her and they walked off together, talking in hushed voices, leaving me alone. I felt isolated. I didn't expect to suddenly be treated like one of the band, but I had no more idea about the underlying tensions than the previous night. The irritation was just taking hold when Leah arrived. At least I assumed it was Leah. It was hard to tell behind the sunglasses. She came towards me, stumbled over a broken pipe, and swore.

"All right?" I asked.

"Yeah, fine," she said. Thankfully their musicianship was infinitely better than their conversation.

After a minute or so of uncomfortable silence, apart from the wind and traffic, Steve and Holly returned. Steve took control. I was grateful. He directed us all to a space on the far side of the building where the light was casting interesting shadows on what was left of an interior wall. He took a can of spray paint from his shoulder bag and started work, writing the band's name on the wall. In some ways, I was quite impressed. It was wanton vandalism, certainly, but hardly likely to lower the tone of the place. And I admired the sense of daring. I just couldn't wait to get out of there.

Leah hardly spoke a word throughout the entire session, but she seemed happy to pose as I directed. I made use of the available natural light and then tried some with a flash, bouncing it off broken ceiling tiles. After the group shots in various combinations I did more of the girls together, and then each of them on their own. Despite everything, I started to almost enjoy myself. I always find photography therapeutic and I love a creative challenge. We tried some other places within the building, and I did some artistic stuff, playing with shallow depths of field and then slow shutter speeds with the traffic behind, blurring it into the background.

After about an hour and a half it was getting dark, I was cold and I was running out of film. Thankfully Steve called a halt.

"That should do," he said. "How are they looking?"

"Decent, I think. There's definitely something there."

"Excellent."

Leah came to stand beside him, but Holly wandered off on her own. It was like the girls couldn't bear to speak to each other. I didn't have much optimism for their future together, but I kept those thoughts to myself.

"Listen, I was going to suggest going to the pub to celebrate, but I think we're going to have to run," he said. "Sorry." He looked genuinely concerned.

"That's okay," I replied. It was a shame. It would have been nice to chat to them, but in other ways I was relieved. I just wanted to get home and get warm. And have a shower.

"How long will it take to process the films?"

"Not long. I'll crack on with it first thing tomorrow."

"Brilliant. Do you want to pop by the rehearsal studio tomorrow afternoon, maybe two-ish, if that's not too early? I can't wait to see them. And we're playing live again tomorrow night if you fancy coming again."

I agreed, said I'd love to, and offered to attempt some live shots. As I was packing my camera away, Holly came over. It seemed completely out of character.

"Can I have a word?" she asked, as though talking to a stranger, rather than someone she'd been working with for the last couple of hours.

"Of course," I said. "What's up?"

She seemed hesitant.

"I just wanted to say thanks. For coming."

I was taken aback.

"That's okay," I said. "It was fun."

"No," she said, shaking her head. "It wasn't. Not really. But that's not your fault. You did a great job. Let me give you my number." She asked for a pen. I took one out of my camera bag and she wrote it on the side of one of the film boxes.

"It was great to meet you," she said. Suddenly her face conveyed a warmth that I'd never seen before. It was all very odd. I was tempted to get the camera out again, but there was no time.

Steve led the way out of the building, back through the broken gate and onto the street outside. I assumed we'd all get the tube back to somewhere together, but instead they said their farewells. I was left to walk to the station on my own.

It was the last time I'd see all three of them alive.

Chapter 8

GRAHAM March took the rear exit from Green Park Underground station, emerging onto Stratton Street, close to Langan's Brasserie. Evening service was just beginning, but despite the culinary temptations, he walked past, heading towards the Albermarle Casino and Gentleman's Club, just off Berkeley Square.

If everything went well, he would endeavour to find a pretty hostess in whom to indulge for a couple of hours, but first there was some business to resolve.

He nodded to the doorman who stood aside so he could enter the marbled foyer. A golden chandelier gave a low, seductive light.

"Good evening, Mr March, wonderful to see you again," said the receptionist from behind the security of her desk. The faked sincerity was almost believable.

"Good evening, my darling," he replied. "Just a quick word with Jacqueline if I may?"

"Of course. I'll just check that she's in."

Of course she was in. She was always in. Where else would she be? But it still paid to employ a gatekeeper.

The receptionist picked up the phone and dialled an internal number. A moment later she turned back to March.

"She's ready for you," she said. "You know the way."

"Thank you, my dear," he said. He unbuttoned his overcoat and headed through the gilt-laden double doors.

"So?" asked Jacqueline, once the drinks were poured. "What's new with Mikołaj?"

"It's all very interesting, my dear."

"Meaning?"

"He's an intriguing young man. Speaks very highly of you, by the way. We had quite the chat about you. It seems he'd like to take you to dinner."

"Well that's not going to happen."

"Really? He was most insistent."

"My involvement is strictly via you. As far as he's concerned I don't need to exist any more. I can't be anywhere near this."

"Of course."

"As long as that's understood."

Understood but highly inconvenient.

"Naturally, Jacqui. On the plus side, he confirmed the imminent shipment, although I wish he wouldn't use that word. I find it slightly dehumanising."

"Christ. First the homeless, now this. You do make me laugh. You're all heart, Graham. I didn't think you had it in you."

"I'm a decent man."

"And I'm the fucking Princess of Wales."

They paused to drink. Jacqueline lit a cigarette, offered one to March, but he declined.

"I'm still off them," he said.

"Good for you."

"Telling you, you're in the company of a new man."

"And I don't believe a word of it. Did he give an actual ETA?"

"Not an exact date, no. I suspect the logistics are complicated, but early next week from what I can tell."

"Good. Did he confirm how many?"

"Anywhere between twelve and twenty."

"Useful. And I can rely on you?"

"I'm shocked you need to ask."

"I'm equally shocked you expect me not to."

"Haha. We know each other too well."

"Okay. Well, I'll still want first look when they get here. See if I can make use of any. And then we can sort things. Okay?"

"Excellent plan."

Twenty minutes later March was heading back towards Green Park. He stepped off the kerb and nearly collided with a cyclist, who swore. He didn't apologise. His mind was elsewhere. He had a keen instinct for self-preservation and could sense trouble ahead.

It hadn't been the time to start befriending a hostess, under the watchful gaze of the casino staff, but instead of entering the Underground station, he continued and turned right on Piccadilly. He'd just pay a quick visit to Shepherd Market and see if he could maybe find a nice French girl for half an hour or so. It would be a much-needed distraction. And then he could decide how best to get out of this alive.

Back at the casino, Jacqueline addressed the two men in front of her.

"Every fucking thing he does and every fucking where he goes. Okay?"

The taller of the two nodded.

"Good. We're done. Start tomorrow and keep me informed. I want to know everyone the bastard speaks to, what he has for lunch, every time he takes a piss. I do not trust the twat. Start from there and work back."

"Understood."

"No excuses, Finn. I don't need to explain why. Concentrate on him. And Logan?"

The other looked up.

"Like we said, make sure you stick close to every other fucker he may be speaking to. Is that all clear?"

"Yes, boss," said Finn. Logan nodded.

"Right, you can go. The pair of you."

They both turned without a word and left the room. Jacqueline finished her drink and switched off her computer. She'd go out for dinner and then decide exactly what to do with March when this was all over.

After a weekend in his Hampshire constituency, opening a fete and discussing the minutiae of Government policy with ill-informed constituents who clearly had no idea of the real issues facing a man of his standing, Samuel Elmhirst-Banks was pleased to return to the sanctuary and privacy of his Barbican flat. Working in Government offered perks and privilege, but having to shake hands and feign interest with those who elected him was a significant and perennial irritation.

He'd just poured a restorative glass of Argentinian Malbec when the phone started ringing. He sighed. It was rarely good news at this time of the evening. The Chief Whip and the spin doctors didn't respect the convention of the working day.

He moved through to the living room and picked up the handset.

"Seb," he said, using his initials as a short-form of his name.

"Hi," she replied. He immediately relaxed at the sound of the familiar female voice, but then stiffened again as his mind switched back to the March conundrum. The man was a liability. The situation needed to be controlled.

"I'm glad it's you," he continued. "How's it going? Anything to report?"

"It's not exactly trouble-free but there's nothing to worry about."

"Do I want to hear this?"

"Probably not."

"Jesus. Spare me then. Just the basics."

"Okay. Don't panic, but we've had a couple of complications on the domestic side of things. Nothing I can't handle."

"For God's sake. Is it bad?"

"No, I'm dealing with it."

"How bad?"

"Honestly, don't worry. Bad, but not too bad. I'm sorting it."

He paused, giving himself a moment to think, but then decided to trust his instincts.

"Good. I trust you. Any more movements?"

"He's been back to the parlour and the casino. Just the regular pattern, nothing out of the ordinary. I've got a plan, though. You'll absolutely love this."

Chapter 9

IT amazes me that a city the size of London, with nearly seven million inhabitants, can sometimes seem so small. I don't take the Underground particularly regularly (may have mentioned it), but I was once on a train that was pulling into Edgware Road station when I looked up and saw two people from my school in Manchester, standing on the platform. How did that happen? I jumped off the train immediately and greeted them like long-lost friends until reality struck and I remembered that I didn't have much in common with either of them, and would probably never see them again.

A similar thing happened on the journey back from Bromley-by-Bow. It's an open-air station. I walked to the back of the platform in order to improve my chances of getting a seat, and waited in the cold for the train to arrive. The rain had reduced to a light drizzle so it was just about bearable, although it was doing nothing for my hair. There was only one other passenger on my end of the platform. He was about my age, mid-twenties, and seemed well-dressed despite an otherwise slightly rugged appearance. I was particularly impressed by his scarf, which was an almost perfect match for his blue eyes, and tied in a casual

European loop. Not that I'm in the habit of making eye contact with strangers, but he'd looked up as I approached, just before his mobile phone started ringing. He answered the call, but had to end it quickly as the train approached. I didn't take in what he said.

We both got on to the same carriage, and sat on opposite sides, about five seats apart. I didn't have anything to read so tried to collect my thoughts about Danny and Clare, and then the photo shoot and the band. A couple of times I looked up. Scarf man was reading a novel. I tried to make out the title for the sake of something to do. And then he looked up, and caught me, so I quickly averted my eyes, as you do, and may have even blushed a bit.

Eventually the train pulled in to Mile End. I had the option of changing there, but instead decided to stay on and swap to the Northern Line at Moorgate. Scarf man stood up and made his way to the doors, and left the train as soon as they opened. I watched him walk down the platform but then returned to my private world.

I'd been so happy on Friday, laughing and drinking with Katie and Ben. It had all seemed so natural, so easy, so uncomplicated. Colleagues of sorts, having a good time, swapping industry gossip. But now my mood was considerably darker. I wasn't sure quite why I felt so irritated about Clare's reappearance, but just the mention of her name seemed to play havoc with my blood pressure. And I'm normally such a nice, placid person.

I started having thoughts that would have seemed surreal just two days ago. Maybe I had been too hasty with Ben. My feelings for Danny run deep, but it's complicated by the intensity of our friendship. Realistically if we were ever going to get together it would have happened by now, but maybe we just know each other too well. I'm historically useless at relationships, and no matter how much I dream of hearts and flowers, the risk of ruining what we already have always holds me back. On occasions, I get the sense that he feels the same, but we've reached a kind of easy familiarity in which such issues never really get discussed.

Eventually the train pulled in to Moorgate. I got off and made my way to the northbound Northern Line. I moved to the end of the platform again. After an eight-minute wait the train arrived. The carriage was busy, and it was standing room only, although a lot of people got off at Kings Cross and I was able to get a seat for the last few stops. And that's when I noticed scarf man again, at the far end of the carriage, still reading his book.

That puzzled me. How had he done that? I tried not to keep looking but I was finding myself intrigued. He didn't seem to notice me, though, so I tried to think of something else.

A few minutes later, the train pulled into Camden Town and I stood up to get off. I gave him one last glance, but he seemed oblivious. That was probably a good thing. He was still reading.

I got off the train and walked through the station, wishing my bag was slightly less heavy. Eventually I caught the escalator to the ground level, then turned left to get the bus up to Rochester Square and home. And that, I thought, was that.

About half an hour later, I made a decision. I called Ben. What harm could it do? Sadly, however, there was no answer until the voicemail kicked in. I didn't know what message to leave, so I disconnected the call, partly frustrated and partly relieved. In one sense it felt like some great infidelity, but an increasing part of me had decided it was entirely justifiable. At the very least we could have a nice glass of wine, or several, and we could discuss editors and clients and all the sort of fashion industry nonsense that I normally try to avoid, but really should probably pay more attention to.

Danny wasn't home and I was feeling restless. I thought about heading up to my studio to process the films, but I was tired and felt in need of a shower and a lie down. I popped the kettle on but then remembered that we'd used the last of the milk that morning. So, reluctantly, I put my jacket on, and popped out of the flat to get some from the petrol station on Camden Road (and some biscuits, I won't lie).

As I was queuing up to pay, I heard the door open behind me. I paid and took my change, and turned to leave, only to see scarf man walking towards the chiller cabinet at the back of the shop. I did one of those double take things, just as he turned around and caught me looking at him again.

There was a momentary look of puzzlement and then he started to smile.

"Are you following me?" he said.

It was one of those scenes you play back in your mind with all sorts of witty responses, but in the heat of the moment I could only manage a "What? No. Sorry."

And then I thought, hold on, I was in the shop first, so I was very much not following anyone. I pointed that out.

"Valid point," he said. "Although you did follow me onto the platform at Bromley-by-Bow."

"No, I didn't. You just happened to be there when I arrived. That's different."

"Okay, but you were looking at me on the train."

"Don't flatter yourself. I was trying to see the title of your book."

"My book?"

"Yes."

"Right."

"It looked familiar and I was bored, all right?"

"If you insist." He started laughing. Normally that would have annoyed me but actually I didn't mind. I could see the funny side.

"So, what was it?"

"My book?"

I nodded.

"The Shipping News."

"Ah, okay. I've heard of that. Is it good?"

"I think so." He looked down. "Anyway, I should leave you to your, um, biscuits."

I followed his eyes to the packet of overpriced chocolate digestives and suddenly felt guilty. I hoped my choice of comfort food didn't scream desperation.

"Yes, well, thank you. Nice meeting you. Again."

"My pleasure. See you soon." It was said with a genuine smile and a twinkle in his eyes.

"Not if I see you first," I said, but didn't mean it. I was just leaving the shop when he called after me.

"So, what were you doing in Bromley-by-Bow?"

I stopped, letting the door close on its own.

"Taking pictures. And you?" He took his change from the shop assistant.

"I was at 3 Mills."

"3 Mills? Should I know that?"

"Possibly. I don't know. It's a film studio."

"Ah, very impressive. So, you're what? A film star?"

"I wish. No, just the odd bit of acting but nothing you'd have heard of. Not yet, anyway."

That was my next question answered.

"What's your name? I'll look out for you."

"Mitch Hennessey. And you are?"

"Anna. Anna Burgin."

"Pleased to meet you then, Anna Anna Burgin, so good they named her twice," he said, offering me a handshake. I accepted. His hand was warm and the grip firm, but not overly so.

"You can let go now," I said, but part of me didn't mean that either. What was happening to me? First the thoughts of Ben, and now this. Maybe it was my subconscious deciding it was definitely time to move on. Or at least definitely show Danny what he was risking.

"I don't suppose..." he started, then paused. "No, sorry, I shouldn't."

"Shouldn't what?"

"I was just going to say, if you're so intent on stalking me, maybe you could fancy going for a drink some time?"

"Ah," I said.

"I'm sorry."

"No, don't apologise. I'm flattered."

"Really? So you would?"

"I didn't say that. Just I was flattered to be asked. And just to reiterate, I'm not a stalker."

He laughed.

"Ah okay. Sorry. I was getting carried away. Boyfriend?"

"It's complicated."

"Understood."

"Nice meeting you, though." I turned to leave.

"Let me give you my number," he said. "Just, you know, in case it gets any, er, less complicated."

I turned back. I *was* flattered. I liked him. God.

"Okay," I said.

He took a card from his wallet. It said Mitch Hennessey, screen actor, and had a mobile number below.

"Very impressive," I said.

"Call me," he said. "Any time. And I'll lend you the book when I've finished."

"Okay," I smiled. "I may just do that."

I didn't give him my mobile number in return, not least because I can never remember it. But this time, I really did leave the shop, and headed home with slightly more of a spring in my step. There was suddenly even more to think about, but the possibilities were intriguing.

Samuel Elmhirst-Banks looked at the clock. It was nearly ten. Maybe too late? It was worth a try. He dialled a number. It was answered on the third ring.

"DS Cranston."

"Amy! How are you? It's Seb."

"Seb. Hi. What's up?"

"Just a quick call. Is it a good time?"

He doubted there ever a good time for an unsolicited call from a politician, but he'd met DS Cranston several times in the course of his Home Office duties and they knew each other well.

"It's fine. I was just running a bath. What can I do for you?"

"Nothing urgent. I need to talk to you about a friend of yours."

"Of mine?"

He laughed.

"Okay, not a friend. Graham March."

"Oh God. What's he done now?"

"That's what I need to talk to you about."

"And?"

"He seems to be putting himself about a bit."

"Hold on, let me just turn the taps off."

He refilled his glass while he waited for her to return. One more wouldn't hurt, although it was looking like a busy day tomorrow. There was never a quiet one in Government, just seemingly endless firefighting, committee meetings, and covering of tracks. Talking of which...

"I'm back," she said after a moment.

"I do apologise. This won't take long."

"Do I need to take notes?"

"No, you're okay. It's off the record at the moment. It's just, well... Delicate."

"How come?"

"It's just March. How's the investigation going?"

"You know I can't tell you that. It's an internal enquiry. I'm not involved except as a witness, but even if I was, I wouldn't be able to discuss it. You know that."

"I do. Of course. But I don't need to tell you the sensitivity of the situation. Can I be frank with you?"

"Of course."

"Okay. Look, I probably shouldn't say this but I'm being leaned on, if you know what I mean. You've seen the papers, I assume?"

"Which ones?"

"All of them, just about. Conspiracy theories about corruption seem very much in vogue."

"I've noticed."

"Exactly. And those above seem to expect me to - how can I put this - keep a lid on things, if you catch my drift. Anything new could be *very* bad PR, and we can't have that, especially at the moment."

"Sorry to hear that, but he's suspended while the investigation continues. There's nothing more I can tell you."

"I know. And I'm sure it'll be very thorough."

"It will. It is."

"Of course."

It was time for a different approach.

"Are you keeping an eye on him in the meantime?" he asked.

"Not personally, no."

"Is that not within your remit?"

"Not really. Why? What's bothering you?"

"I'm just concerned, Amy. The rottweilers are circling and they don't need any encouragement. Who's the guy who broke the original story? Danny someone. You know him?"

"Danny Churchill. Yes, I know him."

"What do you make of him?"

"He's straight up. Thorough but decent."

"Is he still on the story?"

"I don't know, but probably."

"But you haven't heard anything?"

"No."

"Okay. But listen, Amy, could you do me a favour? If you hear anything about it, or about anything that March is up to, can you let me know? Within the realms of whatever you can do without breaking any rules, of course. I need to make sure it doesn't get any worse. I could do with knowing what he's up to."

"Okay," she said. "Just don't pin your hopes on it."

"I won't."

They ended the call. DS Amy Cranston returned to her bath. Seb took his glass through to the kitchen. There was progress of sorts, but he still felt uneasy. Maybe it was time to start thinking about insurance.

Chapter 10

"MORNING stranger. How was Germany?" Derek Hughes, one of the Daily Echo's longest-serving sub-editors, looked up from his desk as Danny walked across the open-plan newsroom, towards his corner office.

"Cold," said Danny, pausing momentarily. "Good, though. How are things here?"

"Ah, just the usual. Mike's on the warpath."

"Again? God."

"Definitely in your interest to pop your head in. Word to the wise."

"Cheers, Derek. Shall do." It was good to have someone looking out for you, especially when deadlines were being missed.

With a deep breath, Danny crossed to Mike Walker's office. His editor had been supportive since Danny had taken over as the head of the Special Investigations Department, but his mood could fluctuate in a heartbeat. He handled stress by sharing it equally among his staff, with added venom when a front page was at stake. Danny knocked on the open door. Walker looked up from the newspaper he was reading.

"Danny, come in," he said. A seat wasn't offered. It never took long enough to get comfortable.

"Did you want to see me?"

"No, I didn't want to see you. I wanted to see your fucking copy."

"I'm working on it, Mike."

"What the exact fuck use is that? Shall I call the press hall? Tell them not to bother today because the golden boy's been fucking off round Europe on a jolly? And then call accounts and ask them to express your expenses because you're skint after running up a massive fucking bill trying to find whatever the German equivalent of a wild goose is?"

"No, I'm sorry. But it's taking time."

"To do what? March is as guilty as the fucking Kray twins. How much more time do you need?"

"Is that rhetorical?"

"What?"

"Just asking."

"No, go on. How much longer?"

"It's hard to tell."

"Oh, for fuck's sake." Walker shut the newspaper and threw it on his desk. "What's the delay?"

Danny closed the door without asking.

"I'm going to have to ask you to trust me on this."

"Go on."

"It's getting bigger. I had a hunch he wasn't spending his suspension looking after the garden, so I started looking deeper."

"And?"

"It seems like he's got some very naughty friends from eastern Europe."

"Can you get to the point?"

"Yes, sorry. Okay, he seems to be getting involved in people trafficking. Sex trafficking to be exact."

"Jesus."

"Exactly. He's working with a guy from Poland but there's a network. And then yesterday I found out he's got an involvement in a homeless shelter."

"A *what?*"

"Exactly. Says it's his charitable side, putting the world to rights, but does that sound feasible? I don't think so."

"So, what are you thinking?" Walker's tone was softening. He could recognise a story.

"That he's using the shelter as some form of a front. Either taking girls from there and passing them into his network, or somehow using that to bring them over here from Poland, Bulgaria, wherever. Either way it needs looking into."

"The filthy bastard. So why did you go to Germany?"

"The girls come from the old Eastern Bloc but they get funnelled through Cologne before ending up here. I'm getting close but it's hard to pin anything on him. There's definitely something in it, though. There's talk of a group of girls coming over this week, or if not, soon after. I want to follow him, see what he's up to. See if I can establish a link then bang. We've got him."

"Jesus. Legal's going to have a field day with this. Okay. Do you need any help? Photographer?"

"I'm all right at the moment but I'll let you know."

Walker sat back in his chair, thinking.

"How did you hear about the homeless shelter?"

"He told me himself."

"What?"

"He rang, asked to meet me. I met him yesterday. Wants me to run it as some sort of good news story to help clear his name."

"Well, that's a lot of bollocks. He must know you're getting close, though. He's trying to cover his tracks, or lead you up an alley."

"Possibly literally."

"Exactly. Be careful, Danny."

Walker stood up, came around his desk, and patted Danny on the shoulder.

"Good work. Keep me informed, okay? And on my desk by the end of the week."

"What? The whole thing?"

"Got a problem with that?"

"I don't know, I... It depends how it goes this week."

"You're playing with the big boys now, Danny. The longer you take, the more chance of a leak or the more chance he'll get away with it. I'll give you to the end of the week, then I want him on his sword. Okay?"

It wasn't a question so much as a statement. Danny nodded and left the room.

There were still two desks in the Special Investigations Department. Clare's was now covered in books, newspapers, magazines and clutter but there was an order to everything, below the superficial appearance of chaos. Her Atex terminal had been removed. Danny had thoughts of hiring an assistant of his own, but as yet hadn't had the budget approval. In any case he was doing very well on his own, with occasional support from elsewhere within the editorial department. Clare's nameplate had also been removed from the door. It was like she'd never existed.

There were two phones on his desk - the black one for calls through the switchboard and a red one that served as a direct line for those to whom he'd given his number. Danny picked up the black one and started dialling.

"DS Cranston," said a voice, as the call was answered.

"Hi Amy, it's Danny. Good time to call?"

"Possibly excellent as it happens. How are you doing, Danny?"

He'd met Detective Sergeant Amy Cranston during the search for Clare. Despite him being a suspect in the disappearance, and being on the receiving end of several police interviews, Danny found that he could trust her. She was straight, and had believed in him when her former boss, DCI Graham March, was trying to accuse him of murder. They got on well. They both wanted to see March pay for his corruption. For Amy, it was a question of pride in the police service to which she'd devoted her career.

They made small talk for a couple of minutes and then Danny got to the point.

"Can I talk to you off the record? About March?"

"Of course, although he seems to be the flavour of the month at the moment. Were your ears burning last night, by the way?"

"Mine? No. Why?"

"Nothing to worry about. I just had a call about you."

"Me? Who from?" Danny was immediately on alert.

"A guy called Samuel Elmhirst-Banks. Calls himself Seb for short. Have you heard of him?"

"He's a politician, isn't he? Home Office or something?"

"That's the one. Junior minister."

"Why was he interested in me?"

"He wasn't originally. He called to discuss March. He seems absolutely paranoid about bad PR for the Met. I got the impression he'd rather we brushed it all under the carpet than bring March to justice and face a media backlash. Which is where you came in. He asked if you were still pursuing him."

"What did you say?"

"I said I didn't know but it was possible."

"Well done."

"I'm telling you, I don't owe politicians any favours. All I'm interested in is the truth and justice. I don't appreciate being leaned on, especially by some Tory twat, if you pardon the language."

Danny chuckled.

"I know what you mean."

"Anyway, how can I help?"

"It's delicate. I just wanted to bring you up to speed on a couple of things I'm working on, and see if you'd heard anything. Obviously, discretion is paramount."

"Of course."

"Have you heard about this homeless shelter thing?"

"Ha. Yes. I suspect we both have our suspicions, though, and similar opinions about leopards and spots."

"Exactly. Listen, are you doing anything tonight? Could we meet? It's not really something for a phone call."

"Not tonight, sorry. I'm working late. Tomorrow lunchtime, though, if it can wait?"

Danny gave a thought to his deadline. That could still work.

"That's perfect. I'll keep digging. In the meantime, if you hear anything can you let me know?"

"You as well. Okay Danny. I can't promise. I can't reveal details of ongoing enquiries."

"Understood. Just grapevine though? Unofficial?"

"Leave it with me."

They said their farewells and Danny turned to his terminal. He started looking on the wire for stories about people trafficking. Since the fall of the Iron Curtain it seemed that business was booming. It was a depressingly familiar story. And it was already evident this was potentially his most dangerous investigation so far.

I thought about trying Ben again, but then remembered the way Mitch had smiled at me and decided against it, for now. It was weird. Normally I keep myself to myself, but suddenly I was spoilt for choice.

That said, I decided not to call Mitch either. There were two main reasons. Despite the obvious appeal of an uncomplicated relationship with somebody new, unencumbered by the expectations of friendship or work issues, my heart still very much belonged to Danny. I'd had offers before. In fact, we'd both been on dates before. I went out with an anaesthetist once but it was really boring. He sent me to sleep. Ultimately, though, Danny and I seem to have a connection that goes beyond anything I've ever known, and I just can't imagine that with anyone else.

The second reason? Danny was still very much on the naughty step, and if he had anything at all to do with Clare, ever again, I'd be quite prepared to rethink all of the above and frankly he could go and stuff himself, devotion or not. I was that pissed off. And in that eventuality, it would pay to keep Mitch waiting, to make him even more grateful and even more keen to see me when I finally picked up the phone.

So, either way, a call was out, but I made sure Mitch's business card was in a safe place on my desk at Passion Fruit - my photographic studio. I can't deny that I occasionally cast a glance in its direction, pondering the possibilities. And it would be a fib to deny that I'd copied his number into my phone memory already, just for safekeeping. Where was the harm in that? Part of me was flattered. But a further part of me seemed to be curiously smitten. And that part was nudging me in the direction of recklessness.

I developed the films from the previous day, made contact sheets of the lot, and quick 10x8 enlargements of a few of my favourites. I hung them up to dry then made sure of it with my hairdryer. It's never ideal as the heat can mess with the resin coating of the paper, but better that than having them stick together. Once that was done, it was time to head to the rehearsal studio in Hackney.

I didn't fancy public transport - even though it was an overground train from Camden Road rather than the tube - so I took my Honda Prelude and arrived exactly on time, if you use a fairly loose definition of the term "exactly" and allow a fifteen-minute margin on top.

I pressed the button for the doorbell. It was a fairly bleak-looking place, in a side street, near a parade of shops. I tried to listen for music as I waited for the bell to be answered, but I could just hear traffic, and a passing train.

After a moment, the door buzzed and seemed to become unlocked. I pushed it and it gave way. I found myself in a musty hallway with a set of stairs at the end leading down to a cellar that presumably served as the rehearsal space.

"Hi," I called, but there was no answer. I made my way to the stairs and just as I reached the top, a door opened below. Holly appeared.

"Hi, Anna, good to see you," she said. "Come on down."

She held the door open for me at the bottom of the stairs. I found myself in a room with several sets of big speakers, several flight cases, a couple of keyboards on stands, a desk with an old-looking computer, and a microphone in the middle. There was a sofa against one wall, and the walls themselves were painted black but decorated with newspaper cuttings, all sorts of foam shapes that were presumably for sound reasons, and the occasional picture. There was a mustiness about the place, coupled with the distinctive aroma of marijuana. Curiously, nobody was there apart from Holly.

"Are the others not here?" I asked after she'd offered to make me a cup of tea. She seemed on reasonable form, although she still had a slightly spaced-out look, as though she'd taken something earlier in the day.

"No, sorry," she replied. "I'm not sure what they're up to. They were supposed to be here but I've not heard anything from them."

"That's a shame. I've brought some pictures."

She seemed enthusiastic to see them. Far more enthusiastic than she'd been to have them taken, anyway. I laid them out on top of one of the keyboards. It said Roland on the front and had an array of knobs and nice coloured switches. Danny would have recognised it, I'm sure.

"Wow, I love them," said Holly, as she examined the contact prints. She pointed out her favourites. It was good to have feedback but I was a bit miffed the others weren't there to see them as well. We chatted for a while, although she seemed reluctant to talk about the band. On the upside, she was considerably friendlier than I'd expected. Maybe she just took time to get to know someone before opening up, and there's nothing wrong with that.

"We're playing again tonight if you're interested in coming down," she said, eventually.

"Yes, Steve said. Definitely."

"The others can see the pictures then. Sorry again they're not here. They should be. We're supposed to be rehearsing." She wrote the venue details on a piece of paper and handed it to me.

"I said to Steve I'd attempt some live shots, if I don't get crushed."

"Wow, yes, that would be amazing. Are you sure?"

"Of course." I remembered a night in a night club, elbowing my way through the crowds, taking pictures. The bruises lasted a few days but it had been lots of fun, and the challenge of capturing the energy and mood of the performance intrigued me.

"Thanks, Anna," she said. There was the merest hint of a wobble in her voice.

"Is everything okay?" I asked. It was worth a go.

"In terms of?"

"You know, with the band. I thought there seemed a bit of tension."

Her expression changed. I couldn't work out if it was annoyance or a warning in her eyes.

"We're fine," she said. That was it.

"Okay," I said, in the absence of anything more constructive.

"Right," she continued. "I'd better get on. There's some programming to do even if nothing else."

"Of course. I'll leave you to it. Keep the pictures and show the others and I'll chat about them tonight." I moved towards the staircase. She opened the door again.

"Press the buzzer by the door upstairs and it'll open," she said. There was a definite sense of being rushed out. But then, as I started climbing the stairs, she spoke after me.

"We just work hard, you know?"

I turned.

"Sorry?"

"We work hard. It's a creative business. Of course, there's tension occasionally. Don't worry, Anna."

I walked back towards her. I still couldn't read her eyes but there was definitely something there.

"Are you okay?" I asked with genuine tenderness.

She nodded. I stepped forward, arms extended. She seemed in need of a hug.

"Call me any time you need me, or if you just want to talk," I said.

"I will." She smiled, but it was the sort of smile that hid a hundred secrets. I made my way back to the door. She stayed, leaning on the door frame, as I ascended the stairs.

"Thanks again," she said as I reached the top. I wasn't sure what she was thanking me for: just the pictures or the olive branch of friendship. Either way, I left her there alone. There's often something self-destructive about creative genius. It was bothering me for reasons I couldn't explain, let alone begin to understand.

Chapter 11

I ARRIVED home before Danny and was having a bit of a snoop on the computer, trying to find any evidence of communication with Clare, when I heard him open the door. I quickly stopped and pretended to be tidying the desk, then picked up several teacups and headed in the direction of the kitchen.

He followed me in. We hadn't seen much of each other the previous evening and there was still an air of an unresolved argument. I gave him a hug, but it was less enthusiastic than normal. I think he noticed.

"Cup of tea?" I asked. He nodded.

"Thanks, Anna. Good day?"

I brought him up to speed on the visit to the studio and mentioned the gig later that evening. He said he'd love to come with me, which I took to be a positive. At least he wasn't meeting her, then, not that I'm paranoid. (I am.) In return Danny filled me in on the latest with Graham March, his meeting with his editor, and the looming deadline.

"Is there anything I can do to help?" I asked.

"Well," he began, "I want to follow him. See where he goes. And photographic evidence would be a massive help..." He was grinning.

"Do they not have photographers at the Echo?"

"They do, and I've been offered one, but I'd rather be with you. If you're interested, of course."

"Danny, I'd love to help but that's a bit like you being asked to concoct a poem just because you're a writer of crack investigative news stories. Different discipline. Just because there's a camera involved, it doesn't mean that anything I've learned shooting fashion is in any way relevant to a stake-out."

"Oh," he said. He looked genuinely upset. "Is that a 'no' then?"

I did one of those "what do you think" faces.

"I'm sorry to have asked. I should have thought."

I couldn't help a grin from surfacing.

"Of course I'll help," I said, punching him on the arm, harder than was strictly necessary. "Just no promises that I'll be any good. Okay?"

He gave me a hug. Then, as he let go, I noticed him rubbing his arm and I felt a bit guilty, but neither of us mentioned it again.

"When do we start then, Poirot?" I asked. I called him that occasionally, much to his annoyance.

"How are you fixed this week?"

"Completely free if you need me. I've finished everything I needed to do for autumn-winter, so unless a commission comes up I'm yours."

"Fantastic. Tomorrow then?"

"I'm on."

Danny took his tea through to the living room. I stayed in the kitchen and loaded the dishwasher.

"What time are we heading out tonight?" he called after a few minutes, through the open doorway.

"In a couple of hours. Just over. We need to be there about 8.30-ish. Is that okay?"

"Yup, perfect," he replied.

A few minutes later I walked through to join him. He was typing on the computer keyboard, but as soon as he spotted me he grabbed the mouse and minimised the window he was working in.

I didn't say anything. I didn't need to. Sod the pair of them. I continued past, straight to my room and closed the door with considerable vigour. I had a phone call to make.

Forty minutes later I emerged. This time I really had made an effort. Best outfit, impeccable make-up given the time constraints, new tights without any snags, and shoes that you wouldn't want to walk very far in.

"Change of plan," I said. "The gig's off. I'm going out."

"Anna?"

"Don't wait up."

"Anna? What's up?"

I ignored him, grabbed my jacket and headed out into the night.

"Sorry about the short notice," I said, taking a sip of my first glass of Sauvignon Blanc. I didn't think it would be the last.

"That's okay. Spontaneity is good," said Mitch. "Cheers." He had a pint of some sort of lager. I don't know what - he'd paid for them. We chinked glasses.

"At least I don't need to worry about you following me if I know where you are," he said with a smirk.

I laughed.

"Here we go, starting already. Do women often follow you? Is that something to do with you being a film star? And just for the record, *again*, I wasn't."

"No, just you. And I'm not a film star."

"Yet."

"Probably never, but it's fun trying."

"So, what do you do when you're not on the silver screen?"

I have to confess, I should have been paying full attention at this point, but inwardly I was still fuming, my mind full of dark thoughts. He mentioned something about a petrochemical company which I'm sure was a lot more intriguing than I would give it credit for, although when he then went on to mention marketing, a part of me died inside.

"Basically a salesman then?" I said, hoping I hadn't missed anything important.

"Haha, no, not a salesman. I get involved in brand extension, business development, all that kind of stuff."

"And business development isn't sales because...?"

"God, are you always this awkward? Been single long by any chance?" I was warming to his sense of humour. This was exactly what I needed.

"Tell me about this band then," he said, when I'd got our second round of drinks.

"They're called Lumière Rouge, which means red light I think."

"Seedy."

"Indeed, but with added French-ness to give the illusion of sophistication, I expect. The singer's my friend's brother. Then there are two keyboard players who both look like they're on drugs most of the time, but they're good."

"Sounds encouraging."

"That they're on drugs?"

"No, that they're good."

"Ah, yes. Well, it's probably all backing tapes with a bit played over the top, but the singing's live. That's who I was doing the pictures of in Bromley-by-Bow yesterday."

"The singer?"

"No, the three of them."

"Got you. How'd it go?"

"Better than I thought it would, actually. The girls are a bit strange."

"Girls?"

"Yes, sorry. The keyboard players. Leah and Holly."

"Ah, I'm with you. And the music is...?"

"Kind of goth-y but with synthesisers. Actually, surprisingly decent."

"I can't wait."

"Play your cards right and I'll introduce you. I was supposed to be doing some pictures tonight as well, some live shots, but I left in a bit of a rush and didn't bring the camera."

"So, it's a night off then?"

"Looks like it."

"That's good. We shall make the most of it."

We rushed the second drink and then left the warm comfort of the pub for the short walk to the venue. I don't often come to Islington, but I still knew enough about the area to suggest a meeting place not far from our final destination. We walked up to the front of the queue and I explained to the doorman we were on the guest list. He allowed us through to the ticket desk inside.

"Name?" asked the girl on reception. She had rather impressive bright red hair and dramatic eye make-up, but then a spike through her lower lip that looked particularly painful. I wondered how she managed to kiss anyone without stabbing them.

"Anna Burgin," I said.

She looked down the list, then turned to me.

"You're not down here," she said.

"Sorry?" I said. "I must be. I'm with the band."

"Hold on."

She grabbed a second list from further along her desk, and started working her way down it.

"Anna Burgin?"

"That's me."

"I'm sorry. You were, but it's been crossed through. Look." She showed me my name, very definitely crossed out.

"That's got to be a mistake, surely?" I said. My confusion was second only to my mortifying sense of embarrassment. How not to create a good impression on a first date.

"No, I don't think so. I'll see if I can get their manager for you."

"Thank you."

She disappeared behind a curtain. Their manager? I didn't think they had a manager.

"Sorry about this," I said to Mitch. He put his arm round me, which in other circumstances may have seemed a bit forward, but I was grateful for the moral support.

"That's okay," he said. "I'm sure we'll get it sorted."

A couple of minutes later she reappeared.

"He's on his way," she said. I thanked her, and we moved to the side to wait.

"If we can't get in we can always go back to the pub," said Mitch.

"I know, but it's just so embarrassing. I'm sure it'll be okay, though."

But it wasn't okay. A moment later the curtain was pulled back. A man stood silently, arms folded, grinning at me.

"Here he is," said the girl on reception.

But none of it made sense. I recognised him immediately. The last time I'd seen him, he was trying to arrest me for a murder that I hadn't committed, and which, in fact, had never taken place. The band's new manager was the former DCI Graham March. He turned away without saying a word and disappeared back into the venue. What the fuck?

Chapter 12

DANNY was still up when I got home, just after midnight.

"Anna, I've been so worried," he said. "Where were you?"

"Just out with a friend," I said.

In truth, the issue with the guest list hadn't done much to dampen the "friendship". Quite the reverse in fact. We thought about just buying tickets but the queue was long so we returned to the pub and soon both started to laugh about it. I proceeded to have slightly too much to drink, and our conversation flowed. I tried to ask intelligent questions about the petrochemical industry, but I think he knew I didn't have a clue what I was talking about. He was decent about it, though.

In turn, he asked me lots of questions about my career, and the world of fashion photography. To his eternal credit it wasn't just the obvious ones about models and the usual misconceptions about some kind of party lifestyle with beautiful people in far-flung locations. He wanted to know how commissions worked, about the interaction between brand owners and magazine stylists, and my views on how developments in technology would change working practices over time. It was thought-provoking stuff. He seemed intelligent, and refreshingly charismatic; genuinely interested in me rather than being side-tracked by the glamorous fluff that seems to obsess the less enlightened.

By the end of the night my mood was dramatically happier than at the start, and after many glasses of wine I was possibly bordering on the wrong side of tactile. And then Mitch offered to share a taxi home at his expense, and in the back of the cab I let my guard down further and kissed him. And it was actually very nice indeed, but I wasn't inviting him in for coffee, or anything else for that matter, for rather obvious reasons. I did, however, agree to meet him for dinner on Wednesday.

"What happened with the gig?" asked Danny.

It all seemed so long ago.

"They wouldn't let us in. Bastards."

"What?"

And then I realised that wasn't what he meant.

"Who wouldn't let you in? And who's us?" he persisted.

"I'd been crossed off the guest list. They seem to have a new manager."

"So you went to the gig?"

"Yes."

"I thought you said it was cancelled?"

"No, very much not cancelled although I don't actually know, now I think about it, as we couldn't get in."

"Anna, you're not making any sense. Are you drunk?"

"A little bit."

"Jesus."

"What's your problem?"

"My problem? I don't have a problem except I've been worried sick. You weren't answering your phone."

"Hmmm. Sorry, I didn't hear it. The pub was quite loud."

"Which pub?"

"The one I was in, obviously. If another pub had been loud it wouldn't have mattered because I wasn't there. I was in the one I was in."

"For fuck's sake."

"Oh, don't go getting all sweary with me. I'm home now. Thanks for waiting up but I suspect you've been busy chatting to your girlfriend."

"What?"

"Don't deny it, Danny. But don't worry, I've had a lovely evening anyway. And now I must go to bed."

"Anna, what are you talking about? Please just try to be sensible for a moment."

"Me?"

"Yes, you."

"You want me to be sensible?"

"Yes."

"Danny, I think I've had the most sensible night I've had in a long time. I have very much seen the light."

"What *are* you talking about?"

"Goodnight, Danny."

"Anna!" He actually shouted at me. I could see hurt in his eyes. I'm not a bitch. I stopped and decided to talk to him, albeit leaning on the sofa for support.

"What?" I asked.

"Can we go back to the start?"

"All right. We met when we were students, and then got on well so we ended up sharing a house and then I fell in love with you."

"Jesus, you are pissed."

"Probably less than you think."

He ignored that.

"I meant the start of this evening," he continued. "One minute you're telling me we're going out and the next it's off but you went anyway."

"That's an accurate summary. You should become a reporter."

"Very funny."

"But you missed out the bit whereby I caught you emailing your girlfriend and then tried to hide it by minimising the window."

"What are you talking about?"

"Don't deny it, Danny. I saw you."

"When you came in from the kitchen?"

"Ah, you remember. Top of the class."

"And by my 'girlfriend' do you mean Clare?"

"Obviously."

"Jesus, Anna. I was not emailing Clare."

"There's no need to hide it, I don't actually care any more." That bit wasn't strictly true. "I saw you close the window."

"I wasn't emailing Clare."

"Who then? Have you got another one on the go as well?"

"You're being ridiculous. If you must know, I'd just been sent a picture from a guy I met in Germany that was horrific. I didn't want you to see it. I closed it down because I thought it'd upset you."

"Oh," I said. And stopped leaning on the sofa, and collapsed into it instead.

"Oh", I said again.

"Would you like a cup of tea?" he asked. I nodded. I wasn't sure my brain was up to actual sentences for a moment.

By the time he returned I'd started to think a bit more clearly.

"So, who did you go with?" he asked.

"Just a friend," I said.

"Which friend?"

"Does it matter?"

"Not really but I'm just curious."

"That's okay then."

"Which friend?"

"You said it didn't matter."

"It didn't matter until you started making an issue out of it."

"Until *I* started making an issue out of it? Thanks for the tea, by the way."

"You're welcome. So?"

"So what?"

"So which friend."

I really wasn't sure about this.

"Mitch," I said.

"Mitch?"

"Yup, Mitch."

"Who on earth is Mitch?"

"Just a friend."

"I've never heard of Mitch before."

"I've only known him since yesterday."

"What? This gets worse."

And so, I told him about scarf man on the Underground and how I'd bumped into him later in the garage and he'd given me his number and that he seemed like a really nice guy. I didn't mention the kiss, though. That would have been awkward.

"But you couldn't get in anyway?"

"No, the fucker crossed me off the guest list."

"Who did? Someone at the venue?"

"No, their new manager. Oh, I should probably have mentioned that earlier. It was your mate, Graham."

It didn't make any sense to Danny either. And now I thought about it, it was utterly bizarre. What on earth was Graham March doing there? It couldn't be a coincidence, surely. But what did he even know about music?

"The bastard," said Danny. "He said he'd tell me about his involvement in 'the arts'. Presumably that's what he was referring to. What is he playing at?"

"I'll call Holly in the morning, if she'll talk to me," I offered. "I'm sure we'll get to the bottom of it."

"If you could, it'd be appreciated."

And then my phone started ringing. I searched for it in my bag, but it stopped before I retrieved it.

"What time is it?" I asked.

"Just gone one."

"Who's calling at this time of the morning?"

"Probably Mitch."

That was a bit cheeky.

And then it started ringing again. I pressed the button to connect.

"Hello," I said, cautiously.

There was a lot of noise on the line. I could hear sirens and shouting. I was on the verge of ending the call when I heard someone say my name.

"Hello," I said again.

"Anna?" said the voice. "It's Holly." It didn't sound like Holly. She sounded tiny and distant, voice cracking, as though she was crying.

"Holly? What's up? What happened tonight?"

More noise. More shouting.

"Anna?" she said again.

"Yes, I'm here. Is everything okay?"

"No," she said. "It's Steve."

"Steve?" I asked. "What about him?"

"He's dead," she said. And then the phone line went dead as well.

Chapter 13

Tuesday, April 5th, 1994

DANNY hit the phone to try to find out what had happened while I discovered just how quickly such traumatic news could help sober me up.

Eventually he managed to speak to someone who had a few of the details. I'm not sure if it was a colleague at the Echo or a contact within the police. My thoughts turned to Colette. Did she even know about her brother? Who would tell her? She was away on a modelling assignment and I didn't even know in which country. I didn't know how I could contact her, but equally wasn't sure it was appropriate for me to break the news. And yet I just wanted to speak to my friend, to comfort her, and be there for her in any way I could.

According to Danny, Steve's body had been found washed up in mud on the bank of the Thames near the South Bank. It had been spotted by a couple of French tourists on their way back to their hotel after a romantic night out. They were traumatised, and I understood why. It was just too horrible to contemplate. The police weren't releasing much information, officially, but apparently at the moment they were looking at the possibility of a tragic accident, possibly as a result of a drug overdose, although something more sinister had yet to be ruled out. I couldn't believe the drug theory. I'd only met Steve a couple of times but he didn't seem the type. The girls, maybe, but him? It was another thing that just didn't make sense.

We went to bed around 4am. I didn't think I'd sleep very well, but I must have drifted off eventually. I came to just before eight, disturbed by movement in the flat. Danny was up, getting ready for work. I wanted to catch him before he left so I dragged myself up, feeling awful as a result of the evil triumvirate of alcohol, sleep deprivation and shock.

He was just logging off the computer when I walked through to the front room.

"Any news?" I asked.

"No, not since last night. How are you feeling? You look awful."

"Thanks. I feel it."

I put my hand on his shoulder and gave it a squeeze.

"What on earth was March doing there?" asked Danny, mainly of himself. "And then the singer turns up dead the same night. Coincidence?"

"It's too much."

"Exactly. This wasn't an accident. I don't care what the police think."

"What's your plan? Assuming you have one."

"I'm going to the office. I'll brief Mike. If nobody else has spotted a connection with March, it's something else that needs investigating. Then I'm meeting Amy at lunchtime if she's still free."

"DS Cranston?"

Danny nodded.

"I'll see what she knows, what she can tell me. It's bigger than just a news story now. He's got to be stopped, whatever it is he's up to."

"I did have a thought," I said.

"Go on."

"It's probably nothing but you mentioned this homeless shelter thing."

"Yeah?"

"Could that be the connection? Leah was homeless. Maybe she was there. Maybe she met March somehow and that's how he got a connection to the band."

I could see Danny's thought process.

"Do you have a number for her?" he asked.

"No, but I've got one for Holly."

"Could you ring her? See if you can get a number for Leah?"

"Of course. On it, Poirot."

"Let me know. Cheers Anna. You're a star."

That made me smile. Then suddenly I had a flashback to the previous evening and kissing someone else. Oh God. What had I been thinking?

Danny left for work and I tried to inject some semblance of humanity back into my body via the medium of the shower. It was only a partial success. Tea and toast were very much a requirement.

Just past nine I called Holly. There was no answer. I didn't leave a message. I always think that gives the initiative to the other person. Once you've left a message, there's no need to ring again, even if they don't call you back. Don't leave a message and you can keep trying.

My phone rang. I jumped at it, hoping it was Holly calling back anyway.

"Hi," I said.

"Hi, Anna, it's Mitch." Oh God.

"Mitch, hi. Look, I don't want to be rude but it's not a good time."

"Sorry about that. Are you okay?"

"Yes, fine."

"Are you sure?"

"Kind of."

"What's up?"

"Nothing. Just some personal stuff."

"That doesn't sound good. Anything I can help with?"

"No. I just... Oh, I can't do this now. Sorry."

"Hey, it's me who's sorry. Is it something I said? Or did?"

"No, not at all. I've just had some bad news."

"Really? Shit. Nothing serious I hope. God. Can I do anything?"

"No. I'm going to have to go. I'll call you later, okay?"

"Of course. Just Anna?"

"What?"

"Thank you. For yesterday. I really enjoyed it."

"Me too." Why did I say that?

"Call me if you need me, okay?"

"I will."

I ended the call and tried Holly again. No answer again. I thought back to the photo shoot, remembered meeting Steve. He seemed such a nice guy. A great singer and so down to earth. The only one of the three I immediately warmed to. And yet there was definitely something going on that I was being excluded from. Where were they yesterday? And why, of all the people in the world, and all of the shady characters in the music business and hanging around its periphery, did they end up having anything to do with Graham March? I tried Holly again. This time it was answered.

"Holly!" I said, my heart beating slightly faster. "It's Anna."

"Holly isn't here," came the reply, in a fragile-sounding voice.

"Is she okay? When will she be back?" I asked.

"I don't know, sorry. She's gone. This is Leah."

"Leah, hi! It's Anna." I was repeating myself but she sounded as though she was in a world of her own. Understandable, I suppose.

"Hi Anna. Have you heard about Steve?"

"Yes. It's just a tragedy. Are you okay?"

"No, not really. I..." Her voice drifted off into silence.

"Where are you? Leah?"

"Yes?"

"Is there anything I can do? Where are you now?"

"He's dead," she said. This wasn't going to be easy.

"I know. Have you heard any more? From the police?"

"No, I.... Just... Fuck."

"Listen, Leah, talk to me. Where are you? Don't hang up. I need to talk to you."

"Why to me?"

"I just want to help. What happened yesterday? I came to see you last night but I couldn't get in. And Graham March..."

"That *wanker*."

"Exactly. What was he doing there?"

"Fucking everything up. Fuck, Anna, I've got to go."

"No, listen, Leah, please don't hang up. Can I come to see you?"

"I've got to go."

"Leah, where are you?"

"I'm nowhere. And on the fucking edge."

"Okay, but listen. I don't believe Steve was an accident."

"No, not an accident. The bastards."

"Who are the bastards, Leah? What happened? What can you tell me?"

"Oh, Anna. You don't want to know. It's all just so fucked up. And Steve, I just can't... He was just an innocent guy."

"Please, tell me. What do you mean? Innocent?"

"He was just a guy. Not his fault. And he's... The bastards."

"Leah, have you taken something? I'm worried about you."

"I'm okay, Anna. Just being careful."

"Can you tell me? What do you mean? What's going on, Leah?"

"I can't tell you. Not now."

"Is it the band?"

She laughed.

"The band? I haven't even thought about the band. That's completely fucked."

"So, what then?"

There was silence on the phone. I thought she'd gone.

"Leah?"

"Yeah?" She was still there.

"Tell me."

"I'll meet you. Tonight."

"Tell me where."

"The studio. Seven. Anna, it's all just worse than you could ever imagine. I'll talk to you then. I'll tell you. Can't now. Got to be careful. Got to go."

"Leah?"

But the phone was dead. I tried calling back but it just rang and rang. At least she'd arranged to meet me, if she remembered. She sounded all over the place. I thought there was a very slim chance she'd actually turn up, but it was the best I had. I called Danny's number but there was no answer there either. I left a message with the Echo switchboard for him to call me, urgently, as soon as he was free.

Chapter 14

DANNY left his editor's office, having brought him up to date on the latest developments. He'd asked for a deadline extension, but it was a triumph of hope over experience and it hadn't been granted. He returned to his office and started compiling his notes so far, bringing together everything he'd found out about March since the initial suspension, information he'd gathered on people trafficking from his fact-finding trip to Germany, questions about the homeless shelter, and observations about his apparent contacts. He started to draw a flow chart of connections, but still not much of it made sense. It seemed like he was getting somewhere and nowhere, simultaneously.

He opened the CompuServe account on his notebook computer and dialled a connection. No new messages. He clicked the icon to create one and typed Clare's address.

Subject: Easter Bunny

Clare,

I've tried not to contact you but here I am. I hope all is well. Things are getting serious with the EB and I wonder if I can pick your brains a bit. Are you around? Can we speak? He's turning up in all sorts of new places and I would appreciate your input in putting the links in place. I'd prefer not to discuss it via email if there's an alternative.

Despite everything it was great to see you. You're looking well. There again, you always did look amazing. I think I can say that now.

All is good here, although Anna seems a bit freaked by your reappearance. She's been acting a bit strange and even seems to have been on a date with someone last night. Not at all happy about that if I'm honest, although I suppose it's my own fault.

Anyway, let me know if you're around if you get this message.

Take care,

D.

He clicked "send" and then sat back in his chair, mind drifting. Who was Mitch? How did that even come about? What did he look like? Where did he live? He might be a nice guy with the best of intentions, but immediately Danny felt on edge. What if they started getting serious? He was bound to want to see her again. Of course he was. She was funny and cheeky and wonderful company, and he was a man. A predator.

When he'd first seen her across the student bar, she'd seemed so completely unapproachable. Exotic, intriguing; one of the cool students that everything seemed to revolve around. A goth of sorts: tiny but trendy with a black leather jacket, fishnets and dramatic make-up but with big rock hair. It was a confused look, but no less endearing for that. He'd fallen for her instantly. But when he finally picked up the courage to speak, he eschewed the chat-up clichés and - maybe because of that - discovered, instead, an immediate connection that would develop into a deep and lasting friendship rather than a short-lived student romance.

The goth look had gone. She now embraced the fashion industry she was a part of: trendy photographer meets sophisticated businesswoman. The hair was slightly shorter, but still with an attractive curl. Above all else, she was still the brilliant friend she'd always been and, in his line of work, one of the very few people he felt he could really trust.

The relationship, then, had bypassed the initial buzz of the new, and in so doing they'd avoided the inevitable messy break-up. But now it was almost like they were brother and sister. With the pace of modern life, they'd settled into a comfortable routine, sharing a flat and secrets, and a deep bond and friendship that transcended anything he'd ever experienced before. Could he ever really risk all of that by trying to take things further? Could it ever even be appropriate to try now, after so many years had passed? It was just something he was resigned to, but what, now, if he was losing her anyway?

It was only one date. There was no need to get carried away. She'd been on dates before. So why did this one already feel different? How was it possible that things could change so quickly? Ben had asked for her number, she'd said, and she'd laughed it off, but now only a few days later she'd met someone new and she'd already been out with him, staying out till late, returning home after seemingly having had a wonderful time. She'd looked stunning last night. Clearly she was dressing to impress, but that just made things worse. And all because of a misunderstanding over Clare. Losing Anna would be a life sentence for a crime that he hadn't even committed.

It was nearly lunchtime, but Danny's appetite had gone. He had a hollow feeling inside, as though something was going terribly, irrevocably wrong.

He phoned the flat, just to hear her voice. She answered on the third ring.

"Hi Anna," he said.

"Danny! I've been trying to call you." Her enthusiasm was

reassuring, but equally almost painful. She sounded happy. He wanted her to be happy. He wanted her to be happy with him. He didn't ever want anything to come between them.

"Everything okay?"

"Yes, all good. I spoke to Leah."

"Fantastic. Any news?"

"She was out of it, but she's agreed to meet. At the studio, tonight at seven if that's any good. Are you free? I've got no idea if she'll turn up but it's got to be worth a go."

"I'll be there, definitely. Did she say anything about March?"

"Oh Danny, she was all over the place. She said March was a wanker, but kept referring to Steve and saying it wasn't an accident and she had to be careful. There's something going on, definitely. I kept asking where she was but she was on a different planet."

"Well done, though. That's brilliant. I'll be home about six and we can go from there if that's okay."

"Perfect."

He didn't want to ask, but he had to.

"Have you heard from Mitch?"

There was a noticeable pause. Above all else he just wanted her to be honest with him. The thought of not knowing was far worse than knowing for sure.

"I have, yes."

"And?"

"And nothing, really. He just called to thank me for last night."

"He hasn't asked you out again?"

"Danny..." The silence that followed spoke more than words.

"Sorry, I shouldn't have asked." It was as bad as he'd feared. "I'll see you at six, okay?"

"Looking forward to it."

"I just... You're brilliant, Anna. You know that?"

"What brought this on?"

"Just sometimes things need saying, that's all."

"Well, you're brilliant yourself. Take care and hurry home."

"I will."

He ended the call. And immediately just wanted to hear her voice again.

"You're not eating?"

"No, I'm not hungry."

"Are you all right? Not coming down with anything?"

"I'm fine, just a bit stressed. There's a lot going on. But you order and I'll just have a cappuccino."

"If you're sure."

Danny nodded. DS Amy Cranston examined the menu. There wasn't a huge choice. It was just a cafe really, albeit with a side order of pretentious artificial grandeur. A waitress came over and took their order.

"So," she said, while they waited, "what's new?"

"It's just basically March. Did you hear about the body they fished out of the Thames?"

"Last night?"

"Yes, early hours."

"I did. It's not one of mine but I've heard about it this morning. Why?"

"I knew him. Kind of. I met him the other night. He was a singer. Anna was taking pictures of the band."

"Really? That's tragic. Is she okay?"

"She's upset, of course, but here's the thing. She was supposed to see them again last night but she couldn't get past the door. Their new manager crossed her off the guest list."

"That's weird."

"Exactly. And do you know who the manager was?"

"Go on."

"Graham March."

"*What?*"

"Exactly."

"What does he even know about music? Hold on. *Our* Graham March? Is she sure?"

"Hundred percent."

"That doesn't make any sense."

"I know. And a few hours later the singer's dead."

"Bloody hell. If you pardon the language."

Danny looked behind him to make sure there was nobody in earshot.

"And there's more. One of the girls in the band was homeless. Anna spoke to her this morning. She knew March apparently, possibly through the shelter. We don't know yet, but she called him a wanker. We're meeting her this evening. Apparently she's saying it wasn't an accident."

"What's her name?"

"Leah."

"Surname?"

"I'm not sure."

"I assume we're speaking to her too but I'll check. That's good work, Danny. She may be more open with you. Let me know what she says, okay? Bollocks to the whole protecting your sources bullshit. This is March we're dealing with here. Understood?"

Danny nodded.

"What else did you want to ask me about? I assume it wasn't this, as it only happened this morning."

"I just wanted to run a couple of things by you. I appreciate there are limits to what you can tell me. But like you said, this is March. Special times."

"Fire away. I'll let you know."

Danny looked around again. Another customer had come into the cafe, but the table directly behind them was still free. Danny leaned forward and lowered his voice so it was barely audible above the background noise. The food and coffee arrived.

"No mentioning this to anyone, okay?" he continued. "Especially not your politician friend."

"Of course."

"Right. Well, I've been investigating, as you know. I've made a few connections and started to notice a few coincidences. His name kept cropping up not too far removed from some pretty bad things."

"What kind of bad things?"

"I was expecting the usual. A bit of vice, a bit of protection. Hiding of evidence and all that kind of stuff. But then it seemed to get noticeably darker." Danny paused for a moment, then lowered his voice still further. "Trafficking."

"Shit. Drugs?"

"No. People."

"You mean?"

"Girls from eastern Europe, promised a new life in the west, great job, prospects. Everything from nannies to models. Except when they get here they're heavily in debt, kept against their will, passports taken, families threatened..."

"And forced into prostitution."

"Precisely."

"And this is March because?"

"That's what I'm trying to find out. But I've just been to Germany. It seems to be centred in Cologne. I met some people there who would talk to me. They confirmed he was involved."

"Who did you speak to?"

"That I can't say at the moment, but..." Danny paused. He suddenly looked hesitant.

"What's up?"

"It's nothing. I just need to know that this is off the record."

"Of course. Unless you tell me something where life is in immediate danger."

"No, it's not that. It's something you'd be interested in. But you can't act on it. Not yet."

"Okay. Tell me."

Danny took a deep breath.

"When I was in Cologne I bumped into someone."

"Go on."

"Clare."

"*Clare?*" She put down her fork.

He nodded.

"She's still alive, then."

"Clearly."

"And on the wanted list in several countries. How was she?"

"Looking well, although she's changed her appearance a bit."

"I don't suppose she told you where she was living?"

"No, but she knew about March. Knew what I was over there for. She knew about the trafficking."

DS Cranston resumed her lunch.

"You don't think she's involved?"

"No, it's not her style. But she said she could help me. Save me time. I've sent her an email."

"You've got her email address? We could probably trace her location through that if we know her ISP."

"Indeed, but you can't. Not yet. And she's not stupid. She'll be hiding that somehow. Either way I didn't want to trust her, but, well, as she said, it's a murky world."

"Listen, Danny, if you want my advice, you'll treat anything she says with extreme caution."

"I will."

"It's interesting, though. Speak to her again. Find out what she knows. But for God's sake be careful."

"Of course. Then there's one more thing."

"Even worse than that?"

"Not worse, but weird. I got back on Saturday. On Sunday March called me, wanted to meet."

"He did *what?*"

"That's what I thought. I went to see him in a coffee shop. That's when he told me about his homeless shelter. He wanted me to write a story to clear his name."

"Some chance of that."

"I know." Danny took a sip of the coffee. It was still too hot, but he barely noticed. "But why would he do that? Why even draw my attention to it? Why put himself in the line of fire?"

"Unless he's trying to derail you."

"It doesn't make sense. And then last night Anna went to see the band play, and he was there. Made sure she saw him. What's he up to?"

Amy arranged her knife and fork, then pushed the plate away.

"I've lost my appetite as well. Listen, Danny, there's not much I can tell you at the moment. But I'll keep my eyes and ears open, okay? If there's anything that'll help that I can tell you, I'll be in touch. Okay?"

"That would be much appreciated."

"In the meantime, let me know about tonight. And if you hear from Clare again. We'll stop the bastard."

"Are you worried about the politician? Seb?"

"No, not really. He's leaning a bit. Could make things awkward, career-wise especially, but we don't do cover-ups."

"That's good to know."

She took a purse from her bag and withdrew a ten pound note.

"This one's on me," she said. "It's good to see you, Danny. We'll keep in touch."

Danny drained his cup. They were about to say their farewells when his mobile phone started ringing. He looked at the number and then at DS Cranston. It was another call from March.

Chapter 15

DANNY connected the call.

"Graham," he said. "To what do I owe the displeasure?"

There was hollow laughter on the line.

"You're a cheeky boy, Danny. That could be your undoing one day. You should watch that. But I'm calling because I need to speak to you."

"Clearly. Because otherwise you could have simply not called me. Mission accomplished."

"And clever with it. Although all things are relative. You could go far, which perhaps speaks volumes about the standard of your contemporaries."

"I'll take that as a compliment. What did you need to speak to me about?"

"Not here, Danny. Over coffee. Same place, in an hour. Can you do that?"

"Wow, you must be missing me. I'll just check my diary." He paused. "Yes, nothing on this afternoon apart from a short-notice meeting with a bent bastard who's clearly up to something. But that's you."

"Funny boy, Danny. I'll see you there."

The call ended. Danny looked across to DS Amy Cranston.

"He wants to meet again."

"Be careful, Danny," she said again.

An hour later, Danny was reading a newspaper in the corner of the coffee shop, with a cappuccino by his side, when March pushed through the door and then headed in his direction. Again, they didn't shake hands. March sat down, lit a cigarette and blew the smoke in Danny's direction.

"Cheers for that," said Danny.

"Just toughening you up, lad," said March. "There's a long way to go, though. We're not setting off from what I like to call a particularly strong starting point."

Danny ignored the insult.

The waitress came over and March ordered a pot of tea for one. When she left, Danny spoke.

"You needed to talk to me."

"I did. There's been an unfortunate development."

"Really, with you around?"

"Cut the crap, Danny. This is serious. I met young Anna last night."

"She told me."

"Out with a very handsome companion, as it happens. I always thought you two were going to be an item but clearly she's fond of them with a bit more muscle, if you don't mind me saying."

This was the last thing Danny wanted to hear, but he hoped it didn't show.

"Apparently you crossed her off the guest list."

"Ah, just an administrative misunderstanding. I tried to sort it out but she disappeared. Too loved up to notice, I expect. Who was he, by the way?"

"No idea."

"Well she's done well, but she's a lovely looking girl. You want to lower your sights a bit. Just a bit of friendly advice. But anyway, about last night."

"Yes?"

"There appears to have been something of a tragedy."

"Steve."

"You heard? I thought you might have. Such a lovely boy. It's a terrible waste."

"Graham, I have to ask. What the fuck do you know about the music business?"

"I beg your pardon?"

"You're a copper. Were a copper. And a particularly corrupt one at that. You're what? Early sixties?"

"Fifty-one."

"What?"

The tea arrived. March poured a cup and added milk but no sugar. Conversation paused until the waitress left them alone.

"You're never fifty-one," Danny continued.

"What are you saying?"

"Just that you're not fifty-one."

"I am, but it doesn't matter. Your point is?"

"My point is, what do you know about the music business? Anna tells me you're claiming to be their manager, but I can't understand what on earth they'd gain from that, every offence intended."

"I'm a man of many connections."

"So I gather."

March shot him a look then took a sip of the tea. It still looked too hot, but it didn't seem to bother him.

"I know people, Danny. I get things done. And I'm a philanthropist."

"A what?"

"I do apologise. That was a long word for the Echo, so I

shouldn't have expected you'd understand. I'm a good guy, Danny. I've told you. Friend of the homeless and patron of the arts. All part of my new image, putting right the public misperception."

"Can you stop talking shit for once?"

"I'll pretend I didn't hear that. Anyway, it was looking very rosy until the poor silly boy took something naughty and went for a swim."

"And that's your line, is it?"

"What?"

"That he was on drugs and it was an accident?"

"So I've been told. But that's why I need to see you. It's a delicate time, Danny."

"Clearly."

"I just think the boy needs to be shown some respect. Not have young guttersnipes poking around in his business. I'm a heartbroken man, Danny. We were on the verge of greatness together. I'm just protecting his reputation."

"And so, you want me to not look into it?"

"There's nothing to look into. Just a tragic accident. I told you."

"Which kind of makes me want to look into it all the more."

March leaned forward, his eyes boring into Danny's.

"And I'm just telling you, that wouldn't be wise."

"Because?"

"Because we wouldn't want you to have a similarly tragic accident, would we?"

"Are you threatening me?"

"Threatening, Danny?" March leaned back again. "Nothing could be further from my mind. I'm appealing to your good nature. Let the boy rest in peace."

"I'll bear that in mind."

"You'll do more than bear it in mind."

"Will I?"

"Just make sure you do."

March stood up and went to the counter to pay for his drink. As he took his change, he turned back to Danny.

"We still need to arrange your trip to the shelter. Good news sells papers, Danny. Mike would be proud of you."

"I'll bear that in mind too."

"I'll be seeing you, Danny." And then he turned to leave.

Chapter 16

I WAS standing opposite the coffee shop, partially hidden by a white van that was parked on double yellow lines. As soon as March emerged I was poised with my camera, ready to make a move, just as Danny had requested. He'd rung me with clear instructions just after his call with March, once the meeting had been arranged.

Danny followed close behind him, then ran across the road towards me.

"Come on," he said.

"Everything okay?"

"It's fine. Ready with the camera?"

I nodded.

We let March build up a bit of distance and then we started to follow. Danny filled me in on their conversation. March crossed the road towards Mornington Crescent station, but he wasn't heading onto the Underground, thankfully. The station had been closed for years. Instead he walked past and then turned left, opposite Greater London House, the former Black Cat cigarette factory. He turned onto Eversholt Street, heading in the direction of Euston station. There were lots of buses and taxis. I feared he'd get into one and we'd lose him, but instead he just kept on walking, albeit crossing over to the left-hand side of the road.

"When do I start taking pictures?" I asked, not unreasonably in my opinion.

"I don't know," Danny replied, not altogether helpfully. "Just keep following and let's see if he does anything interesting."

We carried on walking. And then we had to stop. Up ahead, March paused outside a shop, looking as though he was about to go in, but after a moment he continued.

"That was close," I said.

"The old perv," said Danny.

"Who? March?"

"Yes."

"Why's that, then? I mean we know, obviously, but specifically now?"

"Because he was going to go into the porn shop."

"The porn shop?"

"Yes, look." As we approached we saw a shopfront claiming to be a "book shop" with smaller signs underneath offering magazines, and videotapes for sale and exchange.

"How did you know it was a porn shop?" I asked.

"Just look at the signs."

"I can see that now, but I couldn't from where we were. So, at the risk of repetition, how did you know it was a porn shop?"

"It's famously a porn shop."

"Well, it's not that famous. I live about two miles away and I've never heard of it."

"Everybody's heard of it."

"Clearly not."

"Anyway, it is."

"Anyway, that's avoiding the question."

But before Danny could come up with another excuse to explain his rather alarming knowledge of Euston's filth merchants, March stopped again. We stopped too. Up ahead we saw him press a doorbell. I managed to take a picture, although I doubt it was brilliant. Then the door opened and he disappeared inside. We carried on, walking past, but took a good look at the building he'd entered. The neon sign outside flashed "sauna" and then "massage", alternating between the two, in garish pink and blue. Danny smiled.

"Now you can take some pictures," he said.

"Of March in a sauna? I haven't got a bloody wide angle with me."

"You do know that it's not actually a sauna, don't you?" he asked.

"Yes, I'm not completely stupid."

We crossed the road and hid in a side goods entrance that seemed to lead into the back of Euston station. I think it may have been a mail depot. There were lots of Post Office vans in the vicinity. I trained my camera on the door, ready for his reappearance from the brothel.

"How long do you think he'll be?" I asked.

"Is this another test?" asked Danny.

"What do you mean?"

"Checking to see how well I know the working practices of massage parlours."

"Now you mention it."

"Well, I don't know, do I? I've obviously never been in one. But probably half an hour, hour maybe. Depends on how long his appointment is."

"And do you think he's... Really?"

"It doesn't even bear thinking about."

But in reality, we didn't have long to wait at all. I was just starting to get nervous, in case anyone saw us casing the joint, when March reappeared, barely ten minutes after he went inside. He was doing up his jacket as he emerged.

"That was quick," I said. "PE do you think?"

"What?"

"Premature eja..." But Danny cut me off.

"Can't have been. He'd have barely had time to get undressed. That, I strongly suspect, was not a social visit."

"Business then?"

"I'd bet my mortgage on it."

"If you had one."

"The principle applies."

March continued down Eversholt Street and then crossed over. He started ascending the steps into the Euston station concourse. We sped up to get closer. Discretion was paramount, but it would be easy to lose him in a busy mainline train station.

"Let's split," suggested Danny. "We'll be less obvious if we're separate and it gives us double the chance of keeping up. We'll call each other if one of us loses him." It seemed a sensible plan.

March moved across the concourse and seemed to be heading towards the escalators that led down to the Underground station. Brilliant. Danny followed. I held back a bit, but then thought I'd better be brave. All I had to do was follow Danny and I'd be okay.

Luckily, the station was busy, so it was quite easy to go unnoticed. March was heading to the southbound Victoria Line. As I reached the opening to the platform, I saw Danny with his hand out to stop me. I stopped. He's so masterful like that. Putty in his hands.

"He's walking down the platform," he said. "Wait till the train comes in and then jump on."

Two minutes later I felt the familiar gust of wind as the train blasted into the station. The doors opened. A few people got off but the train was still quite crowded. Just before the doors closed we jumped on.

"What now?" I asked as it started to pull away.

"Stay by the door, then we just look out at every station and hope we see him getting off."

"Do you think he's heading home?"

Danny told me his address, but we were heading in the wrong

direction. Warren Street and Oxford Circus passed without incident, but when the doors opened at Green Park, we saw March's familiar bulky form emerge from a carriage two down from ours.

We followed. Again, the platform was busy. That made it easy to hide, but increased the risk that we'd lose him. We split again. Danny stayed behind this time, following me. I was quite pleased at my espionage skills. March was a way ahead, but I only lost sight of him at the top of the escalator as he approached the barriers. I moved to the left and sped up the final few steps, just in time to see him turn right and leave the station by the rear exit.

Danny caught up, and we continued to follow, through the backstreets into Berkeley Square, where we saw him disappear into a casino.

"We're good," said Danny. I had to agree. I gave him a hug. It was just like the old days.

"What now, Poirot?" I asked.

"Same procedure. We hide opposite and wait. Shit, what time is it?"

"Nearly five."

"Okay. How long to get back to Leah?"

"From here? God knows. Not my forte. It's not even on the Underground."

"Where is it, then?"

"The studio? Near Hackney Central but it's overground only. We'd have to change at Highbury and Islington I suppose. I drove last time."

I could see Danny thinking.

"We could probably do it in forty minutes but to be safe we'll give it an hour," he said. "Does that sound right? That gives us till six. Hopefully he'll be out by then."

"Is he the gambling type?"

"I don't know. Are casinos even open at this time of day?"

"It's a valid point. So, you're thinking…"

"Another meeting? Maybe."

We found a bench in Berkeley Square itself, appearing to all the world like a couple of tourists or young lovers, but with a good view of the casino entrance just off a side street. I was ready with the camera as soon as it was needed. It was cold but thankfully the rain had stopped. I snuggled up to Danny to keep warm. Neither of us spoke. I couldn't hear the famous nightingales. If they were there, they were being drowned out by the sound of traffic and the construction that was underway on the other side of the square.

"What do you think he's up to?" I asked at last. There was still no sign of his reappearance.

"I don't know," said Danny. "I've got a theory but it seems too obvious."

"Sometimes the obvious answer is the right answer."

He nodded, deep in thought.

"It's just too straightforward though. I mean, we know he's trafficking, somehow, although whether as the ringleader or just a go-between, we don't know."

"Okay."

"And that's essentially bringing girls over and turning them into prostitutes."

"And he has a business meeting at a massage parlour?"

"That's the point, exactly. Is he giving them first look? Drumming up custom? Either way it all fits, exactly as you'd think. But it just seems too obvious somehow. Too basic. Too easy."

"He's not the brightest, is he?"

"But he is, though. Not Clare levels of super-bright, but he's far from stupid."

I wasn't particularly happy about that specific comparison. I sat up straight, putting a slight gap between us. I don't know why, exactly, but just the sound of her name rankled. I could feel Danny looking at me.

"What now?" he asked.

"Nothing."

"Is it because I mentioned Clare?"

"No."

"I'm not playing this again."

"Well then."

"Good."

Neither of us spoke for probably twenty seconds, but it seemed like longer. Then I just had to ask.

"Have you heard from her again?"

"No."

"That's something."

"But I emailed her."

"Right."

"Oh, come on, Anna," he said. "I told you I was going to do that."

"Did you?"

"Yes."

"Fine. And?"

"I've not heard back yet."

"Ha."

"Oh, just get over yourself."

I turned to look at him.

"Me? Me, get over myself?"

"I'm sorry."

"I just care, Danny. I care about you. I don't want you getting involved with some mental mass murderess, leading you God knows where."

"She's hardly that."

"Really? How many people do you have to kill to qualify? I'd say she was the absolute epitome."

"It's not like that."

"Well, we can agree to disagree. I can't believe you're defending her."

Danny sighed. I turned away from him again. I started having nostalgic thoughts about the previous evening, and how simple and refreshing it had all seemed. How uncomplicated. And then I remembered I'd agreed to go for dinner with Mitch tomorrow night. My first thought was what a disaster and how I could get out of it, but almost immediately it seemed like the thing I most wanted to do. I wanted to call him there and then, just to reconfirm. I'd been short with him earlier. I regretted that now. God, my head was a mess.

But before I had a chance to even evaluate the pros and cons of that little conundrum, Danny spoke again.

"You're not going to like this either," he said.

I took a moment to respond.

"What?" I said eventually.

"I need to go to the massage parlour."

I took another moment.

"Why?" I asked, eventually, my mind already thinking things it didn't want to.

"To see for myself. See if I can find out who he spoke to."

"Am I hearing this?"

"Oh, Anna. Don't be like that."

"Like what?"

"I'm a bloody investigative journalist. It's what I do."

"What? Shag prostitutes?"

"I'm not going to be shagging a prostitute."

"Oh right. Quick massage and a happy ending then?"

"Jesus."

"Jesus yourself."

"There's no talking to you at the moment."

That was just brilliant. Blaming me. I was the one trying to maintain a sense of decency.

"Fine," I said again, for want of anything better.

"Listen, I'll be careful. I'm not shagging anyone. I'm not having a massage. I'll make my excuses and leave. But I've got to go in there, see if I can find out what he's up to."

"And how do you propose to do that?"

"I don't know yet. Play it by ear."

"Okay. And when do you hope to do this exactly?"

"As soon as."

"Tonight?"

"Possibly. Depends how long we're with Leah. If not, tomorrow."

"And you're putting it on expenses, are you?"

"If necessary, yes."

"Oh well, that'll look good." It was at times like this that I fancied a fag.

Movement at the casino entrance stopped any further discussion. I raised my camera. But it wasn't March. It was somebody else. He turned up his coat collar and headed in the opposite direction.

"We should go," said Danny, after a moment, looking at his watch. I agreed. I'd had enough of this anyway. I didn't know then that this was to be the highlight of the evening. Things were about to get far worse.

Chapter 17

WE left Berkeley Square and headed back to the tube at Green Park. It was frustrating not to have seen our target, but I suspected this was the life of people undertaking stake-outs. Long periods of waiting, punctuated by brief moments of excitement, or, as in this case, nothing at all.

It was peak time on the tube and the carriage was packed. For once I didn't mind. At least it gave us both an excuse not to talk to each other. I realised, deep down, that I was being childish, and of course Danny had to follow up every lead. But I just didn't like it, and the thought made me queasy. The annoying thing was just how unapologetic he seemed about it. That was the bit that upset me. Oh yeah, and his seeming enthusiasm to hang out with prostitutes in their place of work, when he wasn't fawning over a certain murderess.

We changed at Highbury and Islington and caught the overground train. It was still busy, but it was only a short journey. We were close-ish together, although there was still a distance between us. I was just getting annoyed by the sound of a mobile phone ringtone when I realised it was mine. With considerable embarrassment, I took it out of my pocket and answered the call, earning several disapproving glances in the process.

"Hi," I said.

"Hi Anna, it's Mitch," came the reply. "Is it a better time to call?"

"Hi," I said again, feeling a slight case of butterflies. "Much better, yes, although I'm on a train and have to get off in a moment. Sorry about earlier."

"That's okay. Are you all right? I've been worried."

"Ah, don't worry. I'll tell you all about it over dinner tomorrow."

"Are you still on for that?"

"Of course." I'm ashamed to admit I did a little girlish giggle.

"That's good. I was worried I'd lost you."

"No, not in the slightest. I had a great night. I've been wanting to call you but I've been out working."

"That's okay."

"I'm going to have to go again in a minute, though. I'm just arriving."

"Where are you off to? Anywhere nice?"

"Hackney Central."

"Fair play. Work or pleasure?"

"Kind of work. Just helping out Danny, really." I couldn't remember how much I'd mentioned about my flatmate's career choice, but I think I'd covered the basics.

"Sounds exciting. Are you on a mission?"

"Something like that. Oh, I'm sorry. Got to go again. I'll call you tomorrow to make a plan, okay?"

"Can't wait. Take care, Anna."

"You too."

And that was the end of that. Immediately, however, my mood was lifted. Two can play at this game. Danny was giving me a funny look.

"We're here," he said, and then turned away.

I followed him off the carriage and along the platform. He wasn't speaking.

"It's only about a five-minute walk," I said, as much to break the silence as anything. He just shrugged. Fine, I thought. By the time we reached the exit, though, I'd had enough.

"What's the matter?" I asked.

"Nothing," he said.

"God, are you doing that thing I do, just to be annoying?"

That, at least, raised a smile.

"Come on," he said. "Lead the way."

I stopped.

"Come here," I said. He came towards me, looking slightly confused. It was big hug time.

"Can we stop falling out?" I said, as much to myself as Danny. He stepped forward and gave me a peck on the cheek. I put my arms around him, then squeezed him hard.

We climbed down the steps and onto the main road, passing under the railway bridge. I led the way. We tried to make small talk but without much success. I changed the subject to Leah as we walked past a parade of shops.

"I just hope she shows up," I said.

"Do you think she will?"

"God knows. It was a weird call, completely off her face most of the time with moments of lucidity. I'll tell you what I don't get."

"What?"

"I tried to play piano when I was little and it was really bloody hard. How come musicians can do it when they're absolutely hammered? It's like they're superhuman. I'd appreciate your expert knowledge here."

"I was never a great keyboard player."

"What? I heard some of your demos. They were decent."

"I know. And thanks for that. But it was all programming of sequencers. If I had to play it all live, I'd be rubbish."

"Fair enough. Anyway, if she does show, it'll hopefully help explain the March connection."

I looked at Danny but his mind seemed to be elsewhere. I stopped walking. Eventually he noticed and turned back to me.

"What now?" I asked. He was smiling.

"I was just thinking about what you said. About the piano. You might have just had a stroke of genius."

"*What?*" I was confused.

"I'll explain when we see her, but you're good. Come on, we've got to get going. Tell me what she said about March again."

"Not a lot, just that he was a wanker, but that's nothing new. She just kept referring to 'bastards' and said she'd have to be careful. There's been something going on ever since we first met them. God. That was only like three days ago. Seems like ages."

We turned off the high street. It was dark now. It all looked different at night. I was pretty sure I had the right road, but there was still a nagging doubt. Then, in a moment of triumph, I recognised one of the buildings. Along the road I could see the entrance to the studio. Somebody was sitting on the pavement, leaning against the wall. Leah. Thank God.

We quickened our pace. But as we got closer, something didn't look right. Was she asleep? Had she passed out? And then as we got closer still, I started to feel a sense of absolute dread. There was a pool of darkness next to her. It was growing. She wasn't moving. The blood caught the light from a street lamp, giving it an other-worldly sheen.

"Oh my God," I said, as I ran towards her. "Leah..."

But she didn't answer. She wasn't moving. Her chest was caked in blood, where it had run from the wound on the side of her head.

I panicked. My first aid training is minimal, but I immediately knelt down to cradle her. She was still breathing, but it was shallow. Danny was beside me. Everything drifted out of focus. I heard Danny saying something about calling an ambulance. I felt my heart beating faster. I should have been alert to danger but instead I just froze. Everything seemed surreal.

"Leah, talk to me," I said. But she was silent. Not moving. Not speaking. Hardly breathing.

"Come on," I said. "Leah. You're okay now. We're with you. What happened? Can you hear me? Squeeze my hand if you can hear me." But she didn't squeeze my hand. Her eyes were focused somewhere in the distance. They looked glassy. I could see the life trying to leave her. Her breathing got shallower still.

"Leah!" I began to lose my mind to shock. Danny joined me. I felt his arm round my shoulders. And yet he was cradling Leah too. Nothing made sense. The world starting spinning. I felt light-headed. My grip on reality was fading.

"Leah!"

From behind me I could see flashing lights, bouncing off the wall. I could hear a siren. And then I was being led away. Paramedics were taking control. Two people in green uniforms were crouching beside Leah. More lights. More sirens. And then voices. A stretcher. Leah was being wheeled away. She had an oxygen mask. Where did that come from?

I was shaking. Where was Danny? There. He was there. Talking to a policeman. And then they were coming for me. And I felt the earth move beneath me. Suddenly I couldn't see. I couldn't stand. I couldn't focus. I was hit by an overwhelming sensation of nausea, but couldn't find my voice to warn anyone. I couldn't hear what they were saying to me. I thought I could see three faces, looking at me. Talking to me. But I didn't hear their voices. My hands and feet were suddenly so cold. I leaned back, against the wall. But the wall wasn't there. I felt myself fall. Everything seemed to slow down, as though the world had stopped spinning. Nothing made sense. Nothing to hold on to.

And then everything went black.

Chapter 18

"ANNA!"

I came to. All I could see was Danny, looking at me. Why was he so close? What was happening?

"Anna, are you okay?" It sounded like Danny. But then I started to focus. It wasn't Danny. It was someone in a uniform. A woman. She was looking at me. Talking to me. And then the full sense of panic seemed to hit.

"Where's Danny?" I asked.

"I'm here," he said. I turned and there he was. And I realised he was holding me.

"What's happening?" I said. "Leah?"

"We're taking Leah to hospital. You need to come with us," said the woman. She was wearing green. But behind her were more blue lights. Flash, flash, flash. And more uniforms. Police. I started to sit up.

"Danny..."

"You're in shock," he said. "We're going to the hospital with Leah. They want to look at you too. Come on."

Danny helped me stand. He supported me. I felt drunk. I hadn't had a drink in days. Well, a day. I could do with one now.

Then I could feel drunk. That would make sense. Nothing made sense any more. And then I was in the back of a car, and my eyes started to close. And I felt my body shut down. I could feel somebody holding me. And then I felt myself drifting. I started to dream. The dreams didn't make sense.

Suddenly the car stopped. The door opened. The cold air hit me. Woke me up.

"Come on," said Danny. "They need to look at you."

At me?

I stood up. I took a deep breath. Everything seemed alien. Why was I at a hospital? And then it all started coming back to me. Leah. Shit. I had an overwhelming urge to talk to a doctor.

"Danny, I need to see the doctor."

"We will," he said, trying to comfort me.

"No, about Leah. It's urgent. Get me a doctor. Now." He looked at me as though I'd gone mad, but something about my tone of voice seemed to register. Before long a doctor was approaching us. He started to talk but I cut him off.

"You don't understand," I said. "You've got our friend here. Leah. Sorry I don't know her surname. It's just I think she may have taken drugs before being attacked. I thought you should know."

"Drugs?"

"Yes. No idea what. I spoke to her earlier. She was out of it. I just didn't want you giving her some painkillers or something and giving her an overdose."

Clearly my lack of drug knowledge was a disadvantage in these circumstances.

"I just... I just want her to be okay," I continued. My voice sounded feeble, even to me.

The doctor gave me a reassuring smile, thanked me, and left in apparent urgency. I don't know if it made any difference. I felt better for saying it though.

We got set for a hard night in A&E. By the time somebody

came to see me, the shock had worn off. I felt fully back to normal, aside from a slight shakiness, as though I hadn't eaten for days. I'd like to say the cup of tea from the vending machine helped, but in truth it was bloody awful. Never trust a vending machine when it comes to tea. I'm pretty confident that's the first rule of life.

Once I was given a clean bill of health, our thoughts returned to Leah. She'd been rushed through to intensive care. We moved to the waiting area next to her ward. I tried to call Holly, but again there was no answer.

At about 2am a doctor came to see us.

"Are you the next of kin?" he asked.

That sounded ominous. We explained we were friends. I didn't know if she had any next of kin. All I knew was that at some point she'd been homeless. I realised I didn't really know anything except that it was becoming an ever-bigger mess.

"How is she?" I asked. Danny gripped my hand.

"She's unconscious, but alive," he said. "She's in the very best place."

"Oh, thank God." Obviously it wasn't good, but it was a whole lot better than it could have been.

"You should go home," he continued. "She's stable. She's going to be here a while."

"Can we see her?" I asked.

"Not tonight. Call us tomorrow and we'll give you an update. With any luck, she'll be okay for visitors in a couple of days."

"A couple of days?"

"She's in a bad way, I'm afraid. She's going to be drifting in and out of consciousness and heavily sedated. It could be longer. Call us and we'll keep you updated."

I thanked the doctor. Danny called for a cab to take us home. It was just after 3am. He looked pale. Worried. We didn't speak much on the journey in case we were overheard. When we got in

I was keen to talk, but Danny insisted we should go to bed. I tried to protest but I was exhausted. I didn't think I'd sleep. That was my last thought until morning. Given what followed, it was good that I'd had a chance to recharge.

127

Chapter 19

Wednesday, April 6th, 1994

SAMUEL Elmhirst-Banks was watching the BBC breakfast news when his phone rang.

"Seb," he said.

"Are you watching the news?" she asked.

"I've just seen it."

There was silence. He broke it.

"What the fuck is happening?"

"It's not what you think."

"No? So what exactly do I think? Come on, tell me."

"It doesn't matter what you think. It's under control."

"I'm sorry?" The clipped words betrayed the growing anger in his voice.

"I didn't mean it like that. Of course it matters what you think."

"Let me tell you this. I'm trusting you to be my eyes and ears in this. And what I *think* is that it's fast turning into a fucking disaster."

"It really isn't."

"Really? Because from where I'm sitting, we've got one person dead and another in intensive care and March is still doing whatever the fuck..."

"Just don't panic, okay?"

"Don't *panic*? Is that what you think I'm doing? That I'm panicking?"

"No, I'm not saying that. Just trust me. It's under control."

"Really? Which bit of staying out of the news equates with being the lead fucking story on the BBC?"

"It's not like that."

"You'd better not be bullshitting me. Do I need to reiterate just how fucking serious this could be if it all gets *out* of control?"

"It won't."

"You're telling me."

"I'm on it."

"Too fucking right you're on it. Stick to him like superglue and everyone he speaks to. And especially any fucking journalist who shows an inkling. Start with this Churchill bastard. And call me. Regularly."

"I will."

"Damn right you will." He slammed down the phone. Outside, it was raining heavily. The dark clouds loomed ominously, but they paled to nothing compared to his ever-worsening mood.

I was barely out of the shower when I heard the doorbell. That's weird, I thought. And then I had a sudden feeling of dread that it'd be a big bouquet or something from Mitch, which was just about all I'd need. I grabbed my bathrobe and was heading towards the door, trying to think of excuses for Danny, while at the same time trying to work out why I thought I'd even need an excuse. God, I was confused. This is why I don't do relationships. I can barely look after myself at times.

Danny had already opened the door. It wasn't a bouquet. It was DS Amy Cranston and a colleague I didn't recognise. They looked serious. He was letting them in. I made my excuses and said I'd get dressed and join them. It was very much a jeans and sweatshirt morning. I felt like I had a hangover, though it was purely the lack of sleep, and the memory of the horror of the night before.

By the time I made it back through to the living room, Danny was in an armchair, with the two police officers on the sofa. Amy introduced her colleague as DC Anil Jachuck. He seemed to be the appointed note-taker. They all had a cup of tea, and Danny indicated one he'd made for me, too. The angel.

"I was just explaining about last night," he said.

"How is she?" I asked. "Any news?"

"She's in a bad way," said Amy, "but it's a bloody good job you turned up when you did. Any longer and, well, it doesn't bear thinking about."

"Any idea who was responsible?"

"That's why we're here. Did anyone else know you were meeting?"

"Not that I know," I said. "I hadn't told anyone other than Danny. I don't know who she spoke to. I wasn't even expecting her to be there, to be honest."

"And yet it was Leah who suggested the meeting?"

"Yes, but she was completely out of it. She sounded off her head on something."

"Ah, we need to ask you about that." It was DC Jachuck.

"Anything I can do to help."

"You spoke to a doctor, apparently," he continued. "Said she might be on something?"

"Exactly. I didn't know what they'd give her as a painkiller or a sedative or whatever, but I was worried there'd be a reaction. I thought they ought to know."

"And yet we've seen the results of the preliminary blood tests. She was completely clean."

"What?"

"The full results will take a few days, but as far as we can tell, there was nothing in her system at all. Not even a trace."

"Are you sure?"

"Completely. Not even alcohol."

"Wow. Is it accurate?"

"There's a limit. If she'd taken something a few days ago, it mightn't show. But anything in the last forty-eight hours would, depending on the drug. Even the fastest would still be there for twelve hours or so. She definitely wasn't on anything yesterday."

"But she sounded completely hammered."

I looked at Danny. That had floored me. Maybe I'd misjudged her completely. He regarded me with a quizzical look.

"She did!" I protested.

"Well, unless she was just trying to sound like a cool rock star, it may have been grief," continued Amy. "Or probably, more likely, fear. If she had any indication of what was going on, she must have been terrified. Did you ever see her take anything?"

"No, not as such. Actually no, not at all. I just kind of assumed. Jesus."

"So, you arranged to meet?" Amy continued.

"Yeah, I called her. Actually, that's not true. I called Holly when I heard about Steve but there wasn't any answer. Eventually Leah picked it up and said Holly had gone away."

"Can you talk us through that call?"

I did my best to summarise, wishing I'd taken notes.

"So, she said she'd tell you what had happened to Steve?"

"Along those lines. She said it was worse than I could imagine but she'd tell me later."

"And she mentioned March? Did you ask her about him or did

she mention him first?"

"I did. I just couldn't understand why he was anywhere near the band, but I'd had a theory."

"Which was?"

"Apparently she'd been homeless. I wondered if that was the connection. Maybe she'd met him at this homeless shelter thing he's involved in."

DC Jachuck was writing at speed, trying to keep up.

"Okay. I'll look into that. Did she give you any indication of how he came into it?"

"No, she just called him a wanker." I felt a bit embarrassed using the term. Part of me was nervous about swearing in front of a police officer. "I was going to ask more about that yesterday, too."

"How did you come to be involved with the band in the first place?" That was DC Jachuck.

"I'm a photographer. I knew Steve's sister. She's a friend of mine. She asked if I'd take some pictures. That's a point - have you managed to speak to Colette?"

DC Jachuck shook his head.

"No, she's away in Sicily apparently, but we've contacted the parents and broken the news."

"Any idea on when the funeral will be?"

"Not at the moment. It'll be a while before we can release the body."

"But can you say anything about it? Does it look like an accident?"

DC Jachuck looked at Amy. She took over.

"We can't say much at this moment. But he was clean as well."

That was a relief, of sorts. But then I'd never been in any real doubt where he was concerned.

"It's not likely he fell in on his own, then?"

"I'd say that's still a possibility but we're definitely pursuing other lines of enquiry."

"Amy?" started Danny. "Actually, is it okay if I still call you Amy while you're here officially?"

"Of course, Danny."

Oh, here we go. Were they flirting as well? Was this another one I had to worry about? Obviously I appreciate the double standards, given that I was the one with the date tonight, but I could justify that in my own way, even if I'd have difficulty persuading anyone else.

"Do we have any idea what March is up to?" Danny continued. "I met the band on Saturday. They were on top of the world, on stage, gig packed full of fans. Everything seemed to be fantastic. But then two days later March turns up and within two days of that, one of them's dead and another's on life support. And we've got no idea where Holly is. Have you tracked her down, by the way?"

"Not yet," she replied. "But we're looking. As for March, Danny, you know as much as I do."

"I know, but isn't it weird?"

"I can see why you'd think that."

"Actually, I don't think it was all fantastic," I said. All eyes were on me.

"What wasn't?" asked Amy.

"There was something going on. The girls were hardly talking on Saturday. Steve said it was hard trying to keep up the momentum, trying to keep everyone happy. Then when I did the pictures on Sunday, there seemed to be some sort of massive tension. At the end Holly came over to speak to me and I said it had been fun, but she said it wasn't, not really."

"Did you have any idea what it was about?"

"No, but then when I went to the studio on Monday to show them the pictures, there was only Holly there. The others should have been but they weren't. Holly said they were supposed to be rehearsing but she hadn't heard from them."

"She didn't know where they were?"

"No. That's the point. But then, as I was leaving, she said not to worry. That they worked hard and just had creative differences. So it could just be that - but she just didn't look right. She looked sad. Troubled."

"We'll look into that too."

"And I've still not managed to speak to her. I keep calling but there's never any answer. The only time there was an answer, Leah had her phone and said Holly had gone, but didn't say where. I don't even know if Holly's still got the phone."

"She possibly hasn't," said Amy. "We'll keep trying to track her down and when we speak to her I'll let you know, okay? Just to put your mind at rest."

I thanked her. The interview drew to a close. Amy and her colleague thanked us in turn for our time, and then they left us in peace.

"How are you feeling?" asked Danny, once we were back on our own.

"I'm still tired," I admitted. "I think it's the shock on top of everything. Are you all right?"

"I'm fine, just worried." He left it at that. I didn't delve further as I thought I knew what he was referring to. Perhaps he wasn't, in retrospect. "I'm going to phone the office, tell them I won't be in and see if they've heard anything."

While Danny made the call, I took the cups through to the kitchen and started loading the dishwasher. Eventually he came to join me.

"There is one other thing," he said. "It's following on from what you were saying last night."

"Go on."

"It's just this. You mentioned playing the piano and how it's really hard."

"Ah yes. My alleged stroke of genius?"

I still had no idea what I'd said that was supposedly so clever.

"Exactly. Bear with me. Presumably if you're going to be any good at piano, you need lessons. And lessons are probably really expensive if you have a lot of them, which is what you'd need if you wanted to do it professionally."

"Agreed."

"So, Leah, at some stage, has presumably had supportive parents who spent a lot of money on her. And she's not very old, so it probably wasn't all that long ago."

I could see Danny's thinking.

"So how do you go from there to being homeless in London?" I asked. "It's not like she was an orphan growing up in a children's home, presumably. Has there been some big falling out? Has she discovered a rebellious streak and run away? Or is it something more?"

"Precisely," he said after a moment. "We need to know more. I just hope she's okay. She's clearly the key to this and yet..." He drifted off.

"And yet what?"

"Well, I just don't know how it all connects, or even if it does. I can't see how it has any connection at all to the trafficking stuff. So why are they getting attacked? And who's doing it? It's only because of March that there's even a link. And even then, it's tenuous. He may be using the shelter as a front in some way, but even so, what's that got to do with the band?"

"Nothing as far as I can see."

"Exactly. So even if he met Leah there and decided to get into the music business, which is possible but weird, how does that explain anything else? Why did someone kill Steve and try to kill Leah? And where's Holly?"

We were about to find out the answer to that, and it was far from what we expected.

Chapter 20

M Y phone started ringing. I ran through to the front room, expecting Mitch, but when I answered the call I could only hear background noise.

"Hello," I said again.

And then I heard a voice, and it definitely wasn't him.

"Anna?" She sounded upset. Shaky.

"Holly?"

"Oh God, Anna, I'm so scared."

"Holly, where are you?" Danny heard me and came running through.

"I've got nowhere to go," she said. "I just don't know what's going on. It's Steve, Leah..."

"I know. Where are you now?"

"Waterloo. I can't go home. They'll find me."

"Who'll find you, Holly? Who's doing this?"

"I don't know. I don't know anything any more."

"Listen, can you stay there? We'll come to you. We can be there very soon, probably half an hour. Can you do that?"

"I can't stay here. Too many people. They'll be looking for me."

I was thinking out loud.

"Can you get on the Underground?"

"Yes, but I can't go home."

"No, don't worry about that. Can you get to Camden Town? Straight up on the Northern Line."

"Yeah, I can do that."

"Do it now, and we'll meet you there. Take the left exit. It'll take you twenty minutes. We should be there by then. I've got Danny with me. If we're not there just wait, okay? We'll only be a few minutes. We'll set off now."

"Thanks, Anna," she said. "But hurry."

"I will."

She rang off. Danny was already putting his shoes on. I followed suit. We grabbed our jackets and keys and headed down Camden Road towards the station.

We arrived before Holly. The wait was interminable. What if she didn't show? What if they'd got to her first? What if right at this minute she was being scraped up, having been pushed in front of a train? Why hadn't I suggested a taxi for God's sake? I hate the bloody Underground at the best of times and this was far from that.

But just as the panic was starting to really take hold, she appeared at the top of the escalator, carrying a nylon holdall. She saw us and gave a very brief wave, looking terrified. She came through the barrier and ran straight into my arms.

"I'm just so pleased to see you," I said.

In fairness, she looked terrible. She'd clearly been crying, but I could only imagine the trauma she'd been through. Danny took her bag.

"Come on, we'll take you home," I said. "You'll be safe there."

Within fifteen minutes we were back at the flat.

"I can't go home," Holly said again.

"That's okay," said Danny. "You can stay here."

"Really?"

"Of course. We're just so pleased you're safe. We've been so worried about you."

"You can have my room," I added.

"No, I can't do that. Can I just stay on the sofa?"

"Seriously, it's no bother. I can share with Danny." I looked at him. We'd shared a bed several times while looking for Clare and it had always gone surprisingly well, even if there'd been a regrettable absence of anything sordid. Things might have been a bit frosty over the last few days, but secretly I was pleased at the prospect. Obviously, I wouldn't mention it to Mitch. God, I wasn't cut out for this level of subterfuge. Danny nodded. That was agreed then.

"Have you got clothes and things?" I asked.

"Just what I've got in the bag," she said. "It's all right, though. Just till I can get something sorted."

"You can stay as long as you like," I said. "Don't worry. We'll make sure you're okay."

I offered to make tea and she accepted. Everything always looks better with a nice cup of tea, but in truth it could hardly look any worse.

"Have you got any idea what's going on, Holly?" I asked, when we were all back in the living room.

"I don't know. I really don't know," she said.

"Who's looking for you?"

"I don't know. I don't know anything any more."

I moved to sit next to her on the sofa, and held her hand.

"I've got so many questions," I said. "Are you up to talking?"

"Of course. But I don't know that I'll know the answers."

"Don't worry. But first, have you spoken to the police? Do they know you're safe? They're looking for you."

She shook her head.

"I'll call Amy," said Danny, and he went to get his phone.

"What happened on Monday?" I asked. "I came to the gig but I couldn't get in. And Graham March. What was he doing there?"

"Oh God. The old fat guy? Fuck knows."

"But how did he even come to be involved?"

"I don't know. It was the first time I'd ever laid eyes on him. That's where Leah and Steve were that afternoon, apparently. Meeting him, without me. The first I knew about it was that night. Apparently he knows lots of venues and stuff but I think it's bullshit."

"They went without you?"

"Yeah."

"Why?"

She just shrugged. It was interesting, though. The two who'd been with March were the two that had been attacked. What had they seen? What had they got involved in? Danny had been listening in from the doorway and he seemed to be thinking the same. He looked at me. He keyed a number into his phone. I assumed it was Amy's, and then, when he made the connection, he left us, pulling the door closed behind him.

"Holly, can I ask you a difficult question?" I said.

"Ask anything. I don't mind."

"It's just when I saw you at the studio you told me there were some creative tensions but it was just because you all worked hard. Sorry to go on about it again, but what did you mean? Is that all there is?"

She looked at me for a moment but didn't speak. It was as though she was deciding whether or not she could trust me.

"And during the photo shoot, too," I added. "I said it had been fun, but you said it hadn't, not really. Was something else the matter?"

There was a rueful smile.

"Oh, Anna," she said.

I didn't want to pry, but it seemed important.

"What is it? You can tell me," I said, almost in a whisper.

But instead of answering she had a question of her own.

"Do you know how the band came about? How we met and how we started?"

"No, not really. I just assumed you were all friends."

"Sort of. But it was more than that, originally."

"In what way?"

"Steve and me. We were, well, together. Going out. The music was a hobby. But then we met Leah one night in a bar and got chatting to her. She seemed a bit lost and I felt sorry for her."

"Was that when she was homeless?"

"Yeah, kind of. I don't know really. She didn't really talk about it much but she seemed to have been through a lot. We kept in touch. Then one night she came to see us at our flat, and started playing on one of my keyboards. She was brilliant. It was a revelation."

"And then?"

"Well, you can guess the rest. She started having feelings for Steve. It seemed mutual. And the next thing you know we're arguing and then we split up and eventually those two got together."

"Wow, that must have been hard."

I suppose it made sense, though. I'd been thinking all sorts, but ultimately it was a classic old-school love triangle. Cupid has a lot to answer for.

"It was. And then recently it's been getting worse. As though they thought they'd be better off without me. You know, Leah's the gifted musician. Steve's the singer. Why have your ex hanging round?'

"But on stage, you were brilliant."

"Ha. Thanks for that. I loved it, you know? But a lot of it was tapes and stuff. The rest was just for show. They probably would have been better off without me, to be fair to them, but I still loved what we were doing. I just didn't love the situation and the thought of the two of them together."

"No, I can imagine."

"So yeah, there were tensions."

"Understandably."

"Don't get me wrong. I didn't wish them any harm, though."

"No, of course not."

"And I just can't believe…"

There were tears in her eyes. I went to get her a tissue.

"Can I get you anything else?" I asked. "Something to eat, drink?"

"No, honestly, I'm fine."

"Okay, but if there's anything, just ask, okay?"

She nodded. Danny came back into the room.

"I spoke to Amy," he said. "Told her you're safe. She wants to come to see you. She should be about an hour or so."

"Well done," I said. Then turned to Holly and added: "Amy's nice. She's a detective sergeant. You can trust her. Listen, I'll leave you with Danny for a bit and I'll go and sort the room out." I thought it would be good to give them time to talk. He was the one writing the story, after all.

By the time I'd changed the sheets and packed a few things into a suitcase, even though I was only moving to the room next door, Amy had turned up. Danny and I retired to the kitchen.

"What do you think?" he asked.

I recapped our conversation, with particular attention to the meeting between Leah, Steve and March.

"She didn't say who she was hiding from?" he asked.

"No, she doesn't seem to know anything, but it's a natural reaction I suspect. You're in a group of three, and of the other two, one's dead and the other's in intensive care. Of course you're going to be worried."

"She must be terrified."

"I would be."

We let that thought sit between us for a moment.

"She's going to need looking after," Danny said eventually. "Are you around today?"

"I am. Until this evening, anyway."

"Brilliant. And is that okay?"

"Of course. If she says anything important I'll let you know. Otherwise I'll just make sure she's safe."

"Call me if you need me, okay?"

"Shall do. Will you be at the office?"

"Possibly. I'm going to see Mike. See if I can talk deadlines."

"What else are you are up to? Do we need to follow March again?"

"Ideally, but we can't really leave her, especially today. I've got an appointment this afternoon so I'll give you a call after that, though. We'll see how she is."

"But you'll be back by this evening?"

"Definitely. Why? Where are you off out to?"

"Oh, just meeting a friend."

"A friend?"

"Yes, a friend."

"Okay."

I was pretty sure he wanted to ask, and equally pretty sure I didn't want to say. I hastily changed the subject but soon regretted that too. Heavens.

"What's your appointment?" I asked.

"Ah, it's nothing," he said, sounding immediately shifty.

"Really? How can you have an appointment about nothing? You wouldn't actually need to turn up." I meant it as a joke, albeit not one of my funniest, but I'm aware it sounded more accusatory.

"It's nothing, just an appointment."

"Very mysterious."

"No, not really."

"What is it, then?"

"Nothing."

I gave him one of my looks, arms folded, the works. Then waited.

"What?" he said. His tone of voice had changed. I could hear the frustration. But still I remained silent. He wasn't getting off the hook that easily. (Double standards? Me?)

"Oh, for heaven's sake," he said eventually. "It's at the massage parlour."

I continued giving him a look.

"It's research, Anna," he said, in a failed attempt to reassure me. "Nothing's going to happen."

"And you need an actual appointment, do you?"

"Not exactly."

"Right."

"Okay, no, I don't need an appointment. I'm just going to turn up, see what I can find out."

"Right," I said again. "Ah well, good luck with that. Try not to catch anything too nasty."

"I'm not going to be catching anything. I'm not actually going to do anything."

"Apart from get your kit off and get worked into a frenzy and then 'make your excuses and leave'?"

"Not even that. I'm just going to talk."

"Like that won't arouse suspicion."

"You're the expert now, are you?"

"No. But it's common sense."

"Look, it's not ideal, I'll give you that. But I haven't got an option."

"Fine."

"Anyway, I'll be back around six, hopefully. Is that early enough for your 'friend'?"

"Perfect."

I was done with conversation for the time being. I edged

closer to the living room door to try to eavesdrop on Amy and Holly, but that nearly backfired badly as the door opened just as I got there. Amy emerged.

"Can I just have a quick word?" she asked.

"Of course."

I took her back through to the kitchen, where Danny was sitting at the table, looking guilty. Or just glum, perhaps. Not his usual chirpy self, anyway. DC Jachuck followed closely behind.

"She's very fragile," she said in a low voice. "She's been through a lot. She doesn't seem to know much, but she's very scared. Are you okay to keep her here for a bit?"

I explained our plans. Amy seemed pleased.

"If she says anything, or anything changes, I'll give you a shout," I said. "Let me know if you track down Colette though. I'd love to speak to her. And obviously if Leah comes round."

"I will."

They made their way to the door, but just as she was leaving, Amy came back and said something to Danny. I don't know what it was. At this juncture, I'd just like to point out that I'm not the jealous type. Like to, but it would be a fib. There were a lot of things I didn't understand. I had a strong sense of the world being off-balance. I yearned for the quiet life, but had a feeling things were going to get a lot worse before they'd achieve any semblance of better.

Chapter 21

ANNY wasn't sure what constituted "rush hour" in the massage parlour trade, but he was pretty sure it wasn't 4pm. That was good. He wanted it to be as quiet as possible to give himself the best possible chance of discovering something of value.

He took the tube to Euston and then walked back up Eversholt Street to the Central Sauna parlour. But as he got closer, so the nerves grew. What exactly was he going to do, and what was he trying to achieve? There wasn't a clear plan. Play-it-by-ear was all well and good but there was plenty of scope for embarrassment, at best, and abject disaster at worst.

Still, he was a seasoned journalist now, fearless in pursuit of a story, trained by the very best. Or at least that's what he told himself. But it didn't explain why he walked straight past at the first time of asking, rather than dare to darken the doors.

He turned and tried again. This time he got as far as the door, took a deep breath, and pressed the buzzer. There was no going back now. The door opened and he was inside. Immediately, and surprisingly, the nerves dissipated. He was struck by a chemical aroma: air freshener perhaps, or maybe just bleach? He imagined there was a lot to keep clean. There was a middle-aged woman behind a reception desk, asking him if he'd been before, smiling at him.

"Don't be nervous," she said. "We're here to make sure you leave completely relaxed."

He was shown downstairs to the basement where two masseuses were sitting on a sofa, listening to a radio, reading magazines and smoking. They were both dressed in perilously short white tunics that revealed expanses of nylon-covered thighs.

"This is Dominika," said the receptionist, indicating the tall redhead on the left, "or there's Aurelia. Take your pick."

Aurelia smiled and winked at him. The decision was made.

He introduced himself and was then shown to a treatment room and told to undress. He was given a towel and a small bag for any valuables, and was offered the use of a shower.

"Would you like a glass of water, Danny?" Aurelia asked. She seemed to have an accent. Possibly Polish?

He said he would. The situation was already rapidly heading out of control.

Aurelia left, saying she would be back when he was ready.

Now here was a conundrum. To undress and potentially make yourself vulnerable? Or stay fully clothed and arouse suspicion. Anna maybe had a point. Danny took off his clothes, wrapped himself in the towel and quickly headed to the nearby shower cubicle, taking his watch, keys and wallet with him in the valuables bag, just to be on the safe side. He took a very brief shower and returned to the massage room. He was nearly finished drying himself as Aurelia came back, carrying a glass of water that she put on the table beside him.

"Have you been here before?" she asked.

"It's my, ah, first time," said Danny.

"Don't be shy. Everyone starts somewhere. I will make sure you enjoy it. Would you like oil?'

"Oil?"

"For the massage."

"Ah, yes. Yes please. Oil is good."

"Okay. Lie down for me please, face down. We won't be needing this."

She indicated the towel. Danny passed it to her, and then, acutely aware of his nakedness, quickly lay down, wondering what exactly he was going to do now. An attractive young woman was about to start work on his naked torso. In another time and place he wouldn't be objecting, but fundamentally this was wrong. It was all happening so fast.

Aurelia poured a small amount of oil between his shoulder-blades and started work.

"Have you been working today?" she asked. Her hands were soft. Experienced.

"Kind of," said Danny.

"What do you do? You seem very tense. Your shoulders are knotted."

"I'm a... er, work in a record shop." Record shop? It was first thing that occurred to him.

"Really? That's interesting." Her voice was soft and soothing. The low light was relaxing. New age music played softly in the background. In his peripheral vision, he could see his own reflection in a full-length mirror that ran alongside the massage table. Aurelia had undone her tunic, revealing matching underwear and black lace-top hold-ups. She poured more oil into the palms of her hands and started working on his arms, working the muscles in his biceps. She was good, no question about that.

"Is that okay or would you like it firmer?" she asked.

"No, that's good."

She moved to the end of the bed and trickled cold oil over his legs, and started to knead the muscles in his calves, occasionally letting her fingertips brush lightly against his thighs. The small talk continued. The clock kept turning. As she worked her way up she leaned close to his ear and started to whisper, revealing a menu of added extras and the associated charges. It was now or never.

"My friend recommended this to me. He said you were good," he said.

"Satisfaction is guaranteed," she said, with a smile.

"I think, maybe just stick with the massage for now, though."

Aurelia was used to this with the nervous ones.

"Do you not like me? Have I not done a good job?"

"No, you've done a great job. I'm just..."

"A bit shy." She finished the sentence for him. "Turn over and let me tell you more about some of the things I can do for you. Maybe that will make you less shy." She ran her fingertips down his spine, as soft as raindrops.

"No, really, just the massage for now," Danny insisted. "Maybe I'll be braver next time. My friend said how good you were."

"And did your friend explain about the happy ending?"

"Not exactly. But he spoke very highly of you, er, Aurelia. How do you spell that, by the way?"

She spelt it out for him.

"Ah, that's right," he said. "You especially."

Danny could see she doubted that. Something in her expression had changed. And then it occurred to him. Maybe she made her living from the added extras. If the house took the basic massage fee, then she was working for nothing unless she could tempt him with more. To her he'd just be a time-waster. And yet she seemed like a nice person. Intelligent. Attractive. What was she doing in a place like this? What damage was it doing?

"I'll tell you what," he said. "Maybe I pay you for the extras but we can just talk, okay?"

"Okay," she said. She was used to the talkers, too. Sometimes they just wanted someone to listen to them.

"Where are you from?" he asked.

"Poland."

"Wow. That's a long way. Whereabouts in Poland?"

"Łódź. Do you know it?"

"Woodge?" he said, repeating her words without any awareness of the Polish characters. "No, sorry."

"It's an industrial city. In the middle."

"What brought you to London? Have you been here long?"

Was that sadness in her eyes? She ignored the first part of his question.

"Nearly two years," she said.

"And how did you end up working here?"

"You have a lot of questions, Danny."

"I'm sorry, I'm just curious."

"Let's talk about you. How long have you worked in the shop?"

"The shop?"

"The record shop."

"Ah yes. About two years too."

"And what is your favourite music?"

Danny reeled off the names of a few bands. He mentioned Lumière Rouge to see if there was any reaction, but there wasn't. He was desperate to return the conversation to Aurelia and the parlour, aware that time was ticking. He sat up and started to get dressed.

"What are your ambitions? What would you like to do?" he asked.

"I'd like to be an artist. I like to draw, and paint. But there's no money in Poland. It's very hard."

"Is that why you came here?"

She looked at him.

"Maybe."

Danny started to do up his shoelaces.

"Maybe you know my friend?" he said. "I think he comes here often."

"It's possible. What's his name?"

"Graham. Graham March."

Suddenly the atmosphere changed. She stood up, her expression hardening.

"Wait here," she said, and left the room.

Danny finished getting dressed. He took some money from his wallet to cover the fee, then sat on the edge of the table, thinking. Was she here against her will? Was she also a victim of trafficking? He had so many more questions, but she seemed reluctant to talk. He needed to earn her trust but it wasn't going to be easy. Maybe he would come again. It hadn't been so bad. His honour was still, vaguely, intact. Like many he'd had preconceptions about prostitutes, but ultimately they were still people. People with thoughts and passions and problems and dreams. He decided to ask her which days she worked, to make sure he could see her again.

The door opened. But it wasn't Aurelia. It was a man. A giant of a man, and he didn't look happy. He grabbed Danny by the collar, twisting the fabric in his fist.

"What the fuck is your problem?" he asked in broken English.

"Sorry?" Danny was shocked and scared in equal measure. He hadn't been expecting this.

The man pushed him to the door, then shoved him in the direction of the stairs. He could see Aurelia, back on the sofa. She looked terrified too. Danny tried to protest his innocence, but just received another shove for his troubles. He climbed the stairs, the man behind him. He was pushed towards the door.

"Fuck off and don't come back. If I see you again, you're a dead man."

The door was opened, and Danny was forcibly ejected. It slammed shut behind him. He stood in the street, momentarily dumbstruck. He looked back at the door. At the parlour. What had just happened? And why did the mention of March have such a dramatic effect?

Danny ordered a cappuccino and tried to collect his thoughts. There was a lot to take in. So, March was certainly well-known, but had he been ejected because they thought he was a friend? Or because he was asking questions? Either way they had something to hide, and March seemed to be at the centre of it.

His mobile phone rang. He connected the call.

"Hi, it's Amy," said the voice.

"Amy, hi. Any news on Leah?"

"No, not yet. She's still in a bad way. It's just a quick call."

"Okay, what can I help with?"

"It's more how I can help you."

"Sounds good."

"Don't get your hopes up. I've made a few enquiries. About March."

"Okay. And?"

"It seems you're not too far wide of the mark. He's definitely involved in something, and I've heard the word trafficking mentioned."

"That's good. Well, not good exactly, but you know what I mean. Are they close to nailing him?"

"I can't tell you that. Listen Danny, keep digging, okay? I'm extremely light on resources here. It's good to have you working on this. Just keep me informed. Deal?"

"It's a deal. Any more word from your politician friend?"

"Oh God. He called me again. I didn't answer it."

"Pressure's still on, then?"

"Looks like it. But I don't care about preserving reputations. The bad guys are the bad guys."

"Agreed."

Danny thought about mentioning his trip to the massage parlour, but before he'd had a chance to assess the possible implications, Amy drew the call to a close.

"I've got to go," she said. "Phone me. Any time."

"I will."

He ended the call. A minute later the phone started ringing again. The number was withheld.

"Danny Churchill," he said after pressing the green button.

"Danny," said Clare. "We need to talk."

Chapter 22

I'D gone through as many changes of opinion about the wisdom of keeping the dinner date as I had changes of outfit. Clearly it was madness, and I was needed at home, and my prime responsibility was to look after Holly. But at the same time, I needed something to take my mind off things, and it could be fun. And while I was having all of these thoughts, I was aware that Danny was getting up to all sorts of unimaginable delights in a massage parlour, and I have to admit that clouded my judgement considerably. I opted for a short dress with the significantly uncomfortable shoes again, abandoned it for jeans and DMs (can't go wrong) and then compromised with a different, slightly longer, yet still stylish dress and different shoes that were still not hugely comfortable, but slightly easier to walk in.

Holly seemed much calmer. I'd plied her with tea and biscuits and raided the fridge to make her an afternoon snack. I promised Danny would organise a takeaway when he returned. She seemed curious about my date, and my relationship with Danny, and just things in general. I was happy to talk, to take her mind off things too, although in truth I expect she found it all rather dull. In return, I asked her about her background. She'd grown up near Winchester in the south of England, but moved to London as a student (didn't we all) and now combined the band with a bit of temping to help pay the bills. She was a bit reserved on the family side of things, but I didn't pry.

I'm not sure we'd ever have been friends if circumstances hadn't thrown us together. She was, as Colette had said, a little bit posh, although I hate to generalise. I'm not one to judge. I've found my first impressions aren't entirely reliable. I used to *almost* have a fondness for Clare, until she did her disappearing act and went rogue on us. And I used to think Danny was near perfect until he started spending his spare time fraternising with murderers and prostitutes.

By 6.30pm I was ready to go out, but there was still no sign of Danny. Presumably he was having a whale of a time, although I tried not to contemplate the details. It was a bit annoying, though, because on top of everything he was now going to make me late.

"Don't worry, you can go. I'll be fine here," said Holly when she'd got bored with me pacing up and down. I'd tried to phone him without success.

"I can't just leave you," I said. "I'm supposed to be looking after you."

"Of course you can," she insisted. "I'm not a child. In any case I'm sure he'll be home soon."

I decided to let fate make the decision for me. I phoned for a minicab. If it came before Danny got home, then so be it. I'd leave Holly to fend for herself. I was sure she'd be safe. Ten minutes later I heard a car horn, looked out the window and saw the car waiting on the street outside.

"Are you're completely sure you'll be okay?" I asked.

"Of course. Now go."

I grabbed my jacket and keys and headed out into the evening.

"It sounds like you've had an interesting time," said Mitch as we started to look at the menu, awaiting our drinks order. He'd made an effort with his appearance; the crisp white shirt seemed to emphasise his glowing skin tone and he looked every bit the possible film star. "Is everything okay now?"

"Interesting's one way of putting it," I said. I gave him the summary as the drinks arrived, without hopefully betraying any confidences. And leaving out Danny's more sordid exploits.

"Wow. I'm so sorry to hear all of that," he said. "I'm honoured that you still agreed to come out with me."

"Believe me, I've been looking forward to it. Although excuse me if I attempt to get hammered."

We did the cheers thing with the glasses.

"How's the world of petrochemicals?" I asked. "Have you managed to find any oil in Camden?"

"Haha. No, but it's okay, you know? Busy."

"I've been thinking about this."

"Oh God. Go on."

"Well, it's just it covers a lot of things, doesn't it? I mean, you dress it up as marketing within a petrochemical company but for all I know that could mean you work behind the till at a garage, on the night shift. I'll be popping in for a tank of unleaded and there you'll be, in front of a wall of fags, trying to hide the magazine you've pinched from the top shelf, and asking me for my Switch card."

He laughed, which was nice.

"Are you always like this?"

"Like what?" I adopted my innocent look, which, it's fair to say, is not one of my naturally most convincing.

"You know exactly what I mean. And no, I don't work in a garage, but work's just work anyway. It pays the bills. The screen acting's the passion."

I wasn't finished.

"Okay though, but tell me. Super unleaded. Advertising con, or do I need it?"

He laughed again.

"Do you want the technical explanation or the marketing one?"

I realised I was possibly being annoying. Luckily, a waiter came to take our food order. I hadn't really consulted the menu, but made a quick decision to go with tagliatelle and then almost immediately regretted it, as it was almost impossible to eat with any degree of elegance. Too late.

The meal progressed and we chatted more. Mitch asked me about my work, my plans and ambitions, and in turn, when prompted, opened up about his past. He'd grown up in a small village outside Nottingham, then moved to London after he'd graduated with a BSc in petrochemical engineering from Heriot-Watt University. He told me about studying for his private pilot's licence and apologised if that made him sound like a show-off. Since he was making me laugh, I was prepared to forgive him.

He revealed more about his acting exploits, his ultimate ambition to star in a major drama, and the need to create a showreel, before giving me the low-down on Meisner training. This seemed to involve standing next to someone, repeating exactly what they'd just said to you, until one of you cracked. Apparently it taught the importance of listening and reacting in the moment. The "reality of doing". He was certainly a good listener. By the time we'd finished the food, we were also the best part of our way through our second bottle and I was feeling a bit tipsy. Well, more than a bit. What do you take me for?

"Can I ask you a question?" he began, after a rare lull while the table was cleared.

"Of course."

"Just are you sure... How can I put this?"

"What?"

"Well, that you and Danny. You're not a couple?"

I laughed.

"Again, we have our moments, but no, not a couple."

"I don't want to tread on anyone's toes."

"Relax. I'm single. And glad of the company. We're best friends. That's all. Really."

"Okay, it's just if he's a big guy and he thinks otherwise..."

"He's not a big guy. He's what? Five ten? You don't need to worry. We look out for each other but we do our own thing."

"Glad to hear it. As long as you're sure."

I nodded.

"I'm sorry if I can't provide the same level of excitement," he said. "I can talk you through various isotopes and bore you to death with hydrocarbons, but it's probably not as much fun as being on a stake-out."

"Oh, don't worry about that. It has its moments, but normally it's just two separate worlds really. We meet up over breakfast, or occasionally in the evenings for a drama on BBC1. Although now I'll be looking out for you, too. My famous friend!"

"Haha. You do sound like a married couple."

It was my turn to laugh.

"I look forward to meeting him," said Mitch, with a wink, much to my surprise and obvious horror.

"Really?"

"Yes, I'd like to meet all your friends."

"Well, play your cards right and I'll see what I can do," I said, while thinking I must absolutely make sure that never happens, ever.

The bill came. Mitch insisted on paying, which seemed incredibly decent given the Brobdingnagian scale of the thing. And that's an incredibly long word after a couple of bottles of Sauvignon. Five syllables. My mum would have been proud, but let's not even get started on that one. I offered to split it, obviously, but he was insistent. Good lad.

"So where now?" he asked as we left the restaurant.

I looked at my watch. It was already past ten. Where had the time gone?

I gave him a hug.

"I hate to put a dampener on things, but sadly I really should be getting home," I said.

"Are you sure?"

"Yes. I'm sorry. I've got to make sure Holly's okay and that Danny's not up to anything indecent with her." God. The thought of that hadn't even occurred to me until that moment. Surely he wouldn't? There again, given his current form, who knew?

"I understand," said Mitch. And he went to give me a kiss on the cheek. I moved just in time so it connected with my lips. So much better.

"Thank you again for another lovely evening," I said, when I came up for air.

"My absolute pleasure. When can I see you next?"

I thought for a moment. Mustn't look too keen, even though I increasingly was.

"Friday evening?"

"Perfect."

"I'll call you. Should we share a cab again?"

"Excellent plan."

He hailed a black cab. We got in and the journey home passed all too quickly. By the end I had a serious case of longing for the night to continue to the early hours. Alas, I knew I had to be sensible. He dropped me off in Rochester Square, and wouldn't take any money for the taxi either. As I stood outside my door waving him off, it was with a curious sense of longing to see him again already, even though we'd just said goodbye.

Danny was still up. It felt a bit like coming home to my parents, trying not to get caught, but failing miserably.

"How's Holly?" I asked, trying to pre-empt an interrogation.

"Fast asleep," said Danny. "She's exhausted, I think."

"I'm not surprised. Was she okay this evening?"

"Kind of. I'll talk to you about it."

That sounded a bit mysterious.

"Let me get a cup of tea and you can tell me."

I put the kettle on, then checked in on Holly. As Danny said, she was fast asleep in my bed. I took the opportunity to grab my bathrobe from the back of the door and then quickly got changed into it. By the time I got back to the kitchen, Danny was already there, stirring two mugs.

"Good night?" he asked.

"Reasonable," I replied. Now was not the time to go into details, not that he'd want to hear them anyway. "Massage went well?"

"Reasonable," he replied. God, it's annoying when he tries to be clever.

"Are we going to be like this forever more?" I asked.

"Like what?"

"I don't know. Cagey. Secretive."

"You started it."

"Okay, add childish to the list."

He laughed.

"Well, you did."

"I had a reasonable evening. There's nothing more to say. We had a lovely tea and a nice bottle of wine and then I came home and here I am. Any further questions?"

"Plenty, but they can wait."

"Such as?"

"Such as, where did you go? What did you have? How was he? Are you seeing him again?"

"You're right, they can wait. And the massage?"

"Still just reasonable."

I threw a tea towel at that point. He caught it.

"Come here," he said.

"You come here."

"All right then."

So he did, and he gave me a hug. Normally that would have been my happy place, but this time it just felt different. More distant. There was so much going on inside my head. I put it down to drink and resolved to work out my emotions in the morning.

"Ugh," I said after a minute, taking a step back.

"What now?"

"I forgot. I may catch something."

"By hanging out with strangers you meet on the tube? You should take precautions."

"Very funny. So, did you?"

"Did I what?"

"Go through with it? Or make your excuses and leave?"

"I got thrown out."

"What?" Now it was my turn to laugh. But as Danny filled me in on the details I soon realised it wasn't funny. I understood the seriousness of the situation and the questions that it raised.

"So, what now?"

"I need to speak to Aurelia again. Find out what happened. But that's not going to be easy."

"I'd offer to go for you but I suspect it would look a bit odd. What are you going to do?"

"The only thing I can think of is to wait outside and catch her leaving work for the day, but that's not exactly sophisticated and would just scare the wits out of her."

"And ensure you get beaten to a pulp. In any case, Danny, these people don't just clock on and off like a normal job. Not that I know, obviously, but I'm imagining it. I can't think she knocks off at 5pm and goes back to a cosy pad in Kentish Town or somewhere."

We needed a better plan, but none was immediately forthcoming. We took the tea through to the living room. Danny closed the door behind us, which was unusual, then beckoned me onto the sofa.

"I need to talk to you about Holly," he said in a low voice.

"What's up?"

"It's just, how well do you know her?"

"Me? Not at all, really. I had a chat this afternoon and found out a bit, but I still don't know really know her as a person."

"Do you think she's straight?"

"Straight as in not-taking-drugs straight?"

"Just generally straight. Trustworthy."

"I've got no idea. She seemed okay this afternoon. I wouldn't put the drugs thing past her, given her appearance backstage on Saturday and inability to get off the sofa. But then I thought that about Leah, too, and it transpires she's never touched the stuff. I extrapolate. Why? What happened?"

"Nothing too specific, but when I came home she was here on her own. And the first I saw, she was coming from the bedrooms. I think me coming back seemed to give her a bit of a shock. She looked flustered."

"She was probably just trying to have a snooze."

"Possibly, but then I went to my room and, I don't know, it just looked like things had been moved."

"That was probably me. I moved some things in. Assuming you're still okay with that and you don't want me to go on the sofa."

"Of course I'm okay with that. It'll be like the old days. I'm looking forward to it, as long as you don't start snoring again. But you don't think she was looking for something to pinch?"

"Holly? I wouldn't have thought so. She seems terribly posh.

She's got money, I think. Why would she be looking to steal anything? And where would she go with it? And I don't snore."

"I don't know. And you do, especially after a drink."

"Don't. I don't know, you're probably just paranoid after this afternoon. I'm sure she's fine."

"I expect so."

"Look, we'll keep an eye on it. She doesn't look the type. But then if she's got a secret drug habit, you never know. Was she okay apart from that?"

"Yeah, fine."

"She's had a hard time. We can't even begin to imagine it, really, but we'll be careful, okay?"

Danny agreed. He crossed to the desk and turned off the computer. And then, for the first time in maybe a year, I prepared to go to bed alongside him. It was one of those things we did out of necessity from time to time, usually when we were travelling together or - in times like this - when circumstances dictated. We were the best of friends. It's the sort of things friends do and it didn't have to lead to any untoward behaviour. And up until the last few days that was a source of abject frustration. One day, I hoped, things might return to normal. But any hope of that in the near future was about to be smashed to pieces.

Chapter 23

Thursday, April 7th, 1994

THE Harlem Yacht Club was neither in Harlem nor a yacht club, but instead a pub with a pretentious name in the Farringdon district of central London. Popular with staff from a nearby magazine company, and a few stragglers from the similarly-nearby Guardian newspaper, it was nevertheless quiet at 11am. Danny opened the door, walked inside, and was looking for the person he was supposed to be meeting when his attention was taken by his mobile phone ringtone.

"Hi," he said, after frowning at the withheld number message.

"Okay, Danny, so far so good. I can't meet you in a pub full of journalists, for obvious reasons, but you're not being followed, which is good. Now look around, show your frustration, then walk straight back out, turn right, walk up through Exmouth Market, then turn right on Rosebery Avenue towards Sadler's Wells. Got that? I'll catch up with you."

Meeting Clare was never going to be straightforward. He didn't know in how many countries she was officially a fugitive, nor in how many others she was officially deceased. He was walking up the road as instructed when a number 38 Routemaster bus stopped just a few yards in front of him. A striking-looking woman with shoulder-length brunette hair, black knee-high boots and long black overcoat stepped off the open platform at the back. She raised an umbrella and then stood on the pavement, looking at him.

"What kept you?" she said, with a grin.

"For heaven's sake. Why can't you just be normal?" he asked, but it was obvious from his tone that he was extremely pleased to see his friend and former colleague. "We meet in some very strange places."

"Indeed we do. Let me take you for coffee. Somewhere we can't be overheard."

They crossed the road, heading in exactly the opposite direction to the nearest coffee shop.

"What brings you to London?" asked Danny as they walked, close together, both sheltering from the rain.

"The truthful answer or the made-up one?"

"Truthful."

"Well, you're out of luck there then. It's better for both of us if I don't tell you. Sorry, give me a minute."

She passed Danny the umbrella and then paused to light a cigarette. She looked questioningly at Danny, but he shook his head.

"We're not supposed to smoke where we're going and you know how I hate to break the rules," she said by way of explanation. "And that was a joke, by the way, before you start."

"You're looking well again," said Danny as she resumed walking. "I know it's less than a week..."

"But a lot has happened."

"It has. Do you need me to bring you up to speed or are you fully on top of everything, as ever?"

They turned right and crossed the road again.

"Not as on top of everything as you are, judging by your little afternoon excursion yesterday." She winked.

"I was thrown out!"

"Probably just as well."

"But I wasn't doing anything anyway, for your information. I was fully clothed at the time. We were just talking."

"I know, I'm just teasing you."

"You know? How do you know? How do you know everything?"

"Wait, we're here."

They stopped outside a residential property in the middle of a row of terraced houses. Clare flicked the cigarette away and then took a bunch of keys from her pocket. She undid a mortice lock first and then a Yale lock above it. Even then she had to give the door a shove to open it. It was stuck slightly in its frame.

"Excuse the dust," she said.

"What's this place? Have you got another flat I didn't know about?"

"No, it isn't mine, but it belongs to a friend. I can use it if I need to. She's away a lot."

"Looks like it."

There was a pile of post and junk leaflets in the hallway. Clare flicked on the light and led the way through to the kitchen. The house was cold. She turned the central heating to manual, and the boiler fired up.

"Tea or coffee?" she asked. She opened the fridge door and took out a pint of semi-skimmed milk and waved it at him. "It's fresh today, don't worry."

"I thought you said nobody had been here?"

"No, that was your assumption. Be careful with those, Danny."

She put the kettle on then turned to look at him.

"Okay, so here are the ground rules."

"For?"

"This. Everything. Number one: you don't keep asking how come I know everything. It'll get tedious as I'm not in a position to tell you."

"Okay."

"You're never going to be able to quote me anyway, as officially I'm not here."

"You're dead in fact."

"Precisely."

"And rule two?"

"I don't think there is a rule two. Just that. Don't ask me questions that I'm not going to answer - not because I don't trust you, because I obviously do, but because others have trusted me not to break a confidence. Understood?"

"Understood."

"There is a rule 1b, actually. Obviously I'm allowed to ask you questions, but it's up to you whether to answer them or not. I may well know anyway so it's just a question of confirming where you're up to."

"And what if you think you know something when you don't? What if you get something wrong or make a mistake? And what if somebody finds you?"

"I'm not saying it won't ever happen, but it hasn't yet and I've got no intention of letting it happen now."

The kettle came to the boil. She put tea bags in two mugs then added water, and started to stir. As the tea brewed she opened the milk.

"Can I ask if you're working alone?"

"No. Although I am."

"And your motivation is?"

"You know what my motivation is. I want to nail March so we can finally draw a line under all of that, and I want to help you and make sure you're safe. Nobody's paying me. I do it because it needs to be done. And because I like to think I'm good."

"And you're repaying your debt to society?"

"Something like that."

She removed the tea bags, added the milk, then handed a mug to Danny.

"Can I ask you personal questions? Like where you're based?"

"No."

"Have you got a boyfriend?"

Clare laughed.

"No."

"No I can't ask or no you haven't?"

"No to both. Let's go and sit down."

She led the way through to a sparsely furnished living room. The walls were bland magnolia, the art anonymous and inoffensive. Danny recognised some as IKEA prints. A small television sat on a unit in the corner, close to the window, which in turn was covered by a plain net curtain. There wasn't much else aside from a sofa and an armchair, with a small table between them. Double glazing muffled the traffic noise from outside. Danny sat on the sofa while Clare took the armchair.

"This reminds me of Geneva," she said. "Although we're missing Anna for the full reunion. What's this about a date, by the way?"

"You know about that as well?"

"You told me in your email."

"Of course, sorry."

"So, is it serious?"

"Oh, God knows. She was out again last night."

"Wow, she's keen. What do you know about him?"

"Not a lot. They met on the tube, which is weird in itself because she hates the tube."

"Do you want me to look into it for you? Make him go away?"

"What? Not if you mean what I think you mean."

"I just mean find out a bit about him and see what he's hiding. Everyone's hiding something."

"Still no, but thank you. Jesus. You know what? I don't know whether to be scared stiff or just bloody glad you're on my side."

"Told you, I care about you."

"Well, that's very much appreciated, but Anna is Anna and whatever will be will be. I'm not going to pretend I'm happy about it but there's nobody else to blame. If I've fucked up I'm just going to have to live with it."

"But you make the perfect couple."

Danny looked to the ceiling, just long enough to try to conceal his emotions.

"It's kind of you to say. We just know each other too well, I think. You and I made the perfect partnership at work, and look what happened to that. Anyway, back to the point. How long are you in London for?"

"Long enough."

"And will you disappear again?"

"I've already answered that."

"You did. Try not to, though."

"Oh Danny, will you miss me?"

"You know I will. I idolised you."

"I know, you said, and it was deeply flattering. I'm really nothing special."

Now it was Danny's turn to laugh.

"I'm not, though," she continued. "I'm just observant, and thorough. I analyse things. I don't have magical powers."

"Right."

"I don't! Well, maybe a few. But it's just hard work and a bit of lateral thinking."

"I'll take your word for it."

"Good. Tell me where you're up to and we can compare notes."

· · ·

Danny began, explaining how he'd started investigating March, and found links to criminal gangs from eastern Europe working out of Cologne. He booted up his notebook computer and showed her documents and photographic evidence he'd compiled, with timelines and interviews, both on and off the record, from sources he'd been nurturing for the last few months.

He explained about how March had called him. About their meetings, the mention of the homeless shelter, and the assumption that it was being used as a shield or front for the trafficking operation. About following him from the massage parlour to the casino, his involvement with the band, Steve's death and the assault on Leah. His own trip to the parlour and subsequent eviction. His conversations with Amy and the pressure that was seemingly being exerted by the Government for a cover-up. And the deadline of the following day.

"You've been very thorough, but all in all, a bit of a mess then?" said Clare when he'd finished.

"Not so much a mess as a giant jigsaw. Most of the pieces are there but just with a few still missing. And I'm still not sure of the bigger picture."

"That's good."

"What? That there's so much missing?"

"No, I was talking about the metaphor."

Clare sat back, looking thoughtful.

"I expect you knew all of that already," said Danny eventually.

She shook her head.

"No, not all of it. You've done well. There are a few things that obviously stand out."

"Such as?"

"Such as you're never going to make the deadline tomorrow."

"Cheers for that."

"Have a word with Mike and I'm sure he'll understand."

"Are you taking the piss?"

"Haha. Maybe. That's the one thing I don't miss. But

seriously, ring him at least. I think you're close but it's evolving. There's not a chance of getting it all wrapped up today, though."

"I'll look forward to that this afternoon, then."

Clare took a sip of her tea.

"The other thing that's missing from Geneva is the champagne," she said. "I'm sure I could find a bottle, but let's keep it for when we've got something to celebrate. I'll tell you what I know, and then we can see where the gaps are, okay?"

"Okay."

"The trafficking links are definite. He's been seen out there. And he's been mixing with some very bad people."

"I know."

"Just be careful, though, Danny, these aren't your ordinary British villains. These are seriously nasty, violent and dangerous bastards. They've got different values entirely. They make me look like an angel."

Danny reached for his cup. It was easy to forget she had blood on her hands. That the person in front of him, with her generous smile, intelligent eyes, and impeccable clothing was capable of acts of intense ruthlessness in the pursuit of self-interest. She could be dangerous. Just being in her company could be dangerous. There was so much he didn't know about her, about how she worked, and about what she'd been through in recent years. Was she even sane? Aristotle said no great mind has ever existed without a touch of madness, and it was hard to argue.

"I agree, the homeless shelter sounds iffy," she continued. "I'll look into that. And I don't know much about this Seb person, but if the Government are wanting to brush things under the carpet to protect the reputation of the Met, they're going to need a bloody big brush and an even bigger carpet."

"What about the massage parlour? I won't ask how you knew I'd been there."

"It wasn't hard. I watched you go in."

"You did what?"

She smirked.

"Oh come on, don't act surprised. I've got to keep an eye on you."

"Shit. I don't know whether to be flattered or offended."

Clare leaned forward and rested her hand on his knee.

"Danny, listen to me. I've come to terms with what I did before. You know what? I did it after a lot of thought and a lot of planning, and I'd do it again in a heartbeat. All of it. But I do regret absolutely some of the things that happened to you in the process. And Anna, of course. I do regret putting you in danger, and I genuinely lose sleep at night worrying that I was anything other than completely straight with you."

Danny sighed.

"Oh, but Clare. Why? You were brilliant. You were perfect."

"I wasn't. That was just your opinion of me because I suppose, if I'm honest, something in me inspired you. But everyone has their faults, Danny. Me particularly."

He started to protest but she waved it away.

"But listen, that was the past. I've told you. Nothing can change it. It's done. Just know I'll never do that to you again. I'm not going to pretend I've changed but I have learned a few things about myself along the way, and I've learned what it's like to feel absolutely isolated, cut off from everything and everybody. But that was my choice so I'm not complaining."

"It's got to be tough, though."

"Tougher than you'd believe. But I also know what's important to me. I had to give up everything. My flat, my job, my friends, relationships, everything."

"So you did have a boyfriend then?"

"Haha, and again you assume. I'm not going there. But you, Danny. You are important to me. You're a good guy. I won't let you down again. And rule 1c: let's never mention this again."

Danny smiled.

"Okay," he said. "I'll try."

"Make sure you do. I'd hate to have to shoot you." She paused. "And that was another joke, by the way."

Danny wasn't so sure.

"How's it going?" Samuel Elmhirst-Banks had woken early, and was at his desk in the Norman Shaw South building by 7am. He'd spent the morning fretting. No news wasn't necessarily good news. Eventually he'd gone down to the riverbank to make a call.

"Slow in some respects, but surprisingly well in others." Her voice was quiet, as though she was also nervous of being overheard.

"Meaning?"

"Meaning I'm getting close to sorting it. It came pretty near to disaster as well, but don't worry. I'm speeding it up now."

"Christ. I don't want to know. Time's running out. You do realise that?"

"I do. I'm managing the situation."

"And the shipment?"

"Confirmed. Late Sunday."

"But nobody's talking about it?"

"Not as far as I've come across."

"Thank fuck. At least that's something. Right, redouble efforts."

"You don't need to tell me. I'm very much aware."

"I know you are. But we need to get there first. Get me the details. Everything."

"You're panicking."

"Do you blame me? Fucking March is a liability and if I don't control this I'm as good as dead. I've got to stand in front of the bloody Home Secretary this afternoon. Try doing that if everything's turning to shit."

"You're so dramatic."

"I don't know if you get this."

"I do. It's your job, your reputation. Your career in Government."

"Exactly."

"We'll sort it. Don't worry."

"I wish I had your confidence."

"You should do. I'll be in touch."

The call ended. He looked at his phone as though it might bite him. It was time to start thinking about a contingency plan in case this all got out of hand. His brief was simple, but the fear of failure was beginning to overwhelm his confidence in those he usually relied on. It was time to tackle March head on.

Chapter 24

"I'VE been making a few enquiries about the massage parlour," Clare continued, lighting a cigarette.

"I didn't think you were supposed to smoke in here," said Danny.

"I'm not. But hey, force of habit. It helps me think."

"You do know that's a myth?"

She gave him a look of bemusement.

"Get me an ashtray from the kitchen, would you? Wall cupboard next to the sink."

Danny left the room, returning a moment later.

"Thank you," she said.

"So, the parlour?"

"Yes. It's run by a hard bastard called Mikołaj Gawlinski. He's from Poland."

"I think I met him."

She shook her head.

"No, that would have been his muscle man, Tomasz Dulinski. You did well to come out with your limbs intact. He'd shoot his own mother, just for something to do."

"Jesus. And something tells me this time you're not joking?"

"Sadly not."

"Brilliant."

"Danny, do me a favour. Don't go anywhere near the place, okay?"

Danny frowned.

"What's up?" she asked.

"Nothing. It's just, oh I don't know."

"Just what?"

"Aurelia. She knows something. I just think it would be good to see her again, to find out what happened."

"Ooh, do I detect the first stirrings of romance?"

"What? No, of course not."

"Now Anna's got a boyfriend you've lost your heart to a hooker?"

"For heaven's sake."

"I'm teasing. But whatever she knows, it's not worth getting killed over, okay?"

"Agreed."

"But I have given her your number and asked her to call you."

Danny laughed.

"What the fuck? How on earth have you done that?"

"I think that comes under the terms of rule 1a. Just hope that she does. She seemed less than keen on the idea. God knows what would happen to the poor girl if they caught her talking to you. It doesn't even bear thinking about."

"Indeed. But seriously, how did you manage that?"

"Danny?"

"What?"

"I wasn't joking about the rules. Okay?"

"Okay."

He sighed. It wasn't going to be easy.

"Thank you," he said. "However you've done it."

"My pleasure."

Clare stubbed out her cigarette then walked through to the

kitchen to wash her hands.

"Are we agreed we're assuming the parlour's involved in the trafficking too?" she called through the open doorway.

"It makes sense if it's not too obvious."

"Good. Although what have I told you about assuming things?" She walked back into the living room and retook her seat.

"Not to."

"Genau."

"Ge-what?"

"Sorry. I lapsed into German. I meant 'exactly'."

"So are you living in Germany now?"

"Danny?" She raised two fingers and pointed them at him, making a clicking sound like a gun being cocked.

He raised both hands in mock surrender.

"Sorry," he said.

"You're forgiven. Just. But yes, don't ever make assumptions unless you're willing to challenge them, revisit them and turn them inside out."

"But it does make sense."

"From where we're looking, agreed. You said you followed March to a casino?"

"Just off Berkeley Square. I don't know how long he was there for but it was at least an hour. We had to leave to go to meet Leah."

"And the name of the casino?"

"Albermarle. I think the full title was Albermarle Casino and Gentleman's Club."

"That figures. So, strippers and gambling. He's a classy guy. What do you know about it?"

"Not a lot yet. The whole Leah and Holly thing took precedence yesterday."

"Okay."

Clare started to smile. Danny noticed, and then realisation hit.

"Go on then," he said.

"I thought you weren't going to ask. It's run by a woman called Jacqueline Glover. On the face of it, she's a respectable businesswoman, which is an achievement given the nature of her business. Late forties, looks older, dresses in animal print and too much gold but probably thinks it looks sophisticated."

"Do people still do that?"

"Apparently."

"Okay, that's on the face of it. But there's more?"

"Of course. Would it be really bad if I had another fag?"

"Yes."

"Ah well." She lit one anyway.

"So, Jacqueline Glover?" continued Danny.

"Bear with me."

Clare took her phone from the pocket of her coat and dialled a number. She listened for a few moments then ended the call.

"Wrong number?" asked Danny.

"Answering service. Don't worry, I'm back with you."

"Sure?"

"Yes. Okay, so Jacqueline Glover. Never married, owns properties, significantly wealthy but hard as nails. What do you get in casinos?"

"Roulette tables? Blackjack?"

"Cash, Danny. Lots of it. There are rumours that she's been involved in a bit of laundering, and March used to be on the payroll until his untimely expulsion from the Force, so we can probably assume, for want of a better phrase, he was being paid to turn a blind eye."

"That figures."

"Have you turned American all of a sudden?"

"No, sorry. That makes sense. Better?"

"Much."

"I'd say 'awesome' but you probably would shoot me."

"Don't tempt me." She raised the fingers again. Danny

laughed.

"I promise never to say that again."

"Glad to hear it. We don't joke about the English language. Let's get back to being serious for a moment and I can decide what to do with you later."

"Okay."

"So, she's not exactly squeaky clean, but that's just the casino. We mustn't forget the Gentleman's Club."

Danny clicked his fingers.

"Yes!" he said. "Could that be a front for prostitution? In which case, she'd maybe be interested in some of the girls coming over too?"

"That's what I'm thinking. So that explains why March is visiting. He's like a glorified salesman. Not that there's particularly any glory in it."

"It all makes sense, though."

"But there's one thing we're missing."

"Which is?"

"Old Jacqui isn't without her enemies for obvious reasons. She fended off a hostile takeover of the business a couple of years ago, and by hostile I mean in the most literal sense. She's also been known to have to do the odd bit of debt collection. Which means?"

"Presumably she's got help. Minders?"

"Correct. I've managed to get names of two: Finn Convey and Logan McDonagh. They're both Irish. Convey's from Dublin. He's the right-hand man and enforcer, typical kind of wouldn't-want-to-meet-in-a-dark-alley merchant. McDonagh's from just outside Cork. He's supposedly more intelligent but he sounds a nasty bastard too. I wouldn't suggest messing with either."

"Christ. March knows how to choose his friends."

"It's a dangerous business, Danny. All of it. Which is why you need me, keeping an eye on things."

"And again, I'm not going to ask how you manage to do that."

"Good, you're learning. Anyway, the point is, Convey's been keeping tabs on March, following him. Presumably reporting back. No doubt McDonagh's out there too, doing much the same. Either way, if the girls are coming in on Sunday, things are going to be hotting up over the next couple of days. And let's just hope that Mikołaj and Jacqueline can sort things out between them in terms of who gets who, or it could be an almighty bloodbath."

"Jesus."

Clare took one last drag of her cigarette and stubbed it out.

"Have you got a plan of action?" she asked.

"Stick close to March, hope Aurelia calls, keep vigilant."

"Very wise."

"We're getting there. The main thing is we need to find out more about Sunday. Anna's helping with pictures when she's talking to me, so that's handy, although if it gets dicey I'll get a staffer in."

"Why isn't she talking to you?"

"Long story."

"Elaborate away."

"Can I make that rule 1d?"

"No. Obviously. I set the rules."

"That's not fair. What did you say in Cologne? I was the boss now, and you were my assistant?"

"I did, but there are limits." She had a devilish sparkle in her hazel eyes. "So? Do I have to threaten to shoot you again?"

"For heaven's sake." Danny laughed and clutched a cushion to his chest as a kind of shield.

"Come on, seriously? What's up? Is it the boyfriend thing?"

"No, that's the result rather than the cause. If you must know, she was pissed off that I was talking to you, and gets more pissed off every time I mention you."

"Why?"

"She calls you my mental mass murdering girlfriend."

"Ooh, that's a bit harsh."

"It is kind of true."

"I was talking about the girlfriend aspect."

"Oh, cheers."

"Haha. No, I just mean you could do much better."

"Right."

"No, seriously."

"Ah, Clare..." Danny stopped. There were raw emotions at play. Things he wanted to say. Things he knew he shouldn't. And years of thoughts and dreams, before everything changed that fateful morning, when she walked out of his life, seemingly forever. She was still an enigma, and still on a pedestal, despite everything he'd learned in the interim. Maybe even because of it. What was going on inside her head? But he knew she was more out of reach now than ever. He knew that every moment he spent with her could be the last one ever, that he'd never get to know her, not really, deep down, inside her mind. And that there were so many things he would never understand.

"Listen," he said, "there's something I should say, in the interests of full disclosure."

"Borderline American, but I'll let it pass. Go on."

"Today, it's been just like the old days. Discussing, planning, thinking. Working with you. I love it. Every minute. Always did."

"It's been fun."

"It always was. We were good. I miss you. And you know what? It absolutely breaks my heart when I think about you, not knowing where you are, not knowing that you're safe, knowing that there are things about you that you'll always keep secret from me. But I'm glad you're here. I do think you're brilliant, despite everything. Maybe just lay off on threatening to shoot me all the time?"

Clare smiled.

"I'll try," she said.

Unfortunately for Danny, Clare wasn't the only one with him in her sights.

Chapter 25

IT felt strange waking up in Danny's bed, and even stranger that he wasn't there to talk to. It took me a moment to remember why I was there, which was just enough time for the headache to hit from the previous night's drinking exploits. But then I had a warm, fuzzy feeling, remembering the good bits, of getting to know Mitch, holding his hand as we left the restaurant, snuggling up close to him in the taxi home. And, of course, the second rather memorable kiss goodnight.

Then I remembered he'd offered to take me up in a little private aeroplane as soon as he got his licence. It was another item on the agenda of things that I will never let happen, ever.

I crept out of bed in case Holly was still asleep and retrieved my bathrobe from the floor. I decided to attempt to have a shower without disturbing her, and then I'd pop my head round the door to see if she was up and wanted breakfast.

On my way to the bathroom, however, I heard movement from the living room. Either Danny was still here, Holly was an early riser, or it was much later than I'd realised. It transpired it was the latter. But as I approached the door I could see Holly sitting in my chair, at my desk, looking through one of my drawers. The blue light on the front of the computer base unit was lit, although the screen was blank.

"What are you doing?" I asked from the doorway. Holly turned, clearly shocked to have been disturbed. She pushed the drawer closed, and looked at me in what appeared to be a combination of panic and something approaching fear.

"Nothing, nothing," she said. "Just looking for ibuprofen or a paracetamol or something. I've got a banging headache."

"In my desk drawer?" Suddenly the previous evening's conversation with Danny raced through my mind.

"Sorry. I didn't mean to... I just thought you may have some. Really sorry. I thought you were asleep. I didn't want to wake you."

"So you thought you'd look in my private desk drawers rather than the kitchen?" I was struggling to keep the anger from my voice. The hangover didn't help.

"Sorry, I didn't think."

"Have you had a cup of tea this morning?"

"Yes, I helped myself when I got up. I hope that was okay. You said it was okay to do that."

"It is. But you didn't notice the ibuprofen packet in the cupboard, on the same shelf as the mugs?"

"Really? No, sorry. But I didn't have a headache then. Look, I didn't mean..."

"Have you been on my computer?" I was on a roll, and getting crosser.

"Your *computer*?"

I looked at the screen behind her. She followed my eyes then turned back to face me.

"No, of course not. Why would I be on your computer."

"I don't know, Holly, but it was turned off last night. I distinctly remember Danny turning the power off."

"It's still off now."

"The screen is. The base station's on."

"I'm sorry, but that wasn't me. Maybe he only turned the screen off, or he was on it before he left for work."

"Why would he do that? He's going to an office full of computers. And even if he did, he'd know how to turn it off again."

"Well, it wasn't me."

I pressed the monitor's power button, but when it sprang to life it just showed the Windows desktop. I saw Holly's expression harden. It was a side of her I hadn't seen for a couple of days.

"Sorry, but I don't know what you're accusing me of," she said, her own voice rising.

"I'm not accusing you of anything. I'm only asking you," I said.

"Well it doesn't sound like it."

"I come in here, and find you going through my drawers. I think I've got a right to ask."

"What do you think I'm up to?"

"Nothing. I'm just asking you what you're doing."

"Fine," she said, then got up and stormed through to the bedroom. My bedroom.

I swore to myself, and maybe called her a name or two (actually, there was no maybe about it), then decided to make a cup of tea before getting in the shower. There, on the shelf, next to the mugs, was a packet of ibuprofen, as I thought. I popped a couple to help with my own headache and downed a glass of water while I waited for the kettle to boil.

I was just trying to work out whether I had the stomach for toast when Holly appeared in the hallway, jacket on, bag over her shoulder.

"Holly?" I called. She turned towards me. "What are you doing?"

"I'm leaving," she said. "Thanks for putting me up, but I'm going now."

"What? Where to?"

"I don't know. But I'm clearly not wanted here."

"What the fuck? What are you talking about?"

"You made it fairly obvious."

"I just asked you what you were doing."

"Yeah, well I don't like being accused of things. So, thanks again but I'm leaving."

"You can't just go. You've got God knows who trying to find you."

"I'm going."

"Where to?"

"I don't know. See you around. Say goodbye to Danny for me. He's cute." And with that she disappeared out of the front door, pulling it closed behind her, although stopping short of the full slam.

Several things bothered me. First of all, I was supposed to be looking after her and I'd clearly messed that up completely. But then, just as that thought entered my head, a bigger concern arose. I hadn't asked to check her bag before she left. If she'd stolen something she'd be getting away with it, and short of chasing her down the street in my bath robe I was powerless to stop her. And thirdly, she'd clearly had her eyes on Danny. It was just as well she was going. Overall, though, I was just shocked by the cheek of the woman. We'd gone out of our way to help her and I didn't expect or deserve that kind of outburst. Well, she could fend for herself. I hoped she was safe, and I knew I'd worry, but if she felt better off on her own then so be it.

I abandoned the toast and headed to the shower. Then I'd have a thorough check of my room to see if anything was missing.

Clare stood up, walked to the window, drew a corner of the net curtain aside, and looked out into the street. It only lasted a moment. Then she turned back to Danny, retook her chair and lit a third cigarette.

"I'll tell you what I'm going to do," she said.

"Okay." Danny was grateful for any assistance. "Sorry if I overstepped the mark, by the way."

"Don't worry, you're fine. We are where we are. There's nothing we can do about it, but we can do something about March."

"Fingers crossed."

"Oh, we will, Danny. You've done well but I'm very pleased you contacted me. I'm actually quite honoured."

"You're honoured?"

"Yes. Genuinely. And it's good to be back with a project. I miss that too. Would you have tried to find me, by the way, if I hadn't come to see you in Cologne?"

"I wouldn't have had the first clue where to start."

"Which is the answer to a different question to the one I asked."

Danny laughed.

"You want the truthful answer? I don't know. I'd gone looking for you once and found you eventually but it didn't go exactly as planned. It was hardly the big reunion. Would I have done it again? I don't know. I thought you'd gone. Of course I thought about you. All the time. But I didn't think you wanted to be found and I knew I had to respect that. I can't pretend I've ever stopped thinking about you, so I suspect that eventually I'd have had to go looking. Does that answer the question?"

"It does."

She put the cigarette in the ashtray, blew smoke at the ceiling, then leaned forward.

"Come here," she said, voice softening.

Danny leaned forward. She took his hands in hers. He could feel the edges of her sapphire ring in the flesh of his fingers. He looked up into her face.

"Where are we up to in the rules?"

"1e I think."

"Okay, 1e. This one is non-negotiable. You must agree to believe me when I say I'm sorry for what I've done to you. I will regret that forever."

"Apology accepted," said Danny, equally as softly. "And I won't forget, I promise."

"I miss you too. You know that?"

"Wow... What's brought this on?"

She smiled, but it was a smile tinged with regret.

"I just want you to know. It's a lonely world sometimes, Danny. Remember what's important. Remember who you care for. When it comes down to it, everything is about people, and especially those we love and who love us in return. You should take Anna to dinner before it's too late. Before you lose her forever."

She let go of his hands, sat back in her chair and picked up the cigarette.

Danny stayed leaning forward.

"I'm never going to change you, am I?" he said at last.

Clare looked away, as though expecting to find answers in the corners of the room. When she turned back, she avoided the question.

"That dinner with Anna thing. That's non-negotiable as well. 1f."

"I think you've maybe broken 1c."

"Which was that?"

"The one about not mentioning how much we mean to each other, I think. I've got a bit confused."

"There you go then. Point proven. I'm a bad person, Danny."

She smiled but thoughts filled the space between them, regrets not far behind.

Danny sat back in his chair. Clare took a paper handkerchief from the pocket of her coat and dabbed the corners of her eyes.

"Anyway," she said, changing the mood. "I was about to say what I was going to do."

"You were."

"I'm going to speak to some people I know back in Germany. Find out what I can about Sunday. And keep looking into Mikołaj and Jacqueline. Today's going to be hectic. You're out tonight, but I'll be in touch later, or if not first thing tomorrow."

"Where am I out tonight?"

"Dinner with Anna."

"Oh, am I? Even assuming I asked her, there's no guarantee she'd come."

"You will. And she will, trust me."

"We'll see."

The conversation was interrupted by the ringtone on Danny's phone. Clare nodded for him to answer it. The number wasn't familiar but it had the London prefix. He pressed the green button to accept the call.

"Hi," he said.

"Hello? Danny?" The voice was female with a foreign accent.

"Who is this?"

"It's Aurelia."

"Aurelia!" Danny looked at Clare. She leaned forward to try to overhear the call. "Thank you so much for calling me. Where are you? Are you safe?"

"I shouldn't call you, Danny. I'm scared. They will kill me, but I was told I need to talk to you. I don't have long."

"I really appreciate it. And please don't worry. I'll look after you in any way I can. Can we meet?"

"We have to be quick. I don't have much free time, but I'm allowed to go to the shop. I can see you but we must hurry. In 30 minutes?"

"I'll be there. Where are you?"

"Do you know the Friends House, on Euston Road?"

"The Quaker place? Of course."

"Meet me there. In the cafe. You get in via the garden on the side. I'll be there unless they're watching me. If they see you they'll kill you too. Hurry."

Danny ended the call.

"You'd better go," said Clare. "I'll be in touch."

"You're not coming with me?"

She gave him a quizzical look.

"You're good, Danny. But you've got an awful lot to learn."

Five minutes later Danny was in the back of a black taxi, making its way through the backstreets towards Euston Road. Within twenty he'd arrived. He found the cafe and scanned the tables. There was no sign of her. He ordered a drink and took it to a table in the corner, giving a good view of the door.

It was still early for the lunchtime trade, but a few customers arrived: friends meeting to socialise, or maybe colleagues discussing business. He didn't know. Didn't care. He waited, watching the door, ready to get up the instant she arrived.

Ten minutes passed. She was late. Where was she? Another ten. Danny's coffee sat on the table, untouched. The door opened, but again it wasn't her. An elderly couple walked in, glanced in his direction. The woman found a table while the man went to the counter.

More minutes passed. Where was she? More importantly, was she okay? He knew how dangerous this could be if she was discovered.

He thought of what she'd said.

"I'll be there unless they're watching me." Maybe that was it. Maybe she'd been followed and had to abort. Maybe they'd discovered what she was up to and now they were watching him as well. Then he remembered the rest of her conversation. The ominous part.

"If they see you they'll kill you too."

The door opened. A man walked in. He was huge. Dressed in black. He stopped, scanning the room. He paused when he saw Danny. Was that a look of recognition? He started to approach, his hand disappearing into the inside pocket of his black leather coat.

Chapter 26

FINN Convey didn't like it when his boss seemed this anxious. It was never likely to end well. She turned away from him, then ran her hands up her face and through her freshly dyed black hair.

"It's out of character," she said at last. "And that makes me very nervous."

"But I can't make stuff up," he said. "If he's stayed at home all day, that's what he's done."

"I know. But it's not right."

"He's got a phone. It doesn't mean he hasn't been making calls."

"That's fuck all use to me."

She turned her chair back towards him.

"At least he hasn't met Danny Churchill again."

"Not since Tuesday, as far as we know."

"What the fuck is he up to? And while I'm on, how's Logan doing? And where the fuck is he?"

"I spoke to him this morning. He's working hard. We both are."

"He should be here."

"He's on his way. Says he'll be here this afternoon."

"Jesus, the pair of you. Just make sure he does as he's told. Understood?"

"Jacqui, it's all fine. Honestly."

She didn't look convinced. No, more than that, she looked different. Stressed. He hadn't seen her quite like this before.

"I'm not going to defend March, but maybe he's just finalising stuff," he continued. "Have you tried calling him?"

"No." She looked at him as though he was stupid. "He's supposed to contact me. That's the deal."

"I'm sure he will if he needs to."

"If *he* needs to? Since when the fuck has this been about what March needs?"

"Sorry, I didn't mean..."

"Get yourself out of here."

He looked at her. There was no point arguing. He turned to leave. When the door was safely closed, she picked up her phone and dialled a familiar number.

"Hello Mikołaj," she said when he answered. "I think we may have a problem."

The man took out his mobile phone, answered a call in a broad Welsh accent, and took a seat at the adjacent table. A moment later a woman arrived, also on the phone. They ended the calls simultaneously and embraced like lovers. Danny breathed out, but recognised the warning signs. Whatever the reason for Aurelia's non-appearance, it could mean extreme danger for both of them.

The sound of his phone brought him back to the moment.

"Danny, it's Mike." This was not good. "I haven't seen you and it's making me nervous."

"Mike, hi, sorry. I've been out finalising the details."

"Is it written?"

"In the process of being written. It's evolving by the minute."

"What does 'evolving' mean?"

"It's changing, growing."

"Danny, are you taking the piss? I know what the bloody word means. I mean in relation to the deadline."

"Ah, sorry. Of course. It's a crazy time. Look, I'm about to do an interview. Can I call you later?"

"I should hope there's no need. I just need your copy."

"I know. In reality, though, I think it's going to be Monday."

From the silence, that seemed to have gone down as badly as he expected.

"Everything's happening on Sunday," he continued eventually. He knew it sounded like an excuse.

"Call me later and tell me why," said his editor. "And it had better be bloody good."

The call ended. It was clear Aurelia wasn't going to show, and sitting here waiting was achieving nothing. Danny decided to head home. It was time to talk to Anna.

His wife wasn't talking to him, but that wasn't anything new. She'd shown remarkable tolerance over the years, he had to give her that, but normally he was out of the house most of the time. Since his suspension, however, he'd been forced to spend much more time at home, and the long-suffering Mrs March was beginning to have had enough of it.

"What are you smirking at?" she said at last, breaking the silence that had lasted into the afternoon.

"Ah, my dear Raphaela," he said. "Just enjoying the day."

"Well, enjoy it somewhere else, would you?" she said. "You're taking up a lot of space."

He was used to that kind of comment. It had long been a

marriage of convenience. He supposed they must have loved each other originally, but now, after more than 30 years, the passion had long since gone. The initial justification for their separate rooms had been so that she wouldn't be disturbed if he was working late. Neither had thought to change the arrangement since the start of his enforced absence. It suited them both.

March's room doubled as an office. He'd spent a lot of time there over the last couple of days, working on a plan. He was a master at self-preservation, but this was the most challenging yet. At least now he'd managed to get Danny interested, by telling him not to investigate. It was so easy to manipulate a journalist.

Within three days the deal would be done, but that could be just the start. Coming away unscathed would be one thing, but that was far from a certainty. It was a risk, of course, but preparing a contingency for every eventuality could be the difference between success and a life behind bars. Or, indeed, no life at all.

But now there was another dimension. The phone call had been unexpected but the possibilities were intriguing. Well, well, well. In some ways it was perfect. He just needed to make the most of it.

"You shall have your wish, my darling," he said. "I am going out for the afternoon. Don't worry about dinner, I'll get something while I'm out."

He picked up his jacket and headed out. He didn't say goodbye. His mind was elsewhere. Yes, he was smirking, and with very good reason.

Chapter 27

NO sooner had Danny descended the steps at the entrance to the Friends House cafe than he felt somebody come up close behind him, walking in step, and getting closer. With a rising sense of fear, he turned, ready to confront his assailant, and instead looked straight into Aurelia's terrified eyes.

She didn't speak. She didn't need to. Instead she turned and headed further into the garden, then through a gate at the far end, and eventually into Endsleigh Street. Her pace slowed. As Danny caught up she pulled him into a doorway, out of sight as much as you could be in a city as well-populated as London.

"Are you okay?" he asked urgently, but he could see she wasn't. She looked close to tears.

"I must be very quick or they will look for me," she said. "Can you help me?"

"Help you? Of course, but how?"

She looked different outside the parlour. Smaller. More vulnerable. And so very, very tired.

"I was promised a job. Come to London, we have a good job. They made me pay lots of money. My family in Poland worked hard to send me, for a better life. But then when I got here they tell me I owe them more money and I have to work for them, and until I pay them they take my passport."

"And hence the parlour?"

She nodded.

"Jesus. How long have you been there?"

"Nearly two years. But I still owe them money. They charge me rent but it's a terrible room. Every day I owe them more. And I have to work all the time, doing terrible things."

"Aurelia, I'm so sorry. Can you go to the police?"

"The police will arrest me, and if I get away they'll kill me."

He knew the threat was serious.

"Can you help me?" she asked again.

"Of course, in any way."

"They have new girls coming Sunday. You have to stop them."

"I know, I'm working on that. Do you know where?"

"Somewhere, East End. I heard them talking."

"Who's them? Mikołaj and Graham March?"

"Yes, you know them?"

"I know March. That's why I asked yesterday. I'm trying to find out what he's up to."

"He's a bad man. He makes me do terrible things."

"I can imagine." The thought was stomach-churning. "What happened? You disappeared then I got thrown out."

"They watch, through the mirror. They're listening. I had to go. I'm sorry."

"Don't worry, there's nothing to apologise for. I'm sorry to cause you problems."

She shrugged but still looked close to tears, as though she was terrified of a world completely out of control.

"Can you stop them?" she asked.

"I'm going to try. Do you know where it's happening?"

"No. But they're meeting on Sunday. You can follow them."

"At the parlour?"

She nodded.

"What time?"

"Evening. Seven. But be careful. They are very dangerous men. I must go now. They will be looking for me."

"Don't worry. But thank you. I'll do everything I can." He wasn't sure if she heard the final words as she ran back down the street, in the direction of hell.

Danny paused for a moment to let everything sink in. It was every bit as bad as he'd imagined. The date and time were progress, even if the location was still elusive. But really, what could he do? He couldn't walk in there alone, unarmed. It would be tantamount to suicide. What had Clare said? These aren't your British villains. They were violent. Brutal. They operated under different rules, placing zero value on human lives apart from their own. He'd have to talk to Amy, tell her everything, and then just be on hand to capture the exclusive. And even then, it could be deadly.

He needed to speak to Clare but he didn't have her number so email was the only option. He turned to head home. Everything was still three days away. There was still time, but things were getting tense. And he still needed to talk to Anna. Would she want to go to dinner? How could he even think about that now - and yet he knew it was perhaps the most important thing of all. Was it even the right time to ask? Whatever the state of their relationship, her friendship was still hugely important to him. It couldn't hurt to ask, just to show his appreciation if nothing else.

He arrived home, expecting to find both Anna and Holly, but neither was there. Where were they? He knocked on Anna's bedroom door, and then, when he got no answer, he opened it to look inside. That was weird. Her suitcase was back on the bed. It looked like she was moving back into her own room. But in that case, where was Holly? And why hadn't she phoned to let him know what was happening? The first familiar pangs of unease began to mount.

He checked his phone again. There were no missed calls, but he dialled his voice mail, just in case she'd called when he'd already been on the phone.

She had. There was a message.

"Hi Danny, only me. Please don't be cross but Holly's gone. I think you might have been right about her. She was going through my desk this morning. Anyway, we had a row and she moved out. No idea where to, which is a worry, but it's probably for the best. I hope she's okay. Anyway, I'm going out but I'll see you tonight. I don't know what time. I hope you're having a good day. Take care. See you."

Well, that answered that. But the thought of Anna with Mitch gave him a hollow feeling. Suddenly all thoughts of dinner were cast aside. His appetite had vanished. Again.

Danny emailed Clare with an update on his meeting with Aurelia and then tried to call DS Amy Cranston. She wasn't there so he left a message saying he needed to speak to her urgently. But after that his mind was blank. He was supposed to call Mike but it was getting late. He'd do that tomorrow. He just kept picturing Anna with this unknown man. Smiling at him, laughing with him. And God knows what else. It was too much to bear. He went to his room and lay on the bed. Her pillow still had an indentation from where she'd spent the night. He traced the shape with his hand, picking up a stray hair that she'd left behind. The hollowness began to grow, consuming him. He closed his eyes. He just wanted everything to be back to normal, like the happy times they'd shared until so recently. How could everything go so wrong so quickly?

He came to when he heard a knock at his door. It opened and there was Anna, grinning at him.

"Wakey wakey, sleepy head," she said.

He tried to shake himself awake.

"What time is it?"

"About half past six."

"In the evening?"

"Yes, obviously. How long do you think you've been asleep for?" She laughed.

He propped himself up.

"I thought you'd gone out," he said.

"I did."

"No, I mean for the evening."

"I didn't know how long I'd be. But no, I'm back now. And you haven't got time for sleep. I've been busy."

"Doing what?"

"Get up and I'll show you."

She disappeared. Danny climbed off the bed, trying to clear his head. Then he followed Anna through to the living room. She'd arranged a selection of prints and contact sheets on the desk.

"I think you're going to like these," she said.

He started to look, but couldn't quite believe his eyes.

Chapter 28

I HAVE to confess, I was pleased with myself. Danny looked at the pictures and I could see the questions forming in his head. Hopefully I'd just made him proud of me.

"What are these? Sorry, I don't understand," he said.

"It's Graham March," I said.

"I can see that. But who's he with? And where are they from?"

"I've got no idea who he's with, but they had a very long chat."

"But when? And where?"

"This afternoon, over drinks."

"But... How?"

I found it hard to suppress a smile.

"I decided to use a bit of, well, initiative," I started. "I didn't have much on, and Holly had gone, and you were out at work so I thought I'd go on a bit of a stake-out."

"You did what?" Danny's expression was hard to fathom, but it looked like a mixture of bafflement and affection. I'd accept that.

"I just thought it might help. I went to March's house and parked up with the camera, waiting to see if he did anything. To be honest, I'm not completely sure I was the only one. There was another car there that seemed to be watching him too, but that one went after a while."

He seemed momentarily lost for words but eventually found his voice.

"Anna, these are incredible. What happened?"

"I waited for about an hour and a half. Maybe more. I was just deciding it was probably pointless when he went out. So, I followed him. Then he met this guy and I started taking pictures from the car, through the window, and then more when they left. Any idea who he is? Is it important?"

"Oh, Anna, come here," he said, and gave me a giant hug. Which was nice. "I don't know who it is but he looks familiar. I can't think but it might be dynamite. It's a good job I didn't know or I'd have tried to stop you, but I'm bloody glad you did."

He kept studying the pictures while I went to put on the kettle. Then thought better of it and returned with a bottle of wine and two glasses. I waved them at him in a questioning manner.

"I might have a better idea," he said, looking up. "Are you free this evening?"

"At the moment."

"Could I take you to dinner? To say thank you? Your choice."

It didn't take much thinking.

"Yes, that would be lovely."

"Are you sure? I just thought it would be nice after all that's happened over the last few days. I hate falling out with you, and obviously to say thanks for this."

"Of course I'm sure. I'll put the wine back and get changed. Italian?"

"You're on."

I left Danny trying to scan one of the pictures with a handheld scanner that looked a bit like a cross between a hairdryer and one of those things that does barcodes. He said he wanted to email it to a couple of people to see if he could get help identifying the other man. I was so pleased I'd been able to help. It might all amount to nothing but it felt good to have done something positive, and it took my mind off Holly for a bit. She'd taken nothing of ours away with her as far as I could tell, but I supposed it could be a while before we noticed anything was missing.

By the time I was ready, Danny was turning off the computer, and ten minutes later we were heading out. The mood was refreshingly good. It's amazing, sometimes, how quickly things like that can turn.

Danny brought me up to speed on developments. He explained how he'd spent the morning in the office and then had a phone call from someone called Aurelia who he'd met at the massage parlour, and was not so much a prostitute as a victim of some form of slavery. It sounded horrific. I didn't ask how she'd managed to get hold of his number, although thinking about it now, it was a bit weird. There were lots of things that didn't seem to make sense to me, but maybe I was just increasingly living in a world of my own. Everything seemed to be building up to Sunday. He seemed nervous, but excited in some ways. In fairness, if it all came off, it would be a hell of a story.

The starters arrived and we had the first glasses from a bottle of Valpolicella, which started the evening off nicely. It was good to be out with Danny, but there was still an atmosphere between us. It definitely wasn't quite like the old days, but I was determined to make an effort.

We talked about music. I mentioned the new Sparks album, and then, turning to cinema, I said I'd like to try to catch The Hudsucker Proxy while it was still on release. He suggested coming with me. I'm pretty sure he did that just to make sure I didn't arrange to go with Mitch instead. And yet as I was having that thought, so I was thinking how nice it would be to let Mitch take me, on a proper date, without the baggage of everything Danny and I had been through.

As the main course arrived (I went for pizza, Danny the gnocchi), I couldn't resist asking the question that had been on my mind all day.

"Any more word from your murderous friend?" I asked, dropping the "girl" from the final word.

"Clare? Can you not actually bring yourself to say her name?" he replied, grinning at me. The grin annoyed me, despite my efforts to be friendly.

"She has so many," I replied. "I forget which is current." And mentally patted myself on the back for such a legendary display of wit. She'd used all sorts of names while up to her previous misdemeanours, which, let it be remembered, were fairly severe.

"It's still Clare at the moment," he said.

"Oh, so you have then. How is she?"

"I daren't tell you whether I have or not, or you'll go off in a huff."

"I will not go off in a huff!"

"Yes, you will. And anyway, I don't think she does the name thing any more."

"*Really?*" I was tempted to make some sort of leopard/spot observation, then decided it was a cliché and I should come up with something more creative, but the wine was getting the better of me.

"Yes, really."

"Well, have you?"

"Do you promise not to get in a bad temper if I have?"

"I promise to try. But Danny, you know what? I only get upset because I care about you."

"I know and that's lovely, but you mustn't worry. She'll disappear again soon, I'm sure."

"Will you stop avoiding the question?"

He laughed, and that annoyed me even more.

"I did get a response to my email," he said. "She's looking into things for me."

"So you were emailing her! I knew it!"

"What? No, not then. Honestly. It was the next day from work."

"Right."

"Honestly. Anyway, you've got nothing to be jealous about. I, on the other hand... How are things with Mitch?"

I definitely wasn't in the mood for that.

"They're okay," I said.

"Just okay?"

"Well, better than okay. He seems a nice guy."

"And?"

"And what?"

"And everything. Are you seeing him again? Do I need to start thinking about a suit for the wedding?"

"Danny. It's been two dates."

"So?"

"It's still early days then, isn't it? I'll tell you what, though, he's got lovely arms."

"Oh, here we go."

"Well, he has."

"Arm perv."

"I'm not an arm perv. I just like nice arms. They're kind of muscly but not stupid bodybuilder big."

"How do you know that?"

"How do you think?"

"I try not to think."

"Well, I'm just saying."

Danny paused, to refill our glasses.

"So, has he, you know, tried to hold your hand? Peck on the cheek?"

I gave him a look that hopefully left no doubt I wasn't going to answer that one.

"When are you next seeing him?" he continued when the message got through.

"Tomorrow."

"Wow. You're keen then."

"He's a nice guy. He's interesting. But can we talk about something else?"

Tomorrow was beginning to seem like too long away.

"So he's an actual film star?" Danny asked, ignoring my request. I sighed.

"Not yet, but heading that way. Maybe."

"I shall expect to see you on the red carpet."

"In your dreams. It'll all be over once he gets a glimpse of all the Hollywood starlets, and I'll end my days a sad, lonely spinster."

"That's never going to happen."

"Yeah, well, I may as well do, for all you seem to care." This last bit was under my breath.

A noise at the front of the restaurant stopped our conversation, probably just in time, as I was starting to get belligerent. We looked up. There seemed to be a bit of a scuffle.

"What's happening there?" I asked.

But before Danny could answer we saw a man pushing his way through, past a waiter who went sprawling to the floor. There was shouting. He looked like a giant, with a shaved head and a determined expression, and he was coming our way. I looked at Danny but he suddenly seemed very pale, with a look I'd never seen before. And then he started to get up and was shouting at me to follow him.

It was all happening so quickly and yet time seemed to stand still. Danny stood and reached for me, but then stopped and just told me to run. I looked at the man. He was staring at Danny and coming towards us at speed. And then I noticed the gun. I screamed, and ducked, trying to get away. I saw Danny run towards the back of the restaurant. Then I heard the sound of gunfire. More screams. The acrid bite of propellant in the air. More gunfire, but different, louder. More shots. Danny had been hit. It was all so surreal. And then I saw a sight that chilled me to my core. I watched as he fell. Just fell, lifelessly, hitting the ground, a bloodstain forming on his crisp blue shirt, where at least one bullet had entered his body.

Chapter 29

I 'M not sure exactly what happened next. The man left as quickly as he'd arrived, leaving panic and chaos in his wake. I tried to rush to Danny but my legs lost all co-ordination. I was dizzy, shocked, feeling sick. I didn't faint again but I came bloody close. I grabbed the table to stop myself falling. People were gathering round him. Someone shouted for somebody to call an ambulance. Anybody. More people rushed towards him. I couldn't see what was happening. I had to move. However horrific, I had to know. I wanted him to see my face as his final memory. To hear my voice as his final words. I tried again. I gathered strength from untapped reserves and pushed forward, hating that I wasn't taller, angry with all these people standing in my way, and terrified of what I'd find when they moved to let me through.

Danny was lying on the ground. Somebody had turned him on his side. Somebody else was tying a ripped section of tablecloth to his shoulder, as tightly as they could, trying to stem the bleeding. Danny's expression was cold. Deathly. I couldn't stop the flow of tears as eventually I knelt down beside him, reaching for his hand, telling him how much I loved him.

And then, from nowhere, there were sirens and more shouting. The people behind me moved away. I looked up to see paramedics running towards us. I tried to speak, but words wouldn't come. There was no need. They could see the pleading in my eyes.

I knelt back to let the professionals do their work. An oxygen mask appeared. Danny wasn't moving. Two, three, four people in uniform, working so hard, doing everything they could. Police arrived. A stretcher appeared. Danny was lifted onto it. And then they were rushing back towards the door, holding Danny between them, towards the waiting welcome of the ambulance and its open doors.

Somehow, I managed to follow. Somebody asked if I was the next of kin. I think I said yes. Either way, I was in the ambulance with them, sirens calling as we sped through the streets of London. And still the paramedics worked.

"How is he?" I asked, but I don't think they heard me. I tried to get close but I knew I was just getting in the way. They were the longest moments of my life.

And then, the paramedics stood back. There was a moment of silence. I had the most terrifying sensation of utter panic. I'd lost him. They'd given up trying to save him. He was lying there, my most amazing, wonderful, irreplaceable friend, gunned down when he had so much still to live for. I didn't scream. Every part of me just started shutting down.

I felt a hand reach out for me. Then another. They were holding me, stopping me from falling. And I could see Danny, looking so peaceful in a moment of such ultimate violence. I just wanted to hold him. To touch him. To be with him. To breathe my life into him, to bring him back to me, if only for a moment.

And then his eyes opened. He looked at me. And when he saw me he smiled. A weak but unmistakeable smile. That's when the tears really started. I knelt down on the floor of the speeding ambulance, just to be close to him, just to hold his hand. And then I heard his voice, muffled through the oxygen mask. I couldn't hear what he said. I urged the paramedic to remove the mask. I had to hear his final words. To hear him say goodbye.

I pulled the mask aside myself, before they could stop me. I knelt closer, cradling his face in my hands. I leaned close. He opened his mouth to speak again. I leaned closer still. And then he spoke to me, and it was the most beautiful sound I'd ever heard.

"That fucking hurt," he said. And he smiled at me again.

The paramedics took over. The mask was replaced. I turned to the person closest to me.

"Is he... going to be okay?" I asked, hardly daring to speak the actual words.

"He'll be fine," she said. "He's been very lucky. An inch further over and we'd have lost him but it's basically a flesh wound."

The sense of relief was overwhelming. That's when I did collapse to the floor. The tears were still flowing, but I couldn't help smiling too. Danny reached out a hand towards me. I grabbed it. I felt him squeeze.

The ambulance arrived at Euston Free Hospital. It was my second visit in forty-eight hours after the drama with Leah. The doors were opened and Danny was wheeled away at speed. I followed, trying to keep up, not wanting to let him out of my sight. Never wanting to spend another moment apart. Eventually I was stopped and told to wait while he was rushed into an operating theatre.

The hour that followed was perhaps the loneliest I'd ever known. All sorts of thoughts went through my head. What had happened? Who was the man with the gun? Was he really trying to kill Danny or did he just mistake him for somebody else? And what if there were complications in the operating theatre? You hear about people having terrible reactions. The shock causing cardiac arrest.

Eventually a doctor came to see me. She did her best to reassure me. She confirmed that the damage would heal in time, although it was a good job the ambulance had arrived so quickly. Danny was going to be okay. I just wanted to hug her. I wanted her to be my mum.

Danny was taken through to a ward where he was given a private room. Apparently he was going to be sedated and kept in overnight at least, and reassessed in the morning. I was allowed to stay with him. There was a police guard at the door. The chairs were uncomfortable but I didn't care. He was all strapped up but looked so beautiful and calm, sleeping away the pain.

I rested my head on the mattress beside him. The sense of shock started to ebb away. A nurse brought me a cup of tea, which was a lovely gesture, but in truth it was bloody awful. As Danny slept on, I started to feel my own eyes go heavy. I leaned back in the chair, feeling uncomfortable but just delighted to be there. Sleep came to take me.

I was roused by the sound of a gentle female voice.

"How is he?" she asked. I looked up and couldn't quite believe my eyes. There, standing before me, in all her dubious glory, was Clare.

Chapter 30

I T took me a moment to register. Her hair had changed. Where it used to be blonde it was now dyed a deep chestnut brown, but she was still as immaculately dressed as usual, from what I could tell in the dim light of the hospital room.

What on earth was she doing here? *How* was she here? There was a policeman standing outside the door and she'd sailed straight past him. Shouldn't he be dragging her away in a pair of handcuffs to begin a life sentence? Presumably she knew that I could destroy her liberty in a heartbeat. Part of me was impressed by the brazen self-confidence of the woman, while the rest was struggling to contain an intense animosity. And yet none of that seemed important at just that moment. My only priority was Danny. I could stick more pins in my mental voodoo doll later.

"He's sleeping," I said, rather stating the obvious. "But he's going to be fine." I tried to keep the ice-cold venom out of my voice, but suspect I may have been unsuccessful.

She reached out and stroked his hand. It was the tenderest of touches. I wanted to slap her hand away.

"Thank God," she said, her voice barely more than a whisper.

Then I noticed the tears in her eyes too. And despite everything I'd said, and every bad thought that had formed in my head over the last year or so, a part of me softened. Whatever she was doing here, simply coming must have represented a huge risk, and yet she'd done it to be close to Danny. To make sure he was okay. Don't get me wrong, I still had a strong sense of entirely justified loathing, but part of me recognised the humble humanity in the situation. We both stood there, not speaking, just looking at Danny who in turn seemed thankfully oblivious to all of the evil in the world. And especially that standing right beside him.

Eventually Clare asked me if I had a tissue. I passed her a box from the cabinet at Danny's bedside.

"Thanks, Anna," she said, dabbing her eyes. And then she looked at me with such an expression of vulnerability I could hardly believe it was the same person I'd last met all those months ago. The self-centred monster I'd demonised in my mind ever since.

"Are you staying with him?" she asked.

I nodded.

"They've said I can," I said. "I just don't want to leave him."

"That's good," she said, in a voice so soft it was like the aural equivalent of being wrapped up in a duvet. In the middle of a cloud. And then she came around to my side of the bed. She opened her arms and hugged me. The whole evening was so surreal I didn't even flinch. Instead I just heard her say thank you, and I stood there, with so many questions, but no idea where to start. The hug ended and she took a step away.

"I didn't think I'd see you again," I said at last. My civil tone took me by surprise as much as anyone.

"No, I suspect not," she replied. And there seemed genuine regret in the way she said it.

In the room there was a quiet hum of electrical equipment,

and the gentle sound of Danny's breathing. It was remarkably peaceful. Clare didn't seem to be in any rush.

"How come you're here?" I asked eventually.

"I just had to come. I had to see him. I thought he'd been..." She didn't need to finish the sentence. I knew. I saw her shudder.

"But isn't it, you know, a bit risky? Shouldn't you be living in exile somewhere? Brazil or something?"

She paused before answering.

"Did Danny talk to you?"

"About?"

"About what I said to him."

"What you said to him? He said he'd spoken to you in Cologne, but I don't remember anything specifically. Why?"

"Oh, it's hard." She paused again. "I'm just so sorry, Anna. Sorry for everything I put you through..."

I put my hand up to stop her.

"Sorry. Not interested," I said. "All I want to know is why?"

"Why I did it?"

I nodded.

"Weakness, I suspect. And I can't ask you not to hate me, but, oh, I don't know. It's a cruel world sometimes."

Danny lying in a hospital bed was evidence of that.

"But are you not worried? About getting arrested? There's a policeman right outside that door, and one word from me could see you locked up for ever."

"I know. But no. I hope you won't do that, although it's probably all I deserve, and I couldn't complain if you did. That said, I don't think they're actually looking for me any more."

"After the crash?"

"Exactly. I still have to be careful, though."

"Obviously."

"Are you going to?" she asked, after a moment.

"Get you arrested?" I paused, while my mind tried to catch

up, thinking of how many problems she'd caused, before finally shaking my head. I couldn't believe what I was doing.

"Thank you."

Clare fetched another chair and put it down next to mine.

"Let's sit down," she said.

We took our seats and then she started speaking again.

"I'm not asking you to like me, Anna, but you *can* trust me."

I tried not to laugh but it came out as a bit of a snort.

"Clare, don't take this the wrong way, but we're doing fine. I'm sure you're a lovely person deep down, but I've kind of moved on. I don't wish you any harm, but equally if I never saw you again, I'd not exactly be upset."

"I know. I do understand. But, equally don't take *this* the wrong way, but you're not really."

"Not what?"

"Doing fine."

"I assure you we are."

"Oh Anna, look at us. We're in a hospital. Danny is lying there, having been shot at, and by all accounts he's had a bloody lucky escape. You've got two friends who've been attacked. One's dead and the other's in intensive care. I'm not saying you're not dealing with it and doing a brilliant job, but equally I don't think everything's 'fine' and I do think I can help you. All of you."

"Right."

"Will you let me?"

That was enough to get me started. I'd tried really hard but I could feel my irritation begin to surface.

"Can I just point something out?" I said, voice rising. "You met Danny when? Last Friday? Everything was working well, he was writing a story, everything was under control. And all of the bad things you just mentioned have happened since. So, don't even start getting me to think about it, or I'll start drawing conclusions that it's all somehow connected with your reappearance, because - and don't take *this* the wrong way either -

trouble seems to follow you around. So no, thank you for the very kind offer, but your help is the very last thing I need."

That seemed to shut her up. I was quite proud of myself.

"It's not like that," she said after a moment, again, almost in a whisper.

"Well, it seems like it to me."

"Can I just tell you what happened?"

"What? Your side of the story? Getting your excuses in early?"

"No, nothing like that at all. Everything that's happened was going to happen. Danny just asked me to help him piece it all together so we can make it stop."

"Danny asked you, did he? When? Did he have some sort of amazing premonition?"

"How do you mean?"

"Because when he spoke to you on Friday, none of this had happened."

She shook her head.

"Sorry," she said. "It wasn't Friday. It was today. This morning."

"He spoke to you this morning?"

"Didn't he mention it?"

"No, he didn't."

I have to confess, that came as a bit of a surprise. If Danny had been awake, and hadn't just been shot, I'd have been having a word.

"He's dealing with some very dangerous people, Anna. It's too dangerous to do it on his own. That's why I was there tonight."

That came as a bit of a surprise too.

"You were there? Where?"

"At the restaurant. Not actually inside the restaurant, but outside. Keeping an eye on things."

"Ah, well that was a bloody big success." My voice was getting louder.

"No, it wasn't, but I stopped it getting any worse."

"What do you mean? It couldn't have got much worse than being fucking shot at."

"It could. He could have been killed."

"Yeah, well that was more by luck than judgement."

"No, it wasn't."

"What?"

And then she told me what had happened, and even though I didn't want to believe a word of it, part of me felt compelled to listen.

"I saw him go in," she started. "The gunman. And I just suddenly had a very bad feeling. Did you hear two sets of shots?"

I tried to think back. I remembered now. The second ones had been louder.

"Actually, yes, now you mention it."

"The second of those were me."

"*What*? You shot Danny?" I couldn't quite believe what I was hearing. "What the fuck?"

"No, I fired into the ceiling. That's what stopped him. The guy with the gun. That's why he ran. If I hadn't, he'd have finished the job."

"Hold on, hold on. You fired into the ceiling?"

"Yes."

"Why not just shoot the twat with the gun?"

"I couldn't do that. It was too dangerous. I'm not a great shot and there were too many other people. If I'd missed him it could have hit anyone."

"So you just shot the ceiling?"

"It's all I could do. But it worked. He looked and saw me, saw the gun, and ran for his life. If I hadn't been there, Danny would have been killed."

"Just let me take all this in for a moment."

I leaned forward, resting my elbows on the bed and my head in my hands.

"I..."

"Shhh." I needed time to think.

Eventually I had a deep breath, then turned to look at her. I was having trouble picturing the woman in front of me as the Clare I knew from old, and equally struggled to picture this version as some sort of gun-wielding nutcase.

"Okay," I said at last.

"I called the ambulance too. And the police. As soon as I saw what was happening. That's why they were so quick on the scene."

"It's a good job they were. But just tell me. If you saw what was happening, or knew it was going to happen, why not just stop it?"

"I couldn't. I didn't know what was going to happen, but as soon as it did, I put an end to it."

"So basically, you're saying you saved Danny's life?"

"Basically, yes. And yours."

Suddenly I started to feel very faint yet again. I hadn't even considered that I'd been at risk. Part of me was still assuming it was some sort of mistaken identity thing. Clare passed me a glass of water. It helped but I'd have preferred something stronger.

"I don't know what to say," I said, when my breathing began to resemble something approaching normal.

"There's nothing *to* say. I just wanted you to know, so you know what you're dealing with."

"I..." I paused. The next bit wasn't something I ever thought I'd say to Clare.

"Thank you," I said, at last.

She reached out for my hand and I let her hold it.

"You don't need to thank me. It was the least I could do."

It was one of those moments where you suddenly have to reassess everything you know to be true. It was far too much for me to process at this time of the night, after the day I'd just had. I just wanted to sleep and make it all go away.

"Where's the gun now?" I asked after a while.

"It's safe. But I can get it if I need it."

"I may be glad to hear that." I tried to smile, but it wasn't altogether successful. "Where are you staying?"

"At a friend's house. But I won't be far away."

"I'm glad to hear that too," I said, surprising myself yet again.

"I'm not invincible, but I'll do everything I can to protect you. Both of you. Just be careful though, won't you? This will all be over very soon but we all need to take care in the meantime."

"I will. And I'll make sure Danny does too, you can be damn sure of that."

"That's good. Listen, the police will want to talk to you tomorrow about what happened. I'd appreciate it if you didn't mention me, for obvious reasons."

"No, of course."

"I'll give you my number and email address. Let me know if you need me or there's anything I can do. I understand if you burn them, but I'm on your side now. If you let me."

She took a fresh tissue from the box, wrote the details on it and gave it to me. I looked at it, then folded it and put it into the pocket of my jacket. Even her handwriting looked sophisticated. She stood up, then reached down over Danny. I thought she was going to kiss him, but instead she just brushed a stray hair away from his eyes. She squeezed his hand, then turned and walked away. Just before the door, she turned, giving Danny one last look.

"Take care, Anna," she said. And then I was back on my own.

I had so much thinking to do, but before I could try to assess everything, I drifted off into a fitful, uncomfortable sleep, dreaming dreams of being chased, and of a world spinning ever further off its axis.

Chapter 31

Friday, April 8th, 1994

I WAS awoken by the nurse checking in on Danny before the onslaught of breakfast activity. It hadn't been the most comfortable of nights. I was still wearing my dress from the night before, I had a stiff neck, and I was badly in need of a shower, but if Clare was to be believed, I should be grateful to be alive. I was desperate to talk to Danny but had to wait while his dressing was changed and his temperature taken. Eventually the nurse said the doctor would be along soon, and left us alone. I took my chance.

Danny was still feeling groggy, but he smiled at me. I reached for his hand.

"Have you been there all night?" he asked.

"I have. You're such a drama queen. Anyone would think you'd been shot," I joked.

He laughed and then winced. It may have been only a flesh wound, but it was evidently still a painful one.

"What actually happened? It's all a bit vague."

"That's a good question. Depends who you talk to."

"Meaning?"

"On the face of it, we were just having dinner when some nutcase barged in and took a shot at you."

"Christ. I ran, didn't I?"

"You did, although you didn't get very far."

"Sorry about that."

"Don't apologise, I'd have done the same. There is, however, another version."

"Really?"

"Yup. In this one, much the same happened, except we were both saved by your guardian angel who turned up, shot a hole in the ceiling, and caused your man to scarper before finishing the job."

He looked at me as though I was speaking a foreign language.

"What are you talking about?" he asked, frowning.

"Clare. She turned up, apparently, and saved the day. And us, as it happens."

"You're going to have to go back over that. Sorry. These painkillers are stronger than I thought. Clare did what?"

And so I told him about her visit, and how she'd stroked his arm with tears in her eyes, and then explained how she'd managed to intervene and stop the gunman in his tracks.

"Do you believe her?" he asked.

"You know what? Painful though it is to admit, I actually do."

"Jesus. Thank God she was there."

"I mean, it could all be nonsense, and maybe she was the one who actually shot you, but I think she was telling the truth. We had quite a chat actually. I think I saw a different side of her."

"You're going to have to go slowly, here. You hate Clare."

"I think hate's a bit strong."

"Loathe then, if that's not the same thing."

"Again, possibly overstating it."

"It's exactly one of the words you use."

"Yes, in one sense, although primarily back in the day."

"As recently as yesterday."

"Yeah, all right." This was a bit awkward for me. "I just think maybe she's shown herself in a different light, kind of."

That made him smile.

"So, you don't now hate her?"

"Let's change the subject. How was your, ahem, morning in the office yesterday?"

"My morning in the... Ah."

"Indeed."

Colour started returning to his cheeks, which I took to be a good sign, medically speaking.

"Kind of surprising," he said.

"The surprise being you didn't go anywhere near it?"

"I suppose that's one way of putting it."

"Quite."

"Oh, I can't win. If I'd said I'd been with Clare you'd have gone all moody and refused to go to dinner with me. At least, you would have done yesterday, before you two became the best of friends."

"Danny?"

"What?"

"Couple of points there. One, I do not go moody, and two, Clare is not my best friend because you are, even though you clearly can't be trusted. And equally as clearly, it seems I can't let you out of my sight."

"You definitely do go moody though."

"I definitely don't, although I might do in a minute if you don't behave yourself."

The conversation was halted by the arrival of the doctor. I was surprised to see it was the same one as the night before, either on a long shift or starting a new day after not much sleep. Either way I have nothing but utmost respect for the NHS and all those who work within it. While she examined Danny, I took the opportunity to visit the bathroom and splash my face with water, but gave myself a fright in the meantime. I looked dreadful: tired, grubby and with the remnants of make-up smudged in all the wrong places. I checked my phone. There were no missed calls and so no voice mail messages. I did as much as I could to make myself look presentable and then headed back.

A familiar voice called out to me as I approached Danny's room. I turned. It was DS Amy Cranston and her sidekick DC Anil Jachuck, approaching from the reception desk.

"How is he?" she asked.

"Not bad, considering. The doctor's with him now. How's everything at the restaurant?"

"Chaotic, as you'd expect."

"Do you know what happened or who it was?"

She glanced at DC Jachuck, as though unspoken words were passing between them.

"Investigations are ongoing," she said. Annoyingly and ironically, she was too straight to give me a straight answer. "We've come to take statements from both of you."

"Any news of Leah?"

Another glance.

"Still the same. She'll pull through but she's in a bad way. Is Holly still with you?"

I gave her the summary, leaving out the bit whereby I'd suspected her of stealing things. I didn't want them to arrest her, purely on the strength of a hunch, although I doubted that would be top priority in any case, given the current climate.

The doctor emerged as we talked.

"How's he looking?" I asked.

She knew me, but hesitated when she saw the other two. Amy and DC Jachuck showed their warrant cards as identification.

"He's pretty good," she said at last. "I'd like to keep him in today just so we can keep an eye on things and make sure he doesn't develop a temperature, but he should be okay to go home tomorrow, all being well. Assuming he keeps making progress."

"That's fantastic news," I said. "Thank you so much."

"My pleasure. It's always good to have a successful one." She gave a wry smile. "He's going to have to take it easy for a few days. I've signed him off work for a fortnight and then we'll see how he is, okay?"

I hadn't even thought about work. That wouldn't go down well, with Danny, let alone with his editor. I made a mental note to call the newspaper and let them know what had happened, and then thought they'd probably already have people on top of it. Nature of the beast.

The doctor left us to continue her rounds, and we all went into the room. I arranged chairs for the other two and propped myself up on the bed. After a couple of minutes of informal chat, Amy got down to business, asking us what we'd been doing, what had happened, did we have any idea who was responsible, and all that kind of thing. She reiterated that we'd been lucky that something seemed to spook the would-be killer as he'd fled halfway through the task, but I managed to avoid any mention of Clare. Thankfully Danny did the same. We didn't lie to the police, as such, we just didn't answer a question that hadn't been directly asked.

"The only thing I can think," said Danny, "is it's something to do with the story - but I'm coming on to that. Did you have any success with the picture, by the way?"

"The one of March?" asked Amy. Danny nodded. "I know exactly who it is. It's very interesting. How did you come about it?"

"That was me," I said. "I followed him yesterday and just took pictures. I didn't know if it'd be important. Who is it?"

"It's our friendly politician, Mr Elmhirst-Banks. Or Seb to friends."

"*Really?*" That was Danny, and it was Amy's turn to nod. "But isn't he trying to force a cover-up? To save the Met a scandal?"

"I said I got that impression, but I can't comment officially Danny, you know that."

I could see Danny's mind working hard through the fug of the painkillers. He propped himself up, winced, and decided against it. I helped to arrange his pillows to make him more comfortable.

"But this could be huge," he continued, when he was settled down. "I've got loads to tell you on March, but if this Seb guy's colluding with him to try to bury things, then it's a fantastic conspiracy." He turned to me. "Oh Anna, you've done very well."

I winked, feeling very pleased with myself.

"We don't know what they were discussing, though," said Amy. "It could have been anything."

"It could, but it's a definite new angle. But Christ, if he knew the shitstorm that's about to hit March, he'd be keeping a million miles away. I almost feel sorry for the guy."

"So, what have you got on March?" asked DC Jachuck. It was refreshing to hear him speak.

"I hardly know where to start," said Danny. And then he brought the detectives up to speed on how we'd followed March to the massage parlour and then the casino, and our theories about both. He mentioned his own visit to the parlour and how he'd been thrown out, and his subsequent meeting with Aurelia. Then, with a final flourish, he revealed as much as he already knew about the forthcoming events of Sunday. Amy did whatever is the modern police equivalent of a low whistle.

"I suspect that's all got something to do with what happened last night," he finished.

"Bloody hell, Danny, why didn't you come to me with all this earlier?" she asked.

"A lot of it I only found out late yesterday. It was the first thing I was going to do today."

She looked at DC Jachuck, who was writing everything down.

"We'd better be getting back," she said. "You're going to be out of action for the next two weeks, according to the doctor."

"Officially."

"But if you hear anything more, let me know. Utmost urgency, okay?"

"I will. And likewise?"

"As much as I can."

"Oh, come on, we're working together on this."

"Danny, I'll do what I can. We'll speak soon."

They said their farewells. I looked at my watch. It was still only just past 8am. Danny seemed to read my thoughts.

"Why don't you go back to the flat, have a shower, have something to eat and catch up on some sleep?" he suggested.

"Because I don't want to leave you."

"I'll be fine. There's a policeman outside. I'll fall asleep in a bit. I don't know what they're giving me, but I'm knackered. And anyway, if you do go, could you fetch my ThinkPad and a notepad and pen? And my phone charger."

I didn't need much persuasion. I had the feeling I was going to need to be on top form and that wasn't going to happen if I was sleep-deprived and surviving on leftover hospital rations. There was no way Danny was about to take two weeks off work, doctor's orders or not. It wasn't even worth me protesting.

"I'll call the Echo and tell them you won't be in," I said. "Not yet, anyway. At least you've got an excuse for missing the deadline."

"I wouldn't rely on it. But thank you."

Half an hour later, I was home. It seemed strange to be back there on my own when we'd both gone out the night before. I found a packet of four croissants in the kitchen so put three in the oven for breakfast and decided to leave the fourth one for lunch. It was not exactly what you'd call a balanced diet. That would have been having two for breakfast and two for lunch.

While they were warming, filling the kitchen with a heavenly baking aroma, I phoned the paper and was put through to Danny's editor. He seemed a bit grumpy, but I assured him it would all be for the best very, very soon. I don't think he took kindly to that, but he said he'd send someone out to check in on Danny that afternoon. I imagine he was looking for a first-hand account of the previous night's drama as much as he was concerned for Danny's welfare, although maybe I'm just getting a bit cynical these days.

After breakfast, I started to feel incredibly sleepy. I lay on the bed to get undressed to go in the shower, but made the mistake of closing my eyes in the process. Two hours had passed by the time I came round, to the sound of my phone ringing.

I answered without thinking, half of my mind still asleep and the rest preoccupied with revolving thoughts of the night before. I think I was beginning to suffer from the effects of delayed shock. I'd been so busy with Danny I hadn't had time to process my own feelings, but a couple of hours of sleep had allowed my subconscious to take over. I suddenly felt very alone, increasingly scared, and significantly confused, but didn't have time to begin trying to put any of that in order before I automatically pressed the green button to answer the call.

And that's probably why I didn't recognise the voice, once I'd announced myself.

"Is that Anna?" he asked. "You sound different."

"Yes, it's me. Who's that?"

"It's Mitch."

Mitch.

"Oh hi, sorry, I was fast asleep," I said.

"It's all right for some. I'm sorry. Is it a bad time?"

"No, it's fine. It was just a long night."

"I daren't ask."

"Haha. No, it's okay. I was just up late with Danny. Super-long story though."

"And again, I daren't ask. I look forward to hearing all about it though. Are you still on for this evening?"

"This evening?" I wasn't even completely sure what day of the week it was.

"Don't say you've dumped me already."

"No, not at all. Sorry, just a lot going on. This evening, yes. Well, hopefully." I desperately tried to bring my mind into focus. On the one hand, the only place I wanted to be was at the hospital with Danny. But if he was going to be fast asleep that wouldn't serve much purpose, and a night out might help take my mind off things - especially as I didn't fancy cooking dinner and staying home on my own. I was just so undecided, and therefore shocked when I heard myself saying "yes, actually, of course" before I'd realised fully what I was doing.

"Excellent. You had me worried there for a moment," he said. "Would you like me to pick you up? Or just meet somewhere?"

I took a quick glance around my bedroom. It was in no fit state to invite someone back for "coffee" and I wasn't going to have time to tidy.

"Let's meet," I said. "I'm off out this afternoon and I don't know what time I'll be getting back."

"Sounds intriguing."

"Honestly, you wouldn't believe. Name a time and place and I'll see you there."

He suggested 7pm at an Indian restaurant just off Camden High Street, north of the station. I knew it well. It sounded perfect.

"Any problems let me know but otherwise I look forward to seeing you there," he said.

"Me too."

I ended the call and headed to the shower. I felt a whole world better after that. Then it was the final croissant before collecting the notebook and charger, plus a notepad and various pens and setting off back to the hospital, to see how Danny was doing.

Once I arrived, I approached the door to his room, but was stopped by a new policeman who'd seemingly taken over guard duties since I left. He asked me for ID and the reason for my visit. Through the window in the door I could see Danny already had a visitor. At first I thought it must be his colleague from the Echo, somebody older, maybe a senior reporter or something. But then, when he turned, and I saw his face, I realised just how wrong I was. Short of Graham March himself, this was the very last person I expected to see.

Chapter 32

"ANNA, meet Samuel Elmhirst-Banks," said Danny when I finally gained admittance.

The politician rose from his seat and shook my hand, with just the right degree of firmness to assert his manliness without causing lasting damage.

"Pleasure to meet you," he said, "but please, call me Seb."

As he returned to his seat I tried to catch Danny's eye. What was he doing here? Danny raised his eyebrows in response.

"Everything all right at home?" he asked.

"Yes, all good. I fell asleep, though. Sorry I'm late back." I took a seat on the opposite side of the bed and started doing hand gestures that Seb couldn't see, pointing at him and frowning at Danny.

"That's okay. Seb's just popped in to introduce himself," said Danny. It didn't look like he had much idea what was going on, either.

"Yes, I was at the hospital and I heard what happened from a mutual friend. DS Cranston? I thought I'd pop by and say hello. I'll leave you to it now, though. Nice to meet you Danny. Think about what I said, okay?"

Danny nodded. Seb got up, shook both of our hands again. Slightly firmer this time. He exuded professional schmooze and insincerity. I hadn't met many politicians but this was how I imagined all of them. He said his farewells, and then turned on his well-polished heel and left us alone.

"What was all that about?" I asked once the door closed. "And what does he mean, 'think about what I said'?"

"He was offering me a job."

"*What?*"

"In Whitehall. I don't know really. I wasn't really listening."

"Sorry, he just turned up unannounced and offered you a job? On what basis?"

"He said he'd heard about me. Amy speaks very highly, apparently."

"Okay. But..."

"Ah yes. Well, he seemed to think I may be spooked after being shot at. Possibly thinking about a career change. And apparently they could do with 'a man of my talents' in Government. Something like that. Complete bollocks, obviously."

"Obviously. You don't have any talents." That made him smile. "Doing what?"

"I don't know. I told you, I wasn't really listening. I was too busy trying to work out what he was up to."

"What was he up to?"

"The first thing I learned... The first thing Clare taught me, if I can mention her name now you're friends again, without you going all off on one..."

I gave him a look.

" I do *not* go off on one."

"You clearly do. But anyway, the point is, the first thing she told me was never to assume anything. That said, I assume the job doesn't exist and he's just trying to get me onside so he can try to exert some influence if I look like writing anything about March."

"He didn't actually say that?"

"No, of course not. But I presume it's the first stage of a long campaign."

I thought for a moment.

"Are you allowed to presume things? Or does Clare say not to do that either? And thinking about it, what's the difference between assuming and presuming anyway?"

"Anna?"

"What?"

"Stop trying to be funny. It's painful."

"I'm not, just genuinely curious. It's like the same word, but different."

"Presume is more like an assumption based on the balance of probability."

It still sounded like exactly the same thing to me.

"Right. Anyway, carry on."

He tried to sit up a bit straighter but winced again and gave up.

"*Presumably* he doesn't know how close I am," he continued. "Or that you took pictures of him, linking the two of them together. It's curious timing though."

"Do you think he's linked to what happened last night?"

I could see him thinking.

"I wouldn't have thought so," he said eventually. "I don't see how he could be. Did you remember the computer, by the way?"

I indicated the bag on the floor beside my chair. Danny asked me to plug it in for him so he could lie in bed, tapping away on the keyboard.

"Which bit of having at least two weeks off work is this then?" I asked when he was all set up. He grinned back at me.

"I'm just filling in parts of the jigsaw. Moving things around. Have you got any idea of the scale of the trafficking industry?"

"I imagine it's huge."

"The more I look into it, the more horrific it gets. It's just evil,

evil bastards preying on the vulnerable. When you read some of the stories it's impossible to believe people would do that to another person. Prostitution's the tip of the iceberg. Some of the stuff happening in Africa is just unbelievable."

"What like?"

"You don't even want to know. It's children from refugee camps or just off the street. They make them shoot their own parents then turn them into soldiers, sex slaves, all sorts. They're getting gang-raped, mutilated. It's absolutely fucking unthinkable."

"Jesus."

"The eastern Europeans like Aurelia get offered jobs here, but they're just sucked in. When they get here, they realise they've been done, but by then it's too late. Their passports have gone. They're beaten, threatened, told their families will be murdered if they try to escape. And yet it seems like it's massively lucrative. Governments are focused on drugs, so moving people is lower risk with enormous profits. There's a whole network of gangs. It's huge."

"And somewhere in among it all, there's March."

"Exactly."

"Oh Danny, be careful."

I tried to change the subject but the mood was sombre. Danny booted up his notebook computer. I offered to go to find a vending machine for an awful cup of tea.

When I came back, Danny was clearly engrossed. I was aware I was probably disturbing him.

"How are you feeling, anyway?" I asked.

"Sore but not too bad. I got up and went for a walk to the bathroom this morning. I think they'll let me out tomorrow."

"Is there anything I can do to help?"

He stopped typing.

"I don't think so," he said. "I'm going to speak to Amy again, and try to see if I can connect this thing to a phone line so I can send a message to Clare to see if she's made any progress."

"Couldn't you just phone her?"

"What, Clare? No, it's just email."

"Haven't you got her number?"

"No. She's rung me but withheld the number."

"Oh," I said. I could feel a smile forming and did my very best to suppress it. By the time Danny looked at me, I was failing miserably.

"What now?" he asked.

"Nothing," I lied.

"Tell me."

"No, it's just odd that you don't have her number."

"She doesn't want to be traced I expect."

"I imagine so. It's just, you know, a bit weird."

"What's weird?"

"Nothing really. It's just that she's not even my girlfriend and yet she gave it to me."

"*What?*" Now it was Danny's turn to sound incredulous.

I reached into my purse for the tissue she'd given me the previous night. I dangled it in front of Danny, just out of his reach.

"What's it worth?" I said, laughing.

"I can't believe she did that."

"She's my new best friend, according to you. Well, in the top two, anyway."

"Pass it here."

I moved it further away. I don't know why I enjoy being so annoying.

"Make me an offer. At the very least it's got to be worth dinner. Although no, not dinner, that's too bloody dangerous. A nice pair of shoes perhaps?"

"Are you serious?"

"Maybe not shoes. Maybe being excused the kitchen rota for a week."

"You're taking the piss."

"Ooh, two weeks. Going up."

"Pass it here and when this all gets sorted I'll take you to dinner and buy you shoes and do the full kitchen rota for a week."

"Month."

"Christ. A month then."

"And breakfast in bed every morning for a month too."

"For God's sake. Deal."

I passed him the tissue, grinning to myself. We both knew he'd never stick to it. He hated cleaning the kitchen but it was worth a try.

"What's your plan now?" he asked.

I looked at my watch. It was coming up to twenty to three.

"No plans, really. Do you want me to leave you to it?"

"You could do. I'm sorry there's nothing more exciting. Don't get me wrong, it's lovely having you here, and of course you can stay and chat if you want to, but I ought to try to work for a bit so if you've got something you'd rather be doing, I don't mind."

"That sounds like a plan."

"Do you want to come back this evening? I feel a bit guilty dragging you out all the time."

"I was assuming, presuming, whichever, you'd be having an early night."

"I probably will. I'm knackered already."

"Let's say I won't come back this evening then, although call me if you need me. I'll phone the hospital to see how you are and see what time you're getting released then pop back in the morning to collect you. Good plan?"

"That sounds perfect."

I bent down to give him a kiss on the cheek and made sure he was comfortable before saying goodbye. There was no need to mention the date unless I had to. I didn't see the need to cause any extra worry, although I wasn't in any case planning on doing anything that he'd need to worry about.

I was about to be reminded that things don't always go according to plan.

Chapter 33

THERE was an atmosphere of quiet industry at the Albermarle Casino and Gentleman's Club. The venue was closed for the afternoon, but preparations were underway for a traditionally busy Friday evening. Bars were being restocked and a cleaner was vacuuming the carpets, while the air was thick with the pine-fragranced scent of the fresh polish on the gaming tables. Next door in the dance bar, the stage was being swept and the chrome pole wiped with a chamois leather. An electrician was making adjustments to the main stage lighting rig.

Jacqueline Glover would be down in a few minutes to check that everything was on schedule, just as soon as her meeting had ended, but for now she had even more pressing concerns.

"So, your man fucked up," she said, looking at the person on the other side of the desk.

Mikołaj held up his hands.

"What can I say? He let me down. He'll be dealt with."

"I don't like it. I don't like loose ends. Do I need to send Finn to get the job done properly?"

"Jacqui, let me assure you, there is nothing to worry about."

"Nothing to worry about? March has been meeting some fucker of a journalist, discussing God knows what, and the next thing we know the weedy twat's making a house call to your place for a rub down. And you don't think that's anything to worry about? And all you've succeeded in doing is drawing attention to him without actually eradicating the problem. Maybe I'm old-fashioned but I'd say that was grounds for concern."

"I can see that. But we have to hold our nerve. Two more days, Jacqui."

"And then what?"

"And then the shipment arrives and we can go back to normal."

"I meant about March."

"Don't worry about him. Graham March will cease to exist."

"Fucking glad to hear it."

Mikołaj smiled and took a sip of his whiskey. He had to trust she wasn't recording this conversation, but he didn't think she'd be that stupid. She was ruthless, but not suicidal.

"How's your guy Logan doing?" he asked.

"You let me worry about him."

"Is he making progress?"

"Are you listening to me? Let me worry about him. And he better fucking had be."

"Is he getting close?"

Jacqui glared at the man opposite but relented.

"Apparently. According to Finn. Says he's getting everything he needs tonight. He'd better come here tomorrow with actual progress or he's getting fired at the very fucking least."

She'd had enough of this. It was time to call a halt to the meeting.

"Right, I've got to get on," she said. "Call me as soon as you get word that they're on the way. And if anything else goes tits up I want to hear about it from you. Personally. All right?"

Mikołaj acquiesced. The last thing he needed now was any drama from within.

———

In a quiet corner of the World's End pub, opposite Camden Town tube station, Graham March looked past the pint of Castlemaine XXXX he'd placed on the table, and focused instead on the woman taking the chair opposite. She was in her late twenties, with flowing auburn hair. Dressed casually in a denim jacket, short black skirt and opaque tights, she retained a certain air of seductive sophistication that appealed to his baser instincts. She spoke with a cut-glass accent that smacked of home counties privilege, although he thought she looked tired beneath the make-up, presumably as the result of a tough few days. She was, unquestionably, very much his type, which was why he was delighted when she'd called to invite him for a drink.

"Long time, no see, Graham," she said.

"Ah Holly my dear, indeed it is. Must be what, six days?"

"Six exactly, give or take an hour. Not since the night Steve..."

Her voice drifted off. She took a sip of her martini and lemonade.

"A tragic outcome," said March, keen not to dwell too much on the past. The night ahead was potentially much more exciting.

"Have you heard any more on the grapevine about what they think might have happened?" she asked.

"Me? No. I'd be the last to know, my dear, I'm afraid I am, what I like to call, persona non grata around those parts. For the time being, anyway, until they realise they cannot do without me."

"Surely that can't be long, for a man of your obvious abilities."

He liked the way she smiled at him. If she was trying to turn on the charm he'd be happy to encourage her, despite the obvious danger. But hey, what a way to go.

"Cigarette?" She offered him a packet of Silk Cut.

"Not for me, my darling, thank you. I only smoke in the company of a certain journalist when I want to annoy him."

"Danny?"

"Yes, young Danny."

She laughed.

"And how is he? Have you seen him recently?"

"I saw him on, ah, Tuesday, as it happens. We partook of a swift beverage. I'm trying to interest him in an article on my charitable work, but he doesn't seem to see the benefits quite yet. And, of course, I wanted to stress that it would be unwise to delve too deeply into the demise of our good friend Steve."

"Quite."

"And yourself?"

"Wednesday. They put me up for a night."

"I heard. Was it enlightening?"

"Not as much as I'd have hoped. Strangely they seem to think I hardly know you. I can't think what gave them that impression."

"Holly, you're a very naughty girl."

"The night is still young, Graham." She blew smoke at the ceiling, reached forward, and gave his leg a squeeze under the table.

"Mmm, you are a delectable tease. I must introduce you to my good friend Giancarlo. His carbonara is to die for. And he has a wonderful Vermentino in the cellar."

"That sounds delicious." Her expression suddenly became more serious.

"Talking of Danny, you haven't been to visit him in the hospital yet then?"

March gave her a quizzical look.

"No, not yet. I've been otherwise preoccupied with Seb. But I'm not sure I'd be welcome. It's another terrible thing."

"It's a dangerous world, Graham. We should always bear that

in mind. I was thinking of going, and popping my head in on Leah while I was there."

"Ah, the poor girl."

"Indeed. The prognosis looks bad."

"Really? I heard she was on the verge of regaining consciousness."

Holly raised her eyebrows and stubbed out her cigarette.

"I'd better get a move on then," she said.

March subconsciously felt for the tape machine in his inside pocket. He just hoped the microphone was sensitive enough to be picking this up.

Chapter 34

WITH a free afternoon, and nothing much to do apart from think about Danny and the general sense of mounting chaos, albeit with a slight tingle at the prospect of a romantic evening, I decided I may as well tidy the flat after all, with, ahem, specific attention to my bedroom. And of course, as it was my first night back in my own room since Holly had stayed, I had to change the bedsheets too. Purely for personal hygiene reasons, obviously, and nothing at all to do with inviting anyone back at any point. Or so I told myself, rather unconvincingly.

I kept thinking of things that Holly could have stolen, but each time I checked, they were still there. Maybe I'd done her a disservice. Perhaps it was just a touch of paranoia on my behalf, coming on top of doubts expressed by Danny. I wondered how she was. I didn't really expect to ever see her again, apart from maybe at Steve's funeral, whenever that might be.

Just the thought of the funeral filled me an overwhelming sadness. He had so much to live for. It was so unfair. I wondered if the police were making any progress in finding out what had happened to him. And to Leah for that matter. It had certainly been a traumatic few days. I felt a bit like the last person standing, which made me nervous, but then I was equally unaware of being in any personal danger. I'm just a fashion photographer. Not really a threat to anyone.

By half past five the place was reasonably spotless, and I headed back to the shower. I decided to really make an effort with my appearance, so it was the full treatment with the hair and make-up. I opted for smoky eyes and pale lipstick and then chose some simple jewellery - all to add drama to my best black dress. I ditched the tights in favour of rather sexy lace-top hold-ups, which I had to hope would actually stay up, and then went back to the uncomfortable shoes which were fearsomely high, but that's one of the perks of being little. I couldn't decide if I looked like a seductive femme fatale or a complete floozy, hoped it was the former, feared it was the latter, and then decided that as Mitch was a man he'd probably prefer the floozy anyway.

I drove to the restaurant. There was a logic to this. It was chucking it down with rain again, so it was good to minimise exposure to the elements. Furthermore, I knew I was feeling reckless, so driving meant I wouldn't be tempted to drink. I wanted to remain in control. Unless, of course, the evening went well and we did, by some fluke of circumstance, end up back at my now very-presentable flat which, just coincidentally, I had to myself for the evening. And if that was the case then the couple of bottles of Cava I'd absent-mindedly left in the fridge should help things go very smoothly indeed. Until that point, however, I always had a get-out clause. I don't give myself away lightly.

"Wow, you look amazing," said Mitch as I approached his table. I smiled. It was an encouraging start.

"Thank you," I said. "You look very lovely too." I was pleased to see he'd also made an effort. He had a crisp white shirt again, with elegant double cuffs, just popping out from the sleeves of his beautifully tailored navy jacket. I momentarily thought of his arms, and how much I'd like to be within them by the end of the evening.

"I've ordered wine," he said, as I took a chair.

"Ah, not for me, thank you. I'm driving."

I could see a flash of disappointment cross his face, but he did well to rein it in.

"Could you not leave the car and we'll share a taxi?"

"Not tonight, alas," I said. "Although if you play your cards right, I may offer to give you a lift home."

"Mmm, intriguing. Your place or mine?"

I just winked and left the question unanswered.

"You can drink though, I don't mind," I added.

"I'll see if they'll let us take the rest of the bottle home. If I drink the whole thing on my own I'll be langered."

That was a new word.

"You'll be what?"

"Sorry, pissed."

"What on earth's langered?"

His cheeks seemed to colour slightly.

"Nothing, Just a bit of Irish slang. From a script I'm learning."

"Exciting. New role?"

"Maybe, if it goes well."

"Film, TV?"

"No, it's just a student thing, but it's all good for the showreel if it comes off."

"Fingers crossed then." I had a devilish thought. "Go on then, give me a line. I can't wait to hear your Irish accent."

"No! It's embarrassing."

"Actually, that's a point, I thought you had an Irish accent when I first heard you on the phone at the tube station. I'd forgotten about that."

"Really? I don't know why that was. I'd just been on at the studio though, so maybe I was practising."

I was tempted to press the point but I decided to let him off for good behaviour.

"Okay," I said with a grin. "For your information, I'm not getting 'langered' or pissed or anything else for that matter, but feel free on my behalf."

The waiter came over and I ordered a Diet Coke without ice. The ice destroys the bubbles.

"So," he said, once we were back on our own, "tell me about your long night."

"Oh, you wouldn't believe..."

And then it all came out, although I did my best to be vague, omitting some of the details where I knew there were confidences that shouldn't be betrayed. I didn't mention Clare by name, nor that she'd reappeared and seemingly saved us.

He said I'd been very brave, but I tried to play that down. Then, as the conversation flowed, he told me about a couple of auditions that he'd been preparing for, and explained the secret of learning lines. Apparently it's not a memory test. If you properly analyse the script, and the emotions and motivations, and fully embrace the needs and wants of the character, then the lines you have should be a natural response to whatever the other person is saying. It all sounded very psychological. Clearly there was a lot more to the whole acting lark than just standing up, talking, and occasionally jumping off a moving train.

At some point the waiter arrived and took our order. At some other point the food arrived. And at a third and final point I asked for the bill, only to discover that Mitch had already settled it. It all seemed to pass so quickly. As we stood up to leave the table, he helped me with my jacket.

"So," he said, raising his eyebrows as we arrived at the exit. I reached for his hands.

"Thank you, again, for another lovely evening," I said, acknowledging the unspoken question. "We should go to the cinema some time, if you're up for that. You can point out all the technicalities." I knew what he was really asking but didn't want to look too keen.

"I would, definitely. I like the thought of people thinking you're my girlfriend."

He put his arm around me. We kissed. My resolve weakened.

"It's still only quarter to nine," he said. "The night is yet young."

He was asking again. My last ounce of self-restraint departed at the thought of what might lie ahead.

"Would you like to come back for coffee?" I asked.

He squeezed me slightly tighter.

"Do you mean coffee or 'coffee'?"

I wasn't quite sure what I meant, although secretly I had an inkling, and it didn't involve caffeine.

"Wait and see," I said with another wink, which, knowing my luck, probably made him think I had a twitch.

When characters in films finally make it across the threshold, they usually rip each other's clothes off before even getting fully past the hallway. This was considerably less dramatic. I showed Mitch through to the spotlessly tidy living room, asked if he'd like a glass of Cava or actual coffee, and then asked him to give me a minute while I phoned the hospital to check in on Danny. He suggested Cava, thankfully, so I excused myself and took the phone through to the kitchen.

My first shock came when I got through to the ward and asked how he was. The nurse on duty said she'd check, then came back on the phone a few moments later.

"He's making good progress," she said. "He should be ready to come home tomorrow. His sister's with him now."

"His sister?" Danny hasn't got a sister.

"Yes. She said to let you know if you called. She's been trying to call your mobile apparently."

"Ah, okay. Sorry. It's been a long day. My phone must be off." I reached into my bag on the kitchen table and found my mobile. There were three missed calls, all from Clare's number.

"So she has. My apologies. I'll give her a call now," I said. "Thank you for passing on the message."

"No problem. Hopefully we'll see you tomorrow. The doctor does his rounds any time between eight and ten, so if you come after that you should be able to take him."

"Brilliant. See you then, and thank you."

I rang off, and walked back to the living room, and apologised to Mitch that I was going to take longer than I thought. He said it was okay and not to worry. I think the glass of wine helped. I went back to the kitchen and dialled Clare's number from my mobile, much more calmly and less annoyed than I'd have been a day ago.

"Is that Danny's sister?" I asked when she answered on the third ring.

"Anna, hi. Are you okay? I've been worried about you."

"I'm fine. I've just been out to dinner. What's up? Is everything okay with Danny?"

"Yes, he's good. We've just been going through the case, putting everything in order. Hold on, I'll pass you over."

There was a pause and then Danny came on the line.

"Hi, Anna," he said.

"I didn't know you had a sister."

"Shhh, not so loud. Listen, are you busy?"

"What? Right now?"

"Yes. Have you got much on? I need a favour, although it's quite a big one."

I didn't have the heart to tell him I had considerably more on than I hoped I'd have in a few minutes.

"It depends. What's that favour?"

"I need to ask you in person."

"Right. Can it wait till the morning?"

"Hmmm." He went silent.

"What is it?"

"It's just it would be better tonight."

"*Tonight?*"

"Yeah. Why, what are you up to?"

"Just at this minute talking to you, but I was about to go to bed." Again, elaboration was not required.

"That's a bit early. Have you been drinking?"

"No, as it happens."

"That's good. Would you be able to come in?"

"What, now? Is it not a bit late for visitors?"

"I've spoken to the nurses and they said it's okay as it's a private room."

"I know, but Danny, it's nine o'clock."

"Just gone five to, really."

"All right, Mr Pedantic, but the same thing applies. Can it not wait till the morning?"

"Not really. But you never go to bed this early normally anyway. I wouldn't ask if it wasn't important."

"Jesus."

"Sorry. Look, if it's a problem tomorrow's fine."

"No, it's not a problem. I'll come in. You owe me though."

"Shoes and kitchen rota?"

"A damn sight more than that. I'll be there as soon as I can."

I rang off. Typical bloody men. Inside a part of me screamed.

I went back to the living room. Mitch was looking at something on the desk but stopped as soon as I entered, presumably having a sneaky peek into my private world. I didn't know whether to be annoyed or flattered, but I could feel a bad mood coming on so knew I should probably give him the benefit of the doubt.

"Everything all right?" he asked.

"No, not really. I've got to go to the hospital. I'm so sorry."

"That doesn't sound good. Is he okay?"

"He's fine, I think. But apparently I'm needed."

"Would you like me to come with you?"

I thought for a moment.

"No, thank you," I said. "That's a lovely offer but I don't know how long I'll be. I can give you a lift home, though." I suddenly realised I had no idea where he lived.

"No, don't worry." He sounded as disappointed as I was. "I don't mind walking. The exercise will do me good."

I gave him a hug. I'm useless at relationships at the best of times, but this one seemed like it was suffering from more external challenges than most. It was just such a turbulent time. Maybe completely the wrong time. But my fear was that by the time the moment was right, he'd have moved on, and I'd have blown any chance I might have had for happiness.

"It's not always like this," I said, mainly to try to convince myself. I knew it usually was.

Mitch put his jacket back on.

"Can I still call you?" I asked.

"Of course."

He kissed me on the nose, which seemed remarkably intimate. I showed him to the door.

"Are you sure I can't give you a lift?"

"I'm sure," he said. "You get going, as soon as you can. Don't worry. We'll get a chance. I'll call you tomorrow."

Tomorrow couldn't come soon enough.

Chapter 35

CLEARLY I needed to get changed into something less obviously seductive, but then I thought, Clare's there, so fuck it. I went as I was.

I parked up at the hospital just before half past nine and made my way through to Danny's ward. I was stopped by a security man who told me visiting had finished, but seemed to believe my story about being needed urgently at the bedside of a dying relative. Danny wasn't a relative, as such, but there was a reasonable chance I was about to strangle him, so the story wasn't completely without foundation.

The lights were low on the ward, but a nurse came when I buzzed the entrance door and I was allowed in. I went straight through to Danny's room, nodded to the policeman on guard who recognised me, thankfully, and opened the door without knocking - half hoping to catch them at it just so I could be proved right after all.

Instead, Danny was propped up on the bed. Clare was in the chair in which I'd spent the previous evening. The bed was covered in pieces of paper, both A4 sheets and pages from notebooks, and Danny's ThinkPad was switched on and open on the bed beside him. Clare got up when I arrived.

"I'm so pleased to see you," said Danny. "Wow, you look gorgeous. What's with the outfit?"

"Thank you," I said, ignoring the question. Clare just smiled and gave me a conspiratorial wink, as though she knew exactly what I'd just been up to. Knowing Clare, she very probably did. She hung up my coat and then offered to go to get us all a cup of tea. I think it was just an excuse for her to go and have a cigarette somewhere, but one day, maybe, I'll learn to give her the benefit of the doubt.

"So, what's the big favour and why the rush?" I asked when she'd gone, after taking the chair. I could feel Danny's attention on my legs, so I crossed them, but I think that made things worse.

"Have you been out somewhere?" he asked, rather than answering me.

"I had, but I was home when I called. The favour?"

"With Mitch?"

"Does it matter who it was with?"

"Yes of course it matters. It breaks my heart to think I'm losing you, if you must know."

"Oh, Danny." I reached for his hand. "You're not losing me. We'll always be us. I'm just having a bit of fun because it does me good. But tonight isn't really the time to get into all of that because it's already late and I'm super tired, and you said it was urgent."

"Okay." He let go of my hand and propped himself up in bed. "We should probably wait till Clare gets back, but I'll give you the background. We've been going through all the research, and interviews, everything we know, everything we assume, everything I found out in Germany."

"You've been busy then. What time did she get here?"

"About half an hour after you left."

"Lordy. That's quite a stint. What happened to your early night?"

"That didn't happen."

"Evidently." To be fair to Clare, though, that was quite a commitment. I found myself in deeply unfamiliar territory trying to be fair to Clare, but credit where it's due, she was putting in some effort, and not without considerable risk to her personal liberty. While I was thinking that, the door opened and she came in holding a small tray with three plastic cups of vending machine tea. I tried to detect the aroma of smoke, but there was no more than normal, so all credit to her for that too. No credit at all for the quality of the tea though, which looked awful as usual, but I doubted that was her fault.

"What have I missed?" she asked.

"Nothing really. Danny was just saying you'd been reviewing the evidence, as it were."

"That's good. Should I take over?" She looked at Danny, who nodded.

"Can I stop you if I have any questions?" I asked.

"Of course."

"And can we fast forward to the bit where we get to the favour?"

She laughed.

"We'll be there in a moment. Thank you so much for coming in, though. And sorry for ruining your evening."

Her eyes were sparkling again. She bloody well knew.

"Don't worry about it. I'm sure there'll be others." I looked at Danny, who seemed be suffering a mixture of emotions that I couldn't quite identify, although if I'd had to stake my life on it, I'd say excitement and a degree of jealousy were in there somewhere.

"Let's go back to the beginning," Clare continued, "although I'll try to keep it brief. We were investigating March, as you know, last year."

"Before you disappeared."

"Exactly." She took a deep breath, as though it was a sore point for her too. Never mind. "At the time we thought he was your standard bent copper, into a bit of evidence removal, protection and a sideline in vice."

"Don't forget the bit about being an obnoxious, sexist twat," I added.

"Of course, although sadly, Anna, there are lots of people like that in the world and it's not actually a crime in itself, more's the pity. The other bits are, though, so we investigated, found evidence, Danny wrote a story and that should have been that. However, rather than being sent down as he should have been, he somehow managed to escape with just a suspension after protesting his innocence, while a full investigation took place."

"Which is where we're up to now."

"Exactly."

"I continued doing investigations of my own," interrupted Danny, "and in the process, I discovered that he was spending his leisure time doing things that were far, far worse."

"The people trafficking."

"Correct."

"And that's why you went to Germany?"

"Yeah. And as we know, the girls end up as prostitutes, working out of parlours or for escort agencies, or even at strip clubs where they're forced to offer extras on the side."

"Like the casino?"

"Exactly. Anyway, while I was in Cologne I met some people who confirmed March was involved, but it's been difficult to get any evidence on record. This is our chance, though. It looks like there's a new group of girls coming in on Sunday."

"But that's when we run into a problem," continued Clare, "because not everything adds up."

"Oh. How come?"

"That's what we've been trying to work out. The trouble is, it all seems a bit too easy, and he's a devious bastard, so we just don't think he'd be so blatant - especially when he unquestionably knows he's being watched. And then you've got the parlour and casino, which seem a little bit obvious too."

"But maybe it is just that simple," I said. "Maybe he's so arrogant he thinks he can't get caught, or he's got friends in high places who will protect him. Like that politician bloke."

Clare smiled.

"Now you're getting there," she said, reaching for a notebook. "But the trouble is, it appears to be an awful lot more complicated than even that. Because for some reason Steve got killed, Leah got attacked and Danny got shot. And when we started to look into those, we started to realise that maybe everything we'd assumed so far was wrong."

Mitch had enjoyed his evening with Anna. She seemed like a nice girl and was clearly keen. He liked that. In other circumstances, she was maybe the kind of girl he'd enjoy corrupting, so it was a shame, really, that things had to be the way they were.

Obviously it would have been a perk to have taken her to bed. He'd have liked that. He'd have liked to have seen the fear in her eyes when he'd tied her up. He would have liked to have heard her scream. It would have been thrilling to see the look of panic when she realised she was completely under his control, and then fun to witness the complete sense of terror when she realised what he was about to do to her.

So yes, it was a shame she'd had to go out. It would have been fun showing her exactly who'd she'd been dating over the last few days. Maybe he should spare her for now, so he could go back there one night when she wasn't expecting him, and resurrect the original plan. Maybe as the summer came and she left a window open. It was a delicious prospect.

There'd be others, though. There always were. So maybe he'd just have to kill her in some other way. The job needed doing, whether it came with the added bonus or not. But he could think about that after his meeting. For tonight, she'd already told him everything he needed to know, without ever naming names. She didn't need to. The evidence was there on her desk. That picture of March and the old guy pretty much sealed the deal.

He pushed open the door to Jacqueline Glover's office at the Albermarle Casino and Gentlemen's Club. She looked up as he entered the room.

"Logan," she said. "About fucking time."

Chapter 36

I TOOK a sip of the tea. It was as filthy as I'd feared. I put the cup on the side and decided I'd just go for Diet Coke in future.

"The band thing caused us problems," Clare continued. "It just didn't seem to be connected, but Danny was fairly insistent that it must be. It was all too much of a coincidence."

"Okay, but how?" Not for the first time that evening I was glad I'd managed to avoid alcohol.

"Well, there was their name for starters. Lumière Rouge. Red light. And I don't need to tell you what that's synonymous with."

"But that *is* just a coincidence. Surely?"

"Maybe. Or maybe someone having an elaborate joke. Hiding in plain sight. So, we had a brainstorm and thought: what do we actually know about the band. Who are Steve, Leah and Holly?"

"Steve was my friend's brother. He was all right. That's how I got to meet them."

Clare started leafing through the notebook. She nodded.

"Here we go. Steve Baca. Singer. His background seems quite normal. Grew up in London, did well at school but always loved performing. He was in school plays, joined the choir, took singing lessons and eventually ended up in the band."

"How do you know all this?" I was part curious, part nervous in case I ever got on the wrong side of her.

"Ways and means, Anna," she said, without elaboration.

"I told you she was good," added Danny. Clare laughed.

"There's loads more, but in essence he does indeed seem like a good guy," she continued. "But he obviously knew something or - perhaps even more likely - saw something or someone, and that's what got him killed."

"Jesus. And the same for Leah?"

"Ah, no. I'll come on to Leah. She's key to all of this, but let's look at Holly first. Danny says you both had suspicions she was stealing things from the flat."

"We did, although I spent this afternoon tidying up, and couldn't see anything missing."

"That makes sense. Okay, Holly Rowan. Danny says she told you she grew up near Winchester in Hampshire."

"She did." I gave her a summary of my conversations with Holly, as best as I could remember them.

"Good. And she seems to have come from a privileged background, private school, all the usual. The trouble is, I couldn't find any mention of a Holly Rowan anywhere."

"Maybe she changed her name. Maybe Holly Rowan was her stage name."

"That's exactly what Danny thought. Or maybe she didn't grow up there at all. But apparently she also told you she'd come to London as a student?"

I nodded.

"That's good. But I checked all the universities and old polytechnics and nobody had ever heard of a Holly Rowan there, either. So either that was a lie too, or she did just change her name. I started digging a little bit deeper and then bingo! I had her."

This sounded exciting.

"Go on," I said.

Clare turned a few more pages.

"Okay. I found a girl. She fitted Holly's description, and does indeed come from near Winchester. Private school, very wealthy parents, came to London not really as a student, though, but more to have fun and spend her trust fund before settling down."

"That sounds like her."

"That's what I thought," said Danny, joining in. "So, we went one stage further. Sorry. I'm interrupting."

"That's okay. It's very much a joint effort," said Clare. "But yes, Danny phoned someone he knows at the Standard, and asked her to bike over some shots from the Londoner's Diary picture archive. When they arrived, we had the proof. It's definitely her."

"Excellent. So who is she?"

"Ah, well that's the interesting thing. Her real name is Holly Elmhirst-Banks."

That name rang a bell. And then it clicked.

"You mean like the politician."

"Exactly. It transpires Holly is his daughter."

The phone rang. Samuel Elmhirst-Banks pressed the mute button on the TV remote before answering. He recognised the number.

"Any news?" he asked.

"All still good," said Holly. "I've met him."

"Good girl." He allowed himself a small sigh of relief. "How was he?"

"Complete sleazebag as ever but we've got him under control now, I promise. It's all go for Sunday."

"Sure?"

"Definitely sure. And I'm meeting the Poles tomorrow. Neutral ground."

"Christ's sake be careful."

"I will. Don't worry."

He still had so many questions. He hated being this far away from the main event, trusting others to manage the clean-up, even though he couldn't get his own hands dirty, for obvious reasons.

"Did he mention Jacqui?"

"He did."

"And? Is she going to be a problem?"

"Only insofar as she sees herself as the ringleader."

"Inevitable. But we can work with her?"

"Definitely. She was fine when I spoke to her. She seems switched on."

"Okay. Well, it's your judgement. Keep me informed."

"I will."

"And Leah?"

"Being dealt with."

"Good girl."

He ended the call, replaced the handset and took another sip of his wine. So many things could still go wrong, but at least they were heading in the right direction. It was going to be a very stressful weekend, but oh so worth it, if it all went well.

Holly replaced the handset. She'd tried her best to be reassuring. It didn't help to reveal her growing unease. She'd sort everything. It wouldn't be a problem.

She'd wanted this opportunity. Wanted the chance to prove herself, to show her father that she could be trusted, that she had a place on the top table. She knew she couldn't let him down. And everything had been going so well, so smoothly, so under control. Right until Leah threw her grenade into the middle of everything she'd planned.

She'd known there was something different about Leah from the outset. Thinking back now, it was obvious really. The way she'd introduced herself. The way she'd latched on to Steve, her willingness to do anything to help, her relentless pursuit of a place in the band.

Of course, in some ways it had been a blessing. She was good, no doubt about that. Had everything proceeded smoothly and the band remained an exciting diversion, she'd have added real musical talent and a strong understanding of the importance of the visual.

All of that was good, but of course it was all just a sham, betrayed by the pursuit of the ulterior motive. The only surprise was that she hadn't spotted it sooner. Leah had ruined it now. Ruined everything. Self-torture, however, was counter-productive. Problems were there to be remedied.

She returned to her phone, and dialled a number. She knew exactly who to call. They'd built quite an alliance over the past few weeks. Not that she'd needed to tell her father yet. That would all come later.

"Hi Jacqui," she said when the call was answered. "I've got a bit of a favour to ask. I need to borrow Finn."

Chapter 37

THIS was beginning to sound more and more complicated.

"Hold on," I said. "This Seb bloke suddenly starts taking an interest in March just as his daughter's band hires him as their manager. That makes sense, kind of."

Clare was shaking her head.

"You'd think so, but it's not that straightforward."

"How come?"

"What did she tell you about how he got involved?"

I tried to think back. It was only two days since we'd had the conversation, but so much had happened.

"She said she didn't know him." I paused, trying to remember the exact words. "She said it was all done behind her back. Steve and Leah had met him the day I took the pictures to the rehearsal studio. The first time she laid eyes on him was the night Steve died."

Clare and Danny exchanged glances, both raising eyebrows. It was like a secret passed between them.

"What is it?" I asked.

Danny passed me a photograph. There, looking straight at the camera, was Holly, albeit looking maybe a couple of years younger. She seemed to be at some kind of reception, maybe a charity ball. Standing on one side was her father. On the other, with a sickly smile on his chubby face, was Graham March.

"Oh," I said. "Well, now I am confused."

"So were we," said Clare. "So we kept looking into it and it seems March and Seb are old pals, kind of like family friends. And Holly's what? Mid to late twenties now? Seemingly she knew March very well indeed."

"But why try to hide it?"

"That's the next question. Because if she lied about that, what else was she lying about? Is it conceivable that Steve and Leah were meeting March when you went, but only to meet him for the first time because she'd already got him involved for whatever reason? And of course, she didn't need to go because she'd known him for years. But if that's also true, then maybe everything else she said and did was suspect too."

"Starting with needing somewhere to stay when she was allegedly too scared to go home," I said, thinking aloud.

"Exactly," said Clare. "And you both thought she was stealing something. But what if she wasn't stealing? What if she was looking for something? Like information."

"But what information was she going to find at our flat?"

And then it dawned on me. If March was a family friend and she was trying to protect him, what better way to try to get access to Danny, to find out what he was investigating, than to move in? God. She'd been left alone in the flat. She could have been up to anything.

"Shit," I said. "Oh, Danny. Clare. What a mess."

"And that brings us on to Leah," continued Clare. "We know very little about her except her full name, Leah Haddon, and that she was homeless for a while. We haven't been able to find out anything else about her background. Can you remember what she said to you?"

"What? On the phone?"

Clare nodded.

"God. Let me think. She said Steve wasn't an accident. Something about March fucking everything up. And she referred to 'the bastards' although she didn't say who they were. Shit. Do you think the bastards were March and Holly?"

"That's where we're getting to."

"But how? And why?"

"That's what we don't know. Because before she got to tell you, somebody tried to kill her. And knowing a bit about the way these kinds of people work..."

"As you do..."

"Quite. Knowing a bit about them, I think they're going to try to finish the job before she has a chance to come round again."

"Oh Jesus. Poor Leah." I tried to let that all sink in. "But surely she has police protection?"

"She does. But she's still very much at risk."

Clare looked up at Danny again. He nodded.

"What now?" I asked. "I wish you two wouldn't do that."

"Do what?" asked Danny.

"Keep looking at each other as though you're both in on some sort of grand secret."

"Sorry, Anna. It's just this is where we need the favour."

"I'd forgotten about that. Why do I get the impression this isn't going to be trivial?"

They looked at each other again. I may have sworn.

"Come on, out with it."

"Okay, but please hear me out," said Clare. "If you don't want to do it, that's fine. And please know that we wouldn't ask if there was any other obvious alternative."

"Understood."

"Right." She took a deep breath. "We need to speak to Leah. And sooner rather than later."

"But she's lying somewhere in this hospital, completely unconscious."

"She is. Or at least she was. She's expected to come round very soon. And we need to make sure we get to her first. As soon as she can speak, she's going to be in very real danger."

"Shouldn't we just be trying to make sure that she isn't in any danger?" I asked. "Surely that's the most important thing."

"It is," said Danny. "And I've spoken to Amy and suggested she double up on security. But we need to get in there as well. We need to speak to her first, before anyone, police included. Once the police do an interview, it's going to be very hard to gain access."

"Right. And how do you do that? Presumably you can't just go along."

"No," said Clare. "But we've got a plan." She paused, as though picking up courage. "We need you to dress up as a nurse and then get in to see her."

I looked at her, looking for any hint of a smile, but she looked deadly serious.

"*What?*" I asked.

"Danny can't do it, obviously. He's covered in bandages. And I can't do it either. Well, I could, and I will if I have to, but there's quite a big risk if I do it. If anything goes wrong and I get stopped, and then they work out who I am, I'm in a world of trouble."

"But what if *I* get stopped?"

"It's not very likely, but if you did, the worst that's going to happen is you get arrested."

"Oh, brilliant."

"I know. It's not ideal. But only until Danny speaks to Amy and then you'd be absolutely fine. Honestly, I don't think it would happen."

"I could get somebody from the Echo," added Danny, "but when Leah comes round, she's going to be very confused and quite possibly terrified. She already knows you. She'd trust you. You already know she wants to talk to you."

"Right. But a couple of questions. When am I supposed to do this? And where on earth do I get a nurse's uniform?"

I saw Clare's eye move to a small pile of clothes on a spare chair in the corner of the room. That answered that.

"My size, I assume?"

"I believe so," she said.

"And when?"

"That's a bit harder. She could come round at any time. The bigger issue is to get you in and out of there without arousing suspicion. We were thinking around 6am, towards the end of the night shift, before breakfast kicks in."

"Bloody hell. You're actually serious about this." I was struggling to get my head around it. "Assuming I'm successful and don't actually get locked up, what am I supposed to be asking?"

"Just everything she knows about what happened. Everything about March and Holly. Everything about Steve. I can give you a tape machine to record whatever she says. There are no questions as such. Just ask her what happened."

"Sorry, Anna," said Danny. "We wouldn't ask if there was an easier way."

It took me a moment to let everything sink in. It was terrifying, I had a strong suspicion I'd be useless, and I didn't have any confidence that the plan was actually going to work. But on the other hand, what option did I have?

"Okay," I said. "I'll do it."

Clare seemed to visibly relax, as though suddenly relieved of some great tension. She came over and gave me a hug. Danny just smiled at me and said thank you. We made arrangements for me to be back at the hospital just before six. I said I'd give it my best attempt with no promises.

"I have to go," Clare announced, after a moment, once

everything had settled down. "I've got a job to do. I'll leave you two to have a catch up, but I'll see you back here in the morning."

We said our farewells and she left us. I looked down at Danny. He reached for my hand.

"Thanks, Anna," he said. "You don't know how important this could be."

"Anything for you, Poirot," I replied, with a smile. But in truth I was suffering mixed emotions. Part of me was extremely pleased to be able to help, but the greater part actually found it quite exciting - assuming I could get my nerves under control. I looked at my watch. It was just past quarter past ten. I had just under eight hours, but I knew I wouldn't ever be able to get to sleep. A rather naughty thought crossed my mind. Maybe the night wouldn't be a disaster after all.

I chatted to Danny for a few minutes and then said I'd head home and be back fully rested in the morning. As I made my way across the car park, I dialled a familiar number. It was answered on the second ring.

"Hi Mitch, it's Anna," I said.

"Hey, how are things at the hospital?"

"All good. No big panic. Look, sorry to ring but I was just wondering if you were, you know, still interested in that 'coffee'?" If I wasn't going to get to sleep, I may as well have some rather enticing adult company. And I've always found excitement quite the aphrodisiac.

"At this time of night? Everywhere will be shut unless you want to go for a drink somewhere."

"I was more thinking back at mine. I've got the place to myself all night and I won't get called away again, I promise. And I've still got the Cava."

There was a moment's silence. I didn't know if it was

hesitation or just my imagination on overtime. Finally, he spoke.

"Yes, that sounds wonderful. Perfect timing in many respects. What time?"

"I'm just leaving the hospital. Should we say eleven? If that's too late please just say."

"No, it's perfect," he said. "I've been thinking about you."

"And likewise."

We ended the call and I headed home. I had a quite severe case of the butterflies, but the thought of what might lie ahead was enthralling. And in any case, if I was going to get arrested in the morning, I might as well make sure my last night as a free woman went with a bang...

Once I arrived home I checked my make-up and applied some finishing touches. I was pleased I hadn't got changed earlier in the evening. There wasn't time for another shower, but I hoped I was still reasonably fragrant. I poured a glass of the Cava, drinking it perhaps too quickly, but there were definitely nerves to be settled.

At exactly eleven there was a tap at the front door. I opened it and Mitch came in. We didn't speak. I just looked at him, with what I hoped would be perceived as a naughty smile. He had the appearance of somebody who knew exactly why he was there, and wasn't about to mess around.

This time we didn't make it past the hallway. He was straight on to me, with surprising force. I was almost taken aback by his enthusiasm. But then the force increased and it started to become quite painful. I asked him to be more gentle but the pressure only increased. I started to feel real pain. And then I caught a look in his eyes that I'd never seen before. A hardness. A cruelty. And as his grip intensified again, I tried to scream, but his hand was over my mouth, muffling the sound. It wouldn't have made a difference. There was nobody to hear me. It wasn't supposed to be like this. I suddenly realised that I might have just made a terrible, terrible mistake.

Chapter 38

MITCH dragged me by the hair through to the living room. My arms were twisted behind my back. I was powerless to fight back. He was much, much stronger than me. I tried pleading with him, but he just swore at me and slapped me hard across the face. He pinned me to the sofa, then removed his belt and used it to tie my wrists together, with my arms behind my back. The sharp edges of the leather cut into my skin.

"Mitch! What the fuck?" I cried, but he hit me again. And again. Harder and harder. The brutality increased. I was terrified. I was powerless. He put his hand over my mouth to try to stop me screaming. I tried to bite him but he just hit me again. There was a ringing in my ears where his fist connected. And then I felt his hand on my legs, pulling roughly at my dress, yanking it upwards. Still he didn't speak, but I could see evil in his eyes. I tried to kick him but it was futile. A punch to the stomach winded me. His hand approached the waistband of my underwear.

And then there was a bang. And he stopped. He looked at me. The pressure subsided, and he fell forward, landing on me. I could feel a wetness on my face, as though I'd been splashed with water. Warm water. Water that was thick, and red.

Mitch slipped off me and fell to the floor. And there, standing behind him, at the end of the sofa, gun and silencer in hand, was Clare.

I was too shocked to think straight. But then Clare was with me, comforting me, holding me, saying sorry to me for not acting sooner. None of it made any sense. I saw Mitch, lying on the floor, vacant eyes still staring at me. A pool of blood forming at the back of his head. I cried. I held on to Clare as though she was the only stable thing in the whole insane world. I felt her arms around me, her hand on my head, stroking my hair, telling me everything was going to be okay. When she let go I could see the blood on her hands. I had no idea what was happening any more.

Clare came in from the kitchen with two cups of tea. I'd moved to the armchair. Mitch was still lying on the floor, not moving. He'd never move again. Clare put the cups down on the table, pulled up a chair, sat next to me, and held my hands.

"So that was Mitch?" she said. I just nodded.

"Oh, Anna," she continued. She stroked my arm, shaking her head. Her hazel eyes looked directly into mine. "He wasn't Mitch. He was Logan McDonagh. Absolute fucking psychopath. He worked for Jacqui."

"But..."

"Shhh... Don't worry. I just wish I'd known earlier. I'm so sorry."

"But, what just happened?" My voice was shakier than I'd ever known.

"Hey, you're safe now. Come here."

I leaned forward. Again I felt the comfort of her arms. This was Clare, the woman I'd hated for over a year. Actually, hated doesn't even cover it. Despised, distrusted, detested even the merest mention of. And now, twice in two days, she'd saved my life. I wanted to cling to her like she was my own mother, although part of me wondered why trouble always seemed to follow in her shadow.

"Please," I said. "What on earth is going on?"

She squeezed me tighter.

"That, I'm afraid, is an indication of the people we're dealing with," she said. "He's been playing you. Has he been asking lots of questions? About Danny?"

I took a deep breath and shuddered.

"Yes, but I just thought he was interested in me. He said it sounded exciting."

"I'm sorry, Anna." Clare looked so strong. So calm. So in control. "He was using you. Trying to find out whatever he could. Whatever you knew. He's been lying to you since the very first time you set eyes on him."

I was still finding it all so hard to take in, even though my heartbeat was returning to normal.

"But the acting?"

"That bit was probably true. But that's why he was so good at playing the part."

"But how come you're here?"

"It's just as well I was," she said, smiling.

"You said you were going to do a job."

"I was. I'm sorry. Danny gave me his keys. I was going to stay here tonight. My job was to look after you. To be your bodyguard. We've both been terribly worried about you. I was supposed to hide away in Danny's room, out of sight unless you needed me. We didn't want to spook you and Danny said if he'd told you, you'd have refused. But I got held up on the way, and then when I got here I could hear screaming. I thought I was too late."

"You were just in time."

"In some ways. But you shouldn't have had to go through any of that. I'm so sorry."

A silence developed between us. Eventually I broke it.

"What are we going to do with him? Mitch? Or Logan or whatever he's called?"

"Don't worry. I know some people who specialise in cleaning."

Again, I looked at her. Who was she? Not for the first time I was glad she was on our side.

"Clare," I said, my voice so quiet I wasn't sure she'd even be able to hear it.

"What?"

"Thank you. I'm so sorry too. I've thought so many bad things about you."

"I know, but I understand that."

"Yes, but I just thought what I thought, based on what happened last year."

"Don't worry. It was a difficult time for all of us."

My face softened. It wasn't a smile as such, but heading in that direction.

"I doubted you. I didn't want Danny to have anything to do with you. In fact, I only phoned Mitch - Logan - because I was so pissed off that Danny was even speaking to you."

"You mustn't blame yourself."

"That's easy to say, but it's true."

"No, you didn't do anything wrong. He was playing you. Every moment from whenever you first met him, he's been working you. If you hadn't phoned him, he'd have found another way. It was always going to happen, Anna."

"God, I've been such an idiot."

"No. You haven't. There wasn't anything you could have done differently."

It was kind of her to say, but still I felt terrible. Dirty. I just wanted to lose myself in the shower, maximum heat. I didn't think I'd ever feel clean again. I'd kissed the bastard. I'd let him get close to me. I'd had feelings, for heaven's sake. I was going to go to bed with him. I shuddered again.

"Listen," said Clare, "if this changes things for the morning, I do understand. I don't expect you to go through with it now. You need to rest. I'll go to see Leah."

I shook my head.

"No," I said. "This changes nothing. We're going to absolutely fucking nail the bastards."

Chapter 39

Saturday, April 9th, 1994

I SLEPT for maybe two hours. When I woke up, the reality hit me and a wave of nausea passed through my system. I genuinely thought I was going to throw up. The week's events had played absolute havoc with my system. I got out of bed and staggered through to the bathroom, looked at myself in the mirror, shrank back in horror yet again and then rushed back to sit on the bed to try to shift the terrible light-headedness before I collapsed onto the bedroom floor.

Slowly I regained composure. Deep breaths helped. It was still dark outside. I could hear birds calling out to each other. The bedside clock said 4.27am. My hair was still damp from the shower I'd taken before going to bed, but I just wanted to get back under the water again. And never come out.

I could hear noises elsewhere in the flat. I don't know why, but I didn't feel scared. After last night, I didn't think anything would ever scare me again. I took my bathrobe from the back of the door, wrapped myself in it, and headed for the living room.

Clare was there, repositioning furniture. It looked just as it had early the previous evening. There was no sign of Mitch, and no sign of the pool of blood that had formed on the floor. Whatever she'd done, it was magical.

"How are you feeling?" she asked when she saw me.

"Shaky."

"I'm not surprised. I'll make you some breakfast."

I sat in the armchair, trying to come to terms with everything that had happened. There was one overriding realisation. I now had proof beyond all doubt that I was, as I always knew, completely shit at relationships.

I could hear Clare in the kitchen. I wanted to call out to her, but instead just took a few minutes to sit in silence, to collect my thoughts. How could I have been so stupid? And what on earth would have happened if she hadn't turned up when she did?

I was expecting tea and toast, but not for the first time, I'd underestimated Clare. She appeared through the doorway with a tray containing a plate full of food. Bacon, fried eggs, tomatoes, mushrooms, toast and - of course - a lovely looking cup of tea. There were two bottles: Heinz ketchup and HP sauce. I had no idea how she'd acquired all of the ingredients.

"I didn't know which you'd prefer," she said with a grin.

"Wow. This is amazing."

"I rather assumed you'd say you weren't hungry so I thought I'd force the issue. Nobody can resist the aroma of bacon."

I laughed.

"Thank you," I said. Okay, I admit it, she'd won me over. I just wanted to give her a squeeze. She joined me.

"Do you mind if I smoke?" she asked.

"Absolutely not, you deserve it," I said. And then, in a moment of devilment, I added: "Danny's got a packet of your cigarettes on the desk somewhere."

That made her laugh too.

"It was an empty box," she said. "I've got some new ones."

There was an easy atmosphere between us. It was surreal.

Only a few short hours earlier she'd killed a man in this very room, and saved my life in the process. Now it was like two best friends sharing a joke. I had to pinch myself to remember that this was Clare. She was capable of just as much wanton violence as the worst of them, but it felt enormously reassuring to have her on my side.

"Can I ask you a question?" I asked.

"Oh God. You can ask. Not promising I'll answer."

"I'm just curious. Are you okay?"

"Am I *okay*?"

"Yes. You know, happy."

She gave me a look that was impossible to read.

"I'm happy that I was here for you."

"Oh, me too. But that's not what I meant."

"I know that's not what you meant. How's the breakfast?"

"Lovely, thank you."

And that was the end of that.

I felt much better after food. I headed to the shower again. By half past five I was as awake as I'd ever be, fully dressed, and raring to go. Clare was in the living room, looking as impeccable as I'd ever seen her. I didn't think she'd slept at all, so I had no idea how she'd done it. An ever-dwindling part of me hated myself, because the bigger part was coming to the conclusion that she was amazing.

During the day, the parking options around the Euston Free Hospital were limited, but in the early hours of the morning the meter spaces were both free and readily available. Holly sat in her car, parked in a side street, and briefed the man sitting next to her.

Once he'd received his final instructions, Finn left her there, promising to return as soon as it was done. He made the five-minute walk to the main entrance. Getting past night security wouldn't be particularly difficult, but he was aware of the potential challenges caused by the inevitable CCTV. That's why he was wearing so many layers, to hide his natural body shape, and why his hair was hidden beneath an anonymous brand-free baseball cap, pulled low to cover his eyes.

The main desk was occupied by a bored-looking man in a security guard's uniform, reading a magazine. As expected, he didn't seem to notice the new arrival. The secret was to look like you belonged, like you knew exactly where you were going.

Once through, Finn followed the signs for the intensive care unit until he came to a locked set of double doors. He'd expected this. He didn't want to press the buzzer to gain access. That would only draw attention, and make sure he was noticed. He had to get to his destination without being seen by anyone. Somewhere, very close, lay Leah and her secrets. Holly needed to make sure those secrets were never revealed, and Finn was not going to let her down.

He found a dark corner. Somebody would go through the doors soon. And when that happened he'd sneak through before they swung closed again. It didn't matter how long it took, but he could feel his heartbeat quickening while he waited.

Chapter 40

I T was weird driving through the streets of north London with a wanted murderess in the passenger seat, especially as she'd so recently shown that she hadn't lost her knack, but I was very pleased she was with me. We agreed we wouldn't yet tell Danny the full details of what had happened as we didn't want him to worry about me unnecessarily. Personally, I was feeling surprisingly upbeat. I had my very own ninja assassin to look after me.

We did, however, agree that we'd need to cover the basics as they related to the case: specifically that we'd discovered more about Mitch, that he was a duplicitous shit, working for Jacqui at the casino, and that we'd now blown his cover. We decided to tell him that Mitch's entire pursuit of me had been one big scam and fact-finding mission, but opted to not mention that I'd invited him back to the flat for morally dubious purposes or that Clare had come to my rescue. We may one day have to reveal the last part of that, but I was very keen to keep the former a secret forever.

It felt equally strange to be working hand in hand with Clare on matters of subterfuge. She was, of course, the master of such dark arts. I reconciled it in my head by convincing myself it was a little white lie, designed not for personal gain but instead to protect Danny from any extra, unnecessary stress. And of course, the side benefit would be that he wouldn't think I'd been a complete idiot. I think it will be a very long time before I ever go out on a date with anyone again, although a girls' night out with Clare wouldn't be out of the question. Wow. I could hardly believe my complete transformation over the last thirty or so hours.

The hospital didn't have much of a car park, but there were plenty of spaces outside, so I left the Prelude safely under a street light and together we walked in, past the night security man who only gave us a cursory glance, and then through to Danny's ward. There was another new policeman on duty outside his room. He asked for ID before letting us through. Clare left me to do the talking, for obvious reasons. I was able to show him my bank card and a business card, but he wasn't having any of it. In the end, I just had to suggest he open the door and ask Danny personally if he'd like to see us.

Danny was sitting up in the bed, typing on his ThinkPad. He closed the screen when he saw us and waved us in. I felt like saying "told you so" to the policeman, but managed to resist. The last thing I needed to do was start the mission by alienating anyone that I didn't need to.

"Brilliant to see you. Did you manage to sleep?" he asked.

"For a little while," I replied. "It's been an interesting night."

I took the uniform and hid behind a screen to get changed while Clare filled him in on the details. To her eternal credit she didn't let me down, even when Danny probed for more. She was good, I'll give her that.

I have to admit, a nurse's uniform is not my best look. The dress was cornflower blue with white trim and a zip up the back, and despite it theoretically being my size, it wasn't particularly comfortable. My huge respect for nurses grew again. I stood there, behind the screen, evaluating the madness of the plan before I dared to emerge and face the ridicule of my so-called friends. Eventually, though, I picked up the courage, took a deep breath, and stepped out.

"Don't start," I said, with a look that hopefully conveyed a severe warning to contain their hilarity. To my deep surprise, however, neither laughed. They both seemed to have adopted a business-first, professional detachment. Clare came over to check the positioning of my little upside-down watch and name badge and then started work on my hair, tying it back so it lost most of its usual volume.

"You look perfect," she said, giving me a final appraisal. "Thank you so much for doing this."

I smiled at her. After last night it was the very least I could do.

"I can't promise it's going to work, but I'll give it a go."

"You can only do your best," said Danny. And then he thanked me too. I felt extremely nervous, but proud, in many ways.

"Let me give you this," said Clare. It was a tiny Sony NT-1 voice recorder. "It may not look much but you can fit an hour on each side of the tape. You may not get in at all, or you may only have a couple of minutes, but it's good to know you've got it if you need it."

I felt a bit like James Bond. I was half-expecting her to follow up with a pen that fired poisoned darts, but then realised I was maybe losing my marbles. She showed me the basics of how to use it and then gave me a clipboard with some hospital notes attached.

"What's this for?"

"It's all part of the bluff. If you look like you know what you're doing and you've got a purpose, you're much less likely to get stopped. It's like a hi-vis jacket. It's amazing how many places you can get into just by wearing one of those."

"I'll bear that in mind," I said with a grin.

"Do you know where you're going?"

"I was wondering about that. No idea, sorry."

"Don't worry. She's in the ICU, the intensive care unit."

She drew me a little map. It began to look familiar from the night Leah was admitted, although my memories of that whole episode were vague at best.

"The key thing to remember is to look like you belong there," Clare continued. "As soon as you hesitate or look around you, you'll start to look suspicious. If you're not sure you're in the right place, it's best to continue past and then double back rather than pausing to check. Leah will have a private room, but you'll hopefully spot it because there'll be someone from the police outside. You may have to buzz through to get through to the ward, but just say you've been sent down from admissions to check that she's in there, if you're asked. Blame a mix-up in the paperwork. I don't know. Something like that. I don't think it'll be an issue, though. Getting past the policeman will be your biggest challenge but I'm hoping they'll be used to nurses going in and out at all hours."

"It's not very secure, is it?"

"We don't know. It's probably more secure than it looks. You'll be all right, though. Don't take this the wrong way, but you don't look particularly scary." There was a cheeky look in her eyes.

"What if she's still unconscious?"

"We're stuffed. But you know what? Don't worry. There's nothing you can do. This is all a bit of a long shot. There's probably a 90% chance you'll come back with nothing, but it's worth a try. If we can get to her before the police, we're in business. The most important thing, above all else, is to be careful. First sign of trouble, get out of there. If you start to think your cover's blown, just abort. Okay?"

I nodded.

"Right," I said, when everything seemed in order. "Wish me luck."

Danny levered himself out of the bed and stood up, but looked a bit unstable. He gave me a hug. I turned and gave Clare a rather formal handshake. And then I gave her a hug too. Then I was on my way.

Finn had been waiting for nearly an hour without success. He was fairly convinced he couldn't be seen. The lighting was subdued, although the first rays of daylight were starting to creep in via a skylight further down the corridor. He'd found a hiding place, out of sight to anyone approaching the double doors from the outside, but close enough that he could make a dash for it, if an opportunity arose.

And then, in the distance, he heard a noise like a door closing. He stiffened, heart rate increasing further, but he was used to that. He was a professional. There was silence. Then he started to hear the squeak of shoes on the polished floor, getting closer. He tried to control his breathing, to be as quiet and as unobtrusive as possible. He got ready to make his move.

The footsteps got louder still. Finn shrank back further into the corner. The walking stopped, and he edged his head out of the corner, looking in the direction of the doors to the ICU. A small nurse, with her hair tied back, holding a clipboard, was pressing the entrance button. There was a pause. This was his chance.

A buzzing sound came from the door. The nurse pushed it open. The door opened wide and she walked through. Timing now would be critical. He had to catch it before it closed. The nurse disappeared and the door started to swing back.

He made a dash for it. Progress seemed agonisingly slow and the door was closing quickly. But just as it was about to close completely, he reached out with his foot and caught it, stopping its motion before it could lock again. Now he'd just give the nurse a moment to disappear and then he'd enter in his own time.

The toughest challenge lay ahead, but Holly had stressed the importance of silencing Leah. And now he had the element of surprise.

Chapter 41

S O far, so good. Getting access to the ward was relatively painless. I just pressed the button and the doors buzzed open. The next bit was likely to be trickier. I walked on, trying to look confident, consulting my clipboard to try to avoid direct eye contact with anyone who might see me. I walked past several private rooms with closed doors, but none had a policeman outside, so I didn't bother to look through the windows.

In the distance, I could see the ward sister sitting at the main desk in a darker blue uniform, presumably keeping watch, on call in case of emergency. The ward was almost silent apart from my footsteps, the familiar electronic hum and occasional bleeps emanating from the rooms as I passed them.

By a huge stroke of good fortune, the ward phone started ringing, just as I started to approach. The sister answered it. It was just the break I needed. I could see her looking at me as I walked past so I just nodded, and pointed at the clipboard.

"I'll come back," I whispered. She acknowledged me and returned to her call.

I continued on, trying my hardest to look like I knew what I was doing, but increasingly feeling that it could all go horribly wrong at any moment. I heard a door close behind me, but didn't look back. Any form of hesitation could be fatal to the plan.

I turned a corner. On the right I could see what I thought was my destination. There was a uniformed police officer sitting on a chair in the corridor, reading a magazine. Close to him was a door to a private room. I just had to hope it was Leah's.

He looked up as I approached.

"Good morning," I said, barely louder than a whisper. He returned the greeting.

"Peaceful night?" I asked. I hoped my voice sounded more confident than I felt.

"Very quiet," he replied. I got the impression he wasn't really the conversational type.

I checked my clipboard, to give the impression that I was doing something official, and then my hand moved to the door.

"Sorry, I can't let you go in there," he said. That wasn't a good development.

"To see Miss Haddon? Leah?" I asked.

"Sorry, strict orders."

"Glad to hear it," I said. "Can you come in with me? I just need to check a couple of details before she starts to get prepared for theatre."

He looked at me, assessing me.

"I wasn't told about this."

"I'm sorry," I said. "There was a cancellation late last night. You should have been informed. I can come back, though. What authorisation do you need?"

"What do you need to do?"

"Just check her bloods and temperature readings from last night. I don't need to take new ones. They'll do that before surgery." I had no idea where all that came from.

He nodded.

"Okay then, just for a minute. I'll have to come in with you."

It wasn't ideal, but it was better than nothing. At least I'd know if she was awake or still out for the count.

He unlocked the door and followed me in. Leah was sleeping. She looked terrible, even in the dim light of the room. So pale and small, and so fragile. A drip was connected to the back of her hand. I made a show of reading the reports clipped to the end of the bed, which was difficult in the near-darkness, and copied a few notes onto my own clipboard. Then I moved over to the machines and monitors by the bedside, and pretended to check the various readings. I had no idea what I was doing, but I wrote things down there, too.

"Has she been awake at all?" I asked the policeman.

"Don't know, sorry," he said.

"I'll see if I can wake her," I said, then turned to Leah and spoke slightly louder. "Leah. Leah. Can you hear me?" I rested my hand on her shoulder. Her breathing was steady but she didn't stir. It was hopeless. I hadn't been arrested but I hadn't managed to speak to her either. I was running out of time. I knew Clare and Danny had said it might all come to nothing, but I was so very frustrated. I just wanted to do a good job, but there seemed to be nothing more I could do with the policeman standing beside me.

"Okay, that's everything," I said. "Somebody will be along shortly."

We moved back to the door. He opened it and then followed me through, and then I was back out in the corridor, mission complete, but nonetheless a complete failure.

Suddenly we heard raised voices from further down the corridor. I could hear footsteps. It sounded like somebody was running. A door banged. A moment later the ward sister came running around the corner. She saw us. I thought I was about to have my cover blown completely, just to add an extra layer of disaster. Instead she called out for the policeman, asked him to come quickly, and he ran off in her direction.

This was my chance. I went back into Leah's room. It was now or never.

"Leah!" I called, much more loudly. I gave her a shoulder a more vigorous shake. She moved under my touch. I tried again, and then her eyes opened slightly, as though squinting at the sun, despite the subdued lighting in the room. She looked terribly confused. I just hoped I wasn't doing anything to harm her recovery.

"Leah," I said again, kneeling down beside her. "It's Anna."

Her eyes closed again. I had no idea what painkillers she was on, but I suspected they were keeping her very well sedated. I could hear noises in the corridor outside. I didn't know how long I had, but I suspected my time was running out, fast. More noises outside. Voices. Shouting.

"Leah, can you hear me?" I pressed record on the tape machine, just in case.

I took her hand, urging her to wake up, just for a moment. The noises outside stopped for a moment. I was getting desperate. I shook her shoulder again. Still nothing.

Then she spoke, in no more than a whisper.

"Anna?"

Everything seemed to happen in an instant. There was a noise at the door. I could see the handle moving, so I instinctively ducked down, out of sight. A split second later, the door to the room flew open. This is it, I thought. I'm about to get arrested. But from what I could see it was neither the policeman nor the nurse, but a black-clad figure in a baseball cap. He didn't seem to notice me on the floor on the other side of the bed, but instead rushed towards Leah.

To my absolute shock, he grabbed the pillow from beneath Leah's head, then placed it over her face and started pressing hard. It took me a second to realise what was happening.

"What the fuck?" I shouted, getting up as quickly as I could. I reached forward to grab the pillow, trying hard to pull it away.

The man looked at me, snatched the pillow, then threw a punch in my direction. I got out of the way just in time. More noises from outside. More banging.

The man looked at me then turned to the machines standing beside the bed, and started pulling out wires, trying to create havoc. I rushed to his side of the bed, and jumped on him. He was twice my size and shook me off easily. I got up again, tried to grab him by his jacket, taking a grip on layers of fabric. I pulled hard, trying to drag him away. He turned to hit me again. The blow connected with my ribs. It hurt. I lurched forward, trying to overpower him, but I'm not really big enough for that kind of thing. He pushed me away, then suddenly, as he turned to hit me again, I saw his face properly for the first time. He stopped mid-punch as he seemed to be assessing me too. There was a vacant sense of evil in his eyes.

And then he really did punch me, hard to the face. I was dazed, ringing in my ears. I stumbled, reaching out for the bed, trying to regain my balance. But before I could do any more, he turned, ran to the door, threw it open, and was gone.

Within seconds there was an almighty bang from outside, as though something was being smashed open. A moment later the policeman came running in, looking panicked.

"Where is he?" he shouted.

"He's just gone," I replied. He ran off again.

I had no idea what was happening, but I still had a mission to complete. I lifted Leah's head to replace the pillow. Her eyes opened again, but she looked dazed.

"Leah, talk to me," I urged.

"Anna?" she said again, her voice still barely audible.

"Yes, that's me. Don't mind the uniform. I shouldn't be here but I need to talk to you. I need to know what happened."

But still she looked confused. I tried again. She looked at me. Finally, she spoke.

"Anna, what's happening?"

"That's what I'm trying to find out," I said. "Can you talk to me?"

But then her eyes closed again. It looked like she was drifting back off to sleep.

"Leah," I urged, giving it one final try. "Tell me, what happened to Steve? Who did this to you? Was it March?"

Slowly she started shaking her head.

"No," she whispered. "Steve just saw me. That's why she killed him."

She?

"Who's she?" I asked. "What happened?"

"Holly."

"*Holly*? Holly killed Steve?"

She nodded. It was the smallest of movements but unmistakeable.

"Why did Holly kill Steve?"

"Because he saw us. When I told her."

"When you told her what?"

Her eyes closed again. She seemed to be drifting away from me.

"Leah," I urged. "Told her what?"

"That she's my sister."

"Your *sister*."

That was the end of the conversation. The door flew open again. It was the policeman.

"What happened here?" he asked.

I explained about the pillow, the punch and the machines.

"I'm going to need to take a statement," he said.

"Did you catch him?"

"No, but I've called for back-up."

"Can I just go and get a glass of water?" I asked. I needed to get out of there, fast.

He nodded.

I turned back to Leah.

"Okay Leah, don't worry. I'll look after everything for you," I said. "Try to get back to sleep."

I turned away and headed back up the corridor as quickly as I could without raising any more suspicion. On my left, a door was hanging off its hinges. It looked like whoever he was had managed to lock the policeman in a room. I didn't know how he'd done it but it was just as well I'd been there or Leah would now be dead.

The sister was still on the phone as I passed, voice raised, asking for hospital security, giving out a description. I walked straight past, but looked over as I did so and pointed to my clipboard again.

She called after me, but I carried on walking. Her voice got louder, but I just headed to the double doors, pressed the green button to release them, and then I was in the corridor outside. And then I ran, desperate to get back to Danny and Clare and equally as desperate to avoid bumping into the man again. He was still out here, somewhere. I slowed as I got further away, and then paused, trying to catch my breath.

From behind, somebody reached out and grabbed me.

Chapter 42

I SCREAMED, then turned, ready to fight, ready to lash out to try to save myself. But it wasn't the man, it was Clare.

"Shhh," she said.

"Jesus, you scared me," I replied, although I doubt she heard me over the pounding of my heart.

Clare took my hand, pushed open the door of a storeroom and led me inside.

"You need to get changed," she said, handing me my clothes in a carrier bag. "How was it?"

"Unbelievable, I just..."

She put her hand up to stop me.

"Actually, save it till we get back with Danny. I'm just so pleased to see you. Well done."

Her praise meant everything to me. Who'd have seen that coming?

She looked away as I got back into my normal clothes. I gave her the uniform and she stuffed it into the bag. Then she opened the door a fraction, checked the coast was clear, and led me back to Danny's room.

As we got there, something seemed terribly wrong. There was

no police officer guarding the door, and when we opened it, there was no sign of Danny.

Finn couldn't help but smile. Okay, it hadn't gone quite as well as planned, but he was resourceful. It was far from over. He listened to the noise in the ward from the relative security of somebody else's private room. The poor sod looked in a bad way, but didn't seem to notice his visitor. Not that it really mattered. He'd only be there for a moment.

There was a lot of noise outside. He could see the policeman running back towards Leah's room. Then the nurse appeared from within. They spoke to each other, and then she walked away, passing within inches of his door. He hadn't meant to hit her, but what choice did he have? She'd taken him by surprise. She shouldn't have been there.

The policeman seemed out of his depth. Some young sap posted on watch duty while the big boys were at work elsewhere. Cannon fodder really. Locking him in a storeroom had been fun, but he'd known it wouldn't hold for long.

Finn watched as the policeman rushed back towards reception, talking to somebody on his radio. And then the corridor was empty. This was his chance. Escape would be difficult. He had to hope that a window would open far enough, and if so that would certainly make things easier. But for now, while the corridor was empty, he had to head back to Leah's room and finish the job that he'd started.

Faced with Danny's empty bed, I immediately started to panic. Clare tried to place a reassuring hand on my arm, but I'd had enough shocks and trauma over the last few days to render that meaningless. My mind was in a world of its own, imagining the worst, fearing I'd never see Danny again, a new sense of nausea welling up inside me at the thought of what might have happened to him.

"Don't worry, it's fine," she said, but the words seemed hollow, as though I wasn't really hearing them. As though I was on the other side of a thick pane of glass, while the world rushed by outside.

And then I saw him, walking towards me, albeit gingerly, from the direction of the toilets. He was fully dressed, moving slowly, and waving at me.

"Here we go," said Clare, squeezing my arm. I rushed to Danny to give him a hug, wrapped my arms around him, then immediately felt guilty as he emitted a sharp intake of breath. Clearly being squeezed on a bullet wound can smart.

"What are you doing up?" I asked.

"I'm ready to go home," he said. "Just waiting on the doctor to give it the nod and then I'm out of here."

"That's such good news."

"I can't wait to get back. Especially now you've got a real nurse's uniform."

"Dream on, sunshine."

Clare was arranging the chairs by the bed when we walked back into the room.

"So, how did it go?" asked Danny.

"I'll give you the summary. Holly killed Steve because he overheard Leah tell her she was her sister."

There was a shocked silence.

"What?" said Danny after a moment. "That doesn't even make sense. Fantastic work getting her to talk, though."

"It's what she said, and thank you. Mind you she was half asleep, but I've got it all on tape." I paused. "Oh, and then somebody broke in and tried to kill her, but luckily I fought him off."

Danny started to laugh.

"No, seriously," I said.

He stopped laughing.

"What, really?"

"It's all on the tape."

"Fucking hell. Excuse the language."

"Don't worry, I'm used to it."

"Sorry. Wind it back. What exactly happened?"

And so I told them about pressing the buzzer, gaining access, and then the ward sister having a phone call just as I was approaching.

"That was me," said Clare, looking pleased with herself. "I'm ever so pleased about that. Good timing."

"I won't even ask how you did that."

"I just timed how long it takes to walk from here to the ICU, added a bit to get through the door, and then called on an internal line."

"What if I'd stopped on the way? Needed a wee or something?"

"You'd have been on your own. But you didn't. We're a team."

I felt unimaginably proud when she said that. Then I told them about getting into Leah's room, the policeman being called away, hiding beside the bed, the man breaking in and trying to smother Leah, and then how he'd scarpered.

"What happened to him?" asked Danny.

"No idea. The policeman called for back-up. He said he'd need to take a statement from me, so I asked if it was okay to get a glass of water and then legged it."

Clare asked for the voice recorder. I handed it over, and she rewound the tape than played it through for us all to hear.

"You've done brilliantly," she said. "Better than I ever dared to dream."

"But what does it mean?" I asked. "Why is it such a big deal that Leah's her sister? Why kill Steve?"

"Let's have a minute to think." She sat back in her chair and closed her eyes. I looked at Danny. He shrugged, then smiled at me and mouthed "well done". It would be nice to have him home, but he could sod off if he thought I'd be dressing up for him. At least until he was better.

After a few minutes, Clare opened her eyes.

"Thoughts?" she asked, addressing us both. I was happy to bow out at this stage, and leave it to the experts.

"It depends what she means by sister," said Danny. That confused me.

"Just what I was thinking," said Clare, which confused me more.

"Sorry," I said, "but am I being stupid? How many different types of sister are there? If we discount the kind you find in hospitals."

They looked at each other.

"Go on," said Clare. Danny took over.

"It depends," he said. "Obviously she could just be her sister, straight up, but then how come Holly didn't know about her? So that makes me think half-sister maybe? Seb's playing the field, gets somebody pregnant, does the dirty and abandons her, even assuming he knew anything about it. It could have been a one-night-stand and he had no idea she was pregnant. Either way, Leah's born to a single mother. Life's tough. She gets fostered possibly, then runs away, ends up homeless. She tracks down her real father, finds him, but for whatever reason she decides to get close to Holly first rather than confront him outright. And for whatever reason this causes a big enough problem for Holly that she has to do away with her."

"Could be," said Clare. "But what do we know about Leah? Apart from the homeless thing."

"Not a lot, not really," said Danny.

Clare gave him a look like a bossy schoolteacher addressing a wayward pupil.

"What?" he said.

"She's a gifted musician. We've already said that doesn't come cheap. So, if she was fostered, it was with supportive parents who clearly thought the world of her. Or else she wasn't fostered, and maybe her mum was just well off. We're only assuming life was tough. Maybe it wasn't. There are plenty of single families who do just fine, with children who go on to great things. It's not all about money anyway."

I suddenly remembered something Danny had told me about Clare, that her father had died when she was very young, and she'd been brought up by her mother, ostensibly as a single parent. It was clearly a sensitive subject.

"Granted," said Danny. "Or maybe Seb did know about her and made some sort of financial contribution, but kept it secret from everyone, especially Holly."

"But why would the sudden discovery be enough for Holly to want to kill Leah?" I asked, "unless she was worried about having to split an inheritance, or something." As soon as I said it, I thought it made a lot of sense, but the others seemed unimpressed.

"It's possible," said Clare, "but why the urgency? Why didn't Leah just go to Seb directly? And what was it that she said to Holly that suddenly put her life at risk? That Holly would kill Steve for, just because he overheard it?"

The thoughtful silence returned. Eventually Danny broke it.

"But none of this helps with everything else," he said. "None of it explains March, or the people trafficking or how all that fits together, even assuming it does. It doesn't explain why March suddenly cropped up, pretending to be a music mogul so he could get taken on as their manager."

I looked from Danny to Clare then back again. I was as confused as ever. Then suddenly Clare spoke.

"Oh my God."

We both looked at her, but Danny was nodding.

"Are you thinking what I'm thinking?" he asked, but she was already standing up, reaching for her jacket. From nowhere, the atmosphere had changed completely and she seemed to be in a hell of a rush to get somewhere.

"It's the only thing that makes sense," she said, voice suddenly very serious. "Danny, speak to Amy. Find out what they've got lined up for tomorrow. We've got to stop that handover." She headed towards the door, then turned.

"I've got to go. I'll be in touch." And then, in less time than it takes to think the world's gone completely mad, she was gone.

Chapter 43

"MISSION accomplished?" asked Holly when Finn opened the car door and leaned inside.

"Of course," he said.

"Good man. I was getting worried. What took you so long?"

"One or two complications, but everything's sorted."

"Glad to hear it. Do you need a lift somewhere?"

"No, you're fine. I'll see you tomorrow, though. We can celebrate then."

He stood up and closed the door. Holly watched him walk down the street and then jump onto the rear platform of a passing Routemaster bus. It was good to work with professionals, but equally she knew she'd have to be on her guard. These people were ruthless. Getting on the wrong side of them could be deadly.

She started the engine, put the car in gear, and then edged out of the parking space. Traffic was still light for central London, but she knew it would soon start to get busy, even on a Saturday. She was glad she was heading out of town. The drive to Winchester could take a couple of hours, but that would be useful time to review all the preparations, to go over everything in her mind, and make sure that all eventualities had been thought about. Her father would be so proud.

———

I'd had enough of being attacked, so it was nice to get home for some relative peace and quiet, albeit with an annoying patient who seemed to want me to make endless cups of tea and supply endless biscuits, when I was quite sure he was entirely capable of getting them himself.

I was worried that in the daylight there'd be some evidence of what had happened to Mitch or whatever his name was, but I had to give it to Clare. Whoever had helped with the clean-up had done an impressively thorough job.

We hadn't heard from her since her hasty disappearing act, but as that's something of a speciality, I wasn't overly concerned. I was looking forward to getting back to the world of focal lengths and f-stops. I wasn't cut out for so much drama. I just wanted to take artistic pictures. To get back to my day job, my studio, my sanctuary.

Danny spent the morning working on his computer and trying to get in touch with Amy, but without any success. By midday the events of the last few days had well and truly caught up with me, so I went for a lie down. My previous night's outfit was still lying on the floor. I thought I'd never wear that dress again. Never wear those shoes. They'd always bring back memories of just how close I'd come to disaster, and how inept I was in forming opinions of men. What on earth had I been thinking? And yet it had all seemed so good at the time, so wonderful to be able to have fun and enjoy myself. Well, that wasn't going to happen again.

I couldn't believe it was only a week since I'd been so excited about Danny's return from Germany, how keen I'd been to tell him about the band, and how much I'd been looking forward to a night out in Covent Garden. I closed my eyes, trying to forget about everything, but my mind was haunted by images of Mitch towering above me. I doubted I'd ever have a good night's sleep again.

I was finally just drifting off when I heard Danny calling. I was tempted to turn over and ignore him, but he shouted again and sounded increasingly insistent. And then I could hear someone knocking at the front door. I knew I'd have to get up, whoever it was. No rest for the wicked, even if they're not particularly successful at wickedness.

The knocking was getting louder and more insistent as I approached the door. I was starting to get annoyed by the time I opened it, but all thoughts of a suitable rebuke receded when I saw the thunderous expressions on the faces of DS Amy Cranston and DC Anil Jachuck. I'd been involved in enough over the last twenty-four hours to immediately feel very faint indeed.

"Hi," I said. "Danny's been trying to contact you."

"Can we come inside?" asked Amy. Maybe I imagined it, but her tone seemed less than cordial.

"Of course. He's through here." I turned to lead them through to the front room.

"It's not Danny we've come to see," she said.

No, I definitely didn't imagine it. I started to feel quite unwell.

I led them through to the front room anyway, offered them the sofa, and then a cup of tea. They accepted the sofa, but refused the tea. Danny tried to say hello and how pleased he was to see them, but Amy cut him short.

"This isn't a social visit," she said. "I've just come from the hospital. I'm afraid to say, it's not good news. Leah's dead."

My legs nearly gave way completely, but I just made it to a chair in time.

"Shit," I said, my mind doing somersaults. "Oh my God. That's awful. What happened?"

"That's what we're hoping you can tell us."

"Me?"

I thought I was going to throw up.

"Don't be coy, Anna. We're not here to waste time."

"But... Sorry, I can't take this in."

"Shall I make it easy for you?"

I couldn't speak. Instinctively I raised my hands to my face and closed my eyes. I could feel tears forming. Tears for the stress, the trauma and the tragedy of the last few days. And specifically tears for Leah.

"The ward sister said a nurse came onto the ward shortly after six this morning. She said it wasn't someone she recognised. The policeman on duty outside Leah's room confirmed the same. Both have given independent descriptions of the person concerned. And guess what? They match the description of a nurse seen leaving Danny's room about seven minutes prior. And, strangely enough, also a person seen entering Danny's room several minutes before that, albeit not in a nurse's uniform."

Each word was like a nail being driven into my brain.

"Mid-twenties, short, maybe five foot to five foot two. Dark hair, tied back, but with a slight curl. Sound like anyone you recognise, Anna? Danny? Would you like to look at the stills from the CCTV to see if it helps jog your memory?"

"Oh fuck," I said. "I am so sorry..."

Danny came to my rescue.

"I can explain this," he said.

"I very much hope so."

And so he told them about our plan, about needing to speak to Leah to progress the story, and how he'd asked me to help. He didn't mention Clare, thankfully, although I was pretty sure if they had descriptions of me entering Danny's room they'd have descriptions of another woman too.

I joined in when it came to the bit about the intruder in the baseball cap.

"I've got it all on tape," I said. "I'll get it for you."

I tried to stand up, but my legs wouldn't support me.

"I'll get it," said Danny. Even in his wounded state he was more mobile than me.

We played them the tape.

"And then he disappeared," I said.

"And you didn't think of reporting this?"

"I didn't think there was any need. The policeman already knew all about it and he'd had a far better look than I had. It was nearly dark in there. I just wanted to get back to Danny. Oh God, I know how this looks, but it wasn't anything to do with me, honestly. She was fine when I left. What happened to her? I can't believe this."

"We don't know yet."

"But *I* didn't kill her!" I said, my voice probably bordering on hysterical.

I looked at Amy and then at DC Jachuck, tears forming in my pleading eyes.

"You've got to believe me," I said, voice breaking. Danny came over and put an arm around me. I leaned into him. I wanted everything else to just go away.

"We know," said the DC.

I looked at him, unsure if I'd just heard correctly.

"I'm sorry?" I said.

"We know," he repeated. "But you did see the person who probably did. We're going to need to take a full statement, and take the uniform away for forensics."

They made me go through it all over again, this time with DC Jachuck taking notes. The questions were relentless. Danny and I were both left with the very clear impression that we'd overstepped the mark, with a severe warning about our future behaviour. I felt terrible, but I could sense Danny was getting increasingly frustrated.

"I'm sorry, but I'm not having this," he said as the barrage continued.

"I beg your pardon," said Amy.

"No, it's not right. It's like you're blaming us but actually Leah was in your care. The fact that Anna got into the room is a bad enough breach of security, but to then let someone else in is frankly fucking inexcusable." His voice was getting louder.

"And on top of that, you can shout at Anna all you like but the fact remains, if she hadn't done what she did, we'd now be none the wiser. Whoever killed Leah would have done it anyway, but we would never have known what happened between Holly and Steve. Or the fact that Leah was Holly's sister."

Amy's face seemed to be visibly darkening.

"Have you finished?" she said. He hadn't.

"No. I just think it's pathetic. Sorry Amy, you know I've got the utmost respect for you, but you know what? I think this is outrageous. You should be here on bended knee, thanking Anna for having the guts to do what she did, not treating us like fucking schoolchildren." Go Danny.

"Finished now?"

"For the time being."

"That's good. Because I'm this close," she squeezed her thumb and forefinger together, "to asking you who the other woman was who spent all day yesterday and the early hours of this morning in your room. Do we want to have that conversation, Danny?"

He sat back and sighed.

"No," he said, voice dropping in pitch and volume.

"I thought not," she said. There was a pause while we all started to process our private thoughts. Eventually Amy broke the silence.

"Let's pause it there." She turned to me. "Is that offer of a drink still available?"

I nodded.

"In which case, now would be a good time for a break. I'm not going to apologise, Danny. You've both absolutely pushed the boundaries, but I do take on board what you said. We'll have a break and then we can discuss exactly what's going to happen tomorrow."

"That's why I've been trying to call you," said Danny. "We've worked out exactly what's going to happen, and I think it's going to blow your mind."

Chapter 44

GRAHAM March finished tapping at the keyboard and sat back in his chair. Computers were still alien to him, and typing wasn't really his forte, but the effort had been worth it. He re-read his final few paragraphs, then searched for the print command. A few seconds later, the dot matrix printer on the end of his desk started its rhythmic screech, and the words were committed to paper.

When it was finished, he tore the perforated edges off the paper and added the printed sheets to a manila folder on the shelf beside him. The handwritten label on the front of the folder had the name Holly Rowan. It was one of several on the shelf. Others had been created for Jacqueline Glover, Mikołaj Gawlinski, and Samuel Elmhirst-Banks. It was all just insurance in case anything went wrong. Years in the police had taught him the importance of making sure every eventuality had been considered. Nothing could be left to chance.

The planning had been meticulous. Uncompromising, perhaps, but it can be a cruel world. He didn't like relying on others, but so far they hadn't let him down. Base greed was a powerful motivator, especially if you weren't unduly troubled by a sense of conventional morality. Now, though, the end was in sight. He just had to ensure that everyone understood they were part of a team. If one should turn rogue, the whole thing could come to a disastrous, shuddering halt. There was just one more day to keep control and then the future could look very bright indeed.

A fifth folder, marked "Cologne", had all the details of his contacts there. He'd enjoyed his visits, but after tomorrow he knew he'd get a very different reception. They'd understand him for who he was. The dangerous, ruthless mastermind, never to be underestimated.

And that just left Danny. What exactly should he do about him? None of this would have even been necessary if Danny hadn't interfered. March would have been quite happy seeing out his days in the police force, with a few little sidelines to boost the pension. Where was the harm in that? It was all entirely normal, and the very least he deserved after all the good he'd done in his once-glittering career. Yes, Danny would need to be dealt with, but there was no immediate rush. Payback, when it came, would be severe, but he was happy to consider it a long-term project for now.

There were, of course, sacrifices for the sake of the greater good. He thought of Aurelia, with the closest he could come to misty-eyed regret. She possessed a touch and tenderness like no other, and oh, those beautiful eyes... How he loved to look into those as she worked her magic on his body. Maybe when this was all over he could find her a new role. One in which she could deploy her very special talents, but where he wouldn't need to share her with others. Again, though, that was another challenge, for another day.

His priority, now the folders were complete, was to make sure everyone did what he needed for one final day. And then to ensure he made it through the rest of the weekend alive.

Clare leaned on the concrete parapet of an alcove on Blackfriars Bridge and looked down at the Thames flowing below. She pulled up her coat collar, then took one last drag on her cigarette and flicked the lipstick-stained butt into the dark, threatening water.

The view was captivating and she felt powerless to move despite the omnipresent moisture in the air. The familiar deep sense of melancholy was returning, compounded this time by new thoughts of the helpless victims of the cruellest depths of mankind.

It had felt good to be back working with Danny, bouncing ideas, unravelling a mystery and thinking the unthinkable until the only remaining option was the truth, no matter how unpalatable. But really it was just a temporary respite, little more than an illusion. She'd made her choices and now had to face the consequences, accept the loneliness, and return to her new life, however much she missed the old. It was nearly time to disappear again, although she couldn't pull the same stunt as last time. There are only so many times you can die before it becomes obvious you're still alive.

She took her phone from her pocket, and looked at it for a few moments, aware of the power and potential in her hands. Such was progress. One simple numeric keypad that could link her from this bridge directly to any phone line in the world. One simple opportunity to say something that could never be unsaid. Eventually she called up the familiar number and phoned Danny, for maybe the final time.

"Hi," she said when he picked up the phone. "Just checking how you're feeling."

"Sore, but don't worry. Much more important, have you heard about Leah?" His voice sounded urgent, troubled.

"I have. It's just so, so sad."

"I know. I couldn't believe it. We've had Amy round here for a statement. She knew about Anna getting into the room."

"I bet that didn't go down well."

"Not brilliantly, no. But listen, she mentioned the other woman who'd been in my room. I'm ninety-nine percent sure she knows it was you. I hate to worry you but I thought you ought to know. Please be careful."

"Oh, Danny." Her voice betrayed the sadness that was beginning to overwhelm her. She paused, trying to think of the appropriate words, but none would come.

"Are you okay?" he asked at last. The concern was obvious.

"Yeah, I'm okay."

"Sure? Where are you?"

"I'm just... out and about."

"It's just your voice. You sound different. You sound a bit fed up."

Clare laughed.

"You don't need to worry about me, Danny," she said.

"What *are* you talking about? Of course I worry about you."

"You shouldn't."

"Well, we all do things we shouldn't do, from time to time."

"Indeed we do."

She heard Danny sigh.

"Seriously though, is something bothering you?"

"Lots of things bother me."

"Anything I can help with?"

"No, I'm just feeling a bit blue. It's fine. It happens."

"You worry me."

"I just told you about that."

"Doesn't stop it happening though. Where are you. Can I come to see you?"

"Danny, I'm not dragging you out of the house when you're supposed to be resting. No, there's nothing you can do, and yes, I'll be okay. It just gets to me sometimes."

"What does? Your situation?"

"Didn't we set a load of ground rules about things you could ask me?"

"We did, but I just hate to think of you upset."

"But Danny, if I'm upset it's my own fault. Let's move on."

"This doesn't sound like you."

"I'm just a normal person. Good days and bad."

"Okay. But I'm here if you need me."

"I know. And thank you. Now, have you got everything you need?"

"For the story?"

"Yes."

"Nearly. It's pretty much written. Obviously until tomorrow night we don't know the final chapter, but if we're right then it's ready."

"Excellent. And if we're right, March is even more of an evil bastard than we thought."

"Exactly. Clare, whatever happens, thank you so much for your help. You've been brilliant. I've loved every minute. Of our time, anyway, not all the other shit, obviously."

"It's been my pleasure. Honestly."

"Are you staying in town?"

"When it's over? No, I don't think that would be wise."

"Can I ask where you're going?"

"No, but you have my email address."

"Can I see you before you go?"

"I'm not sure that would be wise either."

There was a brief silence, just enough for private thoughts to surface again.

"Clare, it breaks my heart. I'm going to miss you."

"And me you, too. More than you'd ever know. Is Anna there?"

"She is. Hold on."

Anna came on the line.

"Hi, Clare?" she said.

"Yeah. Hi Anna."

"How are you?"

"I'm okay. Kind of. I'm just calling to say goodbye. It's been great meeting you."

"And you. Surely you're not going already?"

"I have to, sadly. Hopefully you don't hate me quite as much as you did."

"Hey, don't worry. I've seen a different side."

"I hope so. Will you look after Danny for me?"

"I'll try."

"He's a good man. You could do a lot worse."

"Believe me, I know."

"It's been good to see you, Anna. I wish it had been different, but it *was* good to see you."

"Likewise. When will we see you again?"

There was no easy answer to that.

"Soon, I hope." Just one more small lie to add to those of a lifetime.

"Take care, Clare. And keep in touch, okay? And thank you, for everything."

"My pleasure. And I will."

She ended the call, pocketed the phone and lit a fresh cigarette, blowing smoke across the river where it disappeared into nothing in the air.

She knew somebody was standing behind her. She could feel their presence with the sixth sense that warns of nearby predators. She turned.

"We meet at last," said DS Amy Cranston.

Clare gave a rueful smile. She dropped the cigarette to the pavement and crushed it under the sole of her leather boot.

"I'm glad you came," she said.

"I didn't have any option," said Amy. "Come on. We should get this over with."

Chapter 45

A FORD Transit minibus left the Channel ferry at Dover and the driver made his way tentatively towards passport control. He pulled up at the window, and handed the customs officer the group of passports. This was the moment where everything could go wrong.

The customs officer told him to wait there, and then exited his cubicle. A moment later he appeared at the driver's window.

"I need everybody to get out," he said.

The driver climbed down from his seat, then opened the side door, beckoning the twelve girls from his school party onto the tarmac. They all climbed out, full of enthusiasm and fresh-faced innocence, looking forward to their adventures in this new country that they'd heard so much about.

They lined up, laughing with each other, grateful to stretch their legs, happy to breathe the fresh English air.

The customs officer started his checks, calling them out, one by one. Eventually, it was over. He handed the passports back to the driver, and nodded, to indicate that the girls should get back on board.

"Safe onward journey," he said.

The driver resumed his position behind the wheel and restarted the engine. Everything was running smoothly. First-night accommodation was arranged in a hostel near Canterbury, and then the handover would take place tomorrow. He turned on his headlights, flicked the indicator, and pulled out into the early evening traffic.

The evening rush was about to get under way, but the first visitors to the Albermarle Casino and Gentleman's Club were not there to gamble. Not in the conventional sense, at least. At reception, they were given permission to approach Jacqui's office, and when they knocked on the door, it opened, revealing her opulent desk across the plush dark red carpet.

"Thank you both for coming," she said, when they were seated. "Holly, Mikołaj, I assume you know each other."

They nodded.

"That's good. So, no need for introductions. Straight down to business?"

"If you could," said Holly.

Finn turned up with a tray of drinks. The each took one. Jacqui lit a cigarette.

"The agenda is fairly brief," Jacqui continued. "Only two items. Do we continue with the plan, and if so do we need to switch location? And then what, exactly, do we do with March? I assume you both know what he's been up to."

They nodded again.

"I will be happy to deal with March," said Mikołaj. "I've got something special in mind."

"Glad to hear it," said Jacqui. "And can you make it particularly painful, just for me?"

He smiled.

"It will be my absolute pleasure," he said.

Clare and Amy sat opposite each other in a bar next door to the Sea Containers building, overlooking the Thames.

"You do know I should arrest you," said Amy.

"I do," Clare replied. "Although if I thought you'd do that, I wouldn't have suggested meeting."

"It must be important."

"It is."

"Greater good?"

"Something like that."

Clare stirred her drink, watching the bubbles rise slowly up the side of the glass.

"I'm leaving tonight anyway, away from here completely, but I needed to speak to you before I go. It's about March," she said.

"I rather assumed that."

"I know."

"Are you here to fill in the gaps?"

"Maybe. It depends what you already know."

It was Amy's turn to pause. Clare wondered exactly how much she already knew, whether she fully understood the depths to which March would sink to to save himself.

"I know he's involved in people trafficking with a handover tomorrow," said Amy.

"But that's it?"

"I can't go into operational details but that's the summary."

"Okay."

Clare leaned back in her chair, wondering exactly how to break the news.

"I hate to be the one to say this," she said at last, "but you've got that all wrong."

If you'd asked me a week ago whether I ever wanted to see Clare again, I'd have assumed you were either deluded or simply trying to make me cross. But now, having said my farewells, I was already starting to miss her. I agreed with Danny: there was something about her tone of voice that was a cause for concern. She sounded depressed, as though she was on the verge of disappearing completely. I hoped she was okay, and that wherever she was now, she was taking care of herself. I just wanted to give her a big hug, which is pretty much my answer for everything.

"So, everything's nearly finished?" I said to Danny, as he paused typing on his notebook keyboard.

"Pretty much," he said.

"And you've got enough to nail March for ever? How long do you think he's going to go down for?"

Danny closed the lid of the computer.

"It's not quite that simple," he said.

"In what way?"

He just looked at me.

"Things have changed."

"What things?"

He sighed deeply.

"Make me a cup of tea," he said, "and I'll bring you up to speed."

Five minutes later there were two steaming mugs of PG Tips between us.

"So?" I said.

"Do you want the long version or the summary?"

"Summary first, then the long version if it needs explaining."

"Okay, the summary. March is innocent and his life is in danger, so we need to make sure nobody kills him."

"Whoa, stop you there." I wasn't expecting that. "Sorry, for a moment there I thought you said..."

"I did."

"But... What?" I thought maybe I'd fallen asleep and was

having a surreal dream, but then nothing over the last week had made much sense, so any dream was likely to be more logical.

"I know, it sounds ridiculous," said Danny. "But ironically it's the only thing that makes sense."

"But how? I thought he was arranging the people trafficking and murdering Steve and Leah."

Danny was shaking his head, lips pursed.

"Do you want the long version?"

"I better had."

"Okay." He took a breath. "Well it all goes back to last year, when he got suspended. He wasn't far short of retiring but if he'd been found guilty he'd have been locked up at worst, or at the very least thrown out of the force and lost his pension."

"But he was guilty."

"Exactly. And he knew that protesting his innocence was only going to get him so far. He's undoubtedly got friends in high places, but when the time comes he's going to find they disappear faster than, I don't know, a cream cake on a Weight Watchers away day."

"Than a what?"

"Sorry, I was being creative."

"But surely Weight Watchers would be avoiding cream cakes? Isn't that the point of it?"

"It is, but it was an away day. Anyway, doesn't matter, back to March."

"If you could." Although now you mention it, I could have quite fancied a cream doughnut.

"Okay. So anyway, March tried keep a low profile for a bit but then started to fight back. He decided that the only way to fight the allegations was to prove that he was one of the good guys."

"Which he clearly isn't."

"We know that, but we're not the ones making the assessment."

"And hence the homeless shelter?"

"Exactly, although I'll come on to that. On the face of it, it appears he thought a bit of charity work would stand him in good stead at the hearing. The trouble was, it was so out of character, nobody was going to believe him."

"That's because he's a twat."

"Again, an astute observation."

Still none of this was making any sense.

"But you tracked him to Germany. He was at the centre of a people smuggling ring," I said.

"That's what I thought."

"Are you saying he wasn't?"

"No, but it's a bit more complicated. Here's where it starts to get a bit interesting."

I took a sip of the tea. Danny did the same. It was still a bit hot but neither of us complained.

"Fundamentally, he's a detective," Danny continued. "Trafficking's been going on for years. It's grown a lot since the Wall came down, but it's nothing new in itself. It's a huge industry. I thought March was trying to get a slice of it, trying to earn his fortune."

"Surely he was?"

"No. He was coming at it from a different angle. He was going deep undercover, getting close to it so he could blow the ring wide open. It already existed. He was never the organiser. He just managed to worm his way into the group so that when the time came, he could expose the lot of them, proving to everyone that not only is he on the side of the angels, but that he's a bloody good detective in the process. Working freelance to bust a major crime syndicate. That goes in front of the review board and he's reinstated, charges dropped, free to carry on and take his pension."

"Jesus." This was a lot to take in. "But what about Steve and Leah?"

"That's what got us onto it."

"Sorry, I'm missing something."

"It's what Clare always said. Never assume anything, question everything. We couldn't understand why March was getting involved in the band, and thought he was responsible in some way for what happened to Steve."

"And Leah."

"And Leah. He said he was trying to get involved in the arts. But actually, he was just getting close to Seb."

"What's Seb got to do with it?"

"He's as bent as the rest of them. March has known him for years so presumably knows exactly what he's into. And presumably he thought if he could involve a Government minister, then it'd be extra brownie points come the day of the big reveal."

"But that still doesn't explain Steve and Leah."

"No, but here's how that worked out. Leah was the illegitimate child, trying to find her father. Then, as she got close to him, she realised what he was up to. She spent time in a homeless shelter. We thought that's where she met March, but actually it's where she first came across her father. We already know he was the type of guy who'd play the field and get a woman pregnant. It transpires he wasn't averse to exploiting the homeless, taking vulnerable young girls and abusing them until he got bored and moved onto the next one. Developed a bit of a taste for it. The younger the better, if you know what I mean. The shelter was a front. But not a front for March. March got involved as part of his investigation."

"But Holly?"

"Holly thought the world of Seb. She was always daddy's girl, completely devoted to him, utterly blind to any evil. It was like she'd been brainwashed. She just wanted to prove herself to him. Then suddenly Leah turns up, gets close to Holly, reveals she's her sister and she knows what their father's up to. Leah had to go. And poor Steve was a witness to it, so that was the end of him too. Holly had to kill them both."

"Shit. So, where's Holly now?"

"We think she's Seb's representative in the trafficking set-up. Jacqui and Mikołaj are both looking for girls for prostitution. Seb's just looking for himself, because he's an evil bastard with a wandering eye."

"And March?"

"March saw what was going on. He knew them all, independently. Seb was an old friend. I expect he's provided all sorts of services for Jacqui before, protection, whatever. And he's the kind of sleazebag who spends disproportionate amounts of time in massage parlours. So, we think he dropped hints that he'd like a bit of the action and became a kind of go-between. But when the time comes, he's planning to expose the lot, and walk away the hero."

"Fuck."

The tea was definitely drinkable now, but it had taken on a funny taste.

"What happens now?" I asked.

"As far as we know, the handover goes as planned tomorrow."

"And then?"

"At some point March switches sides. Announces to the world that he's the one who's blown the whole thing open."

"Isn't that entrapment?"

"Arguably but not really. I doubt anyone would care. You've got a brothel, a strip club and a paedophile in the heart of Government. I think that trumps everything."

"But can't you prove that's what he's up to? Not only get the others, but also show March up as the kind of duplicitous bastard who'd try to save his own career by sacrificing everybody else?"

"That'd be nice. The risk is, whatever happens he's going to be seen to be the hero and it'll look like sour grapes for me."

I could see Danny thinking. There was something on his mind.

"There's another problem," he said at last.

"Go on."

"It's just that he's playing an incredibly dangerous game. We know what these people are capable of. They've killed Steve and Leah and they tried to kill me. And if they saw March talking to me, which seems more than likely, then just maybe they've realised what he's up to."

"Oh shit." I didn't dare mention Mitch.

"Exactly. Which is why his life's in danger now. He may be a scumbag but he's our scumbag. And bizarrely it's now up to us to save him."

Chapter 46

Sunday, April 10th, 1994

I'M not sure if Danny slept at all, but I managed a few hours, enjoying a dream in which I was walking through the middle of a delicious giant cream doughnut, until I got to the end and a man started shooting at me, which wasn't so nice.

He was on the phone when I made it through to the front room, but ended the call when he saw me.

"Just trying March again," he said. "There's been no answer all morning."

"That's not good. What time is everyone supposedly at the parlour?"

"Aurelia said seven this evening."

"And you're going to follow?"

"I'm going to have to."

"Well, I'm coming with you and that's not up for debate."

He started to protest but I raised my hand to stop him.

"I'll just make tea and then I'll feel a bit more human," I said.

The tea on its own wasn't enough, but after a steaming hot shower I felt as ready to face the world as I ever would be. Part of me was excited that it was nearly over, but a bigger part of me was terrified about all the things that could potentially go wrong. I wished Clare was with us, but understood why she'd had to leave. I'd felt safe when she was with me, but now all we had for protection was our survival instincts.

Danny was just ending another call when I returned to the front room. He looked pale.

"That was Aurelia," he said. "They've moved the meeting forward. It's all happening at one."

"Wow. What's the time now?"

"Just past eleven."

"Shit. I'll get my shoes."

"I'll try Amy."

I've got several pairs of DMs in various colours, and while they all largely do the same thing it's nice to have the choice. They're just so comfy once you've broken them in. I've never been one for trainers. Today was definitely a black day, to match my black jeans and jacket. I could hear Danny getting ready in his room, so took the opportunity to load a film into my new Nikon F4 and attached my 80-200mm autofocus zoom. It's not the equipment I'd normally use in the studio, but the geek in me was deeply in love with it, and it was a good excuse to get it out. It seemed the best for a stake-out, potentially at a distance. Photography was of secondary importance, though. My main objective for the day was just to look after Danny.

"Did you get through to her?" I asked when he reappeared.

"Not yet but I've left a message. I'll keep trying."

"How exactly are we going to do this?" It seemed like a reasonable question, but if I expected a detailed plan I was about to be disillusioned.

"We're just going to park up, keep an eye out for any movement, and then follow them," said Danny.

"Okay. And then what? Assuming they're going to a handover

somewhere, we do what? Just wait outside, taking pictures? We can't exactly barge in."

"No, that's when we need Amy."

"But what if you can't get through to her?"

"We're knackered."

DS Amy Cranston stood in front of the whiteboard in an operation room at New Scotland Yard, finishing her briefing to an assembled team of specialist firearms officers.

"I'm sure I don't need to remind you, but I have to say this," she said. "You may only use such force as is reasonable in the circumstances in the prevention of crime, or in effecting or assisting in the lawful arrest of offenders or suspected offenders. Now, any questions?"

There was a general murmuring but nobody raised their hand.

"Okay. All good. We'll rendezvous at sixteen hundred. Officers will follow from Euston and then radio through their destination, which is where we come in. Take care, ladies and gentlemen. Have a good lunch and I will see you all this afternoon."

The room cleared until the only other occupant was her partner, Anil.

"Nervous?" he asked, walking across towards her.

"Maybe. It's just ironic really. The first big op I've headed up since taking over from March, and guess who's at the centre of it."

He laughed.

"And there was me thinking we were going to take him down. Where did you find out all that other stuff?"

"Just a source. It seems to stack up, though."

"Is he trustworthy?"

Amy picked up her bag and looked at her colleague.

"First, he's a she. And second, no, not in the slightest. In fact, she's one of the least trustworthy people I've ever met."

"Wow. But you've just told an entire room..."

Amy cut across him.

"I know. Because despite what I just said, I do, bizarrely, trust her entirely over this. She didn't have to come forward and it was a massive risk for her to do so." She paused while she put some document folders into her bag. "March is still bent, though. You do know that? And we will have him one day, even if not over this."

DC Jachuck nodded, a smile breaking out.

"I very much look forward to that."

By just after noon we were parked on Eversholt Street about sixty yards away from the front door of the parlour, although I wasn't about to get out to measure it. It was close enough that we had a clear view of anyone leaving the building, but hopefully far enough away to stop us looking suspicious. Thankfully the rain was holding off for once, so the windscreen remained clear. Danny kept trying to call Amy on his mobile while I sat behind the steering wheel, camera in hand, ready to give chase at a moment's notice.

"Where do you think Clare is now?" I asked eventually, to help pass the time.

"Your guess is as good as mine. I don't know. Maybe Germany? She can speak a bit of German, I know that."

"I don't know how she does it."

"What? Speak German?"

"No, stupid. All the travelling. It's like she can just pass through borders, turn up when she wants, disappear when she wants."

"She's very resourceful. I doubt it's too hard anyway. You just hire a car, one way rental, show a passport and you're away. We know she's got access to passports when she needs them."

"And driving licences. What was that one she had in Paddington?"

"Charlotte Sadler."

"That's the one. Do you think we'll hear from her again? Would you ever try to find her?"

"I hope so, but no, there's no point looking. If she wants to disappear she'll do it properly. I wouldn't know where to start."

Danny tried Amy again. There was still no answer but he left another message. I was feeling increasingly anxious. I was rather relying on her turning up with the full SO19 firearms unit, but currently we didn't have so much as a traffic warden.

At just before quarter to one, a large black Mercedes pulled up outside the parlour.

"Here we go," I said.

I got my camera ready, finger on the shutter, ready to raise it up to eye height and fire off some pictures as soon as anyone emerged. But the car just sat there. Nobody got in or out. Time seemed to be passing slowly. As the clock ticked round to one I started the engine, ready to leave the second there was movement ahead of us.

Unfortunately, I wasn't looking behind.

The rear passenger door on the Mercedes opened. I raised my camera, ready to shoot. But suddenly somebody was banging on my window. I turned to look and my heart nearly stopped at the sight of a gun barrel pointing straight at me.

I screamed and panicked, and instinctively dropped the clutch, causing the car to launch forward. I floored the accelerator, ducking my head in case somebody was about to take a shot at us. For a split second, I had visions of a Hollywood-style car chase, blasting through the streets of London, pulling handbrake turns up one way streets, but it was only for a fleeting moment. Within twenty yards I was slamming the brakes back on to avoid hitting the Mercedes that was now parked across the middle of the road. I looked over my shoulder. The first man was walking back towards the car, gun still outstretched, getting closer. I thought about reversing hard towards him but then the bastard shot my tyres out. I hate it when that happens.

"Oh shit," I said. "Sorry, Danny."

He reached out to hold my hand, and gave it a squeeze.

Within a moment my door was being opened.

"Both of you, out," said the man with the gun in heavily accented English. "Get in the car."

We didn't have an option. We got out of my Honda and into the back of the waiting Mercedes.

Another man in the front reached back and passed us two fairly industrial-looking blindfolds.

"Put these on. We're going on a journey," he said.

I looked at Danny. Danny looked at me. Then we both looked at the man with the gun, who was about to get in beside us. We did as we were told. Danny held my hand again, but fear was beginning to completely overwhelm me.

Chapter 47

DS Amy Cranston made her way to the police canteen and ordered a tuna salad with Diet Coke. She took her tray and found a deserted table on the far side of the room, overlooking the car park. She welcomed the solitude, and didn't want to be disturbed. It was a rare quiet moment, and she wasn't sure when she'd next have one of those.

After she'd finished her lunch she took her mobile phone from her bag, deciding, reluctantly, that it was time to take it off silent. She looked at the screen and was shocked to see twenty-six missed calls. Swearing, she tapped in the number for her voice mail. She listened to the messages in mounting horror. By the third, she was already out of the canteen and running down the corridor towards her office, aware that her career might be about to end.

I had no idea where we were when the car stopped, but the journey, at a guess, had taken about forty-five minutes. Maybe more, it was impossible to tell. Eventually, though, after we'd appeared to leave the road and travelled over some rough kind of waste ground, the engine was killed and the door was opened. I felt somebody reaching for me, dragging me out of the car.

Somebody took my arms and forced them roughly behind my back. I felt something being used to tie my wrists together, far tighter than necessary, digging into the flesh.

I was then grabbed by the arm, and dragged away from the car. I stumbled trying to keep up, but something sharp and hard poked me in the side of the ribs. I suspected it was the gun barrel.

A few moments later I heard a giant grinding sound, which I took to be some kind of roller-shutter door. Once it stopped, the blindfold was taken off and I had the chance to take in my surroundings.

The first thing I noticed was Danny, standing beside me. That was something at least. But beside him stood the man with the gun, and he was still pointing it at us. We were indoors. My eyes quickly began to adjust to the semi-darkness, possibly thanks to the blindfold. Talk about small mercies.

It looked like a giant abandoned warehouse, with faint light coming in from filthy skylights high in the roof above. If I hadn't been so terrified I'd have been sizing it up as a location for a photoshoot. No wonder these kinds of places always end up in TV dramas. The Mercedes was parked inside the warehouse, along with a Ford Transit minibus and two other cars.

"Good afternoon, Danny," said a voice to my right. "And to you, Anna."

A figure emerged from the gloom. It was Samuel Elmhirst-Banks.

"I guess this means I've rescinded the job offer." He laughed, but I was struggling to see any humour in the situation. "I'm so glad you decided to join us."

And then I saw Holly, standing beside him.

"Holly!" I shouted, but she just ignored me. At least she had the decency to look to the ground.

"Can you tell us what's going on?" asked Danny. "I'm assuming this isn't a social visit."

He sounded a lot braver than I felt, even though I thought I could detect a slight tremor in his voice.

"It will be my pleasure. But first I must introduce you to a friend of mine."

He beckoned us forward, past one of the cars. Two chairs sat side-by-side, facing a third. And in the third, tied down so he wasn't going anywhere, was Graham March.

"Take a seat," said the politician. "I think you might enjoy the show."

We did as we were told. It's not easy to argue when a man's pointing a gun at you. Our arms were still behind our backs, so it was particularly uncomfortable, and then made worse as further cable ties attached our wrists to the chairs.

I'd never seen March looking quite like this before. He looked terrified, and much smaller than normal, his eyes pleading with us. A pool of something I took to be urine was on the floor beneath him.

"Graham has an apology to make to both of you," said Seb.

March's eyes hardened. He muttered something.

"What was that?"

"I said fuck off, you Tory twat."

That was brave. But then equally looked a bit foolish as Seb's fist connected with his midriff. March bent forward as much as his ties would allow him, coughing and gasping for air.

"I can see this is going to get interesting," Seb continued. "Mikołaj, show us the girl."

The sight that greeted me next is not one I'll ever forget. I couldn't quite believe the brutality. A young girl, stripped naked, body red raw from the severest of beatings, was dragged towards us, trying to walk but stumbling, heels dragging across the cold concrete floor. Her hair was matted, her face covered in blood, her lips split and her eyes half closed.

"This is Aurelia," Seb continued. I heard Danny gasp. "This is what happens when someone meets with a journalist without our permission."

"Bastards," said Danny. I thought I was going to throw up.

She was dragged away again. Seb continued.

"As you can see, we take things like that very seriously. But Graham here took things one stage further, didn't you Graham?"

March didn't speak. Seb punched him hard on the side of the face. There was a sickening crack.

"Okay, he seems to have lost his voice. I'll tell you what he did. He not only met with a journalist, specifically you, Danny, but then he briefed you about our whole arrangement, just so he could save his own skin."

"What?" said Danny, voice rising. "March didn't say anything about it."

Seb just laughed.

"Really? And you expect me to believe that?"

"He didn't! I've been investigating but he didn't tell me anything."

"Ah, if only I could believe you, but sadly, I know that you're lying to me. And unfortunately for you, you're about to see what happens when people do that."

"But he fucking didn't."

"Danny, do yourself a favour and shut up, can you? I know he did because we've watched him meet you. And then we paid a little visit to his house and we came across the folders in which he'd written everything down for you. Luckily Mrs March was out at the time so she didn't have to be a witness, although, if you ask me, she's already suffered enough."

Seb picked up a baseball bat and walked back across to March. He swung it hard and brought it down viciously on his knees. There was another sickening crack, and March screamed in pain. This time I did throw up.

Chapter 48

REPORTS were coming in of an incident close to Euston station. A white Honda Prelude had been found abandoned. The damage to its two rear tyres was consistent with the reports of gunfire. Witnesses had reported the two occupants of the car being driven off in a black Mercedes, although nobody had seen the number plate.

"Shit, shit, shit!" said Amy, banging her fist on the dashboard as Anil sped through the city streets, siren blazing, heading in the direction of Eversholt Street.

By the time their car arrived, two other squad cars were already at the scene and the door to the parlour had been kicked off its hinges.

"Anything?" she said to a colleague who was emerging from the basement.

He shook his head.

She grabbed her radio and asked for an update from a similar team who were performing a simultaneous raid on the Albermarle Casino and Gentleman's Club.

"Nothing, just a cleaner but she doesn't even seem to speak English."

"Fuck!"

She radioed back to the control room.

"Can you get CCTV?" she asked. "We want to follow a black Mercedes car, no idea of the reg, leaving Eversholt Street sometime around 1300. We need to know where it is. And it's fucking urgent."

"We'll see what can we do, but it's not going to be quick."

"What now, boss?" asked DC Jachuck, who was still standing beside her.

"We think. That's all we can fucking do."

Luckily most of the vomit missed my jacket, although the aroma and bitter taste didn't do much to improve the ambience of my surroundings. Not that anybody seemed to care. All attention was on Graham March, who was starting to look like he was in significant pain.

"You see, I've known Graham a very long time," Seb continued. "Obviously I've always known he was a two-faced bastard and couldn't be trusted, but I hadn't realised just how far into the gutter he'd descended. He used to try to pretend he was my friend, although I knew he was only ever doing that in the pursuit of self-interest."

He took the baseball bat again, and swiped it hard and fast onto March's left arm. I wasn't sure if the noise I heard was the arm itself snapping or the ribs underneath. Either way March cried out again. Danny tried to wriggle free of his chair and received a punch in the face from the gunman for his troubles.

"Seb, please," I heard myself say. "Can we please stop this?"

"Stop? I've barely started."

The baseball bat connected again. I thought March must be close to losing consciousness. A patch of blood was growing ever larger on his shirt.

"I mean in fairness, he did introduce me to Mikołaj and Jacqueline. And I have to say the quality of the merchandise is really quite excellent." I looked up at the minibus. I suddenly realised what it was doing there. "But I thought he was doing it for the simple motive of a quick profit. Not because he was trying to save his own miserable career."

There was another giant crack as the bat connected with March's ankles. He screamed out in pain. Still conscious then. I wasn't sure if that was a good thing.

"Anything to say, Graham?"

March could barely speak, but from what I could hear it definitely sounded like another "fuck you". Another punch to the midriff followed, with similar results.

"What happens now?" I asked, but then almost immediately wished I hadn't.

"Graham needs to be shown the error of his ways," said Seb. "That's the first priority. And believe me, when I've finished with him I know Mikołaj quite fancies a turn. Jacqui will be along in an hour or so, and I'm sure she'd like a quiet word also. And after that I'm afraid we just need to perform a bit of a clean-up."

There was a momentary respite as Seb's phone started ringing. He answered the call.

"Yes, he's with me now... No, he won't be going anywhere... Of course. I will. Yes, hold on... I'll just check. One moment."

He walked away, towards a door at the back of the warehouse, opened it and disappeared from view. I thought I caught a glimpse of a young girl sitting on the floor, looking terrified. So that was where they were keeping them.

"Anna, I'm so sorry," said Danny, but got another fist in the face for his troubles.

"Shut the fuck up," said the gunman.

"Go gently, Tomasz," said the guy Seb had referred to as Mikołaj. He'd been standing watching proceedings since dragging

Aurelia back off to a corner. "We want him to enjoy his turn when it comes."

I felt utterly powerless and helpless. I'd gone beyond fear, out through the far side of panic, and was bordering on a kind of silent hysteria, in which the horror was so great my mind was in danger of closing down completely. There were so many things that I didn't understand, and yet equally I understood everything completely.

I understood what March had been trying to achieve, even if it had backfired badly, and I understood how it must have looked, even though it was completely wrong. I understood Holly's involvement and her devotion to her father, and I even understood why we'd been dragged into it and were now facing apparent execution. But what I couldn't understand was what kind of warped madness could make one human being want to do this to another. What kind of animal could drag innocent girls to England from a foreign country only to exploit them and abuse them, either just for money and greed, or to gratify their own abhorrent perversions. What kind of mental sickness gave licence to this kind of abject cruelty and torture. What sort of freak would actually seem to be enjoying dishing out this kind of punishment to another living person, made of the same fundamental atoms and presumably sharing mutual ancestry, if we went back far enough to Adam and Eve. Not that anything I'd seen was doing anything at all to shake my deeply entrenched distrust of all organised religions. What kind of god would give one of his people this kind of power to inflict such pain on one of his others?

My mind was brought firmly back to the present by the return of Seb.

"That was Jacqui on the phone," he said. "I told her not to rush. We can continue our discussion."

He picked up the baseball bat again, and swung it backwards, looking like he was going for the most vicious blow yet. And then there was a bang. It very much looked like his head exploded.

Seb dropped to the floor, the baseball bat rolling away in my direction, not that I could reach it given the fact that I'd lost the use of my arms. Tomasz the gunman and Mikołaj both dived for cover, but not quite in time. Holly started running. There was another bang and Mikołaj took the hit. He screamed and fell. Another bang and a cloud of concrete dust flew into the air where the bullet missed him and connected with the floor. The next bullet did the trick, though. He slumped forwards, motionless. Tomasz had dived behind the car and was now returning fire, but I had no idea what he was aiming at. I couldn't tell where the shooting was coming from. There was the sound of glass shattering as a bullet ripped through the car windscreen, and then more as the side window exploded. I thought I heard somebody running. I turned to look, but couldn't see anyone. But then the bangs seemed to be coming from a new direction. Tomasz turned and fired back too. I'm sure I felt the rush of a bullet millimetres from my face.

There was a momentary pause. And then another window shattered on the car, this time from the other side. I could see Tomasz look round, stunned, then try to get out of the way of this new attack, throwing himself towards the front of the car.

In the distance, I could hear sirens and it sounded like they were getting closer. Inside, though, there was another round of gunfire. Tomasz stood up to return a shot, but it proved to be a fatal mistake. Two bullets in quick succession ripped into him. His body contorted and fell to the floor. The sirens were getting louder and louder.

And then, out of the darkness strode a new figure, dressed all in black. It was somebody I didn't think I'd ever see again.

"Jesus, how many times do I have to save you two?" said Clare. She smiled. And then she was gone.

Chapter 49

WITHIN seconds a police van had smashed through the roller shutter and the place was swarming with armed police. Paramedics rushed to March and cut through his bindings. He was lowered onto a stretcher and taken to an ambulance as swiftly as you can carry an eighteen-stone man. More paramedics attended to Aurelia although she seemed a comparative lightweight.

Danny and I were released from our chairs. The police burst through to the rear office. There was lots of shouting. Lots of weapons, but thankfully no more shooting. A paramedic tried to wrap me in a blanket, but I just wanted to hug Danny so he wrapped it round both of us. A few minutes later Holly emerged from the back room, wrists handcuffed, a big black-clad policeman on either side. And then a group of terrified-looking girls followed, maybe twelve in total, perhaps fifteen, all escorted away. I had no idea what the future held for them, but whatever it was, it'd be a damn sight better than the misery they'd been so close to walking into.

I just hugged Danny for all I was worth. He hugged me back. The cuts to his face looked nasty. A paramedic started work, cleaning the wounds, and applying dressings. And in among all of this there was absolutely no sign of Clare. She'd vaporised just as quickly as she'd appeared. Back to her secret world, wherever that may be. I owed her so much. I just wanted the chance to say thank you, but equally I knew that this time I really might never see her again.

I looked to Danny.

"I'm sorry," I said. "I'm sorry for ever doubting her."

"We've all done that," he replied.

"Where is she?"

"Gone I assume."

I started to cry. Tears of relief, but also a reaction to all of the horror I'd witnessed. And, of course, also for Clare. She'd made a new world for herself but something told me it wasn't without regret. And I cried for her as I wanted her to be happy too.

Danny hugged me again and then let go and took a step backwards.

"What's up?" I asked.

"It's just you."

"What about me?"

"In all the excitement I'd forgotten that you puked. I can't believe you actually did that."

I punched him on his shoulder. It was only a gentle tap, really, but I'd forgotten about the bullet wound. Some things never change.

Amy came over to talk to us.

"We're going to need statements. Again," she said, arms folded. I couldn't work out if she was pleased that it was all over or pissed off with the amount of trouble we'd been at the centre of over the last few days.

Behind her, the clean-up was underway. Bodies were being

covered up. The area was being cordoned off with police crime scene tape. A photographer seemed to be taking endless pictures, which made me wonder what had happened to my lovely Nikon F4 and whether I'd ever see it again. And my car for that matter.

"Did you get my messages?" Danny asked Amy. "I've been trying to call you all morning."

"I was in a briefing. By the time I picked up the voicemail, you'd already gone."

"So how did you track us down?"

"An anonymous tip-off. Let's just say you seem to have a guardian angel."

I looked at Danny. I imagined he was thinking the same as me.

"Although it seems that by the time we got here, you had the situation pretty much under control," she continued.

I wasn't sure what to say, so kept quiet. For his part, Danny just shrugged.

"I suspect it must have been a rival gang," Amy continued. "Somebody they'd pissed off somewhere along the line. It's a shame we arrived just too late but they're probably miles away by now. I doubt we'll ever catch them."

I wasn't quite sure if my ears were working properly. Amy was far from stupid and equally incorruptible and yet I got the impression a deal had been done.

"Something like that," said Danny. "They were big blokes, whoever they were."

Maybe he was in on it too.

"I had my eyes shut so didn't really see anything," I added. In for a penny. It seemed a shame not to be part of it, whatever "it" was.

Chapter 50

Monday, April 11th, 1994

DANNY worked through the night, finally filing his copy just after 5am. He hardly noticed the fatigue and pain from the ordeals of the past few days. It was a huge story, and he was sure Mike would be delighted - perhaps almost enough to minimise the inevitable lecture about the importance of deadlines. He'd be the toast of the newspaper for a day or so, or at least until the next big story came along. There'd be just as many pages to fill tomorrow. Just as much pressure to come up with the next big thing.

Of course, March was still free, and likely to be reinstated once the evidence of his freelance investigation was put in front of the review board. He'd still need watching. He was bound to be back to his old tricks, but that was another investigation for another day. For now, Danny was content with a front page exclusive exposing a sex trafficking ring, with the added scandal of revealing a Government minister as a predatory paedophile. And the real scoop was his own eyewitness report of the final stand-off. It made for compelling reading. There would be follow-up stories in the days ahead, and the other papers would have angles of their own, but his reputation as a fearless investigator was growing.

Jacqui Glover had been stopped on the way to the warehouse, along with her sidekick Finn Convey. She'd been arrested on suspicion of being part of the trafficking ring and for living off immoral earnings. Finn had been arrested on suspicion of being the hospital intruder who had killed Leah. The Albermarle Casino and Gentleman's Club had been raided and was now closed for business and likely to stay that way. The Central Sauna massage parlour had been raided too, with multiple further arrests.

Graham March and Aurelia had both been rushed to hospital. Both were expected to make a full recovery in time, although Aurelia's psychological scars would possibly never fully heal.

Danny would have scars too, but he didn't care about those for now. As he arrived home, daylight was beginning to emerge through the omnipresent clouds. There was something beautiful about a city in the early hours, the birds announcing the clean start of a new day full of hope and possibility. But first of all, he just wanted to check that Anna was safe, and thereafter head to his own bed for the first time in far too long.

Danny left me a note, propped up next to the kettle, safe in the knowledge that would be the first thing I'd reach for once I'd opened my eyes long enough to focus on putting one foot in front of the other. I must work on being less predictable. All was good, the story was done, and he was going to bed, albeit at the time most normal people were waking up.

It was going to take me a few days before I'd be able to return to any semblance of a normal life, without the nightmares or the sense that I was never far away from panic. For today, though, I had a plan. I wanted to do something special for Danny, but didn't dare suggest a restaurant after the last time. The memories of that were still too fresh.

I took my tea to the computer and connected to CompuServe, and then began my search. I was going to demonstrate my cookery skills, where the phrase "skills" is particularly loosely defined. A home-made Indian would definitely go down well if it was even vaguely successful, so I concentrated on finding a recipe that looked both tasty and suitable for a relative novice.

While Danny slept on, I went to the supermarket and stocked up on all of the ingredients, together with a couple of bottles of sparkling wine and a pair of frozen pizzas as a fall-back, in case of disaster. I returned to CompuServe to find out exactly how to make a marinade, and was surprised to see I had a new email. I don't get too many of those. I clicked on it and the words filled the screen.

Subject: I'm going to miss you

Hi Anna,

I know I haven't always been your favourite person but it's been good to get to know you a bit better over the last few days. Hopefully you've seen a different side of me, although it's a shame it took such adversity to bring us together. I'm sorry I had to leave in a rush, but it wouldn't have been wise for me to hang around. Too many questions. :-)

You asked me if I was happy, and I know I avoided the question. I'm just not very good at talking about myself. In truth, I don't really know who I am any more. Let's just say that I've got all that I wanted, but the grass isn't always greener. Sometimes it doesn't grow at all. I made decisions that I have to live with for the rest of my life, however long that may be, so there's no point dwelling on them now.

I must thank you, though. You were exceptionally brave in the hospital. We wouldn't have been able to unravel everything without you. You have my eternal respect and admiration, for whatever that is worth. You don't deserve the trauma you've had to put up with over the last few days.

I don't know if we'll ever meet again, but I will always think of you. Take care of Danny for me. I won't pry into your relationship, but I hope that you have a wonderful future together, in whatever form that takes.

Take care and look after yourself too. You're a very special person.

Love,

Cxx

I felt a wave of emotion as I re-read the words. Tears came again. I knew she only had herself to blame, but still she'd made a lasting impression on me, and she was right, my opinion had changed completely. I hoped we would meet one day, although I suspected that if it ever happened it would be when I was least expecting it, at a time and place of her choosing. I just hoped it wouldn't be too far in the future as I had so many more questions to ask. Not least, how on earth she'd managed to get hold of my email address.

Chapter 51

I THINK I'll stick to photography rather than opening an Indian restaurant, but the meal was at least edible. It was a kind of coconut chicken arrangement with all sorts of spices and fresh chillies and a spot of cream to hopefully mask any deficiencies in culinary expertise. I don't know what surprised Danny the most: the fact that I'd cooked for him in the first place or just that as yet neither of us had been poorly. The night was still young.

I'd set the kitchen table nicely, complete with four candles, and our finest plates and cutlery. There were even little paper napkins. The wine was proving a success too. I was standing by his side, refilling his glass from the second bottle, when I suddenly had a realisation.

"Are you sure you should be drinking?" I asked. "I forgot about the painkillers."

He laughed.

"I think it all helps," he said. "And it was a lovely meal. Thank you."

"My pleasure."

"I didn't know you could cook."

"All the evidence would seem to suggest that I can't."

He put his arm around me and gave me a squeeze.

"I could get used to this," he said.

"Don't push your luck. And you're loading the dishwasher."

"I'd love to but, you know, doctor's orders."

"Well, you definitely shouldn't be drinking any more then." But I refilled his glass anyway.

We took the glasses and the rest of the bottle through to the living room, together with a little box of After Eight mints. Then I went back and fetched the candles. They created a beautiful, warm ambience that was almost romantic. We curled up next to each other on the sofa.

"I'd have missed this if you'd run off with Mitch," he said.

"Well, that was never going to happen."

"I don't know. I think you were quite smitten."

"What? Me? No. He wasn't my type."

Danny started to smirk.

"That was a sexy outfit for someone who wasn't your type."

"What? When?"

"When you came to the hospital."

"Oh that. No, nothing special. I am, in case you've forgotten, a fashion leader."

"Right."

He was giggling at me.

"You had quite the strop though."

"Entirely justified in the circumstances."

"I wonder what happened to him."

That raised alarm bells.

"In what way?"

"Clare said you'd blown his cover and traced him to the casino, but he wasn't on the police report as being arrested."

"Ah."

"You say that as though you know."

"I just…" I wasn't quite sure what to say.

"What?"

"I just think perhaps Clare scared him off."

"That sounds ominous."

"You know what she's like. She doesn't tend to do things in half measures. I don't think you need to worry about him any more."

"That sounds even more ominous."

I cuddled in closer to him.

"How's the wound?" I asked.

"Still sore. Actually, that's a good point. Do you think Amy will give us back the uniform?"

I gave him one of my looks.

"Just because I'm pleased to have you home doesn't mean that I won't cause pain if you misbehave."

He laughed again.

"Clare's all right though, really, isn't she?" he asked.

I thought of her email. I hadn't mentioned it to Danny. It was all for another day.

"I still think you fancy her," I said, avoiding the question. There were too many ways to answer it. "You're allowed to mention her name now, though, if you want to."

"That's good."

We descended into an easy silence. At some point the wine ran out. I couldn't face another After Eight.

"You know what," I said at last. "I think I'm going to do the dishwasher tomorrow. We should get you to bed."

"That's a very good idea."

"If you ask me nicely I may even tuck you in."

"That would be nice. Can you promise me one thing, though?"

"What?"

"Can we agree that we're never going to fall out again?"

I looked at him, lying there, in obvious discomfort, but with such sweet, honest eyes.

"It's a deal," I said, extending my hand. He took it and we shook. I loved the feeling of his hand in mine. I didn't want to ever let go.

EPILOGUE

Wednesday, August 3rd, 1994

The five star Vitosha New Otani Hotel towers over the Bulgarian capital, Sofia, offering views of the city and the volcanic Vitosha mountain beyond. The hotel is famous for its Japanese garden and indeed is known locally as Yaponskiya - the Japanese Hotel.

Just off the opulent, marbled lobby is a wood-panelled cigar bar, offering well-heeled guests a choice of the finest whiskies from distilleries around the world. Never one to bow to convention, the woman in the corner, sitting on her own in a deep brown leather Chesterfield armchair, ordered a bottle of Chablis Grand Cru, together with two crystal glasses.

While she waited for the wine to arrive, she scanned her English-language newspaper. She still thought of England as home, even though it was now over a year since she'd lived there. Of late, the homesickness had been growing in intensity, the lure of the motherland acute. For now, though, her base was Sofia with its yellow cobbled streets and unique architectural mix, from the Roman remains of the original city of Serdica to the stark mass of communist concrete.

The waiter offered her a taste of the wine. She put the glass to her nose and inhaled the mineral scent, then swirled the glass and took a sip. She nodded her approval. He poured her a glass and then left the bottle in an ice bucket that he placed on the table. She sat back in her chair, put the newspaper to one side, and started idly toying with her Ceylon sapphire ring.

The wine was good. She'd developed an appreciation of the finer things. She was not, however, planning on drinking the whole bottle alone. A special guest was due any moment, one she hadn't seen in person since she'd saved his life in an east London warehouse, four months previously. She closed her eyes, losing herself in the familiar thoughts of simpler times, of the days when he'd been a regular part of her working life.

The sound of voices brought her back to the present. She looked up and saw him raising a hand in greeting while walking slowly towards her. She'd been looking forward to this moment. He looked surprisingly well, considering what he'd been through and the injuries sustained. She smiled when she saw him, and indicated the opposite chair.

"Good afternoon, Graham," she said.

"Clare. How delightful to see you. Have you missed me?"

"I have, but I'll take much better aim next time."

He laughed.

"Still not lost your legendary sense of humour, despite the humble surroundings."

"Who said I was joking?"

He lowered himself into the seat.

"This for me?" he asked, indicating the second glass. She nodded. He poured himself a generous measure before topping up hers, almost as an afterthought.

"How are you?" she asked. "Safely back in the land of chasing criminals?"

"Nearly, my dear. Official start date's Monday, although I've been reintroducing myself to what I like to call some of my old acquaintances."

"And the injuries are healing?"

"I can't complain. A bit of a limp as a lasting memento, but it could have been worse."

"It could."

There was no need to dwell on the details.

He waved to attract the waiter's attention and then, when he arrived, asked for a Cuban Montecristo cigar.

"It would seem rude not to, given the surroundings," he said, looking at Clare. "Care to join me?"

"I'm not a cigar kind of girl, but you go ahead. I suppose a small celebration is appropriate."

"Indeed it is."

A moment later, the waiter returned with the cigar. Clare passed March her lighter.

"I suppose I ought to thank you for coming to my rescue," he said when they were back on their own.

"There's no need. I'm a woman of my word."

"You could, perhaps, have maybe come a little bit sooner, though?"

"Or I could have just let them kill you. Made it easier for everyone."

"That's one way of looking at it."

"Believe me, it was tempting."

Clare lit a cigarette, wafting the smoke away with her hand, then took a sip of her wine, admiring the pale-yellow liquid as it caught the light. March took the opportunity to change the subject.

"Beautiful choice of hotel by the way," he said. "Are you staying here long? Should we take this bottle back to your room?"

"Ah, Graham, it's good to see you never change."

"I just like to think I offer a service. I can't imagine it's easy for you to find suitable company, given your itinerant lifestyle. Don't think I'll be offended if you want to take advantage."

"I don't, despite the kind offer."

"I rather assumed that's why you asked to see me."

"You know full well why I asked to see you."

"Well yes, there is that too."

Clare flicked ash, then adjusted the hem of her pin-striped skirt.

"Have you spoken to your German friends?" she asked.

"I have, of course."

"And?"

"They're very pleased with you."

"So they should be."

"And with the delightful Ms Cranston, obviously. It was quite the international clear-up."

She nodded.

"Did they give you anything for me?"

March reached into his jacket pocket and withdrew a lightly padded envelope. He placed it on the table, resting his hand on top.

"Obviously I had to deduct my travel expenses," he said.

"Goes without saying. I assume you flew economy?"

"Oh dear. I knew I'd got something wrong."

Clare took the envelope and placed it into her bag, next to the voice recorder and its illuminated red LED. She paused for a moment, fully in control.

"You know, Graham," she said at last, "I've spent the last few months trying to repay debts. I felt I owed Danny and Anna because of what happened last year, and the trouble they went to, looking for me. I even felt, deep down, that I owed you. Your sheer incompetence, no offence, let me get away with disappearing."

"I'd hardly class it as incompetence."

"Oh, come on. We both know you're only interested in your bank balance and your genitalia."

March laughed.

"You say that as though it's a bad thing."

"There's more to life, Graham."

"Says the woman who made a fortune from fraud and then killed her accomplices."

"It was a bit more complicated than that."

"It really wasn't."

Clare, turned, re-crossing her legs, aware that March was watching them. He was so easy to read. She wasn't finished.

"I wanted to help the Germans, not just because they have some interesting projects, as we both know, but mainly because I just wanted to do good, you know? The trafficking had to stop. I mean, obviously it goes on, but we put a dent into it. Does that make sense?"

"It does. It's all very noble."

"It's not a question of being noble. Just that I wanted to do the right thing for its own sake. Do some good in the world and make a difference. Even if the condition of being allowed to get involved meant saving you when I'm fairly sure you weren't quite as innocent as you pretend. But you know what? I think that I've done that now. In some ways, it just feels like I'm out of the red. Back in the black. Back to thinking about what I want from life, and what's best for me."

"You've never been shy of doing that, if you don't mind me saying."

"I've had moments. But fundamentally I like to think I'm a good person."

March smiled, as though not believing a word.

"What's next?" he asked.

"You go back to work and try to behave yourself."

"And you?"

"You don't need to worry about me."

March leaned forward.

"You do know I could arrange for you to be arrested at any moment?"

"You could, but not now. Not when I know what I know."

He laughed.

"They'd never believe you."

"Are you prepared to run that risk?"

"For the kudos of bringing in the elusive Clare Woodbrook?"

She was suddenly alert, not liking the change in his expression.

"The thing is, my dear," he went on, "I'm afraid there's been a rather significant change in the plan."

She looked into his eyes, leaned forward and lowered her voice.

"Graham, you're not in a position to renegotiate. And just for the avoidance of any kind of doubt, you don't want me as an enemy."

"I was thinking that. And that's why I thought, maybe, it was time to change the rules. I hate to sound cold about it, but you do represent an unacceptable risk."

"Meaning?"

"Well again, not wanting to be coarse, but having you as part of the equation has ceased being, what I like to call, tenable."

He tapped the ash from the end of his cigar and took a large mouthful of the wine.

"Of course, it gives me no pleasure. You're a lovely looking lady so it seems like a terrible waste, but we're all supposed to think you're dead already so it won't come as a surprise. You didn't think I could fraternise with a wanted criminal, did you?"

He leaned back in his chair and looked up, towards the back of the room, and the open doorway that led through to the lobby. She turned to see what had caught his attention. There were four men in dark suits near the concierge desk, each of whom seemed to possess the physique of a steroid-abusing bodybuilder. One was talking to a smartly dressed member of staff. As she caught his eye, the concierge indicated in her direction. The men started to approach. She turned back to March. His expression seemed cold, cruel.

"Obviously Danny will miss you, but it's a dangerous game as we know. If you'd like me to pass on a final message, now would be a good time."

She was momentarily speechless. March seemed to be studying her, maybe looking for signs of fear. The men were getting closer. They entered the bar.

"I'm sorry to be the executioner, my dear, but needs must."

The four men arrived at the table, taking a position on each corner. There was no escape. Clare had been expecting this moment. There was no point in being afraid.

"You are, and always will be, a bastard," she said, looking straight into his hard, expressionless eyes. Then she looked at the men. They were even bigger up close. They looked brutal, intimidating, uncompromising. She took a deep breath.

"Graham," she said, "I'd like to introduce you to four friends of mine."

The End.

SPECIAL THANKS...

Writing Out Of The Red brought back happy memories of the Emap days of 1994. Thanks, therefore, to friends and colleagues of the era - including Louise Duffy, Darren Wallace, Sarah Harron, Paul Smith, Marcus Austin, Joe O'Halloran, Gail Robinson, Paul Bennett, Clare Newsome, Adam Ellis, Dave Cartwright, Roger Gann, Garret Keogh, Mike Hales, Adam Ellis, Max Cooter, Gautam Paul, Neil Ellul, Anielka Briggs, Cass Spencer, Roger Green, Ruth Allen and everyone else with whom I had the pleasure to share moments in the workplace.

As ever, huge thanks to my editor, Carrie O'Grady, for endless encouragement, fresh perspectives, brilliant suggestions and impeccable attention to detail.

Many thanks too, of course, to Mary Cafferkey, for support and inspiration. I hope you like it...

Out Of The Red was largely written by candlelight over many late nights. Special mention again, therefore, to DayBehavior for the ultimate soundtrack. The new album, Based On A True Story, is coming soon and will no doubt underpin book three. :-)

Find them at www.daybehavior.com.

FEEL FREE TO SAY HELLO... :-)

If you enjoyed the book, have any queries, or just want to say hello, I'd love to hear from you via www.davidbradwell.com. While you're there, you can also download a **FREE copy of the series prequel** - In The Frame:

Photography student Anna Burgin didn't expect to be arrested, but she's the only suspect for a series of crimes, and the Police have found damning evidence in her room. But Anna has no recollection of doing anything wrong. Was it a moment of madness? Or is somebody setting out to destroy her? And is the stranger in the bar really trying to help, or just part of an evil conspiracy?

You can also follow me on Twitter: @dbshq - or see what Anna is up to: @AnnaBurginNW1

If you enjoyed Out Of The Red, you should read **Cold Press** - book 1 in the Anna Burgin series.

London. 1993. Investigative journalist Clare Woodbrook goes missing on the brink of unveiling her biggest-ever story. Is it kidnap? Murder?

Worse still, the police investigation into her disappearance is being headed up by a corrupt DCI - himself the subject of one of Clare's current investigations.

Clare's researcher Danny Churchill sets out to find her, and enlists the help of his flatmate - feisty fashion photographer Anna Burgin. But they soon realise that nobody can be trusted. And as the search becomes ever more desperate, suddenly their own lives are very much on the line.

Packed with intrigue, twists, conspiracies, and dark humour, Cold Press is a hugely entertaining British thriller, with a sting in the tail.

Book 3 - **In The Frame,** the series prequel novella, is available as a FREE ebook at www.davidbradwell.com.

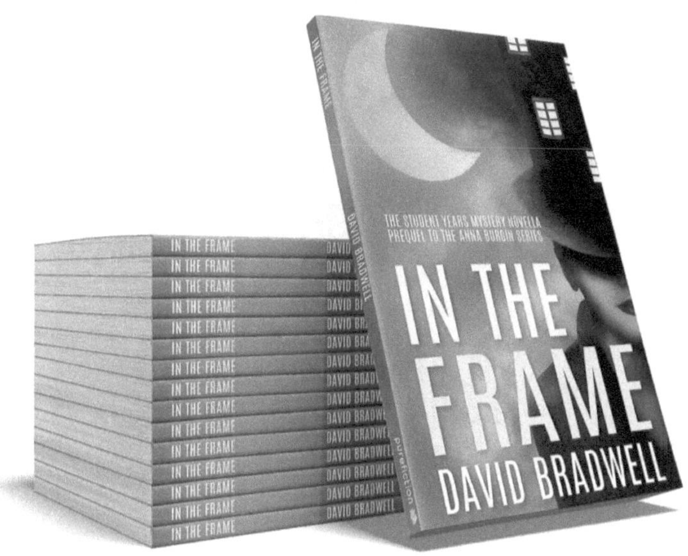

In The Frame takes us back to Anna and Danny's student years and explains how they became friends in the first place.

Photography student Anna Burgin didn't expect to be arrested, but she's the only suspect for a series of crimes, and the Police have found damning evidence in her room.

But Anna has no recollection of doing anything wrong. Was it a moment of madness? Or is somebody setting out to destroy her?

And is the stranger in the bar really trying to help, or just part of an evil conspiracy?

The sequel to Out Of The Red is book 4: **Fade To Silence.**

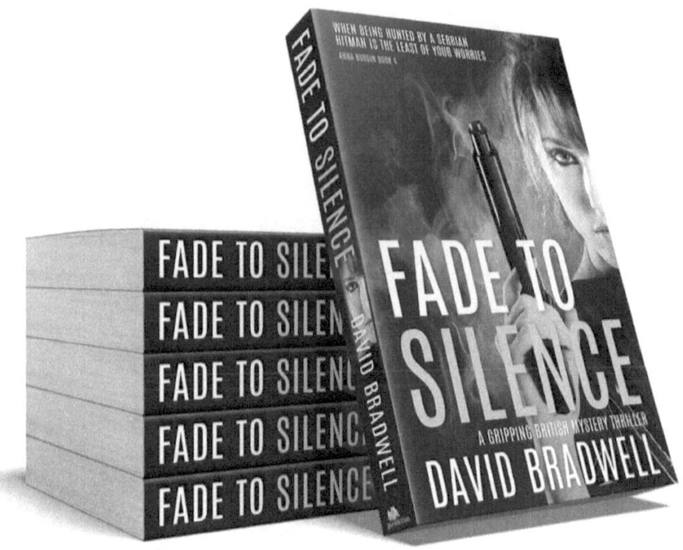

You know you've got problems when being hunted by a Serbian hitman is the least of your worries...

Balkan gangsters, corporate spies and a fugitive killer are all on the loose in London, but when a body shows up, all of the evidence points to the victim's wife.

Journalist Danny Churchill wants to find the truth. But when reports emerge of a huge shipment of weapons heading to the UK, it soon becomes the most dangerous and action-packed investigation so far.

Packed with twists, intrigue and dark humour, Fade To Silence is book 4 in the bestselling Anna Burgin series.